THE MORNING STAR ENTANGLEMENT

Ebonie Wayne

Arc Inkwell Publishing

Copyright © 2021 by Ebonie Wayne

The Morning Star Entanglement is a work of fiction. Names, characters, and situations are from the author's imagination. Any resemblance to real people or situations is purely coincidental.

All rights reserved.

This book or parts thereof may not be reproduced in any form, stored in any retrieval system, or transmitted in any form by any means—electronic, mechanical, photocopy, recording, or otherwise—without prior written permission of the author.

ISBN: 978-1-955386-01-2

Cover Design by: @HerrSmog

Published by: Arc Inkwell Publishing

*Many thanks to Topsie T. and Tolu J.
For your encouragement and honest feedback
during the writing and editing of this novel.*

01 | Trouble

Feyisayo had just walked in from the gym. She was about to change out of her work-out clothes and take a shower when she heard a knock on her bedroom door.

"Come in," she answered.

It was Tutu, her younger sister. She had an uncharacteristically grim expression on her face.

"What's the matter?" Fey asked, leading her by the arm to sit on the bed. She noticed some papers in her hands. On closer inspection, they looked like a bunch of opened mail. "What are those?"

After a few seconds, Tutu finally answered. "I found these in the attic. Mom asked me to go there to fetch you some luggage for your trip."

Fey nodded. A few weeks before, the sisters had both returned home from college for summer break. Fey, who would begin her senior year in the fall, would travel to Germany in a few weeks for a study-abroad semester at the Technical University of Munich (TUM).

Tutu continued, "I got nosey since we hardly ever go up there, you know. And I found this old-looking luggage in the corner. It had the same design as that old keepsake pouch Mom uses as a makeup bag."

"Yeah, didn't she say it's one of the few items she still has, that she brought with her when we moved here from Nigeria?"

Tutu nodded in agreement. "It was old and dusty, so I dragged it out of the corner and opened it up. I found some of Mom's stuff—and these letters from Dad."

Fey snickered. "Eeewww, old love letters between Mom and Dad?"

Tutu shook her head, her expression still as grim as when she walked into the room. "They're letters from Dad—to us."

Fey's face fell. "What do you mean?" she asked as she snatched the letters out of her sister's hands. She quickly scanned the postage dates and addressees of the first few letters and came to the same conclusion as her sister. Brows tightly knit and her heart beating wildly in her chest, she said, "So, Dad *has* been trying to get in touch with us all this time. Why would Mom lie to us?!"

Tears welling up in her eyes, Tutu responded almost in a whimper, "I don't know." She watched helplessly as her sister paced up and down the bedroom. She could see Fey's anger building up, and she somehow felt responsible.

Ever since Fey and their mother had that big blow-up last year, she had watched the two of them grow apart. But in the last few weeks since they had been home from college, Tutu had tried to help mend the relationship between Fey and their mother. She had suggested a surprise birthday dinner for their mother, after which they both began laughing and joking with each other like before. And now all of that was for nothing! She just wanted them all to be a happy family again, but it didn't look like that was ever going to happen.

As she sat there, Tutu thought that perhaps she shouldn't have said anything. Maybe she should've waited until later to mention her discovery. But, was there really a good time to break the news that your mother had been lying to you all your life? Tutu felt betrayed. She also felt like a coward. She knew she didn't have the guts to confront their mother about this, so she told Fey, knowing there was no way she'd keep quiet about it.

Fey, on the other hand, was seething. She also recalled the conversations and arguments she'd had with their mother about their father. For as long as she could remember, it was only the sisters and their mother. And whenever Fey asked about their father, their mother would clam up or get upset.

Fey wished she wouldn't make the subject of her father so difficult. It's just that now that Fey was older, she wanted real answers to her questions. She was no longer satisfied with the usual "Your dad left us and never came back" response. Now, Fey wanted to know why they separated. Did he cheat on her? Or did they just fall out of love?

Her parents both lived in Nigeria before they came to the States, and so her mother had to have known her father's family. Even if he ran off on them, why couldn't Fey and her younger sister get in touch with him? Did he not want to meet his children? Why couldn't they have a relationship with her father's family? Why was her mother keeping them away from everyone? Didn't her father ever try to contact them since he left?

She always had this nagging feeling that her mother was hiding something. She stared at the letters in her hands—proof that her instincts had been right.

Tutu wiped her eyes. "What are you going to do?" she asked.

When Fey turned to face her, Tutu swore she could see the fire in her sister's glowering eyes. The kind that almost choked and burned you at the same time. Fey was enraged. Tutu's breath hitched for a moment, and then as if sensing her sister's discomfort, Fey forced a smile, her anger dissipating slowly. She walked over to sit next to her younger sister and put her arms around her.

"Did you read any of the letters?" Fey asked, her voice shaking as she tried to get her anger under control.

"Just one," Tutu responded, her eyes questioning her sister's sudden calm demeanor. Although she was shocked at the intensity of Fey's scowl a few seconds ago, she was even more surprised at the fact that Fey was trying hard not to stay angry. Tutu wasn't sure if she was relieved or disappointed.

"Let's read them all. Later, we can confront—I mean, *talk*—to Mom about it when she gets home from work tonight. We'll get everything sorted out then."

Tutu nodded in agreement. Perhaps it was good that Fey had a level head than her usual headstrong self. That gave her some hope that tonight's conversation with their mother might not be as explosive as she was anticipating.

***

Adaobi rushed in the door from the pouring rain. The sudden downpour made rush hour traffic quite unbearable, and now that she was finally home, she quickly shed her high heels as she stood in the foyer.

"Feyi… Tutu," she called out to her daughters to announce her arrival. No response. Adaobi padded across the hardwood floor to the kitchen to find them getting dinner ready. "Wow. What's going on here? I thought you both wanted me to make pounded yam for dinner?"

Tutu responded with a smile. "Hi, Mom. We just decided to surprise you." She looked over at Fey, who simply nodded without turning around. She appeared to be busy with something at the stove.

"Oh, ok. Well, I'll go change and be down in a few minutes."

Soon after their mother left, Tutu nudged Fey. "Why didn't you say anything?"

Fey sighed. "I know it was my idea to get Mom in a good mood before we talk to her about the letters. But as soon as she came in, I—I just couldn't look at her. I don't think I can do this, Tutu…"

"Do what? Talk to her about the letters?"

"No! I mean, talk to her without getting mad like I did last time."

Tutu looked at her sister for a moment before she said, "Who said you had to talk to Mom without getting upset?"

Fey raised a brow. She didn't see that coming. Heck, her sister's tendency to avoid conflict at all costs was the reason Fey suggested this whole dinner thing in the first place. If their Mom was in a good mood, chances are she'd be less likely to stonewall them and might open up to them about the letters and the truth about their father. There was no guarantee, of course.

"I think we should go through with dinner as planned and just let things happen as they will. To be honest, depending on what Mom says, even I don't think I'll be able to keep calm this time." Tutu said coolly as she sat down at the table.

Fey smiled to herself. Perhaps her sister was finally growing some backbone after all. "Sounds good."

During dinner, Adaobi noticed that her daughters were quieter than usual. When she asked if they were alright, both girls glanced at each other but said nothing. After a few minutes, Fey spoke up.

"Mom, can I ask you a question?"

"Sure."

Fey took in a deep breath before asking, "Did Dad ever try to contact us—even if it's just once?"

Adaobi stiffened at the question. Her face pulled into a frown, and she stopped eating. "What's this all of a sudden?"

"I need to know, Mom," Fey pressed.

"I don't understand why you always like to bring up bad memories, Feyisayo. We've been doing just fine since you've been back."

"What bad memories? We—" she gestured to herself and Tutu, "—have no memories of Dad, and you won't even tell us anything."

"I've told you what you need to know—"

Fey cut her off. "I just want to know if Dad ever tried to get in touch with us."

Adaobi was silent.

Tutu chimed in, "Mom, I want to know too."

Adaobi stared at Tutu in disbelief. "So, you're in cahoots, ehn?"

Tutu's heart sank. This was the first time she ever sided with Fey, and now her mother was taking a jab at her. Well, there was no turning back now.

There was an uncomfortable silence at the dinner table as all three women stared at each other.

After what seemed like forever, Adaobi spoke. "No, your father never tried to get in touch with us."

Fey suddenly slammed her fists on the dinner table. "You're lying!" she yelled.

Adaobi raised her voice as well. "Don't you dare talk to me like that ever again, young lady. I am your mother, and you will treat me with respect!"

"Sorry, but liars don't deserve any of my respect!" Fey spat in response.

In an instant, Adaobi reached across the dining table and slapped her daughter. She was furious at Fey's audacity. What had come over her suddenly?

Fey immediately reached into the back pocket of her jeans and slammed the attic letters on the table. "Care to explain what these are?" she asked, glaring at her mother.

Adaobi recognized the letters immediately, and in the span of a few seconds, her expression went from shock to anger. "How dare you go looking through my stuff!" she growled.

"Nobody went through your stuff, Mom. I found them in the attic," Tutu responded.

Adaobi glared at her. Tutu could see that she was visibly shaking from the anger and frustration at being cornered. Adaobi placed a hand on her forehead and rubbed her temples with her fingers. A headache was forming.

"You can't continue to hide from this, Mom. We're not little kids anymore. You need to come clean with us," Fey urged.

Tutu joined in, "Please, Mom, talk to us."

After about a minute, Adaobi finally spoke. "I did not want you both to find out like this." She sighed in defeat. "What do you want to know?"

Fey and Tutu glanced at each other.

Then Fey asked, "The first thing I want to know is why you didn't tell us about the letters."

"I didn't want you to ask to see your father or talk to him. He's not in a position to do either of those things."

"Is Dad in the States or Nigeria?" Tutu asked.

"He's in Nigeria."

"Why did he go to Nigeria?" It was Fey this time.

Adaobi sighed. "In the summer of the year that your father completed his master's degree, we received a call from his mother that your grandfather was seriously ill, so he took a trip to Nigeria. And we haven't seen him since."

Fey and Tutu were thoughtful for a moment. It was apparent to Fey that their mother would not divulge everything voluntarily, and they would have to ask the right questions.

"Do you know why he never returned?" Fey asked.

"While he was there, his parents wanted him to take a second wife. He refused at first, but he eventually did, and now he is with his new family."

"Why did they want him to marry someone else? Didn't they like you?"

"They claimed he needed a wife to bear him a son. Even though your father didn't care about any of that nonsense."

"Does he have other children?"

"I don't know."

"When was the last time you heard from him?"

There was another silence. Adaobi looked lost in thought, but she didn't answer the question.

"How can we contact him?"

Adaobi suddenly looked alarmed. "You cannot!"

"Why not?! Are you worried about saving face? That we'll tell him you've been lying to us all these years?" Fey sneered.

Adaobi gave a short, humorless laugh. "No, my dear. At this point, I don't care what your father thinks of me. What I do care about is your safety."

"You make it sound like he's involved in some shady business," Fey quipped.

"You have no idea, child."

"Mom, that makes no sense. Are you saying that Dad is an engineer turned gangster?" Tutu chimed in.

"I can't go into any details, but there are dangerous people who could harm him and us if they knew where we are. The people watching him are very wealthy and very influential in Nigeria. Your dad only writes letters because it's safer that way."

"Can you contact him if you wanted to?" Fey asked.

Adaobi shrugged. There was another silence.

"Mom, I know you must've been hurt when Dad took another wife," Tutu said. "I have a few African friends whose dads have more than one wife, so I get that about the culture. But just abandoning us must've been hard on you financially. Did he ever send you any child support at the very least?"

Adaobi sighed again. "A few months after his wedding to his second wife, your dad started wiring money into a joint account we used to have together while he was here. He has never stopped doing that. That money funds your college education, girls." She pointed at Fey. "And your study abroad trip to Germany."

Fey looked relieved, and she almost smiled. Their father wasn't a deadbeat after all.

Adaobi lowered her head so that her daughters would not see the tears gathering. She always avoided this conversation for this reason. It would eventually bring back all the hurt and pain. Despite all the years, her feelings were still raw. Perhaps it was because she never really got any closure from the whole matter. How was she to get closure from someone who was thousands of miles overseas, whom she could neither talk to nor see? All she had were these damn letters!

02 | Pay It Forward

The next few days after the tense Q&A dinner was wrought with some unavoidable tension in the house. Adaobi expected that the sisters would come back with more questions, but surprisingly they did not.

Soon, it was time for Fey to leave for Germany. Tutu left the house with Ada and Fey, but she did not go with them to the airport. They dropped her off at the mall to hang out with a college friend who was in town. The rest of the ride to Wilmington airport was quiet. Adaobi and Fey were both lost in their thoughts.

Once they arrived, Fey immediately checked in her luggage. Just before she was about to head over to the security search line, she turned around and hugged her mother.

"Have a safe trip, dear. Make sure you call as soon as you arrive in Munich," Ada said.

Fey nodded. Then she reached into her purse and handed her mom an envelope. "If there's a way, and you think it's a good idea, please send this to Dad for me." She pulled her mother in for another hug.

Adaobi took the letter but was silent. She waited until Fey had completed the security search and was headed to her departure gate before she started to head home.

While driving home, Adaobi couldn't help but feel a bit sad. Dropping Fey off at the airport reminded her of the last time she had seen her husband. Just like today, she had taken him to the airport so that he could go back home to Nigeria to visit his ailing father. Little did she know that he would not be coming back.

She placed the letter that Fey had given her on the passenger seat next to her. Should she mail the letter? Was it a good idea? She wasn't sure she could answer those questions at the moment. Temidayo wrote to them via PO Box, which she had kept active over the years. There was a reason she couldn't answer the question from the other night about the last time that he had written to them. It was because she hadn't gone to check the box in a very long time. Why? Because the entire situation became too painful and difficult.

Initially, when Temidayo started writing, Adaobi would write back. Mostly it was her venting her anger and frustration at their circumstances, while he apologized profusely. Not once did he seem frustrated with her or upset with her. In every letter, he reminded her that he loved her, and she flip-flopped between hoping he'd come back to them and wondering why she was holding out hope. It was also difficult to communicate in this way since she had to wait for weeks or months to receive a response from him. Snail mail communication across the Atlantic in those days required a lot of patience and dedication. One day, she decided to stop wasting her time with a man who swore in his letters that she was the only woman he loved, but who was powerless to do anything about reuniting with her.

A while later, when Ada stopped her car, she was parked in front of the post office. She sighed to herself. *Why am I here?* She had subconsciously driven there without realizing it. Was this a good idea? She grabbed Fey's letter from the seat and debated whether to read it. That would be an invasion of privacy, but she was curious to see what her daughter had written. After a few more minutes, she finally summoned up enough courage to get out of the car and go inside the post office.

She located the box and quickly opened it before she convinced herself otherwise. She took all the letters in there and left. When she got home, Tutu wasn't there. She was just about to check the time when she received a notification on her phone. It was Tutu letting her know that she'd be staying out later than planned and wouldn't be home for dinner.

Realizing that she had the next few hours to herself, Ada took a wine glass, her favorite bottle of red wine, and went to the living room. She hadn't done this in a while—not since her daughters had been home for the summer. Occasionally, she would kick back on the weekend and enjoy a glass or two of wine, while watching some of the TV shows she had recorded.

For the first time in a long time, she felt a bit lonely. She was very devoted to her career as a college professor, which didn't give her much time for dating. Not that she was looking for a serious relationship, but it would be nice to just have some company from time to time. Years ago, she'd tried dating again to prove to herself that she had moved on from Temidayo. That didn't quite work out well. She threw herself into her career with determined enthusiasm after that.

Her thoughts drifted to the letters she had picked up from the post office. There was no better time than the present, so she decided to look through them. There were about forty envelopes altogether. Twelve of them were addressed to Tutu, fourteen to Fey, and the rest to Ada. The most recent one was postmarked a month ago. It was a birthday card for Ada. She smiled to herself. Although she hadn't expected anything, she was glad Temidayo hadn't completely forgotten about them—about her.

Looking through the rest of the envelopes, it looked like he had sent birthday cards to all three of them every year, for the last ten years. Although Ada had stopped checking for and responding to his letters many years ago, he never stopped writing as he had promised. She was impressed. She suddenly realized that she hadn't mailed Fey's letter. She'd have to stop by the post office sometime soon. Ada continued sorting the envelopes in three separate piles, one for each of them.

Although she was unhappy about the confrontation a couple of weeks ago, Ada was relieved that she didn't have to keep hiding everything from the girls anymore. However, she wasn't going to divulge information unnecessarily. She still had to ensure their safety after all. She disagreed with his methods, but their father was also keeping them safe in his own way.

***

Fey woke up from her nap. Glancing at her watch, she realized she'd been asleep for most of the second half of her flight. The pilot just announced the plane's descent, and Fey began to feel the butterflies in her stomach. She was finally here, in Germany!

After going through airport security, she took a cab to the *Wohngemeinschaft*, the shared housing accommodation that she would be staying in with her friends. She was the first to arrive. Her best friend Demi and the others would be arriving over the next few days. Even though she would be the only one in the house, she didn't mind. She was looking forward to some peacefulness.

She checked out all four available bedrooms and selected one of the larger ones for herself. Although the rooms were smaller than her bedroom back home, they were still larger than the dorm rooms on the

Georgia Tech campus where she attended college in the States. There were two full bathrooms upstairs and a guest bathroom downstairs. She thought about getting ready for classes in the mornings and hoped that none of the other girls had a habit of taking forever to shower in the morning.

She spent the next two hours unpacking. She flopped down on the bed and reached for her phone to call her mother, who picked up after the fourth ring.

"Hello?"

"Hi, Mom. It's Fey."

"Hello dear, glad you made it safely. How is the boarding house? I hope there are no unwanted surprises."

"No, actually, it's very nice—just like the pictures in the online listing."

"That's good…" Adaobi yawned. "What time is it over there?"

"7:30 PM. I forgot there's a time difference."

"It's about 1:30 AM over here. I fell asleep on the couch in the living room, so I'm glad you called. I would've been sore if I slept here all night."

"Oh, okay. Well, I should let you go. I just wanted to let you know that I arrived safely, and I'm settling in okay."

"Alright, dear. I'll talk to you later. Stay safe, okay?"

"Sure, Mom. Good night!"

After Fey hung up, she decided to get some dinner. She was eager to explore the neighborhood, but could wait until tomorrow. Walking around aimlessly at dusk on your first day in a foreign land was a potential recipe for disaster. She decided to order in instead. Thanks to Google, she found a pizza place nearby that offered delivery.

As Fey settled in bed for the night, her thoughts drifted to the recent news about her father. Based on the postage dates on the letters Tutu found, the last letter was from over ten years ago. She wondered if he had given up on trying to reach out to them. She hoped her mother would mail the letter but more importantly, she hoped he would respond.

She reluctantly pushed those thoughts out of her mind and she focused on her plans for the next few months here in Munich. As a Civil Engineering major at Georgia Tech, Atlanta, she was ecstatic about starting her senior year at TUM. While soaking in knowledge was her number one goal, she was also looking forward to new cultural experiences here in Munich. Maybe she'd even pick up a little

German.

The next morning, Fey woke up to unfamiliar surroundings and was confused as to where she was for a moment. Then she remembered that she had arrived in Germany yesterday. She checked the time. It was a little after 10:00 AM. She dragged herself out of bed, took a shower, got dressed, and went out to explore the neighborhood in hopes of getting breakfast or brunch.

As she walked a few blocks, Fey couldn't help but admire the different building architecture. Being in a big city like this kind of reminded her of downtown Atlanta. Still, it was different—even the air smelled different. Just as her stomach gave a sudden hunger growl in protest, she spotted a cafe that offered a variety of breakfast foods and outdoor seating. She took out the paper with the list of places that the landlord had provided to help his tenants get acquainted with the neighborhood. This cafe was on the list. *The food must be good*, she thought to herself as she walked in.

Once inside, Fey ordered a croissant and a cup of coffee. She tried to pay with her credit card, but the cashier refused it and pointed to a sign that read, 'Keine Kreditkarte, No credit card.' When she looked in her wallet, she realized that she didn't have any cash. She face-palmed herself at the realization that she never got around to converting her US dollars into Euros. She started to apologize to the cashier that she wouldn't be able to buy the food she ordered when someone behind her offered to pay. To her surprise, he spoke English.

"That's alright, Miss. I have some spare change."

Before she could refuse, he quickly stepped in front of her and handed the cashier some bills. Fey stepped aside while he placed his order.

"You didn't have to do that," she protested weakly, feeling embarrassed.

He turned to her and smiled pleasantly. "It's no bother. I've been in your shoes before, and a stranger bailed me out just like this. I'm simply paying it forward. Now, you can do the same for someone else."

Fey nodded and smiled. "Thank you."

"My pleasure," he said with a playful wink.

Fey couldn't help but smile shyly at that. She even felt some heat briefly rush to her face.

While they were waiting for their orders, Fey stole glances at him and took in his features as he answered a call on his cellphone. He was a handsome guy of African descent, but he spoke with a British accent. The man was taller than her by about six inches and was wearing a pair of jeans and a fitted dress shirt, which accentuated his broad shoulders and toned arms. He looked to be a few years older than Fey, and she wondered if his job was nearby. It was a weekday after all, and he was probably taking a lunch break from work.

He was still on his phone when their order was ready. He grabbed his sandwich and drink and gave Fey a slight nod before he exited the cafe. Fey waved goodbye in response, took her order, and a few seconds later, she was seated at a small, empty table by a window. While sipping her coffee, she looked out the window, people-watching. Fey didn't realize how much time had passed until someone sat down in front of her. She looked up to see that it was a middle-aged man who simply grunted something to her in German and proceeded to eat his meal.

Fey looked around the cafe. Yes, there weren't a lot of seats left, but how do you just sit in front of someone you don't know and then pretend that they're not right in front of you? It wasn't like she wanted to start a conversation with the man, but it just seemed too intimate and was just plain awkward. After a few more minutes of sitting in awkward silence, trying not to watch the man eat his meal, Fey left the cafe. She walked around the neighborhood for another fifteen minutes before she went back to the house.

She chatted with Tutu on the phone for a few minutes, telling her about her embarrassing breakfast incident. Then she decided to watch some TV. After a while, she fell asleep and woke up sometime later to the doorbell ringing. Startled, she jumped up from the sofa and went to see who it was. She wasn't expecting the rest of her housemates until tomorrow, so she wondered who it could be.

She opened the door to find her best friend standing there with her luggage.

"Demi?!" Fey shrieked in surprise. "I thought you were arriving tomorrow."

With a smirk, Demi replied, "And I thought you had gone deaf or something. Do you know how long I've been out here ringing the doorbell?"

"Sorry," Fey apologized as she stepped away from the doorway so that Demi could come in. "I fell asleep while watching TV. I guess I'm still jet-lagged."

Once Demi brought in her luggage, she said, "I wanted to surprise you; that's why I didn't call ahead."

The two ladies hugged each other tightly.

"I missed you all summer," Demi pouted.

"I missed you too." Fey hugged her again and held her hand as she led her upstairs. "Come, let's pick out your room."

After giving Demi a tour of the house, she decided on a room. They chatted for a while and then Demi groaned, "I'm so yucky from my flight, I need a shower!" Just before Fey walked out of the room, she added, "Since you got a chance to explore the neighborhood a little during the day, how about we explore the nightlife together once I finish taking a shower?"

Fey raised a brow. "Really? You just got here, and you already want to go clubbing?"

Demi crossed her arms across her chest. "Yes, I'll have you know that is the best way to unwind," she said matter-of-factly. "I'm just so excited to be here!"

Fey chuckled and shook her head. "Fine, I'll go and get ready." When she arrived in her room, she looked through her clothes to see what she could wear. Since it was the time of the year when it starts to cool down a lot at night, Fey opted for a pair of black sequin leggings, a silver blouse, and her one-and-only leather biker jacket. Demi had given it to her as a birthday gift a few years prior because she claimed that not having a trendy leather jacket in her wardrobe was fashion sacrilege.

After getting dressed, Fey waited for another ten minutes in the living room before Demi finally made her way downstairs. She was wearing a floral baby-doll mini dress and heels.

"So, where exactly are we going? I mean, this isn't Atlanta, and we don't exactly speak German."

"I'm glad you asked. There's a bar close to campus that I want to try. I hear it's trendy, and it has a lot of great reviews from foreigners." She glanced at the time. "Our Uber should be here in a few minutes."

03 | Iben

It had been a couple of weeks since Fey's arrival in Munich. The rest of her housemates, Tara and Kiera, arrived a couple of days after Demi. Classes were going to start next week, and the friends were now on their way to the international students' meet and greet. They had spent a couple of days since everyone's arrival getting acquainted with their neighborhood and the bustling city of Munich in general. While Fey didn't mind occasionally hanging out with her friends at the bars and clubs, she was more comfortable at a jazz lounge. Regardless, she enjoyed spending time with her housemates these past few weeks. All four of them were college friends, and they generally hung out together during the semesters. However, the fall semester would be starting soon, and with that, opportunities to socialize would drastically reduce.

After getting off the train, they walked to the venue. It was a short walk, and the friends arrived just as the International Student's Union president was about to begin his speech. They joined several students who were also just arriving. Afterward, they walked around to all the different stands, meeting different people and getting information on where to take crash courses in the local language, best eateries, bars, volunteer opportunities, and so on.

At some point, Fey broke away from her group to find out more about the different volunteer opportunities available. Back in the States, she never took the chance to get involved in serving the community. So Fey thought this was an excellent opportunity to gain experience while meeting with the locals and perhaps experiencing Munich on a different level. Fey intended to make sure that her study abroad time over the next few months would be a memorable one.

After signing up as a volunteer at a homeless shelter, she left to join her group at the agreed-upon meeting place. The bar was a few blocks away, and one that they had visited a few times in the last couple of weeks. Once inside, she found Demi and the other girls, and after a few drinks, they went home.

The next morning was Friday. After returning from a quick morning run, Fey received a text message from one of the volunteer coordinators that she met the day before at the meet-and-greet. She was paired with another experienced volunteer, and she had to meet up with the person around noon for onboarding and to receive details on the coming weekend's activities. Fey was surprised to be contacted so soon but was also looking forward to getting involved.

A few hours later, she was on her way to the meeting address, which happened to be an office building. Perhaps the person that she was supposed to meet with worked there. She finally located the building, and since it was right around lunchtime, she noticed a sudden rise in foot traffic in and out of the building.

As she got closer to the entrance, she slowly got swept away in the rush of people coming in and out of the revolving door entrance. As people moved the door along, she quickly realized that this was probably the fastest moving revolving door she'd ever been through. Before she knew what was happening, the cycle ended unexpectedly as she was nudged forward straight into the lobby. Stumbling while trying to steady herself, she abruptly stopped moving as she bumped into a pair of strong arms. She quickly let go, stepped back to compose herself, and looked up to see a face she recognized. It was the same man who had paid for her meal a couple of weeks before.

"Hi there," he said with a smirk.

"Oh my gosh! This is the second time you've saved me from an embarrassing situation. I was certainly on my way to falling flat on my face if you hadn't stopped me."

He chuckled good-naturedly.

"I'm so sorry I bumped into you. I'm usually not this clumsy. I just got swept away in that madness!" Fey said, pointing towards the door. "Anyway, I'm here to meet someone, so I'll let you get to lunch or wherever you were heading to."

The man raised an eyebrow. "Really? I'm meeting someone here too." He held out his hand. "I'm Iben."

It was Fey's turn to raise her eyebrows in surprise. "Oh my gosh! I'm Fey," she said, accepting his handshake with a smile.

"What a pleasant coincidence," Iben said, holding her gaze and her hand a moment longer before letting go and shoving his hands casually in his pants pockets.

Is he flirting with me? Fey thought to herself. *Nah, I'm probably overthinking it.* "Yeah... so do you work here?" she asked.

"I do. When I'm not taking classes at TUM."

"I'm attending TUM as well. Study abroad semester... So, I didn't see you at the meet and greet yesterday."

"Yeah, it was a pretty big turnout. Easy to get lost in the crowd," Iben said with a slight shrug.

"True... So how long have you been attending?"

"Two years. I'll complete my master's degree this academic year."

"That's great."

Iben looked away and gestured towards some seats in the waiting area. "Why don't we go over there?"

They found an unoccupied sofa in the corner of the lobby and sat down, continuing their conversation.

"So, what's your course of study?" Iben asked.

"Civil engineering."

"Cool. Beautiful *and* smart," Iben replied with a smile, holding her gaze.

Fey gave a short self-conscious laugh. *Okay, he's definitely flirting*, she thought to herself. She, however, realized that she didn't mind. She honestly wanted to know more about him, so she asked, "So, what brings you to TUM... from the UK?" She couldn't miss his British accent and was hoping he'd divulge information about his background. Maybe his family migrated to the UK just like hers had migrated to the States.

"Well, I'm here for my master's degree in intellectual property law. And after I graduate, I'll be heading back home to continue working at my grandfather's firm."

"Your grandfather's a lawyer?"

"No, the company's pretty diverse, and I'll be working with the legal department, overseeing contracts and stuff."

"I see... What about your siblings? They're also working at your grandfather's firm, I presume." Fey realized that she had just asked a personal question, so she hoped he wouldn't be offended. This was the second time they'd met, but there was a cool but mysterious aura about him that drew her in.

Iben paused for a few seconds before answering. "Not at all. But I do have other family members who also work for my grandfather."

Fey nodded.

It was Iben's turn to pry. "So, what about your siblings?"

"I have a younger sister. She's back in the States with my mom. Which reminds me, I need to give them a call this weekend before my mom sends a search party to Munich!"

That earned a chuckle out of Iben. "Sounds like you all are close."

It was Fey's turn to pause. She was enjoying this easy conversation with Iben, and she didn't want to sour the mood by talking about her family drama and how happy she was to be away from her mom. "You know how mothers can be... overprotective and overbearing and such," Fey responded with a light shrug.

"Perhaps... but still, we wouldn't be who we are today if it weren't for our parents. They can be very demanding at times, but we just need to remember that it's all out of love. I try not to take things too personally and just focus on being the best me."

Fey noticed a sad, yet determined look briefly cross his face. *Oh my gosh! That got deep all of a sudden. Good job, Fey. I ended up souring the mood anyway.*

Then Iben asked, "So, what made you decide to be a volunteer?"

Fey was surprised at the sudden change in conversation, but volunteering was the reason why she was here today, after all. "Um... One of the things I'd like to do while I'm here in Germany over the next few months is to experience the country from different perspectives. Of course, I don't understand the language very well, but I do feel that interacting with the locals in some way, other than college students like myself, is one way to achieve that goal."

Iben nodded in understanding. He looked at the time on his phone and then said, "I'm sorry, but I have to get back to work."

Fey was disappointed, but she tried not to show it.

Then he added, "Um—can I get your contact info so I can reach out to you later about the volunteer event for Saturday?"

Fey nodded with a smile and hoped Iben didn't see the relief in her face. After handing her his phone, Fey entered her phone number and email address.

"Thanks," he said and stood up. Fey joined him, and they started walking towards the exit.

"I apologize for having to leave so suddenly."

"No worries. If I hadn't peppered you with questions, we would've at least had the time to accomplish what I came here for."

Iben shook his head. "Don't say that. I really enjoyed chatting with you." He held out his hand for a handshake, and Fey took it.

They said their goodbyes and Iben waited until Fey walked out of the building before letting out a breath he didn't realize he was holding. As Iben walked towards the elevator back to his office, he smiled to himself. He was honest with Fey when he told her that he was pleasantly surprised that she was the person he was supposed to be showing the ropes for the volunteer program.

Since that day, when he met her at the cafe a few weeks ago, he stopped by the cafe almost every day after that to see if he would, by chance, bump into her again. She didn't go there very often, but the few times he did see her there, he had chickened out on approaching her. What if she didn't recognize him? What if she didn't care that he'd bought her breakfast and would think he was just a creep? He berated himself internally for feeling that way. He wasn't one to be timid around women, but there was something about that woman that made him cautious, as he didn't want to scare her off. She had a warm yet confident air about her that drew him in.

While chatting with Fey, he realized that he wanted to get to know her better, and he was not going to let an opportunity pass by. He pulled up her contact info on his phone and sent her a text message.

'Hey, this is Iben. Since it's your first time, we can go to the soup kitchen together tomorrow morning. If it's okay with you, let's meet up at the cafe tomorrow at 6:00 AM.'

A few minutes later, he got a response. *'Sure thing!'*

Iben smiled to himself again. He was undoubtedly looking forward to tomorrow.

***

Iben was already at the cafe when Fey arrived. When she came over to where he was seated, he gave her one of the two cups of coffee he was holding.

"I hope you don't mind your coffee with cream and sugar."

"Not at all, thanks!" Fey responded with a smile.

A few minutes later, they were on the way to the soup kitchen. After a 20-minute train ride, they walked for another ten minutes before arriving at their destination. Iben formally introduced her to the rest of the volunteer team, and then they went about their assigned tasks.

A few hours later, after helping with the cleanup, Fey looked around for Iben. They had been so busy, and she didn't get a chance to chat some more with him as she had hoped, which was silly. After all, this wasn't a social event, and they were there to serve. Disappointed when she couldn't find him, she took out her phone and started to check for directions back to her place. Suddenly, a voice from behind startled her.

"Was I such a terrible companion on the way here that you'd rather go home by yourself?"

Fey turned around to find Iben, peering over her shoulder with a smirk. "Hmmm... you don't know the half of it," Fey joked, and he chuckled. "Anyway, I couldn't find you, so I figured you were either busy or had left."

"You were looking for me?" He smiled, pleasantly surprised.

Fey shrugged nonchalantly. "Are you ready?" she asked.

He nodded, and they started towards the train station. They walked in comfortable silence for a few minutes before they walked past the bar that Fey and her friends went to the night of the campus meet and greet. Demi and her other housemates wanted to go back later, but she wasn't feeling it. She sighed.

Iben heard her sigh and was curious to know what she was thinking. "Penny for your thoughts?" he asked, breaking the silence.

"Oh, it's nothing..."

Iben pressed. "I've been told that I'm a pretty good listener."

Fey smiled politely. "I'm good, really," she insisted. It wasn't like she was thinking about anything interesting or earth-shattering.

"I really must be a lousy companion if I'm making a pretty lady sigh so deeply," Iben said jokingly.

Fey chuckled. "Fine, fine, nose-box." She rolled her eyes. "I'll tell you..." She glanced over at Iben, who was all smiles. He looked pleased as punch with himself. "My friends want to hang out this weekend, and I'm thinking about bailing out on them."

"Why?"

"The bar's really not my scene. But I also don't want to let the girls down."

"So, what would you rather be doing?"

"I'd rather stay indoors, reading a book or watching TV. Classes are starting in two days, and I prefer not to be hungover on Monday."

"I see... so what's your scene then?" Iben asked. This girl was interesting. Most young ladies he knew wouldn't say that they didn't like bars.

"I love jazz music. Back in Atlanta, I had the opportunity to go to a small jazz music lounge once. It was a lot of fun." She smiled at the memory.

Iben watched Fey as she spoke. He didn't take his eyes off her for even a second. He was very attracted to her, and he meant what he said earlier about her being pretty. He continued watching as her face lit up while describing her experience at the jazz club.

"What about you?" he suddenly heard Fey ask, snapping him out of his thoughts.

"What would you like to know?" he asked smoothly, the corner of his lips lifting into a smile.

"Well, what do you like to do when you're not working or volunteering?"

Iben rubbed his chin briefly and then said, "I like cooking, and I sometimes play chess at a Meetup here in Munich."

"You don't look like you can cook at all," Fey said with a look of disbelief.

"I bet I can cook better than you," Iben teased, a mischievous smile forming on his handsome face.

Fey snorted at his response. Even though she wasn't a great cook like her sister Tutu, she believed she could certainly cook circles around this guy. "Don't believe you!" Fey's tone carried a teasing note, her eyebrows raised.

"How so? You're judging a book by its cover?"

Fey stopped walking, turned to face Iben, and said, "Yes, I'm very judge-y right now, and here's why I don't think you can cook." Suddenly, she held his hands and ran her fingers softly across his palms. "So soft, no calluses, smooth... I bet you can only cook... ramen noodles."

Iben watched speechlessly as Fey innocently ran her thumb across his palms to make her point. To his surprise, her touch sent exciting electric currents through his body. He lifted his eyes to meet hers, and for a few seconds, they held each other's gaze. Iben said nothing as Fey's eyes shone brightly.

"Well, am I right?" she asked smugly. She truly believed she'd made a profound point, and that's why there was no response from Iben. She didn't realize what effect she was having on the young man standing in front of her. In fact, she didn't realize that she had suddenly crossed a physical touch boundary with a man that she had only met a total of three times. Somehow, it just felt natural to her.

Looking at the beautiful woman in front of him, Iben had the sudden urge to pull Fey close to him. However, he quickly pulled himself together, shook his head slowly, and said smoothly without missing a beat. "Wanna bet?"

Fey let go of his hands and continued walking. She didn't notice the flash of disappointment that crossed Iben's face. He didn't want her to let go of his hands.

"Are you suggesting a cook-off?" she asked.

Iben caught up to her and said, "Great minds think alike."

"Hmmm... okay," Fey agreed.

"The dish will be rice!" Iben declared.

Fey gave him the side-eye and raised a questioning eyebrow. *Of all dishes, rice?*

"Hey, I can make a mean rice dish," Iben retorted proudly.

Fey chuckled. This guy was too funny. "Rice is rice. How tasty can anyone cook rice?"

"You just gotta be creative."

"Fine... we'll have a rice cook-off," Fey said in mock defeat.

Even after they got on the train, the pair continued chatting and teasing each other like old friends. Before long, they arrived at Fey's stop. She got up and was about to say goodbye when Iben mentioned that this was his stop as well. They continued walking together until they arrived at the cafe they'd met earlier.

"Thanks for the great company," Fey said, smiling.

"Ah... glad I was able to redeem myself," Iben responded, with a smile. He was referring to Fey's earlier comment, teasing him about how he was a lousy companion.

Fey laughed softly and simply shook her head. She couldn't remember the last time she laughed as much as she had with Iben in the previous hour. She glanced at her watch. It was almost 2:00 PM. She realized that she didn't want their time together to end. But, despite how she felt, she didn't think it was fair to delay him any further, as he probably had other commitments. She smiled instead and reached out her hand for a goodbye handshake.

Iben's eyes met hers, and he reached out his hand in response. As soon as their hands touched, he suddenly remembered the moment from earlier when she had rubbed the palms of his hands, and he immediately felt some heat rush to his face. Good thing he was dark-skinned; otherwise, his thoughts would be exposed. *Why the heck am I feeling like a hormonal teenager?!* Iben thought to himself. Still smiling, he said, "I had a great time today, Fey."

"Me too."

Silence.

Iben self-consciously cleared his throat and then let go of her hand. "See you around," he said with a wink before turning around and heading to his apartment.

"Bye," Fey responded before walking the rest of the way back to her place.

04 | Closer

It had been about a month since the semester began and since Fey started volunteering at the shelter. Although they attended the same university, she didn't have an opportunity to see Iben on campus, so she always looked forward to the weekends. They soon settled into a routine. On Saturdays, they'd meet at the cafe, go to the shelter together, and then leave together.

Today, instead of saying their goodbyes after reaching the cafe storefront like they usually did, Iben invited Fey to lunch. She was hungry, so she agreed. They ordered their meals and sat down at a table to wait for their orders to be ready.

"I know we've both been busy lately, but how do you feel about having that cook-off you promised this weekend?" Iben asked out of the blue. He was smiling mischievously.

Fey raised her eyebrows in surprise. She had completely forgotten about that. Indeed, she hadn't taken him seriously since they were just teasing each other anyway.

Fey didn't respond right away, so he quickly added, "Unless you're busy, of course. I know it's short notice..."

"Name the time and place and be prepared to get crushed!" Fey returned his challenge with a smile.

Iben slowly let out the breath he was holding. He was relieved that Fey didn't turn him down. He had gotten to know her a lot more in the past month, and they had become fast friends. He had grown to like her a lot. She was beautiful, smart, had a great sense of humor, and had an aura of quiet confidence. He felt so comfortable whenever he was with her. His gaze fell on her smiling lips. She was wearing light lip-gloss today. Like he'd been doing a lot lately, he wondered what it would feel like to kiss those lips.

"Penny for your thoughts?" Fey asked since he hadn't responded to her.

I really can't tell you that now, can I? Iben thought to himself. He cleared his throat self-consciously before saying, "Your place, dinner tonight, 6:00 PM. I'll bring the ingredients. Your roommates can be the judges."

"Deal! Let's shake on it."

They did, and after lunch, they both went their separate ways.

***

"Wait, what?!" Demi exclaimed in surprise after Fey told her about Iben coming over. "You've been keeping secrets from me, young lady." She pointed an accusatory finger at Fey, who simply laughed at her best friend's dramatic response to the news that she had invited a guy over.

"What secrets? You're acting as if I never mentioned him to you before. Or like you just found out that I have a boyfriend or something." Fey rolled her eyes and continued tidying up the shared living space in preparation for Iben's arrival later that evening.

Boyfriend? "You like him, don't you?" Demi asked, her eyes narrowed in suspicion.

"We're just friends, Demi. If I didn't like him, we wouldn't be friends, right?" Demi said nothing in response, so she continued, "It's unfortunate that you won't be here, though. He was looking forward to meeting you."

"Well, I'm not heading out until around 8:00 PM so I can stay and chaperone you guys until then," Demi finally said with her signature, impish smile.

Fey chuckled and said, "Yes, mother!"

At 6:00 PM sharp, the doorbell rang. Fey answered the door and let Iben in. After introducing him to Demi, she explained that, unfortunately, most of the ladies weren't home; so only Demi was available as a judge.

"Iben, I promise to be as impartial as I possibly can. Although, I am getting a free meal tonight, so take that with a grain of salt," Demi said with a grin.

Iben chuckled. "Sounds fair to me," he said.

"Well, I'll be upstairs. Whenever you guys are ready, just holla," Demi chirped. But just before leaving the pair of contestants in the kitchen, she walked by Fey and spoke in a low tone so that no one else would hear. "Nice catch!"

Fey simply glared daggers at her friend's back as she walked away. She was now suddenly worried that Demi might say something outlandish or embarrassing in front of Iben before the end of the night.

Back to the cook-off.

Iben announced that he would be preparing garlic butter rice for the competition. Fey, on the other hand, said she would be making fried rice. Earlier, she sent a list of ingredients to Iben since he offered to bring them. They chatted while preparing the ingredients.

After Fey washed and seasoned the chicken, she went over to Iben and watched as he chopped the vegetables. She raised her eyebrows in surprise as he quickly and expertly chopped and sliced carrots and onions like a professional chef.

Iben, who had been stealing glances at Fey, noticed her expression and teased, "Bet you wish you hadn't challenged me, huh?"

Yeah, she thought to herself, but she wasn't going to admit that. Instead, she said, "I'll admit, your knife skills are enviable. But that doesn't mean that you can cook better than me."

Iben chuckled and said, "I guess we'll just have to wait and see."

Once they finished prepping their ingredients, they both started with their rice dishes. When the rice in both pots was in the last stages of steaming, Iben began to sauté the chicken breast cutlets that Fey had seasoned earlier. In another 30 minutes, everything was ready.

"You know, Iben, in the many years that Fey and I have been best friends, she has never cooked for me or anyone else I know for that matter," Demi announced as she sat down to eat the delicious-looking meal in front of her.

Fey rolled her eyes in response. *Here comes the crazy talk*, she thought to herself. She turned to Iben and said dismissively, "Don't believe everything that comes out of her mouth."

Iben smiled as he listened to Fey and Demi tease each other. Suddenly, Demi asked with a mischievous smirk, "Just curious, what are the stakes in this cooking duel?"

Iben and Fey glanced at each other at the same time. They hadn't thought about that.

Seeing the expression on their faces, Demi asked, "May I make a suggestion?"

Fey had a bad feeling about where this was going. She suddenly had a flashback to the time when they played Truth or Dare in high school, and Demi had dared her to confess her feelings to a boy that she had a crush on.

"Sure," Iben said before Fey could refuse.

Demi was all smiles at this point, while Fey tried her best to hide her apprehension.

Demi looked thoughtful for a moment. Then, she said, "If Fey wins, Iben, you have to take her to a jazz club." She then glanced over at Fey and added, "If Iben wins, Fey, you'll have to buy him dinner at a restaurant of his choosing." She looked back and forth between both of them, looking pleased as punch.

While Fey was relieved that Demi hadn't suggested anything as crazy as she had feared, one couldn't miss the fact that she was obviously trying to set them up on a date.

Again, before Fey could say anything, Iben responded with a smile, "I'm cool with that. Fey...?"

Fey shot him a glance, and they held each other's gaze briefly before she looked away and shrugged nonchalantly. She didn't notice the confused look that briefly flashed across Iben's face. Even though it was only there for a moment, Demi caught it and thought to herself with a smile, *Interesting...*

Demi finally decided to try the food on her plate. First, she ate Fey's fried rice, and then she tasted Iben's garlic butter rice. Demi tried her best to control her facial expressions so that neither Fey nor Iben would be able to tell which one she liked best. Both contestants watched her intently as she slowly savored the food in her mouth.

After watching Demi eat a few more mouthfuls, Fey got impatient. "Well... which do you like best?"

Demi finished chewing and drank some water. Then she assumed the airs of a pretentious, European food critic. "Iben, I enjoyed the crunchiness of the golden butter-fried garlic chips that accompanied the soft and lightly seasoned Jasmine rice. Paired with the sautéed chicken breast, it was divine."

Iben chuckled. "Thank you, madam," he said with a bow, playing along.

"Don't encourage her," Fey chimed in while trying to stifle the smile that was forming on her lips.

Then, Demi turned to Fey and said, "I enjoyed the burst of flavors from the fried rice. The vegetables were steamed and seasoned perfectly. Paired with the sautéed chicken breast, it was to die for."

"Wow!" Fey responded with an eye-roll.

Demi continued, "And the winner is... drumroll... Fey!"

"Yes!" Fey shouted excitedly, after which she did a silly victory dance where she jumped up and down and side to side.

Iben was all smiles as he watched her act like a little kid. He was enjoying this side of Fey that he'd never seen before. "Congratulations on your win, milady," he finally said with a bow.

Fey laughed. "Thank you, kind sir! Although I will admit that you are a worthy adversary in the culinary arts." Her smiling eyes met and held Iben's for a moment.

"Ahem!" Demi interrupted after a few seconds, causing Fey to feel self-conscious. "Well, thank you both for a wonderful meal. Now, I have to head to my study group at the library." She stood up, turned to Iben, and said, "It was nice to meet you, Iben."

"Likewise, and thanks for indulging us." He smiled warmly.

Demi grabbed her bag, waved goodbye, and left.

"I'm starving!" Fey announced to Iben after Demi left. "Ready to eat?"

"I thought you'd never ask," Iben answered, and then he dished out two plates of food.

They ate quietly, each of them lost in their thoughts, and neither saying much of anything until the meal was over. Afterward, Iben helped with the dishes.

"Would you like some coffee?" Fey offered.

"Sure."

A few minutes later, they were seated in the living room, mugs of coffee in hand, drinking quietly. Iben was the first to break the silence.

"So, when would you like to redeem your jazz club coupon?" he asked with a smile.

Fey dismissively waved her hand, "Don't worry about it. You don't have to feel obligated to do that," she said with a small smile.

Iben looked like he was pondering something for a moment. Then he said, "Actually, I found a nice jazz club in the area, and I've wanted to ask you if you'd like to go with me."

Fey raised her eyebrows in surprise. *How sweet*, she thought to herself. And then it dawned on her. *Wait, is he asking me out on a date?*

Iben looked at her expectantly.

Fey said nothing. She was experiencing a rush of different emotions right now. She was certainly excited to hear that Iben wanted to take her to a jazz club. Also, she really liked him a lot, but she had a feeling that he might just be doing this as a friend, nothing more. She finally put her mug down and started to say something. "Uhm…"

Just then, Iben turned to face her and reached for her hands. This time, he was the one who rubbed the palms of her hands with his thumbs as he spoke. "Fey, I *really* like you... a lot." His deep voice was full of emotion. He continued with a smile teasing the corner of his lips, "I always look forward to seeing you every Saturday so that we can go to the shelter together. I never want you to leave when we get back to the cafe and have to go back home. I always have to control the urge to call you during the week, just so that I can hear your voice."

Fey smiled at his words and shyly bit her lower lip. This made Iben's heart do flips. However, a look of concern appeared for a moment as he thought to himself: *Although she hasn't pulled her hands away yet, I still don't know for sure how she feels about me. She's not saying anything. Is she hesitant or just shy?* He then remembered the weird look on her face after Demi had suggested the winnings of their cook-off. *Maybe she doesn't see me in that way? Aaahhh!* He was driving himself crazy with these thoughts. Instead of making any assumptions, he decided to take a risk and find out.

Still holding her hands, Iben pulled her up so that they were standing just a few inches in front of each other. He quickly closed the gap between them. One hand gently held her by the waist and pressed her body close to him. In response, Fey wrapped her arms around him and buried her face in his chest. Iben swore he could hear his heart beating in his ears. They stayed like this for a while, neither of them saying anything, just enjoying the feeling of being close to each other.

Moments later, overcome with the deep emotions he felt for the woman he held in his arms, Iben lowered his head and gently planted a kiss on the top of her head. *She smells amazing,* he thought to himself as he inhaled the botanic fragrance in her hair. Then, he kissed her forehead. Next, he lifted her chin and looked into her eyes before kissing her soft cheeks. Finally, he kissed the corner of her lips. A breathy moan escaped Fey's lips, which immediately drove Iben crazy with desire. *Mmm, sexy.*

In the next moment, his tongue gently teased apart her lips, earning him another moan from Fey. To his delight, she also responded by parting her lips. Iben couldn't control himself any longer, he dove right in and enjoyed the exotic, sweet nectar of the kiss as Fey kissed him back. Moments later, his desire now satiated to a dull ache, Iben slowly withdrew and gently kissed her soft lips.

His eyes softened as he took in the features of the beautiful woman in his arms. He kissed her forehead one more time, and she fell into his

embrace.
    He finally got his answer.

05 | Passion

The next day was Sunday, and Fey woke up much later than usual. She didn't go for her usual early morning run because she stayed awake till late last night. After Iben left, Fey couldn't fall asleep. The kisses they shared last night, and the warm, tingling sensations she felt as Iben wrapped his arms around her waist kept replaying in her mind.

Now awake, she thought back to last night's events. She had been pleasantly surprised when Iben suddenly confessed his feelings to her after dinner. Without a doubt, the feeling was mutual, but unlike Iben, she probably never would've voiced them. She would've continued to be in denial of the fact that their friendship was turning into something more in her heart. Before last night, she would've continued to be content with hanging out with him on Saturdays after their volunteering, even though she hated having to part from him afterward. As it turns out, they had both wanted to spend more time together but were both worried about coming off as needy or too forward.

Fey's thoughts were interrupted by a notification on her cellphone. It was a message from Iben.

'Good morning, beautiful,' it read.

Fey couldn't help but grin from ear to ear. *'Good morning,'* she typed back.

'Could milady pencil me in for a lunch date today despite her busy schedule?'

Fey chuckled at his teasing. *'Sure, as long as you make it worth my while…,'* she teased back.

'Challenge accepted,' he responded. *'I'll pick you up in front of the cafe at 2 pm.'*

'Cool. See you soon.'

At exactly 2:00 PM, Fey walked into the cafe. It was the same one where they first met. Within a few seconds, she spotted Iben, who was seated at a corner of the cafe and walked over. As soon as Iben saw her, a smile lit up his handsome face. He stood up and immediately pulled her into a hug when she got to the table. This open and public display of affection surprised Fey but in a warm and fuzzy kind of way. Taking in his scent, as her head rested on his firm chest, Fey was just thinking about how good he smelled when they parted.

"Hey," Iben greeted, his voice soft as he held her gaze.

She smiled. "Have you been waiting long?"

He shook his head. "Let's go," he said as he held her hand in his and started walking towards the exit.

"We're not eating here?" Fey asked, puzzled.

"Nope!"

After they got outside, Fey followed Iben to a delicatessen a couple of blocks away. He asked her to wait outside while he went in.

What is he up to? Fey thought to herself, puzzled. *We didn't eat at the other cafe, and it doesn't look like we're eating here either.*

A few minutes later, Iben finally came outside, holding a wicker basket. It had a lid, so Fey couldn't see what was in it. After a couple of seconds, she chuckled in sudden realization, "Is that a picnic basket?"

"Yes, milady. And now we need to get going," Iben responded with a bright smile.

Fey sighed and shook her head in mock resignation as she followed Iben to their next stop. *I didn't eat any breakfast and was looking forward to lunch. At this rate, I'll be starving by the time I get to sit down and eat.* Fey was feeling slightly sorry for herself.

Another ten minutes of walking brought the couple to the entrance of a familiar park - *Englischer Garten*. A few Saturdays ago, the volunteering team had come to the park for an event. Fey didn't get a chance to explore the park at the time, as they were on a mission. By now, she had figured out what was going on. Iben had brought her to a picnic lunch at the park.

As if reading her mind, Iben said, "Last time we came here with the team, you said you'd like to come back some other time. It's a nice day today, so I figured, why not."

Awww... he remembered. How sweet, Fey thought to herself. It felt nice to have someone think about her in that way.

As they walked through the enormous park, Fey took in the scenery. Past the lush greenery, she could see several people who were enjoying a quiet, lazy afternoon at the lake - *Kleinhesseloher See*. It was September in Munich, but the weather was uncharacteristically warmer than usual, which brought many folks out to the park. The sun was bright, the breeze was refreshing, and you could hear the laughter and squeals of little kids playing here and there.

Finally, they found a quiet spot on the lawn, and Fey helped Iben set up their lunch. As soon as the picnic hamper was open, a mouthwatering aroma wafted up Fey's nose.

"Smells so delicious," Fey said excitedly. As if on cue, her stomach let out a loud growl in response.

Iben chuckled as he continued to take out the items in the basket. "Now, I wonder if there's enough food here for a certain someone," he teased.

Fey rolled her eyes. "Well, apparently, someone was secretly trying to starve me this afternoon by dragging me through half of Munich."

"Caught red-handed," Iben joked, raising his hands in mock surrender. Then he added, "I'd like to think of it as my way of helping you work up a good appetite, though."

Fey chuckled.

One of the things that Iben loved about Fey was her sense of humor. She never took his jokes too seriously, and he loved that she could tease back as much as he gave. It was so easy being with her. He couldn't think of anyone else who made him feel so comfortable. Although they'd only known each other for barely two months, they shared a familiarity that made him feel like he could be his playful self, letting down the veneer that he put up every day to face the world.

Fey mumbled something that Iben didn't hear. He had turned away to continue taking out the remaining things from the hamper. When he looked up from what he was doing, Iben realized why he hadn't heard what she had said clearly. It was because she was busy stuffing her face with some of the brownies.

"I'm sorry," Fey mumbled apologetically. "They looked so delicious."

Iben smiled at her sheepish apology. "No need to apologize. Dessert before a meal is cool too." Unlike some of the girls he knew or had dated in the past, Fey seemed to be herself. She wasn't pretending to be so prim and proper, or that she didn't eat more than a few morsels of food. Even the few times they had lunch over the past month or so, Fey always had a healthy appetite. Despite that, she had a slim figure, with gentle curves in all the right places—at least from Iben's perspective.

A few minutes later, they started eating. Thanks to Fey's ravenous appetite, the spread of sandwiches, soup, fruits, and brownies quickly disappeared.

Fey leaned back against the tree under which they were seated and made a show of rubbing her belly to indicate her satisfaction. "Thank you for the meal. I couldn't fall asleep until late last night, and I had just woken up when you sent me a text inviting me to lunch. So, I hadn't eaten anything until now."

"Really? Why couldn't you fall asleep?" a concerned Iben asked.

Fey froze for a second. *Crap! I wasn't paying attention to what I was saying... Well, I certainly can't tell him that it was because I was busy thinking about kissing him!*

With that thought, Fey's eyes involuntarily landed on Iben's lips, which were currently wrapped around a straw as he sipped his drink while waiting for her response. Those were the same lips that had wreaked sweet havoc on her senses the night before. Worried that Iben would be able to read her thoughts, she quickly looked away and nonchalantly shrugged while trying to change the topic. "Were you able to get home at a decent time last night?" she asked.

Iben did not respond right away. He had a thoughtful look on his face before he eventually said, "Yeah... but by the time I did, I was missing you already."

Fey smiled at his cheesy words as she looked at him. He playfully winked at her before reaching out his hand to hold hers. They sat there quietly, enjoying the :comfortable silence.

After a while, they started chatting about the coming week. Now that the couple was on the same page in terms of their feelings for each other, they naturally wanted to spend more time together. Although they were both busy, they could squeeze in some time to have lunch once during the week. Iben usually wasn't on campus during the day classes since he was a graduate student taking evening classes and had a part-time office job. However, on Thursday, it was fortuitous that he had to be on campus around 11:00 AM to meet with his advisor. They agreed to meet up for lunch around noon. By then, Iben's meeting would be over, and Fey would be done with classes as Thursday was a short day for her. She only had two courses, which were in the morning.

After agreeing to a meetup location, they packed up and left the park. Despite Fey's protests, Iben walked her back to her place. At her doorstep, Fey turned to face him. "Thanks for walking me back," she said.

"It's my pleasure, milady."

"See ya," Fey said and turned around to open the door.

However, Iben suddenly said, "Hang on a second."

She turned around with brows raised, wondering what else he had to say. The next moment, he was already in front of her and pulled her in for a hug. Caught by surprise, Fey didn't return the hug right away.

"Can I call you tomorrow?" he asked softly.

Fey could feel his breath against her ear, sending delicious waves down her back down to her toes. "Mmmm," she hummed, returning his hug.

"Can I call you every day?" Iben asked, hugging her a little bit tighter. He was aware that she might think he was corny, but he just didn't want to assume. He was over the moon that their feelings for each other were mutual, and he was very much attracted to her. Still, he didn't want to overwhelm her with unwanted attention from him suddenly.

Fey chuckled lightly at his question. "Of course. Next thing I know, you'll be asking permission to kiss me."

They both stilled.

Fey had blurted out something she was now worried might make Iben feel obligated to kiss her. *Why am I suddenly so loose-lipped around this guy? How embarrassing.*

On Iben's part, he felt that he had successfully distracted himself from the lusty thoughts he'd been keeping at bay all afternoon. He also thought that he probably would've been fine leaving with just a goodbye hug. But now, she was talking about kissing him, and he could slowly feel himself losing his resolve. With his arms still around her, he gently leaned back from the hug to look at her face, as if checking to see if she meant what she just said. Fey was looking up at him with those beautiful brown eyes. The smirk on the corner of her full lips seemed to taunt and dare him. Iben could hear his heart beating faster and faster as he ran his thumb across her lips. *So soft,* he thought to himself. At this point, only one thought was on his mind.

The next moment, he leaned in and captured Fey's lips. She moaned softly as she felt his tongue parting her lips. Fey softened in his embrace as he deepened the kiss. She responded passionately, conveying her feelings to him. When the kiss ended, Iben looked down at Fey's beautiful face and then leaned in to kiss her forehead.

"I'll let you go now," he said almost in a whisper, even though he still embraced her tightly.

"Mmm," Fey nodded.

After Iben left, she went into the house. However, something was bothering her about the moment she and Iben had just shared. She was still lost in her thoughts, trying to decipher her feelings and didn't see Demi, who was sitting in the living room. Fey walked right past her.

"Earth to Fey… earth to Fey." Demi waved her hands and tried to get her attention.

"Oh—hi, Demi. What's up?" Fey asked.

"I don't know. You tell me. Why are you so distracted?" She looked Fey up and down and quickly added, "And where did you go?" When Demi had checked for her earlier and saw that she wasn't around, she assumed Fey was out for her Sunday run. But now she noticed that Fey wasn't wearing workout clothes.

"I went to lunch with Iben."

A bright smile quickly replaced the curious look Demi had on her face moments ago. "You've been holding out on me, my dear," she chirped. She reached out for her friend's hand and quickly led her to her bedroom. Once they were inside and the door was closed, Demi demanded excitedly, "Spill!"

Fey chuckled and shook her head as she took a seat. She knew precisely what Demi wanted to know. How had things progressed between her and Iben since last night?

Demi was her best friend, and Fey had no intention of hiding anything from her. For one, Demi was the only friend she had confided in regarding the issues she'd been having with her mother. They were as close as sisters. Fey narrated everything that happened last night after Demi left. She also told her about how Iben had invited her to lunch at the park, and the kiss they shared moments ago.

"Sounds like things are progressing well between you two. So, are you in love with him?" Demi asked.

Fey chuckled in amusement. "I don't think so. We've only known each other for a couple of months."

"That doesn't matter. Anyway, I think Iben might already be in love with you."

"And you know this because…?"

"Woman's intuition," Demi replied simply. It was apparent that her friend was either dense or in denial. Even she could understand the looks of adoration that Iben gave Fey last night. That was why she tried to come up with a reward to set them up on a date with each other. But she decided that it was probably best that she let Fey figure it out on her own.

Fey scoffed. "Whatever! We do like each other. I enjoy his company, and the physical attraction is there without a doubt."

Demi, who was watching her friend's facial expressions like a hawk, noticed something odd. "But...?"

Fey looked at her friend and knew she had picked up on it. She sighed. "Well, after we kissed just now, he wouldn't even look me in the eye. He just turned around and left." She sighed. "I can't help but think that maybe it's because I kinda instigated the kiss. Maybe he felt awkward after the obligatory kiss, and he just had to leave immediately. Ahhhhh!" Fey flopped on the bed and buried her face in her pillow in embarrassment.

Demi watched her friend's reaction and wanted so badly to tease her. However, she could tell that this was bothering her a lot. "Okay, so do you mind giving some more details on the kiss? Was it like an obligatory, chaste peck on the lips?"

Fey looked up from the pillow. "No, it was very passionate. I wished it wouldn't end." She sighed again.

"Well, you have nothing to worry about, then. I am almost certain that Iben probably couldn't control himself any longer, and that's why he bolted right after. He's quite the gentleman." Demi responded, sounding sure of herself.

While Fey refused to believe her friend's analysis of the situation, Demi wasn't far from the truth.

***

Iben went straight home after he left Fey's place. While kissing her, he could feel himself slowly losing his self-control. He couldn't believe that in the heat of the moment, he had seriously contemplated inviting Fey over to his place right then so that he could execute the lusty thoughts in his head. Thank goodness he kept his sanity and stopped lingering. If he hadn't left right away and he had taken things a step further, she probably would've written him off. He couldn't help replaying the kiss in his head over and over. Her moans, her soft lips, the softness of her skin as he held her close. *Damn, why am I so worked up?* He felt like a hormonal teenager again. It was exciting, yet frustrating. In the end, he took a cold shower to cool himself down. A few minutes later, his cellphone rang. After checking the caller ID, he picked up.

"Yo!" Iben answered.

"Hey, bro," Fola, the person on the call, responded. "How was your date?"

"None of your business!" Iben snapped. "What do you want?"

Fola chuckled, unaffected by Iben's acerbic tone. "I come bearing news from yonder—" he started, jokingly.

"Cut the crap, man! Or I'm going to hang up!" Iben interrupted. Although he was used to his friend's jovial behavior, it was getting on his last nerves right now. Especially since he had a bad feeling about the news Fola was about to give. He and Fola had been close buddies since secondary school, but they only ever called each other for crucial matters. Other times, they'd just send text messages to each other. Only two people could get Fola to deliver a message by calling Iben. One of them was his grandfather.

"Okay, okay," Fola relented before he said, "Vivian's birthday is coming up, and she's invited us to her party."

"I'm not interested," Iben replied immediately.

"Come on, man! I don't want to go by myself. Think of all the ladies we could meet."

Iben scoffed, "Since when did you need me as a wingman? Besides, I'm not interested in the ladies right now."

"Because of your new girlfriend? You know that Vivian is going to be upset."

"Yes, I really like Fey, and I don't want to mess up what we have. But that's got nothing to do with why I don't want to go. Vivian is too annoying, and you of all people know that I can only handle her in doses."

Fola sighed defeatedly. He knew his friend had made up his mind. "If I tell her that you're not coming, you know that's only going to stir up more craziness, Iben," he warned.

It was Iben's turn to sigh. "Maybe, but I'll just deal with it later if it does come to that."

Iben and Fola chatted for a few more minutes before the call ended. Iben tossed his phone on the only couch in his small one-bedroom apartment and sat down. The reason he was irritable with his friend earlier was that he had guessed why he was calling. About a week ago, he had received a text message from Vivian inviting him to her birthday party. He never responded, and he had hoped that she would get the hint. However, he was wrong. Instead, she recruited reinforcements in the form of his long-time buddy. Well, he still wasn't going to attend.

He shook his head to rid his mind of his current thoughts. He got up, grabbed his laptop from his bedroom and started working on the edits to his thesis paper. He needed to get a few things done in time for the scheduled discussion with his advisor later in the week.

06 | Getting to Know You

Thursday finally arrived, and after her classes, Fey walked over to the building where she and Iben had agreed to meet. She'd been looking forward to today. Even though Iben called her every day since their picnic date, Fey still missed him and looked forward to hanging out with him today. When she reached the front of the building, she saw Iben chatting with the president of their volunteer group.

Fey waved to the blonde girl talking to Iben. "Hi, Leni!"

"Hey, Fey," Leni responded with a smile. "What brings you to this side of campus?"

Fey met Iben's gaze briefly, and he winked at her. Every time he did that, Fey felt that he exuded exquisite male sexiness, and she couldn't help but smile shyly. "I'm meeting someone," she responded.

"Oh, so is Iben," Leni retorted. She suddenly came to a realization as she looked back and forth between both of them. *Are they meeting each other?* Leni then noticed that Iben's eyes hadn't left Fey's since she walked up to them. And now, they were gazing and smiling at each other like long lost lovers. Did they forget that she was standing right there? Leni was starting to feel like a third wheel. "Well, I'd better head out. I'll see you both on Saturday," she finally said and excused herself from the awkward situation.

As soon as Leni left, Iben hugged Fey's shoulder in a side hug and planted a kiss on her forehead. He closed his eyes as he inhaled the botanical fragrance in her hair. "Hey, beautiful," he said.

Iben's public displays of affection still surprised Fey. However, she smiled as she looked up at him and asked, "How was your meeting with your advisor?"

"It was good. Making headway on my thesis paper," Iben responded. "Are you hungry?" he asked after checking the time. It was just a few minutes past noon.

"Yeah, I guess."

They decided to have lunch at the school cafeteria. When they got to the cashier, to Iben's surprise, Fey insisted on paying.

"You bought me lunch last time, so it's only fair that I do the honors this time," she explained with a smile.

Iben was ready and willing to pay, and since he was a little old fashioned, he wanted to do things like pay for meals when they were out, especially since he was the one that suggested that they meet up. Regardless, he didn't make a big deal about it. It endeared Fey to him even more. He thought about some of the other girls he had dated in the past. They were all aware of his financial status and weren't shy about taking advantage of it. He didn't mind either. After all, his grandfather is one of the wealthiest business moguls back home. There wasn't anyone there who didn't know of the Ariris.

They found a table to sit down and have their meal.

"What's your favorite color?" Iben suddenly asked a few minutes into their lunch.

Fey looked up from her meal and chuckled internally. *That's not random at all*, she thought to herself sarcastically. "Red, it's my birthstone color."

"Mmmm.... when's your birthday?"

"January 8. When's yours?"

"November 16."

"Really? My sister's birthday is on November 22nd."

"Oh, cool. What's your sister's name?"

"Tutu... I miss her," Fey responded with a sad smile. "I'm going to give her a call this weekend," she added determinedly.

They continued eating quietly for a while until Iben spoke.

"I miss my sister, too," he announced suddenly. His smile was sadder than Fey's. "You share the same birthday as her," he added.

Fey broke into a big smile. "Really? What's her name? Is she older or younger? Is she here in Germany as well? What's she like?" Her excitement at the knowledge of a new birthday mate brought forth a slew of questions.

Iben was a bit taken aback by Fey's sudden excitement. Now he wished he hadn't said anything. He didn't like talking about his sister to anyone as it brought back sad memories. If it were anyone else, he would've just brushed them off. However, he found that for some reason, he couldn't deny Fey.

"Her name is Amara. I'm older... And no, she's not here in Germany." He saw that Fey was about to speak, but he quickly cut her off before she asked more questions. "So, what do you think about Germany, now that you've been here for a few months?"

Fey was caught off guard by the sudden change in the conversation. With a questioning look, she tried to meet Iben's gaze, but he didn't look up from his food. He suddenly seemed intent on concentrating on the rest of the food on his plate, so she said nothing.

I guess there will be other opportunities to ask questions and get to know more about his family, she thought to herself, trying not to be too disappointed.

While Fey was gathering her thoughts, Iben internally sighed. He felt terrible about what he had done. After all, he initiated the personal questions. But he just was not ready to talk about his sister.

For the rest of their lunch, the couple chatted about many things. However, they coincidentally avoided questions that were too personal. By the end of the meal, Iben realized something. He wanted to get to know Fey and about the people dear to her, her family, and friends. But that also meant that he had to be willing to open up about his family and friends as well. It's not that he had anything to hide from her. He was just used to having only a few people close enough to him in that way.

Aside from his buddy Fola, there was only one other person who knew him well. However, he wanted Fey in that small group of people. He just had to get rid of his mental block. He decided that he would stop trying to put up a wall and let conversations happen naturally. Unlike earlier, when he cut off the opportunity to share some of his feelings, next time, he would try to be more open with her.

Fey excused herself to go to the restroom. While she was gone, Iben received a text message. It was from Vivian.

'So glad you'll be coming to my party, Iben. I was worried that you were still mad at me. Anyway, see you next Saturday!'

Iben frowned. *That bastard sold me out!* Clearly, Fola had lied to Vivian that Iben would attend her party. He had to end this business with Vivian once and for all. Although she was an intelligent woman, Vivian was acting dense and ignoring his signals. For his part, Iben realized that avoidance wasn't going to get him anywhere, either. With a frown on his face and his jaw clenched, he made up his mind. This was the expression that Fey saw when she came out of the restroom.

"Are you okay?" a worried Fey asked as she reached out and looped her arm with his. She'd never seen Iben this way before, but now, he looked furious. *What could've happened in the short time that I was away?*

Fey's words jolted Iben out of his thoughts. He looked down and saw Fey's concerned expression. He also realized that she had initiated close physical contact with him. His face softened as he broke into a small smile. "I'm fine now," he said.

As they walked away from the cafeteria, arms still intertwined, Iben suddenly had a thought.

"If you're free next Saturday, would you like to go with me to a birthday party?" he asked.

"Sure, I don't have anything planned. Who's birthday party?"

"Nobody important."

Fey stood still and looked up at Iben with a confused look on her face. "Why the hell are we going then?"

Iben burst into laughter at Fey's question. *She's right, though. Why would anyone attend a nobody's birthday party?* "It's an old acquaintance's birthday," he said. "I'd rather not go, but I'd like to introduce you to a few people who will be there at the party. Some of them I've known since childhood."

Fey nodded. Now that Iben wanted to introduce her to his friends, the weird feeling she had earlier that he was uncomfortable sharing personal information with her slowly went away. But she had a few friends whose ex-boyfriends had friends who were such giant assholes that the couples' relationships didn't last long. Perhaps Iben also wanted her to meet his friends as a test? Her instincts said no, based on what she knew about Iben so far.

Regardless, from her perspective, meeting his friends was an excellent way for her to get some juicy info on Iben. In her experience, close friends tend to enjoy spilling important and embarrassing information about you to your significant other. Fey mentally wrung her hands in excitement as she looked forward to this party.

***

The day of Vivian's birthday party finally arrived. As Fey was getting ready, Demi was chatting with her.

"Stop hovering," Fey chided as she looked in her closet for what to wear.

Demi gasped. "What do you mean by hovering? You're going off to some random party hours away, and you know only one person there. Yet, you tell me not to hover?"

Fey sighed as she decided on a red, knee-length, floral print dress, and a pair of black wedge sandals. She finished off the look with a black leather jacket.

"I know what you mean, Demi. This is the first time that I'm going outside of my comfort zone here in Munich. But it's Iben—I trust him."

"Trusting him is your business. Looking out for your safety is mine." Demi countered.

Fey didn't respond as she got dressed. Then, she grabbed a small, silver clutch, and while transferring her ID and wallet from her everyday purse, Demi, who had left for a few minutes, came back and dropped something in it. It was pepper spray. Fey raised a questioning brow.

"That's the only way I'm going to feel a little bit better about you going to this party." She made it sound like an ultimatum.

Fey sighed, "Yes, mother!" she responded, tongue in cheek. The truth was that she understood her friend's concern, and she would've done the same if their roles were reversed.

A few minutes later, at 5:00 PM on the dot, the doorbell rang. It was Iben. Demi went to answer the door while Fey finished applying her makeup.

"Hi Iben," Demi greeted as she let him in the house. "Fey will be downstairs in a few minutes."

"Hi Demi," he responded with a smile. He walked in and stopped at the foyer, standing next to Demi.

Without skipping a beat, Demi turned to him and asked, "So, where's this party you guys are attending?"

"Salzburg—about two hours away."

Demi nodded, then she asked the question that she wanted him to answer. "Since you're whisking my best friend away to Salzburg, would you mind telling me your full name?" Demi asked. In case something terrible happened, she needed to know who to blame.

Fey heard Demi's question when she came downstairs to join them. "Demi!" she scolded as she walked over to stand next to Iben. She was a little taken aback by her friend's rudeness.

At first, Iben was caught off guard by her question, but he quickly recovered and responded. After all, he had nothing to hide. "No problem. My name is Iben Ariri," he said with a smile. Now that he thought about it, he and Fey never had to mention their last names during their interactions.

Demi froze in shock at the mention of his last name, Ariri. She recognized that name! She stared at Iben for a few seconds. Demi badly wanted to ask if he was related to the well-known business mogul in Nigeria. But she quickly recovered and said, "I am Demi Oke." She felt that it was only fair to give her full name as well. "Please take good care of my friend."

"You can trust that I will bring her back in one piece," Iben promised, placing his hand over his chest.

After Fey and Iben walked out the door, Demi thought to herself, *Ariri—Who would've thought that I'd hear that name here?*

***

As they walked down the street, Iben glanced over at Fey. She looked adorable in a short dress, and also rather badass with the leather jacket. "You look great, by the way," he said.

Fey looked Iben over. He looked handsome in a pair of black denim pants, a light blue dress shirt, and a casual linen khaki blazer. On his feet, he wore a pair of black casual sneakers.

"Thanks! You're not so bad yourself." Fey returned the compliment with a sheepish smile when Iben caught her checking him out.

Iben abruptly stopped in front of a gray Volkswagen Jetta parked on the side of the road and opened the passenger door for Fey.

"You're driving?" she asked, surprised. "I just assumed we were taking the train as usual."

"Salzburg is almost two hours away by car, and we might leave the party pretty late. I think by then, it'll be kind of late for us to be coming back by train. Besides, the train ride back will be about double the travel time. So, I brought a car instead. It'll give us more flexibility."

Fey nodded at Iben's explanation. "That makes sense."

After Iben got in the car and started driving, Fey apologized. "Sorry about my friend's behavior back there."

"No worries. You're fortunate to have such a good friend." Iben looked over at Fey and smiled. Then, he reached out to hold her hand, their fingers intertwined, while he drove using his other hand.

They enjoyed a comfortable silence for a while before Fey said, "In a way, Demi's question got me thinking about us."

Iben looked over at Fey and gently rubbed his thumb over hers. "In what way?" he asked.

"I know we only just met each other a couple of months ago. But I feel like I don't know enough about you. I'd like to know more about the mysterious Iben."

Iben's lips curved up in a smile at the word, mysterious. "Ask me anything!" he declared with confidence, even though his heart was beating faster for some reason. Perhaps, it was because he was about to take a leap and break his all-time rule about getting too close to others. Past betrayals are hard to forget, after all. However, his feelings for Fey made him want to throw caution to the wind in that regard.

Fey nodded, then she asked, "Where exactly is home for you? You're obviously of African descent, but based on your accent, I'm guessing you grew up in Europe, maybe the UK?"

"Pretty decent deductive abilities you've got there, Detective Fey," Iben teased. Then he added, "I was born and raised in Nigeria. When I turned fourteen, my grandfather sent me to the UK. I finished grade school and attended university there."

"What a small world, my parents are from Nigeria as well."

"No way! Where in Nigeria?"

"My dad is Yoruba, and my mom is Igbo. If I remember correctly, my dad is from Ogun State. And my mom is from Cross River State."

"Do you speak either language?" Iben asked.

"Nope. But I do understand a little bit of both. I learned from my mom. She can speak both."

"Now that I know that you're Nigerian, I'm guessing Fey is short for something, right?"

Fey nodded with a small smile. "Yes, my full name is Feyisayo Ademola."

"Feyisayo..." Iben sounded out her name. "I like it!" he added.

Fey looked over at him and chuckled internally at his sudden enthusiasm.

"Have you ever visited Nigeria?" Iben asked.

Fey shook her head. "I was born there, but when I was little, my family emigrated to the States. I don't remember anything from when we lived in Nigeria, though."

"Would you ever visit?"

"Yes, I would love to. Except that for now, I have some family issues preventing me from doing that."

Iben was curious to know what the family issues she mentioned are. However, he didn't pry. This was supposed to be her chance to get to know him more.

"Have you gone back since you left when you were fourteen?" Fey asked.

Iben nodded. "Yes, a few times. Before I graduated from university, I went home once or twice. I worked at my grandfather's company during the summer of my second and third years at university. When I completed my bachelor's degree, I moved back and lived there for about two years before I decided to get a master's degree."

"I see... why did you choose TUM here in Germany instead of a university in the UK?"

"I wanted a change of scenery," was his simple response.

Fey nodded in understanding. She was studying abroad in Germany for a change of scenery as well. She wondered if he had family issues that he was trying to escape from temporarily just like she was.

They were both quiet after that, just listening to the radio, each with their thoughts.

After a while, Iben contemplated whether to ask a question that had been on his mind. His curiosity was getting the better of him. He was dying to know what family issues were preventing her from going to visit Nigeria. Truthfully, when she said her parents were Nigerian, his heart skipped a beat. Was this fate? Now, he imagined a reality where she would visit him in Nigeria. But should he be thinking about this now? Although he liked Fey, he hadn't dared to think about what would happen to their relationship beyond her semester in Germany. Was she even going to agree to a long-distance relationship? He suddenly felt a tightness in his chest. Right then, Iben realized that he couldn't bear the thought of parting with her.

He sighed deeply and looked over at Fey to say something to her. To his surprise, she was asleep! *She must've been tired*, he thought to himself. *I'll tell her later.*

Around 8:00 PM, they reached the Salzburg city limits. They had run into unexpected traffic, so the trip took longer than Iben had anticipated. He drove for another twenty minutes before arriving at the party location. Iben drove into the underground garage and parked the car before waking Fey.

"Fey... we're here," he said as he gently touched her shoulder.

Fey opened her eyes when Iben called her name. She looked at the time, and her eyes widened. She only meant to close her eyes for a little catnap. How could she have slept for the entire trip?

"I'm sorry," she apologized embarrassedly. "I didn't mean to fall asleep. You should've woke me up earlier."

Iben chuckled. "Don't apologize. It just means that you trust me enough to let your guard down around me. I'm happy about that." He leaned in and planted a kiss on her soft lips. "And that's for how adorable you sound while snoring."

Fey's eyes widened, and she smacked him on the shoulder playfully. "I do not snore, mister!"

Iben laughed. "I was just kidding," he said.

"I'll get you back for that," Fey said, rolling her eyes. She looked out the window to hide the smile that threatened to appear on her lips.

"Oh, are we keeping scores now?" Iben couldn't help but continue teasing. "How about we keep scores on something else instead?"

Fey raised a questioning eyebrow. *What is this dude up to now?*

Iben leaned in again and said almost in a whisper, "Let's keep score of how many times I steal a kiss from you tonight." As soon as he said that, he planted another kiss on her lips. This time, his tongue made an appearance, making Fey completely forget her initial ire. Whenever he did that, she couldn't help but turn to putty in his arms. A soft moan escaped her lips, which in turn drove Iben crazy with desire. He deepened the kiss, and Fey wrapped her hands around his neck in response. Iben wrapped his left arm around her waist, pulling her closer to him, while his other hand caressed her cheek. They passionately enjoyed the taste of each other's lips till their hearts' content.

After they had both calmed down from their passionate moment, Fey touched up her makeup, while Iben sat in the driver's seat with his eyes closed. He was slowly evicting all the lusty mental images that had crept into his mind during their kiss. Iben badly wanted to put his arms around her waist again and press her soft chest against him. He imagined his hand slowly sliding down her waist to her lower back, and then... He took a few deep breaths to calm himself down.

"I'm ready," Fey announced a few minutes later.

Iben opened his eyes and turned to look at Fey. His eyes involuntarily landed on her lips that now appeared fuller and more inviting, with a fresh coat of lipstick. He shook his head internally as he fought back the urge to kiss her again. "Okay, let's go," he said instead.

07 | Party Time

Iben and Fey took the elevator up to the street level and entered the party venue. It was a trendy nightclub and bar. The entire second level of the space was reserved for the party. Fey couldn't help but wonder who the birthday celebrant was. He seemed to have very high tastes, and a lot of money to blow. She had an inkling that it wasn't cheap to book this party space.

When they got upstairs, the party was already in full swing. The latest afrobeats music was pounding through the speakers. Green and purple neon discotheque lights illuminated the glossy white walls and ceilings in the space. Some people were at the bar, some were seated on the sofas along the walls, and some were dancing.

"Let's get something to drink," Iben suggested as he led Fey to the bar. "What do you like?" he asked.

Fey leaned against the bar top and ordered a sangria, while Iben ordered a tap beer. No sooner had they gotten their drinks did someone called out behind them.

"Iben! Bro!"

Fey turned around and saw a guy walking towards them with a big smile on his face. He was wearing a fitted t-shirt and a brown leather jacket. The front part of his shirt was tucked into his blue jeans so you could see his belt buckle. On his feet, he wore a pair of brown leather boots. As he got closer, Fey could see the handsome face of the person who was about the same height as Iben, a little over six feet. With each step he took, he exuded a confident, sexy aura. Fey noticed some of the ladies around them checking him out and whispering. She also realized that Iben had suddenly put his arms around her tightly in a side hug.

When the guy got to the bar, he ordered a drink and said to Iben, "I see you decided to come after all."

Iben's face deadpanned as he gave the guy a cold stare. "No thanks to you, of course," he replied.

The guy chuckled and took a sip of his beer. Then, he looked over at the pretty lady that Iben had his arm around possessively, and then back at Iben. "Aren't you going to introduce me?" he asked.

Iben turned to look at Fey. His eyes softened as he broke into a small smile. "This is my girlfriend, Fey," he said, his eyes not breaking away from hers. After a few seconds of intentionally subjecting their only audience to the lovey-dovey looks they were giving each other, Iben finally turned to Fola and said with a flat voice. "And this is my best mate, Fola."

Best mate? Fey thought incredulously. If that was the case, then why was Iben so cold towards him?

"Nice to meet you," Fola said as a bright smile spread across his handsome face. He held out his hand for a handshake. "I've heard so much about you," he added.

Fey shook his hand and said with a polite smile, "Nice to meet you too, Fola."

"I didn't realize that you were bringing a plus one today," Fola said to Iben.

"I didn't realize that I needed to run that by you first," Iben retorted coldly.

Fey looked back and forth between both men. She could not help but feel like she was missing something. *What the heck is going on here? Is this the birthday guy, and he's upset that he has an extra guest that he wasn't expecting?*

Fola turned to Fey and said with a polite smile, "Please excuse us. I need to talk to your boyfriend for a few minutes."

Iben turned to Fey and said, "Don't go anywhere. I'll be right back." Then he leaned in and gave her a peck on her cheek. Before he walked away, he smiled and held three fingers up. He was letting her know that was the third kiss he had given her tonight.

Fey rolled her eyes as she watched the two men walk off a few feet away to have their 'talk.'

Once they were out of earshot, Fola asked, "What are you doing, bro? Why would you bring her to Vivian's party?"

"She's my girlfriend, and I want to introduce her to everyone," Iben said.

"What about Vivian?"

Iben sighed and pinched the bridge of his nose. "You know I don't want anything to do with her. She and I are in the past. Just because she's in denial or has a change of heart doesn't mean that I need to as well. I've been trying to get this across by ignoring her, but she mistakes it for—complacency? Or that I'm playing hard to get? Who the hell knows what's going on in her mind? And now, thanks to you telling her I'll be here, she probably thinks she has a chance. So, I'm here today to make things clear once and for all!"

Fola looked away and scratched his head, feeling guilty. When Vivian kept pestering him, he had lied to her that Iben had agreed to attend just to get her off his back. Based on the phone conversation between him and Iben, he was confident that Iben wouldn't show up anyway. Regardless, he knew what his friend was talking about. Iben and Vivian used to date and were engaged, but Vivian broke it off a few years ago. However, everyone in their circle knew that she was feisty and strong-willed. She was also used to having her way, and now that she had decided that she wanted Iben back, she was unstoppable.

"Okay, but are you sure this is going to work? I know you don't care, but Vivian is going to be livid that you brought a date."

Iben sneered. "Sounds to me like you're worried that she's going to be mad at you for not telling her that I'll be coming with my girlfriend."

Fola sighed. He could already imagine Vivian raking him over the coals about this. *I guess this is karma*, he thought dejectedly. He then had a thought and decided to ask a question that had been on his mind since when Iben told him that he was dating Fey.

"Vivian aside, why go through all this trouble? This relationship with Fey isn't going to last anyway. She'll be going back home to the States by Christmas. And you'll be going back to Nigeria." Fola glanced at Fey for a second before adding, "She seems like a nice girl. It isn't fair to drag her into this. You shouldn't be using her to resolve this matter with Vivian."

Iben sighed and leaned against the wall behind him. He looked over at Fey as he said, "I think... I'm falling for her, man."

Fola's eyes widened in surprise. Never in a million years would he have thought that he'd hear Iben say those words. Even when he was dating Vivian, he never said that.

Iben continued, "I want to be with her all the time and—I don't want her to go back home. I don't know what I'm going to do when the time comes. I can only hope that I've filled up her heart and mind so much by then that she'll at least want to try a long-distance relationship for now. Maybe we can work something out."

He closed his eyes for a moment and took in a deep breath. "When I got a text from Vivian, and I realized you had told her I was coming, I was angry. But then I realized I could kill all this shit with Vivian by coming here today. With Fey here, everyone in our circle, especially Vivian, will know that I'm serious and have no intention of getting back together with her."

Fola quietly listened to his friend. He was shocked, but it seemed like Iben was really into this Fey chick. Enough to go head to head with Vivian. Who was she, and what was so special about her anyway?

"What if she's just getting with you because she knows who you are?" Fola asked. After he and Vivian broke up, Iben had casually dated a few women who only wanted to be with him because of his family status.

Iben shook his head. "She's not like that. She didn't even know my last name until a few hours ago. And she didn't seem to recognize it when I mentioned it. Her parents are Nigerian, but she doesn't seem knowledgeable about the culture. She has lived in the States all her life."

"I see… so, what's the plan?" Fola finally asked. "Since you seem to be serious about her, do you want me to do a check?"

"Not now," was Iben's reply.

Fola nodded in response.

"What about the other stuff?" Iben asked cryptically.

"Still working on it. Her father has done a good job of hiding the evidence, but I still have some leads that I'm looking into."

Iben simply nodded. "Where's Vivian?" he asked.

"She's in one of the private rooms." Fola nodded towards the loft section of the nightclub. "She probably knows you're here by now," he added.

"Got it," Iben said and started walking back to Fey. At some point, during his conversation with Fola, as more people arrived, Iben no longer had a direct line of sight to her at the bar. As he got closer, he frowned at the scene before him. A guy was sitting next to Fey at the bar, and it looked like he was hitting on her.

Fey had been sitting at the bar for a few minutes while Iben and Fola were talking. Some guy who came to the bar to order a drink saw Fey sitting there by herself and decided to chat her up.

"Hey, baby. Can I buy you a drink?" he asked.

Fey tapped on the glass of sangria that she was still drinking and said, "No, thanks. I'm good." She turned around briefly to look behind her and saw that Iben was still talking to Fola.

The guy ignored her response and said to the bartender, "Give the lovely lady another glass of whatever she's having."

Fey ignored him, but the guy continued. "Would you like to dance with me later on?"

For the first time, Fey turned to look at him with an incredulous look on her face. She couldn't believe that he just seemed to be in a world of his own. This situation was precisely the reason why she didn't like the bar and nightclub scene. You have to fend off unwanted attention constantly.

"No, thanks! I'm here with someone." Fey responded curtly and decided that she was going to look for Iben. As she stood up to leave, the guy reached out to grab her hand to stop her.

This was the scene that Iben saw as he walked over. His steps quickened when he saw the guy reach out his arm to grab Fey. Rage welled up within Iben, and he was behind the guy in a flash. Pressing the guy's shoulders down with force, he warned in a threatening voice, "Let go of her!"

Startled, the guy let go of Fey, lifted his right arm, and threw his elbow back to hit whoever was assaulting him from behind. But Iben's response was quick, and he counterattacked by a swift feint leading to a sharp elbow to his attacker's neck. Iben followed through with his attack by slamming the guy's head on the side of the bar counter, sending him to the floor. The guy was livid at this point. Despite his bloody, throbbing forehead, he sprang back up right away and attempted to launch an attack on Iben. However, when he looked up and saw who it was, intense fear etched across his features. He withdrew and staggered back a few steps.

"Ah...I...I... I'm sorry," the guy stammered out. "I didn't realize that she was here with you, Mr. Ariri." He bowed his head apologetically several times and quickly stumbled away.

From Fey's perspective, everything happened so fast. One moment she was trying to fend off unwanted attention, and the next, the guy was on the floor bleeding from his forehead. What surprised her the most was the other guy's extreme change of attitude as soon as he realized it was Iben. She looked over at Iben and wondered what that was about. What was Iben's identity that made the other guy run off in fear like that?

As soon as the guy scuffled away, an unruffled Iben turned around and pulled Fey into a tight hug. "Are you okay?" he asked in a worried tone and kissed the top of her head. "Sorry I took so long."

By now, they had garnered the attention of a few onlookers, so Fey was slightly embarrassed by the sudden intimacy from Iben. She buried her face in his chest, shyly, and said, "I'm okay."

He leaned back slightly from the hug and said, "Come on, I'll introduce you to my friends."

The couple walked away, hand in hand. And within minutes, news of the altercation reached the birthday girl, Vivian.

08 | Vivian

In one of the private rooms in the loft, Vivian looked down from the only window in the room overlooking the party below. She scanned the entire space and finally spotted Iben chatting and drinking with some folks. Of the six people seated at the sizeable semicircular booth, the only person Vivian did not recognize was a young lady dressed in a red floral dress. *That must be the girl from the bar that I just heard about.* Iben was seated between her and another one of their mutual guy friends, Tonna.

Vivian frowned when she noticed that Iben had his arm around Fey possessively, and she leaned into his embrace. Occasionally, Iben would whisper something in her ear, or plant a kiss on Fey's cheek or forehead. It was clear to anyone watching that Iben appeared to be taken with this woman.

The more Vivian watched, the more irked she became. But Vivian, the woman that she is, knew that Iben wouldn't do anything like this without reason. *What is he trying to achieve? Is he trying to make me jealous?* she thought amusedly.

"I think so. Iben must still be upset about your broken engagement," she suddenly heard her best friend, Zara say.

That was when Vivian realized that she had voiced her thoughts out loud. She sighed. "But it's been almost two years since! How can he keep a grudge for so long?" She sounded exasperated.

When she found out that Iben was traveling to Germany, she made up her mind to follow him. She had begged her father to allow her to come to Germany for her master's degree as well. It was all to show Iben her sincerity at trying to work things out between them. If trying to appease his male ego would do the trick, she didn't mind working that angle. But it didn't seem that Iben was softening up at all. She sighed and thought to herself, *when did this guy become so hard to please?*

All this time, she thought she was making progress by not being too pushy. From Vivian's perspective, she had been indulging Iben's anger or whatever he had been feeling after they broke up. She didn't even get mad at him for the string of girls he dated recently, but for him to bring one of them to her birthday party was just too much.

She decided that she was going to have to take another approach. As far as Vivian was concerned, this little stunt of Iben's wasn't enough to make her give up what's hers by right. When they were teenagers and betrothed, she had felt that she did not want to be with Iben. However, she had matured since then and was now ready to take on her role as his fiancée—as his future wife.

"I'm not giving up!" Vivian suddenly announced. Then she turned to Zara and said with a smirk, "Please, let the MC know that I'm ready to come down."

***

Fey was having fun chatting with Iben's group of friends at their table. The incident at the bar seemed a distant memory, even though it happened only about an hour before. At first, when Iben introduced her to his friends as his girlfriend, everyone seemed surprised. However, they all warmed up to her and made her feel comfortable. Fola was the most talkative, and he was telling all sorts of funny stories from when he and Iben were in secondary school.

Suddenly, the MC/DJ turned down the music for an announcement. Since their table was close to the small podium in the party space, Fey and the others were able to see a gorgeous woman in long braids that reached down to her lower back, walk up to the podium and grab the microphone. She was wearing a sleeveless, black and white cocktail dress. The knee-length dress seemed to melt into her voluptuous curves, from the halter neck down to the side slit that stopped midway up her thighs. On her feet, she wore a pair of white three-inch heels. She held onto the microphone and smiled down at everyone, looking very much like a queen about to address her subjects.

"Hello, everyone, and thanks for coming to celebrate my birthday with me. I'm honored to have you all here today." She paused, and there was some light applause. "While you all are great folks, I am most happy that my favorite person in the world, Iben Ariri, who also happens to be my fiancé, is also here to celebrate with me. You all know who I'm talking about, right?" she added with a bright smile.

Several people laughed, but no one at Fey's table did.

"The night is still young, so please continue to enjoy yourselves. And thanks again for coming!" Vivian finished her short speech and regally walked off the podium. The music turned up again, and the partying continued.

When Vivian mentioned that Iben was her fiancé, Fey froze for a few seconds just staring at her drink glass on the table, her heart suddenly pounding furiously in her chest. She wished the ground would open and swallow her up. She slowly looked up at Iben, who was sitting to her left. He was staring down at the drinking glass in his left hand while wearing a very intense facial expression. His jaw was tightly clenched, and you could see the anger in his eyes. This signaled to Fey that he had not expected such an announcement either. Nobody said a word, not even the talkative Fola. She wasn't sure what she was expecting, but Fey couldn't help but turn her gaze to look at the others at the table one after another. Except for Fola, nobody looked her in the eye.

She was about to say something when they suddenly heard a female voice say, "Hey, darling. I'm so glad you made it as promised." Everyone looked up to see that it was Vivian. She smiled brightly and said with confidence, "Can you all please excuse my fiancé and I for a few minutes?"

Everyone but Fey and Iben left. Vivian noticed this and cocked her head to the side before saying to Fey, "That includes you as well."

Fey's eyes met hers, and she could see the ridicule in Vivian's eyes. But Fey didn't look away. Instead, a smirk lifted the corner of Fey's lips. To Vivian, it came off as a challenge, but for Fey, it was a self-ridiculing one. What the hell was she hanging behind for? Even she didn't know why she stayed back. All this time, she seemed rooted to the seat while trying to process what was happening. Clearly, Vivian and Iben had a thing between them, and just now, Vivian made it clear that she was the third wheel. It was a very embarrassing situation to find oneself. Fey was about to stand up when Iben gently tugged her hand back. It was the same hand that had been holding hers under the table since they were seated. Fey only just realized that they hadn't let go of each other's hand.

"She stays... Or we both leave!" came Iben's cold response.

Both Fey and Vivian looked at him in shock.

Fey had mixed feelings about this situation. First, she was happy that Iben wanted her to stay. It made her feel less like a third wheel.

However, she felt like Iben was using her as a cover-fire for whatever issues he had with Vivian. It wasn't rocket science to figure out that there had to be some reason why a woman's supposed fiancé would deliberately show up to her birthday party with another woman. Fey's curiosity got the better of her, and she decided to stay and see how this would play out.

Although Vivian was livid on the inside, she displayed a helpless look on her face. "Fine, if that's what you want," she conceded and sat down next to Iben so that he was seated between both women—Vivian to his left and Fey on his right. Vivian suddenly leaned in, pressed her chest against his arm, and said, "You haven't wished me a proper happy birthday yet. I—"

Iben stiffened at the contact. "What do you want, Vivian?" he said, cutting her off. "I don't have time for your little act, so just get to the point!" he snapped.

"Is that the way to speak to your fiancée in front of another woman?"

"I am not your fiancé," Iben countered. "You broke up with me, remember?"

Vivian was taken aback by Iben's attitude and words. In the past, he would at least give her some face when others were around. But for this girl, he was disrespecting her? What an insult! She was about to respond when Iben cut her off again.

"Despite your little stunt on the stage, nothing changes. You and I are not together. We will never get back together! I came here today to make this clear to you once and for all, and to introduce you to my girlfriend. In the future, please treat her with respect."

Fey watched the show that was unfolding right before her with widened eyes.

Vivian was stunned speechless.

"Then Iben stood up and turned to Fey. "Let's go home," he said.

Fey got up and left with him.

Vivian wasn't known ever to take a loss lying down, and she certainly wouldn't start today. However, she cared about her reputation and didn't want to make a scene, so she played it off by walking away to another table as if she was taking turns saying hello to her other guests. She watched from the corner of her eyes as Iben led Fey away, and as soon as she saw them step out of the party room, she followed them.

Fey allowed Iben to continue holding her hand until they reached the elevator that would take them down to the first-floor lobby. While waiting for the elevator, she forcefully yanked her hand away from his, which caught Iben by surprise.

"Fey—" he started to say.

Fey cut him off. "Save it!" she snapped, holding her hand up to indicate that she wasn't interested in whatever he had to say. "You invited me to your ex-girlfriend's birthday party, and didn't have the common decency to give me a heads up? Why?!" she seethed, glaring daggers at Iben. She had been holding back her emotions and couldn't help but lash out at him now that they were away from prying eyes.

Iben sighed guiltily. "I'm sorry…"

The elevator doors opened, and they walked in. As soon as they got off the elevator on the first floor, Iben and Fey had barely walked a few feet away when the other elevator doors opened. Vivian stepped out and called out, "Iben!"

Fey and Iben turned around at the same time to see Vivian walking up to them, with Fola hot on her heels.

"Stop this, Vivian," they heard Fola trying to talk her out of whatever she was going to do.

Knowing Vivian's temper, Fola had an inkling that she might try to follow Iben after he left. He was right. As soon as he saw her heading towards the exit, he was hot in pursuit and just narrowly managed to get in the elevator with her.

For a few seconds, all four of them stopped in their tracks, staring at each other.

Fola was the first to speak. "I'll ask the valet to get your car."

Iben nodded and tossed his car keys to Fola, who caught them effortlessly and headed to the front of the lobby.

After Fola left, Vivian asked, "Can I talk to you please, Iben?"

Iben didn't respond but instead turned to Fey as if asking for permission.

Fey looked at him and said, "You can talk to her. I'll go and wait in the car." She then spun on her heels and continued walking towards the exit.

As soon as Fey was out of earshot, Vivian spat, "If she had said no, would you have listened to her?"

Iben ignored her question and shot back, "What do you want?"

Vivian smiled bitterly and said, "I just want to know why you are doing this, Iben. We've known each other since we were kids. Who is she, anyway? Why would you choose her over me?" She was exasperated. No matter how much she thought about it, it didn't make any sense.

Iben crossed his arms across his chest in a defensive stance. His voice was cold as he spoke. "Even though we were both betrothed against our will, we dated for many years. During that time, you were rebellious as hell, but I was patient, and I treated you well. In turn, you cheated on me with Damola. I remember that day when you came over to my place and begged me to let you go. You said you were unhappy being with me and couldn't bear to continue a forced relationship. And that you were pregnant with Damola's baby. I realized then that I neither had your heart nor your loyalty—not even as a friend. You didn't even consider our friendship to be worth anything. If you did, you would've done right by me by *first* breaking off our engagement before you hopped into another man's bed."

Vivian looked at Iben's stoic face as he recounted their history. Tears welled up in her eyes.

Iben continued, "I didn't hear from you for almost half a year after that day. And when I did, you had called to tell me that you had a change of heart and was now willing to try and work at our relationship. That was the most ridiculous thing I'd heard in a long time."

"But you never told your grandfather about our breakup, so I thought…"

"You thought I was sitting around pining for you?"

Vivian bristled when she saw the ridicule on Iben's face as he asked the question. "That's enough!" she spat angrily. She was about to go on a tirade when she caught herself. She reminded herself that she had to stay focused. "I was chosen by your grandfather, Iben. He will never accept her over me," she tried to reason.

"He will once he realizes that you were fucking another man while engaged to his grandson," Iben countered with a sneer. Then he added, "Don't forget that I am just like my grandfather. We value loyalty above all."

Vivian let out a short, derisive laugh and said with a smirk, "I'll deny it! You have no proof!"

"I will get proof of your abortion. It's only a matter of time. Do you and your father think you can hide that information from me forever? I am an Ariri after all."

With that, Iben started walking away.

"There are plenty of guys who are lining up to be with me, Iben.

You'll regret this!"

Iben stopped and looked back. "Vivian, thanks to your little stunt today, I now know exactly how I feel about Fey. I also know that she's the one I want by my side, not you."

Vivian was speechless after that.

"You should head back to your party. I need to take my girlfriend home."

***

Even though she gave Iben permission to talk with Vivian, Fey felt a pang of jealousy as she watched them talk from afar. Seeing Iben and Vivian standing together, she had to admit that based on looks alone, they were perfectly matched and looked good together. He was tall and handsome, and she was a voluptuous goddess.

Although Iben had said all those things to Vivian back there, there was always the possibility that the two of them could get back together. Fey's heart sank at the thought. She sighed deeply.

"I'm sure this is one birthday party you'll never forget," Fola said jokingly.

Fey hadn't realized that he had come over to stand next to her until he spoke. "No kidding," she said flatly as she continued looking at the two people talking from afar. Then she turned to Fola and asked, "What's really going on between those two?"

Fola chuckled. "You should ask your boyfriend that question."

Fey sighed. He was right. Besides, she probably wouldn't believe anything Fola said anyway since he was Iben's best friend and was likely to paint him in a good light.

Fola watched Fey as she watched Iben. He'd been doing that all night, observing her reactions, especially when Vivian threw the bombshell announcement earlier. He had to admit that he admired the way Fey handled herself. He had half expected that she would cause a scene or try to show everyone that she was the one with Iben and not Vivian. But to his surprise, she was classy through and through. Her poker face could rival Iben's.

Fey turned around and didn't look back anymore when she saw Iben walking towards them. When he got outside, Iben walked to Fey and put his arm around her, but she shrugged it off and instead turned to Fola and said. "It was nice to meet you, Fola."

Fola nodded and said, "Take care."

Without giving Iben another look, Fey got in the car to wait for him.

Iben watched helplessly as Fey ignored him. That was the second time in a row that she had rejected physical contact with him tonight.

"Looks like someone's in the doghouse," Fola pointed out, with a low whistle.

Iben glared at him. "What were you guys talking about?" he asked Fola as he watched Fey get in the passenger seat of the car.

"She's dying to know the real situation with you and Vivian. But she's obviously upset with you, and her ego probably won't allow her to ask you," Fola responded. He had always been good at reading people. "If I could give you some advice, bro, you shouldn't hide anything from her about you and Vivian. If you're still serious about her, this is your chance to truly win her trust."

Iben nodded once but said nothing.

"Well, now I have to go back in there and deal with the aftermath of our dear Vivian's self-implosion."

Both men said their goodbyes and went their separate ways.

When Iben finally came to the car and got in the driver's seat, he opened his mouth to say something but quickly changed his mind because Fey deliberately turned towards the passenger window and pretended to be asleep. So, he simply started the car and began driving.

09 | Love

As Iben drove back to Munich, his mind was in turmoil. Several times he wanted to reach out for Fey's hand out of habit. But whenever he remembered her prior rejection of his advances, he quickly changed his mind. *Tonight turned out to be a cluster-fuck*, he thought bitterly to himself.

For one, he was happy to put Vivian in her place once and for all. But now, he was nervous because Fey was giving him the cold shoulder. Several scenarios played in his mind as he drove. What if she refused to talk to him the entire drive? What if she refused to speak to him for days? What if she broke up with him over this?

Iben panicked. He couldn't let that happen. So, he slowly hatched a plan in his mind. He'd been driving for about thirty minutes, and it was now 10:55 PM—time to put his plan in motion.

"Fey, I'm going to stop for some coffee. Want some?" he asked.

No response, as he expected. He knew Fey wasn't asleep, though. Her breathing didn't indicate that she was. A few minutes later, he turned off the highway and drove to a coffee shop that was open late. He parked the car but didn't get out right away.

Iben watched Fey as she sat with her eyes closed, her head still facing the passenger window, away from him. Her arms that had been folded defensively across her chest were now simply clasped together and resting on her lap. From Iben's perspective, she appeared to have lowered her defenses a bit. Hope surged in his heart.

"I'll be right back," he announced before stepping out of the car.

He left for some time and came back with two cups of coffee and some pastries. For a few seconds, Iben said nothing. Since Fey still had her eyes closed, he took the opportunity to just look at her. His eyes softened as he visually caressed her beautiful face, from her eyes to her nose to her lips. Those soft lips were going to be his undoing, Iben thought to himself. He wished he could kiss them now, but he knew it wasn't the right time. They had other issues to take care of first. His eyes traveled down her exposed neck, following the plunging neckline of her dress, down to her tummy, and finally to her hands that were resting on her lap.

"Fey..." he called softly as he reached out and gently touched her hands.

Surprised at the unexpected touch, Fey's eyes flew open, and their eyes met. However, she did not shrug off his hand this time.

"I got you some coffee and something to eat. We were drinking a lot tonight, so it's a good idea to eat something," Iben said.

Fey nodded and reached for the pastry bag. It was fudge brownies, her favorite. "Thanks," she said with a small smile and started eating one of the brownies.

About a minute later, Iben said, "I'm sorry I put you in an embarrassing situation today. I should've told you that it was my ex-fiancée's party we were going to. Please forgive me."

Fey nodded and took a sip of her coffee. Truthfully, her initial anger had died down substantially. Earlier, as she sat in silence while Iben was driving, she thought back to everything that happened that night. Aside from the shock of finding out who Vivian was, she had to admit that Iben acted above board throughout. He protected her from the guy at the bar. He also protected her from being bullied by Vivian, and he refused to talk with Vivian alone until she gave the okay. And now, he was thinking about her and even stopped to get her something to eat and drink.

When Iben saw that Fey accepted his apology, his erratic heartbeat began to calm down. Since step one of his plan was successful, it was time for phase two. He was sure that he wanted to be with Fey, so he decided to take Fola's advice and lay down all his cards.

He gathered his thoughts and began, "My parents and my little sister Amara died in an accident when I was little. Afterward, my grandfather adopted me and raised me. It's because of him that I am who I am today."

"I'm so sorry to hear about your family. How old were you when it happened?" Fey asked.

"I was ten years old at the time, and my sister was around seven or eight," Iben responded. "When you told me your birthday, and I realized that it was the same as hers, it brought back old memories."

Fey didn't ask any more questions, so he continued.

"Anyway, Vivian's father and my grandfather are long-time business partners, and my grandfather is very fond of Vivian. So, when he told me that he had found a good match for me and that it was her, I was fine with it. I knew her since we were kids anyway, so it wasn't like she was some stranger. But Vivian is a free spirit, so naturally, she rebelled against the idea. But, she only showed her rebellious side to me. In the presence of my grandfather, she was a different person."

Fey thought about what Iben just said, and she honestly couldn't blame Vivian. She wouldn't want to be forced into a relationship like that either. Parents shouldn't do that to their children.

As if Iben could read her mind, he said. "I know it's probably strange to hear of betrothals in the 21st century, but in the business and political world, things like this happen fairly commonly. Usually, it's to ensure an alliance of sorts."

"So, your family is wealthy?" Fey asked.

Iben chuckled. "You could say that. My grandfather owns Ariri Corporation. He built it from the ground up to one of the largest conglomerates in Nigeria. You're probably not plugged into the Nigerian economic news, but his company is well known in Nigeria and other African countries."

Fey nodded as he spoke. Then she asked, "Were you in love with Vivian?"

"No. I liked her, but I was not in love with her. Honestly, it was more of a duty for me. My goal was to please my grandfather and uphold our end of the business deal. That didn't mean that I mistreated her. At the very least, we were good friends. Fola, Vivian, and I all grew up together. So, in my mind, I was getting to know the person I was going to be married to in the future."

"So, what changed? How did both of you get here?" Fey prodded.

"She cheated on me. And the icing on the cake was that she got pregnant by the guy she was cheating with. She even came to my place to beg me to ask my grandfather to annul the betrothal because she was in love with this other guy. Some months after that, she called me out of the blue to tell me that she wanted to get back together. Obviously, things hadn't worked out with the other guy, and she thought that since I hadn't told my grandfather, that meant I was open to continuing where we left off. I refused, and she kept bugging me—she can be very persistent. So, later that year, I decided to come to Germany for my Master of Laws. I was trying to get away from her craziness, but she followed me here anyway."

"What did your grandfather do when you eventually told him?"

Iben sighed. "Actually, he still doesn't know," Iben confessed.

Fey raised a questioning brow and asked, "Why not?"

"I haven't said anything to him because I need proof. As a businessman, my grandfather is strict about holding up your end of an agreement, unless the other person reneged on their side. Also, he's very fond of Vivian, and it'll be difficult for him to believe what she had done without hard evidence. As you can see from tonight, she's excellent at playing the victim. I'm currently working on the proof of her abortion, though. Her father has worked very hard to seal the medical records, but I have some of my best team of investigators on this, and we should have a breakthrough soon."

Fey listened to him talk about his team of investigators, and he sounded like he truly was the heir to a business enterprise. In her eyes, he'd suddenly gone from the boy next door to a high society, high profile individual.

"But, to everyone else other than you, Fola and Vivian, you're still engaged."

"Not exactly. Of course, people knew that we were dating, but aside from close family, nobody else knew about our engagement. In fact, until today, Vivian had never wanted anyone to know. So, I was shocked that she decided to make such a statement back there. I think it was out of desperation, though. She probably guessed that since I brought you to her party, I must be serious about you. She was probably banking on me, allowing her to keep up appearances so that she could entrap me."

Iben stopped talking, and Fey quietly digested all the info that he had given her while finishing up her coffee and brownies.

"So... what does this mean for us?" Fey asked. She was wondering what his grandfather would think of her once Vivian was out of the picture. She certainly didn't have the pedigree that Vivian seemed to have. And what would happen if his grandfather decided to pick someone else for him to marry? Iben appeared to be a dutiful and loving grandson. Would Iben agree? Would that be the end of their relationship? The thought of that happening caused a tightness in her chest. She didn't want that to happen, but she also didn't want to just bury her head in the sand, pretending that it wasn't a real possibility.

"I love you," Iben suddenly confessed.

Fey's eyes widened when she heard those words. Speechless, she looked at him with a shocked expression on her face.

"Yes, I love you. I want to be with you," Iben said. He held both her hands before he continued. "Meeting you and getting to know you this past couple of months has made my time here in Germany, one of the best decisions I've ever made."

Iben didn't know when or how, but he had fallen in love with the woman sitting next to him. She stole his heart, and there was no looking back. He had never felt this way about anyone else before, so it was both exciting and scary at the same time.

After Fey recovered from her initial surprise, she asked, "What if your grandfather disapproves?"

"That won't happen. But if it does, I will remind him that I went along with his choice the first time, and it didn't work out. Now, I have chosen for myself. And I'm very proud of my choice. Fey, the only way that we can ever break up is if—if you don't want me."

After he said the last sentence, he leaned in and kissed her on her cheeks, next on her lips. Then, he slowly rested his forehead on her right shoulder and sighed as he said, "Tell me you want me, Fey." His voice was deep and full of emotion.

Fey was filled with a surge of emotion as she listened to Iben bare his heart to her. She couldn't help but put her arms around him as he continued to rest his head on her shoulder.

"My mother and my father separated when I was little," she began. "My paternal grandparents wanted him to take another wife so that he would have a son. They tricked him into going to Nigeria, and he just never came back. He stayed behind after he married the woman they had arranged for him. My mom has never been the same ever since. She had to raise my sister and me all by herself. We're talking about the Nigerian culture, so I want you to know that polygamy is out of the question for me. I don't want that kind of life for myself, Iben."

Iben lifted his head and looked into Fey's eyes. "Are you saying that because you do see me in your future?" he asked eagerly.

"Slow down, Romeo," Fey said with a light chuckle. "I was speaking in generalities. But—" she paused for effect, "if ever there's a chance that you might want a polygamous relationship, then... please let me go and let's end this now," she pleaded.

Iben shook his head and declared, "If you will have me, you're the only woman I'll ever want or need."

Fey looked Iben in the eye as he spoke. She saw his sincerity and believed him. She shyly bit her lower lip and lowered her eyes as she nodded. "Okay, I'm in."

At those words from Fey, Iben's heart surged with intense happiness and relief at the same time.

"Yes!" he blurted out, causing Fey to chortle. They both laughed.

After their laughter died down, Fey asked, "So, what's next...?"

Iben sighed when he looked at the time. It was well past midnight.

"First, I need to get you home."

Iben turned on the ignition and started driving. On the second half of their trip, the couple chatted light-heartedly. When they arrived, Iben parked the car by the street and walked Fey to her front door. It was already 2:00 AM.

Iben pulled her in for a hug and said, "I want to see you later on today."

"Okay, what time?" Fey answered as she rested her head against his warm chest.

"Two o'clock."

"Okay—no, wait. I promised to go shopping with Demi in the afternoon, so it'll have to be later. Maybe around six o'clock?"

"Okay..." Iben said, hiding his disappointment. He knew that she had other friends aside from him, and he certainly didn't want to be the kind of guy that tries to monopolize his girlfriend's time.

10 | Future Plans

The next day, Fey went to the mall with Demi, as promised. While shopping, she spent some time filling her in on everything that happened at the party she attended with Iben.

"Wow. What an eventful night for you," Demi said. "That Vivian chick sounds like a handful. Although, I never thought that you would be one for a long-distance relationship."

Fey furrowed her brows at Demi's comment. In the euphoria of solidifying her relationship with Iben, she hadn't thought about that at all. What *would* she and Iben do after the semester ended?

"Me neither," she responded. "Anyways, enough about me. What did you want to talk about?"

Demi sighed. "It's my parents. They want me to move back immediately after graduation."

Fey was surprised, "Why?" she asked.

When Demi was younger, she was very sickly. As the only child of her parents, she was brought to the United States to receive surgical treatment that wasn't available in Nigeria at the time. After her surgery, her father accepted a position at the International Monetary Fund (IMF) in Washington, DC., which precluded a return to Nigeria for many years. Her mother also started working as a teacher at the school that Fey was attending at the time. That's where she met Fey, and they became friends. As far as she knew, Demi's parents didn't have a problem with her staying in the States even after they moved back to Nigeria years ago.

Demi filled her in on the details.

"You know how I want to start my own business after we graduate, right?" Demi began.

Fey nodded in agreement. She knew that her friend was a

fashionista at heart and had always dreamt about starting her clothing line. After completing her bachelor's degree in Business Administration, Demi was going to move to New York and start her business. She already had a catalog of designs that she had created on her own. Her designs were very fresh, merging traditional and modern elements.

"My parents said they will help set up my business if I move back home to Nigeria."

Fey's eyes widened in surprise.

"On one hand, this is a very lucrative deal for me," Demi continued. "But I haven't lived in Nigeria for such a long time. I'd have to learn the fashion industry over there."

She was also concerned about how difficult it would be for her to fit back into the culture where parents have more of a say in what their children do than here in the States. Thankfully, her parents were more liberal than others, but still.

"What do you want to do?" Fey asked.

"I don't know," Demi sighed. "If I stay, I can probably get a nine-to-five job at a consulting firm like Bain or McKinsey. I can try to save money for my dream, but with Dad cutting off all financial support after I graduate, it'll take me a very long time to save enough money to do what I want. If I go back to Nigeria, everything is going to be handed to me on a platter. It almost sounds too good to be true..."

"They're your parents. What ulterior motives could they possibly have? They probably just miss you and want you close to them. You're their only child, Demi," Fey reasoned.

Looks like going back is the best choice, Fey thought to herself.

Demi continued, "I even tried to make a deal with them to continue supporting me for just three to six months after graduation. I was going to use that time to save up some money so that I could stay here and start my business and not have to go back. But my mom saw through my plan. That woman is too clever for her own good." Demi pouted.

Fey laughed. "Sounds more like you want to have your cake and eat it too," she admonished. While she wanted her friend to stay, she also knew that Demi was a bit spoiled.

"Why can't I? Hmmm? Life's not fair!" Demi continued to complain.

Both women were quiet for a while, deep in their thoughts. Demi spoke first.

"If I go back, I'll miss you, Fey. You're my only friend who I can rely on."

Fey smiled wryly. "I'll miss you too, Demi." She reached out to hold her friend's hand. "Don't worry. It's not like you will never be able to come back and visit me."

"I guess..." Demi responded. "So, what are your plans after graduation?" she asked.

Fey sighed. "I'm not so sure anymore. So many things have happened in the last few months. I found out that my father had been trying to reach out to Tutu and me, but my Mom was hiding it from us. Then, there's Iben, who I really like a lot, though I am not sure what we're going to do after this semester is over and I have to go back home. Then, of course, I have my career to think about. At this point, I'm kind of unsure about the future." Then she added jokingly, "Maybe we should swap places, huh?"

Demi suddenly had a thought, and her face lit up. "Yes! That's the perfect solution!" she exclaimed.

"What's the perfect solution?"

"Move to Nigeria with me after graduation!" Demi declared.

"Huh?"

"Think about it. You'll get a chance to meet your dad. You'll get to be with Iben. And lastly, you'll get to be with me, your *awesomest* best friend." Demi was grinning from ear to ear.

Fey scoffed. "That sounds all well and good, but I do not have parents who are willing to bankroll me in a business venture," she said sarcastically. "What would I do for a job and a place to stay when I get there?"

"You can live with me, of course," Demi said matter-of-factly. "You know my parents will be happy about that. As for a job, I'm sure my dad can pull some strings for you."

Fey was quiet for a while as she considered this spontaneous idea of Demi's. Then, she said, "My mom is going to be very unhappy if I tell her that I want to move to Nigeria." She could just imagine the shouting match they would have over this. "As for a job, I don't want to rely on your dad if I can help it. I'd like to try and find one for myself before I go."

The two women continued to discuss and come up with contingencies for Demi's Dip-to-Nigeria plan. By the end of their hang out, Demi had gone from being depressed about going back to Nigeria to being excited about it, now that her friend was considering coming along as well.

Fey texted Iben on their way back. *'I'll meet you at the cafe in 30 minutes.'* When she arrived, Iben was waiting outside.

"Let's go," Iben said after hugging her.

"Where to?" Fey asked. She remembered the last time something like this happened, Iben had surprised her with a picnic lunch. It was already late in the evening, so she wondered what he had planned.

"I'd like to talk to you about something, so let's go to my place where we can have a little more privacy and talk over dinner."

"Okay," Fey replied, wondering what he wanted to talk about. "What's for dinner?" She remembered Iben was a pretty good cook from their cook-off.

Iben smiled, "You'll have to wait and see..."

They walked the rest of the way quietly until they arrived at a high-rise apartment building. They walked into the lobby and rode the elevator up to the fifth floor. At the end of the hallway was Iben's apartment. He swiped his hotel-style key card to unlock the door.

"I'll go and warm up the plates. Make yourself at home," Iben said to Fey as soon as they entered the apartment.

Fey looked around the space. When she walked in, she saw the open kitchen with a bar-style countertop and three stools, straight ahead. Iben was setting up their dinner there. To the right was a small living area with one sofa, a desk with a lamp, Iben's laptop and some books. To the left was a door leading to his bedroom and another to the full bathroom.

Fey admired the whitewashed brick walls contrasted with the dark brown wooden built-in shelf in the living/study area. The entire space, except for the kitchen and bathroom, was carpeted. It felt nice and lush against her bare feet.

"Nice place you got here," she called from the bedroom. She flopped on the neatly made bed and started making imaginary snow angels on it. The sheets felt so luxurious. Just like the apartment building itself, everything she had seen in here so far looked understated or ordinary until you touched it or looked closer and realized that it was high-end quality stuff.

"Glad you're making yourself at home," Iben said with a chuckle as he leaned against the door frame watching Fey roll around in the bed.

Fey looked up and sheepishly smiled before getting off the bed. "My sister used to do that when we were younger. She'd come into my room and couldn't resist making a mess of my neatly made bed. I had to body slam her a few times until she stopped." She smiled at the memory.

Iben chuckled. "You did what?" he asked amusedly.

"Yeah, I had to teach her a lesson, you know." She was now standing at the door next to Iben with a big grin on her face.

Iben shook his head as he wondered what type of kid Fey was when she was younger. Then, he put his arm around her shoulder and said, "Dinner's ready."

Fey followed him to the kitchen and was surprised at the spread in front of her. Baked salmon, bacon-wrapped scallops, spinach, asparagus, baked potatoes, and bread rolls. She looked at Iben and asked, "You cooked all this?"

Iben smiled, "Yes," he said. "Are you falling for me even more now?" he added as he playfully wiggled his eyebrows.

Fey rolled her eyes at him and shook her head. *What a flirt*, she thought to herself amusedly. Iben chuckled. They sat down to eat.

"So, how was your hangout with Demi, by the way?" Iben asked, a few minutes into their meal.

"It was good... We've been so busy these past few weeks, so it was nice catching up," Fey replied. "Her parents want her to move back to Nigeria after we graduate next spring. She's not too happy about it, though. She was trying to convince me to relocate there as well."

At Fey's words, Iben stopped eating and looked at her. Fey relocating to Nigeria would be awesome, from his perspective. But then he remembered that she had mentioned some family issues preventing her from visiting Nigeria. So, Iben didn't think that she could just up and leave. Maybe if he found out more details about this family issue, he could figure out a way to get her to make the decision that would work in his favor. It would seem that the stars are aligning.

Fey continued. "She and I have lived in the States for so long. However, she's visited a few times over the last several years. While I haven't set foot there at all." She turned to Iben and said, "Remember when I told you about my father being in Nigeria?"

Iben nodded.

"Well, I found out just before I came to Munich that my mother had been hiding letters my dad sent to us. My sister and I confronted her about it, and she confessed that she didn't want him to find us or contact us for our safety. Her reasoning made no sense to me. Honestly, I feel that she's just being vindictive about what happened between them and how he took a second wife and abandoned us when we were little. I don't blame her for feeling the way she does about my dad, but

I hated growing up feeling like my father didn't care about us. I was so glad to find out that it wasn't the case. Before I came to Munich, I asked my mother to deliver a letter to him. In that letter, I asked him to reach out to me. I don't have any confidence that she will do it, though."

They both continued eating for a while before Iben asked, "Why don't you go and visit your dad in Nigeria instead?"

Fey sighed. "That's what I would like to do. But I don't even know where to begin my search. I think he's in Abuja, but he may have relocated, and my mother won't give me any clues. At best, I know his name. But how many people named David Ademola are there in Nigeria? It'll be like looking for a needle in a haystack."

Iben nodded slowly in agreement.

They ate the rest of their meal in silence, each with their thoughts. Afterward, Fey helped Iben with the dishes, and they moved to sit on the sofa in the living room. Fey had a bottle of hard cider while Iben had a bottle of beer.

After a few minutes, Iben asked, "You mentioned that you'd like to look for your dad. If you had the means to do that, would you go to Nigeria to find him?"

Fey looked thoughtful for a moment, then she said, "I think I would seriously consider it. Honestly, it would take very little convincing. I really want to find my father. I have so many questions for him. I want to get to know him. Also, with Demi going back to Nigeria, I will have somewhere to stay while I pursue any leads. But I need to find a job and stuff. It's so scary. So many decisions I need to make. I don't want to make them lightly."

Iben hugged Fey to comfort her. His heart was beating fast as he listened to her talk. He couldn't believe his good luck. Here he was wondering how he was going to convince Fey to move to Nigeria so that they could be together. But the stars truly were aligning in his favor.

"And there's also the matter of you and me," she added.

Iben stiffened. Somehow her words sounded foreboding. His heartbeat quickened.

"What are we going to do about us when the semester is over?" Fey asked.

Iben leaned back slightly from the hug to look at her. "I love you, Fey. No matter the distance, I want to continue this relationship with you," he responded.

"I've never been in a long-distance relationship before. I've heard so many bad stories," Fey confessed.

"We can make this work. Please don't give up before we even get started," Iben pleaded. "If you want, we can always revisit this at the end of the semester. If we both feel that it won't work after that, then we can call it quits."

Those last words of his felt like a knife to his chest. Quit? Like hell, he wanted to quit! But he didn't want Fey to feel pressured, so he said that to put her at ease. What he truly wanted was to make this woman his. With that thought, he leaned in and kissed her. It was intense from the start. It was like he was trying to convey all his love, all of his deep, intense feelings for her into this kiss. By the time they parted, Fey was almost breathless. They looked into each other's eyes as Iben said in a voice deep with emotion, "I believe we're worth giving it a try. Do you understand?"

Fey nodded and smiled. "I'm so glad you feel the same as I do," she said as she sighed in relief.

She didn't want their relationship to end either, so it was reassuring to hear Iben's words. Yes, their relationship was going to be a long-distance one at some point in the near future. But what relationship didn't have any risks? She just had to bring it up for discussion, though. That was the kind of person she was. She faced conflicts head-on as best as she could. Was it scary? Yes. But the thought of what might happen if she did not face things head-on terrified her more than the conflict.

Iben sighed with relief at her response. He repositioned himself on the sofa so that he lay his head on Fey's lap. The last few minutes had been a rollercoaster ride for his poor heart. He sighed again. When did he become such a love-sick puppy? This woman was undoubtedly going to be his undoing. As he lay there with his eyes closed, Fey rubbed his head gently. It felt nice.

After a few minutes, she asked, "What was it that you wanted to talk to me about?"

"Oh, right. I had almost forgotten." He opened his eyes and looked up at her. "In two weeks, I have a conference in Regensburg. It's from Friday to Sunday, and I want you to come with me." Iben raised his head and looked at her expectantly.

"Sure," she responded without hesitation.

For a few seconds, Iben's brain short-circuited. He hadn't expected her to agree so easily. He already had his speech planned out to convince her to come along with him.

"You will?" he asked, just to make sure he heard her correctly. "It's a weekend trip," he added in case she missed that part.

"Yeah... why are you looking at me like that?"

Iben quickly composed himself and said, "I'm just really glad to hear that. I'll make arrangements for our accommodations." He smiled happily as he laid his head back down on Fey's lap.

"What's the conference about? Is it for work or school?" Fey asked.

"Remember the thesis paper that I met with my advisor about recently? I'm going to be attending the conference to present my ideas."

"Oh, that's really cool."

"You can bring your books and study while I'm away at the conference. Then we can hang out afterward."

"Okay."

The couple stayed quietly as they were for a long time until Fey spoke.

"Iben."

"Hmmm?"

"I need to get back home."

"Don't go. Stay with me," Iben said—his eyes were still closed.

"It's almost midnight, and tomorrow is Monday."

Iben groaned unhappily at the truth in her words.

"So, I won't see you until Saturday?" he pouted.

Fey rolled her eyes at his antics. "Stop being silly. Isn't this how it's always been?" she chided gently.

"Yeah, but it's different now that we're dating." Iben sighed and reluctantly sat up.

Fey excused herself to go to the restroom. When she returned, Iben was still sitting down. He didn't take his eyes off her as she walked towards him.

"Let's go," Fey said when she stopped in front of him.

She held out her hand to pull him up, but he suddenly pulled her down towards him. Fey let out a surprised yelp as she landed on his lap. He then repositioned her so that she was sitting with her legs spread out across the length of the sofa. A hug and a gentle kiss on her lips followed. Fey put her arms around his neck as the kiss deepened. Iben's hands that were around her waist then slowly traveled up and down her back as he moved to kiss her neck. Fey's breath hitched as his kisses trailed down her neck, sending unexpected waves of pleasure through her. When he reached her collarbone, Fey let out a moan and Iben instantly felt himself harden. *Oh…Damn!*

He abruptly stopped and managed to say, "I think—I should stop." Then, he gently rested his head on her shoulder to calm himself down.

Fey wondered why Iben suddenly stopped kissing her. She had a few guesses, but she didn't ask.

They sat with her arms still around his neck until Iben finally said, "Let's get you home."

Since it was already late, Iben decided to drive Fey home. He led her down to the building garage and stopped in front of a car. Fey recognized it as the same car from their trip to Salzburg and asked, "You still have the rental car?"

Iben answered, "It's mine. I've had it for over a year."

"I see… and you've not been driving it around because…?"

"To spend more time with you," he said matter-of-factly. "Driving meant less time in your company."

Fey gave a chuckle as she got in the car. *This guy is too much.*

***

After Iben dropped Fey off at home, he returned to his apartment. Now that she wasn't here, he missed her. For the first time since he owned the apartment, he felt lonely.

Just as he was about to go to bed, he received a text from Fola.

'*I secured the evidence on Vivian. Check your email.*'

Iben smiled to himself before he responded. '*Good work. What about her father?*'

'*Almost there, I'll have everything for you in about two weeks.*'

'*Cool. I have another assignment for you. I need you to find Fey's father. His name is David Ademola.*'

'*I thought you didn't want to investigate her.*'

'*This is different. It's a favor for her.*'

'*Got it.*'

'*Work hard, and I'll give you a reward.*'

'*Just hook me up with a beautiful chick like your girlfriend, and we're even.*'

'*Fuck off!!!*'

'*Lol*'

Now irritable, Iben tossed his phone on his bedside table and got ready for bed.

***

After Fola sent his last text to Iben, he had a good laugh to himself. He just loved teasing that guy!

Although it was nighttime in Munich, it was early morning in Moscow, Russia, where he was away on a work assignment. Fola had been working in the Financial Crimes Unit at Interpol for some years now. Although he and Iben grew up together, Fola was a few years older. After he graduated college, Iben's grandfather, Edafe Ariri, used his connections to secure him a position at the Economic and Financial Crimes Commission (EFCC) in Nigeria. A couple of years later, the EFCC recommended him for a joint task force position at Interpol. Fola was very good at reading people, combined with his law degree and critical thinking skills, he was an outstanding investigator, and he soared through the ranks at Interpol. If there was a needle in a haystack, Fola would find it.

However, given that Edafe Ariri was his benefactor, he was undeniably loyal to the Ariri family. He would take on extra investigative work like the one Iben had assigned to him regarding Vivian. Besides that, Iben was like his brother, and he would do anything to ensure his happiness. They had both been through a lot since their childhood, and now that they were older, any little bit of personal happiness that had nothing to do with duty or survival was a welcome reprieve.

Unlike Iben, who seemed to be in love with a woman, Fola wasn't ready for that kind of relationship. He enjoyed the freedom of short and temporary romances while he was in whatever city his jobs took him to. Being a good-looking man, he never had issues charming the ladies. Life was good.

One of the things that Fola loved the most about his job was traveling. He was a bit of a daredevil who loved the thrill of traveling to different countries doing investigative work. Now the head of a team of investigators charged with monitoring certain types of financial crimes between Africa and Europe, their current assignment brought them to Moscow, Russia. He looked out of his hotel window and recalled a conversation that he had with Iben's grandfather a few months ago.

"Fola, my son. Remember that when Iben takes over the company, he's going to need you back here by his side. Iben is very capable but still naive about certain parts of our business. I'm sure you know what I mean. In the future, there will be moments when he'll need strength from you. He'll need you to continue to handle those um... unique matters with extreme prejudice."

"Yes, Papa!" Fola had responded.

He had always known that he was being groomed to be Iben's right-hand man—his Consigliere. Now, with Iben finishing up his education next summer, this life he had right now would change. Soon, he would be leaving the bright lights for the shadows. He sighed. *Better enjoy this while it lasts.*

At that moment, his phone rang. *Speaking of the devil,* he thought to himself when he looked at his caller ID.

"Hello, Papa," he greeted.

"Fola, my son," came Edafe Ariri's deep voice over the phone. "Where are you these days?" he asked.

"I just arrived in Moscow yesterday. I hope you are doing well, Papa."

"These old bones are tired, my son," Edafe laughed. "Any news on the shipment?" he asked.

"Yes, I was able to figure out who intercepted it."

"Is it who we suspected?" Edafe asked cryptically.

"Yes. What are your orders?"

"Take care of them and leave no stone unturned," Edafe instructed.

"Understood!"

After the call ended, Fola took out his laptop and signed into a secured network that he used only for Ariri-related tasks. He sent a message over the network. *'Send the drones.'*

Seconds later, he received a response. *'Affirmative.'*

He logged out of the network and put the laptop away.

Minutes later, he received a message from one of the IT specialists on his Interpol team that they had acquired some information on one of their suspects. He smiled to himself.

Time to earn some 'good karma' points!

11 | Intimacy

Two weeks later, it was time for Fey to accompany Iben to his conference.

"So, are you excited about your weekend getaway?" Demi teased as Fey was packing her weekend bag.

Fey gave her a sidelong glance and asked, "Why do you seem more excited than I do?"

Demi chuckled. "I'm just happy that you guys will be able to take your relationship to the next level."

"You don't say," Fey responded dryly, as she continued to pack her toiletries.

"Here you go," Demi said as she dropped a small box in her bag. Condoms.

Fey glared at her. "Seriously?"

"Better safe than sorry," Demi defended herself.

Fey shook her head. "You've gone from giving me pepper spray to condoms?"

Demi shrugged. "Yeah, your boyfriend has grown on me, I guess. So, now I'm rooting for you guys." She smiled cheekily.

"Just leave," Fey pointed to the door.

Demi chuckled and sauntered out of the room.

Iben rang the doorbell at precisely 3:30 PM. Fey was ready, so she answered the door right away. Thinking about the condoms Demi gave her, Fey wanted to make sure that she didn't get a chance to say something crazy to Iben. She quickly ushered Iben out the door so that they could leave right away. Just when she thought they were home free, she suddenly heard Demi yell after them, *"Play safe,* you two."

Before Fey shut the door, she glared daggers at her friend.

After Iben put Fey's luggage in the car, they started their two-and-a-half-hour trip to Regensburg. This time, Fey didn't fall asleep. She was very chatty, much to Iben's delight. She talked about her mother, her sister Tutu and Demi. She also mentioned that Demi had told her about a career-ladder program called the Advanced Management Trainee Program that the Nigerian Government had recently set up to encourage expatriate citizens to return to the country. The program would provide training and a guaranteed leadership position in the government to whoever was accepted. Fey intimated that she would apply for the program and try her luck.

"I've heard of the program. It's very competitive. Let me know if you need a reference," Iben said.

"Thanks. Demi's dad and her uncle have offered to be my references for now. I'll let you know if I need to take you up on your offer."

Iben nodded. "By the way, when we arrive, I'll need to leave for a few hours to meet with my advisor. Just to go over tomorrow's presentation and stuff."

"Okay."

They arrived at their hotel around 6:00 PM, and after Iben checked them in, they took their luggage to their room. The door opened to reveal a very spacious suite with two queen-sized beds, a large sofa, and two desks. The en suite bathroom was very spacious as well, with a tub and a shower. There was also a kitchenette and a fridge.

Iben looked at the time and said, "I need to leave soon. Order room service since I probably won't be back until after dinner."

Fey nodded.

Sometime later, Iben grabbed his laptop bag. "Wait up for me," he said after kissing her. Then he left.

Fey was indeed hungry, so when Iben left, she ordered dinner from room service. After her meal, she took a shower, changed into something comfortable, and got in one of the beds to watch TV while waiting for Iben to return. When Iben came back from his appointment, he found Fey already asleep. She was curled up in the bed, wearing a pair of red jersey shorts and a white tank top.

She wasn't kidding when she said red was her favorite color, Iben thought to himself.

He picked up the bedcovers and gently put them over her before he went to take a shower. When he finished, he put on a pair of shorts, turned off the TV and climbed in the empty bed. However, knowing that Fey was in the other bed, he couldn't go to sleep. After about ten minutes of tossing and turning, Iben mumbled to himself, "Who am I fooling?" Then he left his bed and laid down next to Fey. He positioned himself so that Fey's back was facing his chest, and his arm was around her waist. Soon after, he fell asleep.

A few hours later, Fey woke up. She looked at the time on her phone that was next to her. It was a little past 1:00 AM. She noticed Iben's arm around her and repositioned herself so that she was facing him. She ogled him unabashedly now that he was asleep. For a while, Fey just watched his handsome face as he slept. Before she knew it, her fingers gently traced his lips. Next, she touched his bare, toned chest and then leaned in and gave him a light peck on his lips. She did all of this gently so that she would not wake him.

Suddenly, she heard Iben say in a low, groggy voice, "Are you trying to seduce me?"

Fey yelped in shock and quickly turned around. *Oh my gosh! Was he awake? Ahhh, how embarrassing!*

Iben still had his arm around her, so he pulled her closer to him so that she was now flush against his chest. Then he leaned in and whispered in her ear, "You can't bail now, babe. Now that you woke me up, you should finish what you started."

His warm breath by her ears sent tingles throughout Fey's body. She giggled and said, "Don't be silly. You weren't even asleep."

"But I was... I'm just sensitive to your touch."

Iben sounded so sexy that Fey's heart was pounding in her chest at his words. But she was too shy to respond, so she simply closed her eyes and said nothing.

Hearing no response from Fey, Iben decided to take matters into his own hands. He began by kissing behind her neck and sucking on her earlobe. His warm tongue sent waves of delight down Fey's body, pooling in her nether regions. She moaned in response as he moved his hand from her waist to caress her tummy. His hand soon found an opening under her top and made its way up to her soft breasts. All the while, he continued kissing her neck and ear.

Iben could feel himself getting hard. The woman he loved was right next to him and he wanted her. He pressed his growing erection against Fey and groaned deeply. His hands kneaded her nipples as he continued kissing her. His hands then traveled back down and stopped just below the waistband of her shorts. He didn't go lower. Just rubbing her there, teasing her, drove Fey crazy with desire.

"Iben..." she whimpered.

Hearing her say his name in such a sultry voice caused Iben to immediately stop everything he was doing. He turned Fey over so that she was lying on her back, and he was straddling her. He looked down at her as she looked up at him. She looked so gorgeous and sexy as she shyly bit her lower lip.

"Babe, I want to kiss you," Iben said before he pulled up her tank top, exposing her breasts. "All of you." He then leaned in and captured one of her breasts in his mouth, running his tongue across the nipple, while he kneaded the other with his fingers. Fey moaned with pleasure. A moment later, he moved to kiss her lips, parting them with his tongue. He then slowly left a trail of warm kisses from her neck, to her breasts again, and then to her tummy.

At this point, Fey was writhing with intense anticipation. She moaned with a whimper again as she looked up at him with smoldering eyes, "Iben…"

In response, Iben slid his fingers inside her shorts and found her clitoris, her love button. Fey arched her back in ecstasy and spread her legs to allow him easy access. Iben swiftly took off her shorts and underwear that was now wet from her juices. Now bare before him, Iben imagined himself inside of her and moaned at the sight of her vagina. It looked like a pink rose, wet with the morning dew.

He leaned in and tasted her rose with his tongue. He savored the taste, the wetness, the fragrance. It was amazing. He wanted more, so he stayed there, his head buried between her widespread legs. He licked, he sucked until Fey orgasmed in his mouth.

When he looked up, she was breathing heavily, still raw from the sensations. He repositioned himself and pressed his erection right between her widespread legs. He was now bulging through his shorts so much that it hurt. He looked into her eyes and asked, "Will you have me?"

Fey's response was to gently lift her hips against him, indicating yes. Iben's eyes immediately flashed with intense desire. He stepped down from the bed and took off his shorts. Then he put on a condom.

Fey watched Iben as he climbed back in bed and on top of her. He kissed her lips, then her breasts, as he slowly guided himself to her entrance.

Then, he entered her.

Fey gasped as his hard member slowly filled her core.

Iben moaned deeply as he entered her warmth. He couldn't believe how tight and wet she felt. He looked down at Fey, the woman he was in love with. She looked so gorgeous.

Fey dug her fingernails into his back as the pressure she felt from him being inside her sent pleasure currents through her.

Iben leaned in and kissed her lips as he waited for her to get used to his size. When he felt her arms around him relax against his back, he asked in a very deep and breathy voice, "Are you ready?"

Fey slowly nodded, and in the next instant, Iben started to thrust. First gently, slowly and then he gradually increased his speed. She felt amazing, better than all the fantasies he had about this moment. Iben looked down at the woman beneath him. He enjoyed watching her breasts bounce as he continued to thrust deeply. Before long, he wrapped his arms around her and leaned in so that he was flush against her chest. He wished she could melt into him.

Gradually, her softness, her moans, his thrusts, his moans, soon brought them both to an otherworldly, electrifying orgasm.

Minutes later, they laid next to each other, with Fey against Iben's chest and his arms around her. He kissed her forehead and said, "I love you."

Fey nodded and buried her face in his warm embrace.

Iben didn't expect her to say anything in return. Although he was already on that train, he was willing to wait until she was ready to get on. It was enough for him that she wanted to be with him and give their relationship a chance.

***

The next morning, Iben woke first and watched Fey as she slept. He recalled their intimacy from last night, and a big grin appeared on his face. It was everything he had imagined and more.

She's mine, he thought happily to himself.

Minutes later, when Fey opened her eyes, he said, "Good morning, beautiful."

She smiled when their eyes met. "Hey," she said in a low voice.

Iben put his arm around her, and she snuggled close to his chest.

"What time is it?" Fey asked after a while.

"A little after 8 o'clock."

"When do you have to leave for your conference?"

"In about two hours. I'm not the first one presenting, so I don't have to be there when the conference starts."

Fey nodded and moved to sit up. Iben watched as the bedcovers slowly slid down to her waist. Her perky breasts were now in full view.

"Are you trying to seduce me again?" he teased, as he stared at her bare chest.

Fey's eyes widened in realization. She looked down embarrassedly and quickly pulled the covers back up over her chest.

"I did not seduce you," she objected.

"Oh...? Wasn't it you who touched and kissed me first?" He continued teasing.

Fey opened her mouth to object but realized that it was true. She then decided to explain that she only did that because she thought he was asleep. But she quickly caught herself when she realized that it would just make her sound pervy, so she kept quiet.

"Just so you know, I'm not complaining or anything," Iben added with a wink.

This shameless guy, Fey thought to herself. "Shut it!" she snapped as she smacked him playfully on the arm.

This earned a chuckle from Iben.

Fey gave him an eye-roll and said, "Don't worry, it won't happen again."

"Is that so?" Iben smiled knowingly. This woman was obviously not aware that certain desires, once unleashed, were difficult to keep at bay. Especially when the object of your desire is right within reach.

Iben then watched amusedly as Fey painstakingly reached for her tank top that was hanging off the edge of the bed while trying to keep her chest covered.

Before putting it on, she said to Iben, "Close your eyes."

He raised a brow, "Why?"

Fey glared at him, so he did as she asked, a smirk playing on his lips.

After putting on her top, she got off the bed. As she walked to the en suite bathroom, she suddenly heard Iben whistle suggestively at her. She reached for one of the pillows on the sofa and forcefully threw it at him. "Make yourself useful! Order breakfast or something!"

Then she quickly entered the bathroom.

Iben caught the pillow and laughed.

Sometime later, after they both got dressed and had breakfast, it was time for Iben to leave. He pulled Fey into a hug and said, "When I get back, let's go out on a date."

Fey smiled and said, "Sounds good."

After Iben left, Fey focused on getting her schoolwork done before he returned. She finished up an assignment for one of her classes and then studied for a test that was coming up the following week. Around 3:00 PM, when Iben returned, she was watching TV.

"Hey," Fey smiled when she saw him. "How was your presentation?" She got up from her seat to hug him.

"It went well! Glad it's over though. So now I can focus all of my attention on you." He kissed her forehead as they hugged.

"Did you eat lunch?" Fey asked. "I saved you some sandwiches." She nodded towards the room service tray on the table.

Iben smiled at Fey's gesture. It warmed his heart that she cared about him and thought to save him some lunch. Even though he wasn't hungry, he said, "Thanks, I'll have some." He picked up one of the sandwiches and ate it.

***

A few hours later, they were both ready for their date. Fey dressed up in a pair of black faux leather leggings, a black silk blouse, and a chic army green blazer. She completed her look with a layered beaded necklace and a pair of silver flats. Iben was dressed in a pair of faded gray jeans, a striped t-shirt, and a black bomber jacket. On his feet, he wore a pair of Chelsea boots. Together, the couple gave off a casual, trendy vibe.

Iben refused to tell Fey where he was taking her, as he wanted it to be a surprise. After about forty-five minutes, they arrived at their destination. He gave his car keys to the valet, and he entered the building with Fey.

As soon as they were inside, Fey's face lit up in a bright smile, and she almost squealed in delight. Iben had brought her to a jazz club. The interior was very cozy, with dim lights and intimate seating sections. Along the walls of the space were sofas and tables where couples could relax and have drinks or eat dinner. There was a stage against the main accent wall where the jazz artists would be performing. A few minutes later, they were seated, and Fey perused the lineup of performances for the evening.

"Are you familiar with any of those artists?" Iben asked curiously.

Fey shook her head. "Not really. This is only my second time being in a jazz club. Maybe I'll recognize some of the music covers."

Fey took in the atmosphere as she admired the decor. Pictures of famous jazz and blues artists hung on the walls, along with a few antique horned instruments. Light jazz music was also playing in the background. "I have to say. I *really* love the vibe here." She was all smiles.

Her grin was infectious. Iben couldn't help but smile too as he watched her. "Glad you like it. I've wanted to bring you here since you first told me that you liked jazz clubs," Iben confessed. "Later when we had that cook-off, and Demi suggested I take you to one, I decided that one day, I'd bring you here."

Fey leaned in and looped her arms around Iben's as she sat next to him on the sofa. "Thank you," she said with a smile.

The couple sat like this for a while, after which they ordered drinks and appetizers. As the night went on, different artists and bands performed on the stage, while Iben and Fey chatted.

"So, what kind of music do you like?" Fey asked Iben at some point.

"I listen to just about anything, but afrobeats and reggae are my favorites," Iben responded. "What about you? Aside from jazz."

"Well… country music," she said sheepishly. When Iben raised a surprised brow, she added, "My mom used to listen to country music when I was growing up, so I like it by association. Maybe my love of jazz will rub off on you."

Iben chuckled.

A short while later, their meals arrived and Fey remembered the salmon and scallops that Iben had prepared for dinner a few weeks back.

"How did you learn to cook so well?" Fey asked curiously. "I'll be honest and say that your cooking is on par with this restaurant meal."

Iben smiled at Fey's compliment. "I see you finally decided to bow down to my awesome skills," he teased with a wink.

Fey scoffed at his comment, "You just can't help yourself, huh?"

Iben chuckled and said, "When I was younger, my grandfather had chefs at the house that prepared our meals. I was a very bored and curious kid at the time, so I got them to teach me a few things, and I'd hang out in the kitchen with them. Unfortunately, when my grandfather found out, he sent me to military-style boot camp that summer because he was worried that I was getting too soft and needed to learn how to be a man."

Fey raised a brow, "Seriously? Your grandfather sounds like a very *interesting* man."

"Yeah, he is… Anyway, as I got older and was living on my own in university, I just got better at it."

Fey nodded as she continued to eat. "How old were you when he sent you to boot camp?" she asked.

Iben smiled wryly. "I was thirteen."

Fey's eyes widened. "Wow! In the States, parents would only do something like that when troubled teens needed a serious reality check." Then she added in a teasing tone, "Are you sure he didn't send you there because you were a troublemaker?"

Iben chuckled at Fey's comment and shook his head. "No, not a troublemaker, but it was an eye-opening experience for me. When I was at boot camp, I got to serve at some villages in a remote part of the country and got to see some real poverty. It left an impression on me at that age. Now, I try to help the less fortunate when I can."

"That's why you joined the volunteer program at TUM?" Fey asked in realization.

Iben nodded, "When I take over the company from my grandfather, I plan to start a charity for the less fortunate back home."

Fey's admiration for Iben grew as she listened to him. Not many people with a wealthy background like him would have such an outlook on life. She decided that's why he seemed down to earth.

"How does it feel knowing that you'll soon be taking on such a big role in your grandfather's company?" Fey asked. "I can't imagine what it's like to have such a huge responsibility. It's scary and stressful just thinking about it."

"It can be overwhelming at times," Iben admitted. "But my grandfather has been training me for this role since I was little. And it's not like I'm going to be doing this all by myself. I have a great support team."

Fey nodded before she reached out to hold Iben's hand and squeezed it. "I'll be rooting for you," she said with an encouraging smile.

Iben met her gaze and lifted her hand to his face. Then, he planted a gentle kiss on the inside of her wrist. "Thank you," he said softly.

Iben didn't realize that this action had set Fey's heart aflutter. When he let go of her hand, he asked, "So, what about you? I know you are going to be applying for the expatriate trainee program, but as a civil engineer, where do you see yourself in the next few years?"

Fey looked thoughtful for a while before she answered, "When I was little, I found out that my father was a civil engineer, so I decided that's what I wanted to be when I grew up. I thought it'd be one way to bond with my father whenever I met him." She smiled wryly. "Thankfully, I like what I'm studying. Anyway, I have really enjoyed the transportation and geotechnical engineering coursework the most.

So, I might end up doing something along those lines. Who knows?"

Iben nodded. "Cool," he said. He could already imagine Fey heading up some engineering projects at Ariri Corps. The company had its hands in a few transportation projects, after all. He quickly shook his head to get rid of that thought. As much as he wanted Fey in Nigeria with him, he knew she wouldn't accept such a position even if he offered it. She'd want to do this on her own. She wouldn't even allow Demi's parents to hook her up with a job because she wanted to try it on her own.

Fey could see that he was thinking about something, so she asked, "Penny for your thoughts?"

Iben met her gaze and smiled. "This…" he said before he leaned in and kissed her on the lips.

Fey pushed him away gently and said, "Iben… we're in public."

Iben raised a brow. "So what? No rule says I can't kiss my girlfriend in public." Then he added in a teasing tone, "Are you... shy?"

Fey broke away from his gaze and took a sip of her drink to hide her embarrassment. Of course, she was shy. Hugs and holding hands in public were one thing; kissing was another. Some might see her as a prude, but she couldn't help it. She was private in that way.

Iben leaned closer to her ears and said in a low, sexy voice, "Fine, I'll wait until we get back to the hotel to do what I *really* want."

Fey's eyes widened at his overt flirting. She turned away from him to hide her shyness, and awkwardly tried to change the subject. "You… your food's getting cold," she stammered.

So cute, Iben thought to himself with a smile.

After the date was over, the drive back to the hotel was a quiet one. The main reason was that Fey had drunk a bit more alcohol than usual, which made her very sleepy. She slept the entire drive. Iben chuckled and kind of blamed himself for her current state. If he hadn't continued to tease her by flirting so much through the night, she might not have drunk so much to hide her embarrassment. But her reactions were so cute every time he did, that he just couldn't help himself.

When they arrived at the hotel, Iben parked the car and waited a while before trying to wake Fey. When she woke up, her head felt clearer.

As soon as they got to their room, Fey went straight to the bathroom to change her clothes. When she came out, Iben was already changed and in bed. As she got in next to him, she realized that he wasn't wearing a shirt like the night before.

How distracting. She turned to him and said, "Please, put on a shirt."

He smiled mischievously and teased, "Why? Can't keep your hands off me when I'm shirtless?"

Fey scoffed, "Don't get too full of yourself." Then she turned around so that her back was facing Iben. He didn't see the smile she was hiding.

Unlike the night before, where one of them was asleep before the other went to bed, tonight, both of them were awake and aware of each other's presence.

"Iben," Fey called after a while.

"Hmmm?" he responded.

"I can't sleep," she confessed. She had slept through their drive back and then some, so it was understandable.

Iben couldn't sleep either, but for a different reason. The only thing he could think about was that last night, he had made love to Fey, right here. And now that she was lying next to him, he wanted more. His voice was low and tinged with suppressed desire as he asked, "Do you want me to rub your tummy?"

Hearing those words reminded Fey of last night's intimacy. She remembered how his kisses and the touch of his fingers around her navel put her in frenzied arousal. Although she'd had sex before in a prior relationship, with Iben, it was different—it was electrifying. Every other experience in the past paled in comparison.

Yes, I do, she answered to herself, but would not admit it to him. She knew Iben would have a field day of teasing her about it the next day. So, she said nothing. She would just bear with her desires until sleep eventually took over.

Iben, on the other hand, asked the question because he wanted to put the thoughts of last night's intimacy in Fey's mind. He wanted her to be in the same mind space as he was. Even though she was silent, she didn't refuse him, so he knew he had succeeded.

The sexual tension in the air was almost palpable.

Iben shivered and swore he could feel heat from Fey and he moved closer, like a moth to the flame. Now that he knew what she tasted like, what she felt like, he wanted more. "I want you, babe." His voice was deep, and he spoke right by Fey's ear, sending shivers of delight all over her body.

"I want to kiss you again," he continued as he kissed her behind her neck. He learned from last night that it was one of her erogenous zones.

A moan escaped Fey's lips, and Iben felt himself harden. "I want to... feel you again," he said in a very breathy voice. He then slowly turned Fey over on her back so that he could look at her face. The sultry, seductive look in her eyes was enough indication that they were both on the same page. She wanted him just as much as he wanted her. The next moment, Iben's lips passionately descended on hers.

Before long, they had shed their clothing and were dancing to the rhythm of their desires. Maybe it was because of the newness of their newfound intimacy. Or perhaps the closeness that they now felt towards each other. Whatever the reason, they couldn't help but make passionate love again and again until their desires were satisfied. Hours later, the couple finally fell into an exhausted slumber.

12 | Happy Birthday

"I had a nice time this weekend," Iben said softly to Fey as he hugged her while they were standing at her doorstep. It was Sunday afternoon, and they had returned from Regensburg.

Fey smiled, "Me too."

They broke away from the hug, and Iben tucked something in Fey's hand. "I want you to have this," he said. "It's a key to my apartment."

"Oh… are you sure?" Fey asked as she looked at the key card in her hand.

"Yes, I'm sure." He loved and trusted her. So, he naturally wanted her to feel free at his place.

"Okay," she responded with a smile. Then she added in a teasing tone, "I hope you don't regret it when your apartment becomes my new hangout and study area."

Iben smiled, "You can come over whenever you want." Then he leaned in and gave her a goodbye kiss.

Moments later, Fey waved to him as he left, and then, she went inside the house.

"I see a lovely glow around you," Demi teased as soon as she saw Fey. "How was your weekend?" she asked.

Fey chuckled and gave two thumbs up before going to her room. Once inside, she unpacked her luggage and took out the apartment key card that Iben had given to her. It made her feel warm and fuzzy on the inside, knowing that he trusted her enough to open up his home for her to come and go as she pleased.

Although Fey would hang out at Iben's on Saturdays after their volunteer work, she did not need to go there by herself until Iben's birthday arrived a few weeks later. His birthday happened to fall on a Saturday, so after classes on Friday afternoon, she packed an overnight bag and went shopping for ingredients to cook Iben a birthday meal the next day. Iben was still at work when she arrived at his apartment, so she put the ingredients away and waited for him to arrive.

When Iben got home and saw Fey asleep on the couch, his heart skipped a beat. He couldn't believe that she finally decided to use the key he gave her. He thought about how many times he'd hoped to open the door to his apartment and find her there. And now unexpectedly, here she was. A big grin appeared on his face. He walked over to the sofa and gently tapped her on the shoulder. Fey's eyes fluttered open.

"Hey," she said with a smile when Iben's face came into view.

"I thought you were coming over tomorrow."

"I wanted to surprise you," Fey said as she sat up.

"What a nice surprise." He leaned in and kissed her.

"What time is it?" she asked.

"Around 10:30."

Fey was surprised. "You work this late every day?" she asked in disbelief.

Iben smiled as he sat next to her. "Sometimes… But if I'd known you were coming tonight, I'd have rearranged my schedule earlier in the week. I just had to finish some research and reports for a few cases at the firm before Monday."

Fey looked at him with admiration. *How does he handle all that and his coursework?* she thought to herself.

"Are you spending the night?" Iben asked, hopefully.

Fey nodded. "My bag's in your room."

"You should probably leave some of your things here so that you don't always have to pack a bag whenever you want to spend the night."

"Okay."

Iben smiled happily and stood up. Then he suddenly whisked her up in a bridal style carry. Fey yelped in surprise and reflexively put her arms around his neck for support.

"You're heavy," he teased as he walked to the bedroom and shut the door.

***

The next morning was Iben's birthday. When Fey awoke, she wished Iben, who was already awake, a happy birthday.

"Sorry, I don't have any presents." She couldn't think of what to buy someone who seemed to have everything, so she opted for something with a personal touch, cooking him a meal instead.

Iben hugged her naked body close to his and said in a low voice, "Last night was an excellent birthday present."

Fey smiled shyly and said, "I brought some ingredients to cook you a birthday dinner later tonight. It's not going to be Chef Iben levels, but I'm pretty sure it'll be edible," she joked.

Iben chuckled. "Looking forward to it."

Suddenly Fey's stomach growled loudly, causing Iben to chuckle in amusement. "But first, it looks like I need to feed you," he said as he got out of bed.

Fey watched as he got dressed. She was sure she would never get tired of staring at his sexy physique.

"Shall I flex my biceps a bit more for you?" Iben teased when he caught her checking him out.

Fey giggled and threw a pillow at him.

Iben had a good laugh before he said, "I'll go and get us some breakfast from the cafe. I'll be back soon." Then he left.

Sometime later, Fey heard a knock on the apartment door. Thinking that Iben must've forgotten to take his key with him, she quickly threw on one of his sweatshirts from his closet and went to open the door. To her surprise, it wasn't Iben.

It was Vivian.

And from what Fey could see, Vivian had expected Iben to answer the door. She was standing there with her trench coat unbuttoned and opened wide to reveal her sexy lingerie underneath. She was wearing nothing else.

When Fey saw this, she burst out laughing. "That's cute," she mocked as she calmly leaned against the door frame, looking Vivian up and down, a sneer fixed on her lips.

Embarrassed, Vivian quickly covered herself with her coat and pushed the door open to let herself in. "Where's Iben?" she demanded haughtily as she walked into the apartment.

"He's not here," was Fey's simple response. She shut the door and watched Vivian as she looked around the living room.

Vivian thought that it was a nice and cozy apartment, very simple—just like Iben's style. She thought bitterly that Iben never let her visit him here.

Then, she looked Fey up and down, and noticed that she was wearing one of Iben's old college sweatshirts - it reached down to her mid-thighs, exposing most of her legs. Considering how early in the morning it was, and what she was wearing, it was apparent to Vivian that Fey had spent the night.

Vivian was livid. *What is going on here? How can he allow this bitch to come here and spend the night? What charm does this girl have that I don't?*

"You're the girl from the other day?" she asked, eyeing Fey disdainfully.

Fey knew that she was referring to her birthday party, but she didn't respond. She just stood there with her arms crossed against her chest, a smirk playing on her lips.

For the next few seconds, both women just stared at each other.

"Stop wasting your time with Iben," Vivian finally said. "You're nothing to him. Just a pastime here in Germany till he goes back to Nigeria, and we get married."

"Is that so?" came Fey's lazy response, her facial expression showing disinterest in the conversation topic.

This angered Vivian. It made her feel like Fey wasn't taking her seriously. Not able to control her temper, she lashed out. "Yes, you're just like all those other girls he's been messing around with for the past year. Don't you dare think that because you're here warming his bed, that means that you've succeeded in stealing him from me! You're just a whore that he's using to try and make me jealous!"

While she was talking, she got in Fey's face, waving her finger with an intimidating look on her face. Fey didn't flinch. Instead, she calmly walked to the kitchen to make a cup of ice-cold water with ice cubes. Vivian followed, still barking at her. With the glass of water in her hand, Fey then turned around to face Vivian. She smiled and suddenly emptied the glass of ice-cold water on Vivian's head.

Vivian froze in shock at Fey's action—she glared at her.

"Are you calm now?" Fey asked, with a smirk. Then her voice turned as icy cold as the water she just poured on Vivian. "Now, listen to me. I don't care for your opinion on the nature of my relationship with Iben. It's none of your *damn* business. Is that clear? *You* are just a third party, after all. And the next time you cross into *my* personal space or try and threaten me in any way, I will show you exactly how much *damage* this black belt's roundhouse kick can do to that face of yours."

Vivian was shocked speechless. Nobody had ever spoken to her like that before.

Fey continued, "As for what you *think* is between you and Iben, I'll let him deal with that. Right, babe?" she asked, looking past Vivian.

That's when Vivian turned around and saw that Iben had returned. Vivian's back was to the door, so Fey was the only one who saw him come in. He had witnessed everything that happened from when Fey poured the cold water on Vivian. As he stood there, hearing Fey's threats to Vivian, he raised his brow approvingly.

My girl is a badass, he thought to himself.

Vivian was shocked to see Iben standing there. She hadn't heard him come in at all, but she was glad that he witnessed Fey being mean to her. He would certainly come to her rescue, Vivian thought to herself. It was as if she forgot everything that happened at her birthday party. "Iben, did you see what she did?" Vivian asked, pointing an accusing finger at Fey.

He nodded. "Yes, I did," he said, as he walked over to Fey with the bag containing their breakfast and put it on the kitchen counter. Then he stood next to Fey with his arms around her waist and asked Vivian, pointedly, "What did you do to provoke my girlfriend?"

Vivian's eyes grew wide. "Why would you assume that I did something to her?"

"My baby girl over here is chill unless she is provoked. I know her, and I know you. Fey is not a troublemaker. You are." Iben's response was straight to the point. "That aside, how the hell do you know where I live?" he added with a frown.

Vivian ignored his question and said, "I just came to wish you a happy birthday, Iben. Why are you being like this?" She sounded hurt and aggrieved.

"You should leave," Iben said coldly. He had no time for Vivian's games this morning.

"Can I talk to you in private, please?" Vivian suddenly asked.

Before Iben could respond, Fey raised her voice and said, "Absolutely not!" She could not believe this woman actually thought that she would leave Iben with her while she was wearing that rubbish underneath her jacket.

Both Vivian and Iben were surprised at Fey's sudden outburst. Vivian glared at her while Iben slowly rubbed his hand around Fey's waist as if to calm her down.

"I asked Iben, not you," Vivian spat back at Fey. Then she turned to Iben expectantly.

With his arm still around Fey's waist, Iben said, "She said no. So, you can say whatever you want right here in her presence. You have thirty seconds before I call security."

Vivian was so frustrated that she didn't know what to do. Why was she losing to this nobody of a girl? It almost seemed as if the world was against her.

"I'll come back later," she said as she turned around to leave.

"No, you won't!" Iben snapped. "In fact, I'll find out how you figured out where I live, how you got in here, and then deal with whoever was in cahoots with you. If you do try to come back here again, I will call the cops."

Vivian glared at both of them and left, slamming the door angrily behind her.

After she left, Fey let out the breath she had been holding. For the first time in a long time, she was very annoyed and irritable. She wasn't aware that Iben was carefully watching her body language and facial expressions. "Are you okay?" he asked, concerned.

Fey sighed. "I'm just annoyed that she came here," she admitted.

Iben started setting breakfast on the plates. "You and me both. She's never been here before, so I wonder who told her where I live. Only Fola knows, and he would never tell her. Unless she had me followed somehow."

"I see..."

"Let's eat," Iben suggested. They sat down to eat, but Fey didn't touch her food. So, after a few minutes, Iben asked, "What did Vivian say to you while I was away?" He could tell that something was bothering her.

"Nothing I couldn't handle," Fey responded. Then she added, "I think she came here to seduce you."

Iben snickered at the ridiculous idea. "Doesn't seem like something Vivian would do," he mused.

"Are you defending her?"

"No, of course not," Iben answered, surprised at Fey's question. He realized that things were going downhill quickly, but he couldn't figure out why. He reached out to hold her hand and asked again, "What exactly did Vivian say to get you so upset?"

Truthfully, it wasn't what Vivian said that got to Fey, but what she did. She kept imagining what could've happened if Iben was the one who opened the door when Vivian knocked. Fey contemplated telling him that Vivian had come wearing nothing underneath her jacket. But she decided against it. She didn't want him to have such images of that woman in his head, even if it was just for a second.

"She said I was just a pastime of yours, here to warm your bed until you go back to Nigeria," Fey finally said. Iben frowned and was about to say something to refute it when she added, "Don't worry, I'm well aware that she was just spitting venom."

"Good," Iben responded in relief. The last thing he wanted was for Fey to think that what Vivian said was true. For him, Fey was the woman he loved, and he didn't want any misunderstandings regarding that. "I'll speak with the apartment management and ask them to investigate how Vivian got in the building or elevators without being buzzed up. I think she probably bribed security to get in."

Fey nodded and started eating. "How's it going with the investigation on her abortion?" She couldn't wait to get the woman out of their lives for good.

"We're almost there. Just a few more weeks, and we can deal with both Vivian and her father once and for all," Iben responded confidently.

Fey then decided to stop focusing on Vivian. Besides, today was Iben's birthday, and she wanted him to have a good day.

When they finished eating, Iben reminded Fey that Fola would be coming over, so she went to take a shower and got dressed. After Fola arrived, he and Iben discussed some Ariri Corporation business, after which Iben filled in Fola on what happened that morning with Vivian.

Uncharacteristically, Fola was speechless the entire time as he listened. He wondered what had gotten into Vivian to act like this. *I'll have to get to the bottom of it*, he thought to himself.

Unbeknownst to both men, Fey's mood plummeted again once Iben brought up Vivian's visit. Later, Iben left to go and get ready so that they could go out to lunch. When it was just Fola and Fey in the living room, she said to him, "You know, when I opened the door, Vivian was wearing nothing but lingerie under her coat."

Fola's eyes widened in surprise. Then, recalling the account that Iben had given him on what happened, he said, "Iben didn't mention that…"

Fey sighed. "That's because I didn't tell him," she admitted.

"Why not?" he asked.

"If I did, wouldn't it be the same as him seeing it?" she retorted irritably. "Besides, it's not important in the grand scheme of things."

"It's important enough to bother you and for you to tell me about it," Fola said pointedly. "Aren't you worried that I'll tell him anyway?"

Fey shrugged nonchalantly. For some reason, she didn't believe that he would. What she was hoping for was that Fola could somehow help keep Vivian in check. Fola smiled knowingly, having guessed her thoughts, but he said nothing.

After a few seconds of silence, Fey asked awkwardly, "Were they ever... you know... did they... have sex?"

Fola raised his brows in surprise and was about to say something when Fey raised her hand and quickly said, "Actually, I don't want to know. I'm sorry I asked you that. I'm acting crazy."

She closed her eyes, took in a deep breath, and sighed. *Iben was engaged to Vivian for many years. It'd be unusual if they didn't have sex*, she thought to herself. *What good would having that information do anyway? The important thing is that Iben and I are together now.* With that thought, she slowly calmed her uncharacteristically turbulent heart.

Fola studied Fey and smiled mischievously. "Are you just jealous? Or do you not trust Iben?" he asked provocatively, even though he felt like he already knew the answer to both questions.

Fey scoffed and answered, "Neither."

"So then, you're in love with Iben, and you're jealous that there's an ex who keeps hanging around," Fola retorted.

Fey paused at his words. If she wanted to admit it, yes—she was annoyed that Vivian seemed to find ways to have access to Iben. And the thought of her trying other devious methods to get to Iben really irked her. But was she in love with him? She admitted that perhaps she was feeling more possessive of him as time went by, especially now with Vivian's sudden reappearance. But was that a sign of being in love with someone?

"If I'm in love with Iben, he'll be the first to know, not you," she replied. "So nosey..." Fey huffed as she rolled her eyes at him.

Fola chuckled and thought to himself, *Yeah, she's got it bad. Congrats bro!*

As he sat there quietly with Fey, Fola thought about everything he'd heard today regarding Vivian. He was itching to find out what was going on in her head. Showing up uninvited to seduce Iben? It was laughable. He also wondered how things would play out between Fey and Iben once their time together in Germany came to an end. Would their relationship hold up against the physical distance that would soon come between them? He looked up and saw Iben coming out of the bedroom, so he decided to change the subject a bit and lighten the mood.

"So, Fey—would you mind demonstrating your blackbelt

roundhouse kick?" Fola teased.

"Yeah, do you really have a black belt?" Iben chimed in.

Fey looked at both men and laughed.

"No, I am not a black belt! I was just bluffing to Vivian, and it sounded cool at the time," she finally said, smiling. "But I *can* throw a mean right hook, though. I took some boxing lessons at my gym a while back," she added proudly, holding her fists up.

Both men looked at her in surprise.

Then, Iben's face broke into a smile. He loved the fact that Fey was quick on her feet and not some damsel in distress. He leaned in and kissed her on the cheek before saying, "You are so badass!"

Fey chuckled.

Fola smiled as he watched them. *Iben found him one hell of a unique woman*, he thought to himself.

Before they left for lunch, Fey excused herself to go to the restroom. Fola took the opportunity to say, "I see you've made good progress in your relationship with Fey. I never knew you had it in you, bro."

Iben ignored his teasing and said, "I'm going to need to move to a new apartment after Fey leaves in December." He didn't want Vivian coming over as she pleased. She was like a cockroach that he just couldn't get rid of. And with her behavior these days, he just might murder her out of sheer annoyance!

"I'll contact the realtor," Fola responded.

"Thanks!"

***

After lunch with Iben and Fey, Fola called the realtor to find Iben another apartment. Next, he called Vivian. She picked up on the first ring.

"Are you still in Munich?" he asked right away.

"Yes."

"Let's meet up."

"Okay, I'll text you the hotel address."

A couple of minutes after the call ended, Fola received the address, and he drove about thirty minutes to Vivian.

When Vivian let him into her room, Fola could tell that her mood was down.

"I guess Iben told you that he saw me today," she began after they were seated.

"Yeah, I just had lunch with him and his girlfriend."

At the word girlfriend, Vivian scowled. "I wanted to beat that girl into a pulp today," she said through gritted teeth, as she recalled her earlier interaction with Fey.

"Iben is serious about her. You should leave her be."

"Fola, please help me get Iben back," she begged suddenly.

"Why?" he asked.

"He's mine. I don't want to let him go."

"He's not property, Vivian. Besides, you never wanted him, and now he has moved on."

Vivian didn't respond, so Fola continued. "Is it because he's more valuable now that someone else wants him? When he was yours, he was throwaway. Why the change of heart?"

Vivian pouted and said, "Stop being mean." Then she added, "I realize my mistake."

"Which is?"

Vivian thought about Damola, the man she was going to have a baby with. Just like Iben, he was smart, handsome, and was going to inherit his family's business. The only difference was that she was in love with the guy. She chose Damola, whereas Iben was forced upon her.

However, Damola's family was against their relationship. They wanted him to marry another woman, and even with her pregnancy, they had threatened to disown him and pass him over on his inheritance. So, he caved. Vivian couldn't believe that she had fallen for such a spineless man. While she was willing to burn bridges to be with him, he was unwilling to do the same for her.

That was when she realized that he wasn't good enough for her. She deserved better than him. She was Vivian Ibere, and her future children were meant to be offsprings of a great man, not some spineless jerk. She also decided then that Iben was the kind of man she wanted. So, she had an abortion and has been trying to get back with him ever since.

She just never imagined that Iben would reject her. Despite her indifference toward him before their breakup, Iben spoiled her and doted on her. But not anymore, and she missed that. And now, the more he pushed her away, the more she wanted him. A man who was willing to go against his grandfather's choice to be with another woman. Strong-willed. Independent. Passionate. That's the kind of man she wanted. Iben was that kind of man.

"Why would you show up at his place to seduce him?" Fola asked, suddenly jolting her out of her reverie.

Vivian sighed as she got up to pour herself a drink. "I was just trying something different. When he and I were together, I never let him touch me. So, I thought maybe if I gave myself to him, we would have a chance."

"You do realize that was the wrong move. Throwing yourself at a man like Iben is not going to earn you any points."

Vivian scoffed. "Oh please, he's had girls throwing themselves at him since we broke up. His latest one was even at his apartment this morning."

"His girlfriend," Fola corrected.

"And I'm his fiancée."

"Ex-fiancée," Fola corrected again.

"Whatever, are you trying to upset me right now?" She leaned back in her chair and crossed her legs. "Anyway, I'm not worried. Once he's tired of that girl, I'll have my chance."

Fola shook his head and smiled wryly as he realized that Vivian was a lost cause. *Why would anyone want to take back someone who betrayed them in the way that you did?*

There was silence between them.

"Iben has changed," Vivian mused sadly after a while.

"No, he's still the same. You're just no longer on the receiving end of his graciousness," Fola said pointedly.

Vivian moved to where Fola was seated, and she got on her knees with hands clasped together. "He listens to you, Fola. Just do me this one solid. I just want him to give me another chance," she begged.

"Would you take Damola back, if he came to you and asked?" he asked provocatively.

"That bastard isn't worthy of me!" she spat angrily.

Fola smiled contemptuously. "Yet, you think that you are worthy of Iben. Hmmm?"

Vivian paused and looked away from Fola's piercing gaze. She never thought about it from that perspective. Thinking about it now, Vivian knew in her heart that she was hypocritical. She didn't like that Iben had dated other women since they broke up. But she was willing to put up with it since she had an end-goal. She knew the type of person Iben was. Whomever he was with, he'd be loyal to them. She just had to work hard to make him choose her.

Fola continued, "Anyway, Iben should be the least of your worries. You should focus on your career. Start your own business or something. You never know what might happen in the future if your father's company meets a crisis."

Vivian frowned slightly at his words. It reminded her of what her father had said after he found out that she had irresponsibly broken off her engagement to Iben. He seemed concerned that Iben's grandfather would retaliate. She had shrugged it off, thinking that since Edafe Ariri was very fond of her, he would be forgiving if it came to that. In the meantime, she would focus on getting Iben back.

Fola reached out and gently patted Vivian on the head. He had grown up together with her and Iben since they were young, and despite what was going on between them, he was still fond of her. She was a spoiled princess, with little sense of responsibility. Always thinking of herself only, and they had all indulged her. However, he also knew that in the near future, when Iben unleashed his plans to expose her father's business dealings, she would have nowhere to turn. At that time, Vivian would wish she had never crossed the Ariris. For old time's sake, he decided to give her some advice.

"Vivian," he began. "You're like a younger sister to me. So, listen to your big brother. Focus on getting yourself financially independent. By the time you're done with your MBA next year, you'll need to focus on your career. You like fashion, right? Open a boutique or something. Have your own money. It's not good to rely on your father for everything. And most importantly, forget about Iben. Even if things don't work out with his girlfriend, he will never be yours."

Hearing Fola's words, Vivian slumped dejectedly from her knees to a sitting position on the floor.

Fola stood up a moment later. "Take care of yourself, Vivian," he said before he left.

13 | Merry Christmas

Weeks later, the semester came to an end. Along with it came Christmas and the looming separation between Fey and Iben. Fey rescheduled her return flight to five days later so that she and Iben could spend more time together, and she would still be home for Christmas. After the shared housing lease expired, and the rest of her roommates left, Fey moved her things to Iben's and stayed there until the day of her departure.

In those last days together, the couple toured Munich and the surrounding areas. They visited the Neuschwanstein Castle, which was rumored to be the inspiration for Disney's Cinderella's castle. They also visited a couple of royal palaces in Bavaria. Fey was amazed at the opulence inside these buildings and thought that the ancient Deutsche royalty lived ostentatiously.

After their daytime tour, Iben took Fey to a different restaurant every night for dinner. Since she never asked him for anything, his goal was to spoil her in his own way until she had to leave. He wanted her to have these memories with him. Well, he needed those memories as well. They were going to tide him over until he got a chance to see her again.

While they were sightseeing, they took lots of pictures. Iben thought to himself that he had never cared to take so many photos of anyone or anything in his entire life. But with Fey, he couldn't help himself. He also took Fey to a Christmas Market in Munich, where she bought souvenirs for her mom, sister, and a few of her friends back in the States. Later, when she was packing her luggage, she worried that she might have exceeded the airline baggage limit.

Fey also took the time to apply for the expatriate management trainee program.

"Do you want me to drop that in the mail for you?" Iben asked when she had completed the paperwork.

"Would you? That'll be one less thing I have to worry about. Thanks."

"Not a problem." Iben smiled as he took the sealed envelope and put it away.

Later, as they lay in bed on their final night together before Fey had to leave the next day, she said, "I'm going to miss you, Iben."

"I don't want you to go. I wish you could stay here with me." He sighed. "But since I have no control over that, I'll try my best not to be a nuisance when you get back home. I'll only call you once a week," Iben said, causing Fey to laugh.

She patted him gently on his cheek and said with a smile, "Despite the time difference, I'll make sure to pick up whenever you call."

He gave her a look. "Why do you sound like you're placating a little kid?"

Fey laughed as she watched Iben pout. She thought he looked so cute.

Iben enjoyed the sound of her laughter. He was going to miss that. He was going to miss seeing her smile. He was going to miss talking to her about everything and nothing in particular. He was going to miss her at the volunteer events. He was going to miss having meals with her. He was going to miss her shyness whenever he flirted with her. He was going to miss the feeling of her body close to his. His heart was heavy, and he wrapped his arms around her and held her close. If only he could keep her here. Overcome with these emotions, he started kissing her again, his hand wandering all over her body.

"Iben... we just did... aren't you tired?" Fey said in between kisses.

Iben stopped, looked her in the eyes, and said softly, "You're leaving tomorrow, and I won't be able to see you for a long time. Prepare yourself, my love. No sleep for you tonight." He leaned in and nibbled playfully on her earlobe, causing Fey to giggle. When she stopped laughing, he asked expectantly, "Shall we continue?"

Fey nodded with a smile. This was undoubtedly going to be a night to remember.

***

Around noon the next day, Iben drove Fey to the airport. After checking in her luggage, they walked towards her exit gate. When they got to the security check, Iben pulled her in for a hug.

"I'm going to miss you so much," he said for the umpteenth time.

Fey hugged him back tightly and said, "Me too... Remember, don't work so late all the time. Take breaks. Okay?"

He nodded and said, "I love you," as he kissed her on the forehead. Then he added, "I'd kiss you on the lips, but we're in public, and you're such a prude."

Fey chuckled and broke away from the hug. "I should get going," she said as she picked up her carry-on bag.

Iben nodded. "Have a safe trip," he said as he watched her walk away. He waited until she had cleared security. They waved to each other one last time before he left.

After leaving the airport, Iben went straight home. He started packing up his things for the move to his new apartment. He had collected the keys to the new place for about a week now. He was just waiting until after Fey left before he moved his belongings. Now that she was gone, he didn't want to stay here any longer. Although he already had a word with the apartment management about Vivian, he didn't want to take any chances. That woman was very crafty and resourceful when she wanted to be.

Since the apartment was already furnished when he took possession over a year ago, Iben only had to move his personal effects. As he was packing up his books, he saw a note tucked between one of his law books. It was from Fey. He smiled when he saw it and sat down to read it.

'Iben, Thank you for a wonderful time in Munich. When I first came here, you were the first person I met. I would never have imagined that you would also be the last person I'd see before I leave. I remember when you bought me, a total stranger, breakfast at the cafe. Your kindness and mysteriousness drew me to you like a magnet. I don't know what the future holds for me, but I certainly hope that you will continue to be in it. Merry Christmas, and Happy New Year in advance. Fey.'

After reading the note, Iben's heart filled up with a jumble of emotions. Happiness. Sadness. Hopefulness. He thought about the future. He certainly wanted Fey in his life as well. Of all the women he had dated, she was by far the most independent and straightforward of all. She was confident, fiery when it counted and wasn't pretentious at all. Her drive and determinedness made him want to be better, as well. He could see himself being married to her someday.

Iben paused when the realization hit him. Other than Vivian, he had never imagined anyone else in that role before. And even that was out of obligation. He decided right then that he was going to do all he could to make this dream a reality. First, he had to ensure that Fey would relocate to Nigeria. He looked at the time and decided to make a phone call to Nigeria.

After a few rings, the person on the other line answered cheerily, "Iben, my son."

"Hello, Papa," Iben responded. "How are you doing?"

"I am well. Good to hear from you. I was hoping you were coming home for the holidays."

"No, Papa, I have some work I need to attend to over the next couple of weeks," Iben said apologetically. "I sent you a Christmas gift last week. You should receive it soon."

Edafe laughed heartily, "I got it yesterday. I really like it. Thank you!" he said.

Iben smiled, "I'm glad to hear that." He had purchased some handcrafted smoking pipes as a gift for his grandfather, who enjoyed his tobacco from time to time. He also liked to sample new tobacco blends, so Iben also purchased new types of tobacco for smoking with his new pipes. Edafe Ariri preferred to smoke one kind of tobacco with each pipe, so he had quite a collection.

"How is Vivian?" he asked. "I haven't heard from her in a while."

"I saw her last month on my birthday. We're both busy with our studies and work," Iben answered vaguely.

"Hmmm, I understand."

Iben took the opportunity to change the subject. "By the way, Papa, do you know anyone at the government agency in charge of the Advanced Management Trainee Program?"

"Hmmm… Are you talking about the one where expatriates are given positions within the government?"

"Yes, that's the one."

"Of course. Let me see… Reach out to Kolawole Adebo in the Abuja office of the Ministry of Finance. He should be able to connect you to the right person."

"Okay, thanks, Papa."

"What's this about?" Edafe asked curiously.

"Just looking into it for a friend who is thinking about relocating back home," Iben responded.

"I see… well, let me know if you need anything else."

"This is good. Thanks again," Iben replied. "Well, I know it's getting late over there, so I will let you go. I'll call you again on Christmas day."

"Yes, I will be expecting your call. It's a shame that you won't be here for our yearly celebration."

"Yes, I look forward to the one next year. Good night, Papa."

"Good night, Iben."

The call ended.

Iben immediately wrote the contact's name down on a sticky note and stuck it on Fey's application before he continued packing. By nightfall, he was done. He made a couple of trips to and from both apartments until he had completed his move.

***

After Fey's nine-hour flight, she finally arrived in the States. She immediately sent a message to Iben. *'Hey, babe. I made it back safely.'*

His response came almost immediately. *'Hey, beautiful. Glad to hear it.'*

She hadn't expected a reply until tomorrow, so she asked, *'Sorry, did I wake you? Isn't it like midnight over there?'*

'No, I was waiting to hear from you. I moved to my new place tonight. I'm just about to go to bed.'

'Oh, wow! You must be exhausted. Have a good night.'

'Thanks, talk to you later.'

Fey retrieved her luggage and called her mother to let her know that she had arrived. It was around 6:00 PM so she told her that she would take a cab. By the time Fey got home, it was 7:30 PM, and dinner was waiting. After dinner and the excitement of being back home and seeing her family again wore off, she started to feel the effects of being jet-lagged. With her body still in Munich's time, she excused herself soon after dinner and went straight to bed.

The next day was Christmas Eve, and the family of three each set their presents under the tree as was their tradition for many years. They also decided on their dinner menu for the next day. As they were prepping and cooking, Fey couldn't help but think of Iben's delicious cooking. She'd only been back for one day, and she missed him already. She wondered what he was doing for Christmas and if he would have company over. Other than Fola, he didn't seem to have a lot of close friends. She picked up her phone and sent him a quick message.

'Hey, babe. What are your plans for tomorrow?'

'Hey, beautiful! I'll be at the shelter for a Christmas lunch with everyone. It

should be fun. How are you?'
'I'm good. We're prepping and cooking for tomorrow's Christmas dinner.'
'I miss you…'
'I miss you too. I'll call you tomorrow afternoon.'
'Sounds good. Later.'

For Christmas, Adaobi put the letters from their father that she had retrieved from the post office in small boxes and placed them under the tree for both Fey and Tutu. While she didn't want to have any discussion about their father, she felt that since the cat was out of the bag, there was no point in keeping the letters from them. She had gone to the post office once since Fey left for Germany, but she couldn't bring herself to send Fey's letter. She told herself that as long as their father was reaching out to them, it was enough.

She also didn't want to lie to her children anymore, so when Fey asked if she mailed the letter, she told her the truth. Fey seemed disappointed, but she didn't make a fuss.

From Fey's perspective, she already had a plan to find her father once she moved to Nigeria. She was just a bit hopeful that her mother would've done as she asked, which would make things easier for her.

Later in the evening on Christmas day, Fey and Tutu sat in Tutu's room to share and talk about their letters from their father. There were some letters for each of their birthdays for the last few years. He also sent a birthday card in advance for Fey's birthday next month. This warmed Fey's heart. She became even more determined to find him.

"I'm going to Nigeria to find Dad after graduation," Fey suddenly announced.

Tutu stared at her sister, wide-eyed. "Seriously? Were you able to get in touch with him?"

"Not yet. I'm planning to go with Demi when she moves back home to live with her parents. I've applied for a job there as well."

"So, this is a permanent thing? You're going to be living in Nigeria?"

Fey nodded excitedly. "Yes! It's scary and exciting at the same time…"

"Sounds like you have everything all figured out," Tutu said softly as she absorbed the news. She felt a mix of emotions. Her sister was always a go-getter, and Tutu had always admired her determinedness, but she also felt left out for some reason. Although she knew that her sister might not live at home after graduation, she didn't think she'd be thousands of miles across the Atlantic Ocean. Their family was slowly moving apart, and that made her sad.

Fey noticed her sister's look and reached out to hold her hand. "Don't worry, Tutu. I'll be sure to let you know once I find Dad," she said.

Tutu nodded and forced a smile. "Okay... Anyways, you promised to tell me about your boyfriend," she said, changing the subject.

Fey smiled and happily showed her some pictures of Iben on her phone.

"He's cute," Tutu complimented. "Is he the real reason you stayed back in Germany for a few more days?" she teased.

Fey chuckled and told her all about the fun things she and Iben did together during her last week in Munich. She also showed her the many pictures they took together.

"Are you sure about this long-distance thing?" Tutu asked, genuinely concerned.

"It's not going to be easy, but we're both willing to give it a try. Plus, when I go to Nigeria, we'll be closer to each other."

"Are you in love with him?" Tutu asked.

"Why does everyone keep asking me that?" Fey asked with an amused chuckle.

The sisters continued to chat and catch up with each other until late into the night.

"Please don't tell Mom about my plans to go to Nigeria," Fey said as she got up to leave her sister's room. "I'll let her know when I'm ready."

Tutu nodded. "Don't worry. I won't."

Soon after Christmas and the New Year, the spring semester began, and the siblings each went back to their respective campuses. This was also going to be both Fey and Iben's final semester in their degree programs.

14 | Graduation

Five months later, graduation rolled around. On the evening before Fey's graduation ceremony, she met with her mother and sister for dinner. They had come from out of town to attend her graduation the next day. At some point during their meal, she received a message from Iben.

'Congrats on graduating tomorrow. Remember to take pictures and send them to me. Don't be a slacker.'

Fey chuckled before she sent back a snarky reply, *'I'll think about it!'*

'Don't make me have to come over there...' he joked.

Fey and Iben had been texting each other regularly since she came back from Germany. After Fey's birthday in January, which was the first time Iben called to talk to her on the phone, the couple was successful in their attempts to speak on the phone or video chat at least four to five times in a month. This was in addition to daily text messages. Despite the time difference and their busy schedules, they made the most of it.

A couple of weeks before Fey's graduation was Iben's official graduation from his master's degree program at TUM. While on a video chat with Fey, he mentioned that he would be tying up some loose ends at work before going back to Nigeria.

"I have some good news for you," Fey said in the video. "I was shortlisted for a position in the management trainee program!"

Iben grinned and said, "Congratulations!"

"Thanks," Fey said happily. "Now, I just have to sign up for an interview. I'm probably going to pick a date in August, which is about two months from now. That'll give me time to save up some spending money until I have a job offer. I wouldn't want to burden Demi and her family."

Unbeknownst to Fey, to help her application, Iben had reached out to the Ministry of Finance contact that Edafe, his grandfather, had given him. He had also included himself and his grandfather as references in her job application. As high-profile references, Iben was confident that in addition to Demi's dad and uncle, Fey's package would be given strong consideration by the decision-makers.

He was also hopeful that the weight of having Ariri Corporation references would push her application to be accepted. It was a well-known fact that Ariri Corporation was one of the few companies that provided alternate positions to expats who did not make the cut for the government positions but were still considered valuable resources. In this way, the company partnered with the Nigerian government in elevating the workforce and improving the economy.

"Can you believe that they will also pay for my flight as well? That definitely takes a load off," Fey continued.

"That's good to hear, babe." Iben smiled at all her gushing. He could tell that she was excited about her move. But no one was more excited than he was. Thanks to technology, being in a long-distance relationship wasn't bad so far. Aside from no physical contact with Fey, they were able to communicate regularly and keep their relationship going. But he was undoubtedly looking forward to being in the same physical space as she was.

"So, that means I'll be able to see you soon... in August," Fey added.

"I'm looking forward to that," Iben said with a bright smile.

***

The next morning, Fey woke up feeling extremely happy. Months ago, she had so many decisions to make, with so many uncertainties. And now everything seemed to be falling into place. She was graduating with honors. She had a potential job in Nigeria, which would soon be her new home base. She would finally have an opportunity to find her father, and she would also get a chance to be with Iben again. Her heart overflowed with joy as she thanked the heavens for her good fortune.

All graduates were asked to arrive about an hour before the ceremony started to get acquainted with what would be expected of them during the commencement ceremony. Fey arrived wearing a red and white silk and chiffon knee-length dress. On her feet were a pair of white three-inch heels.

After everyone arrived at their respective departments, they wrote down their names phonetically on sheets of paper. This would ensure that everyone, especially those with non-English names would have their names correctly pronounced as they were called to receive their diplomas. Once they were done, the graduates were shown where they would be seated. The weather forecast boasted sunny skies, so the ceremony was going to take place outside on the lawn. They were then released to go and meet with families and friends that they had invited until the ceremony started.

Fey looked at the time. They had about thirty minutes before the ceremony started. She then called her mom and sister to ensure that they would arrive on time. It was hot outside, so she waited indoors until she received a message from her sister that they had arrived.

On her way to the exit, she had her head down as she was busy texting Tutu. Because of this, she turned a corner with her eyes still focused on her phone and suddenly bumped into someone, dropping her phone in the process. She immediately bent down to pick up her phone and looked up to apologize to the person she had crashed into. The face she saw looking back down at her gave her a shock.

It was Iben.

What?! Fey's apology got stuck in her throat as she realized who he was.

Iben's eyes softened as he realized that the person he was looking for was right in front of him. He smiled and said, "Hey, beautiful…"

At those words, Fey threw herself in his embrace, hugging him tightly. "Iben," she said softly. "You're here…" her voice was filled with emotion.

Iben wrapped his arms around her and kissed her on the forehead. He thoroughly enjoyed her reaction to seeing him immensely. The couple stayed like this until Fey leaned back from the hug to look at Iben again. It wasn't until then that she realized that passersby were looking at them. She became self-conscious and slowly pulled away from their embrace.

"When did you arrive?" she asked.

"Last night. I wanted to surprise you," he responded.

She smiled as she remembered the somewhat misleading text message that he sent her last night about taking pictures for him. She then looped her arm with his and said, "Let's go. The ceremony will be starting soon."

As they walked to the venue, Iben said, "You look stunning in that dress, by the way."

Fey smiled brightly. "Thanks."

By the time they arrived at the venue, the ceremony was about to start.

"You should go," Iben said. "I'll find you afterward."

Fey nodded and went to sit down at her assigned seat in the front. She looked back and scanned the crowds to locate Iben. After a few seconds, she did. There weren't too many tall Black men there wearing a tan blazer after all. Their eyes met, and Iben winked and smiled at her. She smiled back before turning back around as the department Dean started speaking at the podium.

After the Dean gave his welcoming address, the special commencement speaker came up to give his speech. Up next was the class valedictorian, and finally, it was time to hand out diplomas to the graduating class. One by one, as their names were called, each regalia clad graduate stepped on stage to receive a diploma and take commemorative pictures.

When Fey's name was called, she stepped on the stage and confidently walked up to receive her diploma. With each step that she took, she felt a deep sense of personal accomplishment. She did it! She was now a civil engineer about to face the world. She was determined to make her mark, no matter what life threw her way. No matter which part of the world her journey took her.

After the ceremony ended, Iben waited as Fey took pictures with her friends and classmates. When she noticed him, she waved him over and introduced him to her friends.

"Hey guys, this is my boyfriend, Iben," she proudly announced.

"Wait, you're the one from Munich!" one of her friends exclaimed.

Iben nodded with a smile. "Yes... and you're Kiera, right?" he asked. He recalled that she was one of Fey's roommates when they were in Germany the year before.

Kiera smiled. "Yes. It's nice seeing you again."

"Likewise," he responded politely.

Everyone politely took turns, introducing themselves to him and shaking hands.

"Where's Demi?" Iben asked Fey after a while.

"She's at her commencement ceremony. The business school's ceremony is the same time as ours."

"Oh, I see."

"Don't worry. You'll get to see her later. A bunch of us are going out to celebrate later tonight."

After saying goodbye to her friends, Fey and Iben went to find her mother and sister. Thankfully it wasn't difficult to locate them, as they were one of the few people who remained seated after the ceremony ended.

"Congratulations, my dear," Adaobi said as she embraced her daughter. "I am so proud of you."

"Thanks, Mom," Fey responded with a big grin.

Next was Tutu. "Congrats, *Big Sis*," she said with a smirk.

"Thanks, *munchkin*," Fey said, lightly pinching Tutu's cheek, who playfully swatted her hand away.

Iben stood aside quietly as he enjoyed watching Fey interact with her family.

Then Fey finally introduced him to her mother. "Mom, I want you to meet my boyfriend, Iben."

Iben stepped forward and bowed his head slightly as he shook her mother's hand.

"Good afternoon, it's a pleasure to meet you," he said with a polite smile.

Adaobi returned his handshake and slowly sized him up. She met his gaze and thought he was a handsome young man. She couldn't miss his British accent, so she asked, "Where are you from?"

"Mom?!" Fey chided. *How can that be the first thing you say to someone you just met?* she thought in exasperation.

"What?" Adaobi shot back, giving her daughter a sidelong glance before looking back at Iben, waiting for him to answer.

Unperturbed, Iben smiled and said, "Fey and I met when she was in Germany last year. Before that, I've lived in the UK for most of my life."

"I see…" Adaobi said as she slowly nodded.

Fey quickly cut in before her mother continued with a barrage of questions.

"And this is my baby sister, Tutu," she said, continuing with her introductions.

"Hi Iben," Tutu greeted with a smile. "I've heard so much about you. It's nice to meet you finally."

Iben smiled, "The pleasure is mine," he said as he shook her hand.

"Fey didn't mention that you were coming," Tutu added.

"That's because I didn't know he was coming," Fey chimed in as she looked at him, a smile on her face.

"Yes, I wanted to surprise her," Iben said as he met Fey's gaze.

Adaobi watched the interaction between Iben and Fey and gave a small smile. The couple seemed to be taken with each other. Her daughter had never introduced any of her male friends to her before. With the thought that Fey must be serious about him, she said, "We're going to have a small celebration dinner for my daughter's graduation this weekend. Why don't you come over to visit?"

"Absolutely. I'd love to," Iben responded immediately.

Fey looked at him in surprise. "Are you sure? We live in Delaware. It's several hours away from Georgia."

"It's no problem, babe. I'm going to be in the States for the next few weeks. I'm on holiday, you see," he said with a grin.

"Well, that's settled then. We'll see you on Saturday," Adaobi chimed in.

"Let's take pictures," Tutu suddenly suggested.

"Good idea," Adaobi agreed.

Moments later, after pictures were taken, Adaobi looked at the time and said, "We need to get going, Tutu. Our flight leaves in a few hours. I'd like to avoid rush hour traffic."

Fey said goodbye and hugged her mother and Tutu. After they left, she turned to Iben and said, "Let's go to my dorm. I need to get out of these heels," she complained. "They're killing me."

"Sure."

After a ten-minute walk across campus, they arrived at Fey's dorm. Once inside her room, she said, "Make yourself comfortable. I don't have roommates."

Iben nodded as he noticed the single bed in the corner of the room. There were also moving boxes of stuff lying around.

"Sorry about the mess. I'm still packing up my things before I leave on Friday," Fey said when she noticed where he was looking. She then moved some boxes that were in the way, to a corner of the room so that Iben could sit on the only beanbag in the space.

"Let me get you something to drink from the vending machine. I'll be right back."

Before Iben could respond that he was fine and didn't need one, she was gone. In the meantime, he took off his blazer to get comfortable until Fey returned. When she came back, he noticed that she still hadn't taken off the heels that she had complained about earlier. He got up and walked up to her before he suddenly picked her up and sat her down on the bed. Fey stared at him in surprise and watched as he got on his knees and unstrapped the buckle of her shoes before sliding them off her feet.

"I thought you said these were uncomfortable," he said.

Fey smiled at the gesture. She watched as he walked to her dresser to pick up a bottle of lotion.

"I want to give you a foot massage. Is that okay?" he asked.

Fey nodded, and Iben rolled up his sleeves to begin massaging her feet. She began to relax after the first few seconds.

"That feels so good," she said with a contented sigh.

Iben smiled and continued quietly until he massaged both feet.

"Thank you for that," Fey said.

"Happy to do it," he said as he got up to put the lotion back on the dresser. Then he asked, "What time is the get-together with your friends tonight?"

Fey looked at the time. It was almost 4:30 PM. "I think it's around 5:30. I'll check with Demi to confirm," she said.

Iben nodded and walked back to where Fey was seated. He stood in front of her and pulled her up to stand. Then he wrapped his arms around her waist and said, "I can't hold back anymore."

Immediately, his lips descended on hers. He'd wanted to kiss her so badly, since when he bumped into her earlier. But he didn't because he knew Fey would be embarrassed. From his perspective, having a prude as a girlfriend was taxing, sometimes. The kiss was gentle at first. Then Fey wrapped her arms around Iben's neck as the kiss deepened. Iben had missed the taste of her lips. He pressed her closer to him so that he could feel her softness against him. He moaned as desire began to pool within him.

Just then, there was a knock at the door.

A disappointed Iben groaned as he pulled together all the self-control he could muster and promptly ended the kiss. Then he went to sit down while a flushed Fey went to open the door.

It was Demi.

"I heard Iben is here. Is that true?" she said as soon as Fey opened the door. Fey nodded as she let her in.

Demi smiled brightly when she saw Iben seated at Fey's desk.

As soon as he saw her, he said with a smile, "Hi, Demi. Long time no see."

"Hi Iben"

"Congratulations on your graduation."

"Thank you! What a nice surprise. Did Fey know that you were coming?"

"No, I did not. I got the shock of the century when I bumped into him earlier. I thought I was hallucinating for a second."

Iben chuckled at her comment.

"Well, since you're here, you'll be coming to the happy hour, right?" Demi asked expectantly.

"Yes, I will," Iben responded.

"Great! Iben is here. You can let loose tonight. You won't have to be our designated driver today," she said to Fey with a mischievous smile.

Fey rolled her eyes at her. "Whatever... What time are we meeting up anyway?"

"I was thinking we could leave in like an hour. First, I'm going to change. There's no way I'm wearing this all night," she said, pointing to her floor-length graduation dress. "I'll see you guys soon." Then she left.

"I should probably change as well. I don't want to be wearing this all night either," Fey said afterward. She went to the bathroom to change into a simple summer dress with flat, comfortable sandals. When she came out, Iben was lying on her bed, fast asleep.

He must be jet-lagged, Fey thought to herself. *It's almost midnight in Munich right now.*

She quietly sat down next to him, checking social media and playing games on her phone as he slept. About forty minutes later, Fey received a text message from Demi.

'A bunch of us are downstairs in the lobby. We'll wait for you guys,' it read.

'Ok, we'll be there in a bit.'

Fey got up and gently woke Iben up.

"Sorry, I fell asleep. I didn't realize how tired I was," Iben said as soon as he was conscious.

Fey smiled and said, "You just arrived yesterday and haven't gotten used to the time zone here. It's completely understandable."

About five minutes later, they went down to meet the rest of Fey's friends in the lobby.

15 | Shots, Trust and Love

Once everyone assembled, Iben, Fey, and her friends all walked three blocks to a bar that served tapas appetizers. After they were all seated and had a round of drinks and appetizers, they all chatted and joked around with each other. Iben was glad that he was there to see Fey in her element with her friends. It was a different side of her that he enjoyed seeing.

After a while, Demi suggested that they all play a drinking game. They played 'Never Have I Ever,' and Fey ended up drinking a few shots. At some point during the game, Fey noticed that Iben received a message on his phone. When she glanced at it, she could see that it was a text from Vivian. Iben turned off his phone immediately and turned his attention to the rest of the game.

"Who was it?" she asked.

"It's nothing important," Iben said dismissively.

His response caught Fey off guard. *Why would he be hiding the fact that Vivian just sent him a message?* Her mood took a nosedive after that. In fact, she uncharacteristically suggested that the group play a drinking game that every one of her friends knew that she was terrible at playing.

Demi laughed, "You're so bad at this game. Why did you suggest it? You're going to be so wasted tonight."

As expected, Fey ended up drinking a lot of shots. When she was about to down another one, a concerned Iben took it from her and drank it in her stead.

"That's enough for you, babe," he said.

Fey pouted and decided to get up to go to the restroom. But as soon as she stood up, she suddenly felt dizzy, and her legs gave way. In an instant, Iben stood up and caught her in his arms. He decided it was time for them to leave. Iben said goodbye to everyone and left with Fey leaning against him for support. Demi followed them out and handed Fey's handbag and phone to him.

"Sorry you got saddled with this chore," Demi said with a chuckle, "But I'm glad you came. Otherwise, we would never have had the chance to see Miss Prim and Proper Fey get drunk."

"I can still hear you," Fey suddenly said. Her eyes were still closed as she leaned against Iben, her speech a little slurred.

Iben gave Demi a look. He didn't think she sounded sorry at all. He wasn't too happy about the current situation, but he said nothing. One thing was for sure. He preferred the prim and proper Fey. A moment later, their Uber ride arrived. After a fifteen-minute drive, they arrived at the Airbnb condo that Iben was renting during his stay in Atlanta.

Iben effortlessly brought Fey inside and sat her down on the sofa in the living room. He went to the kitchen and came back with a glass of water and some aspirin.

"Here, you should drink this."

Fey did as she was told.

Iben sat next to her and watched as she sat there quietly with her eyes closed.

"Please don't drink like this again," he pleaded.

Fey said nothing for a while, so Iben thought she had fallen asleep. He leaned over and tried to wake her up. Suddenly she opened her eyes, and in a few seconds, she was straddling him on the sofa. Iben's eyes widened, as Fey started to kiss him and her hands reached for his belt and unbuckled it.

So, this is what drunk Fey is like, he thought amusedly. He loved this daring alter ego of Fey and what she was doing to him right now. However, he knew that she was only acting like this because she was inebriated. So, he mentally willed himself to stop her wandering hands, and said softly, "You're not yourself tonight, babe. Come on, let's get you to bed so you can sleep off the alcohol."

At those words, Fey got off him and laughed derisively before she said, "I guess Vivian is the only one that does it for you, huh?"

Iben sat there, stunned by her comment.

"What did you just say?!" he asked in disbelief, as she started walking off to the bedroom. Annoyed, he got up and followed her.

Fey entered the en suite bathroom and locked the door behind her. Iben waited patiently at the door, and after a while, she came out.

Iben's voice was cold as he asked, "What the hell does Vivian have to do with anything?"

Fey scoffed as she walked past him. Ignoring his question, she flopped on the bed and said, "I'm going to bed. You and Vivian can have your secret chit-chat while I'm asleep, and I won't be none the wiser."

Then she closed her eyes and went to sleep. Because of the alcohol, she was asleep almost immediately. You almost couldn't believe that she was awake just a few moments ago. Iben stood at her bedside and glared at Fey as she slept. He was so angry that he wanted to shake her awake and make her explain herself. *Secret chit-chat with Vivian? Where the hell is this coming from?*

For the next half hour or so, Iben paced up and down the bedroom. He tried to think about what could've caused Fey to say what she did. Did she perhaps see the message that Vivian sent earlier? Even if she did, there wasn't anything in it that was incriminating. Vivian had asked why he left Germany without telling her. And as usual, he ignored her message. After a while, Iben decided to go to bed. He'd have to wait until he could get an answer out of her in the morning.

***

The next morning, Iben was up before Fey. He sat up in bed and watched her as she slept. His anger had not subsided, but he schooled his facial expression to hide it.

When Fey finally stirred, she groaned in pain. "Ugh... my head," she complained.

Iben sighed helplessly as he got up to get her some aspirin and a glass of water. He originally had half a mind to let her suffer a bit more for her behavior last night. But he couldn't bear to watch her continue to suffer the effects of her hangover. Besides, he needed her sober and clear-headed for when they discussed her comments last night.

When he came back with the medicine, he handed it to her and said, "Here, drink this."

She downed the aspirin and said, "Thanks."

She fell asleep again and woke up a few hours later, feeling much better. She sat up in the bed and noticed that Iben was staring at her. "What's the matter?" she asked cluelessly.

"Do you remember what happened last night?" Iben asked coolly.

She furrowed her brows as she tried to recall the events of last night. After a moment, everything came back to her. She looked up and met Iben's icy gaze.

"Secret chit-chat with Vivian?" he asked coldly. "Please explain."

For some reason, his question annoyed Fey. Why was he acting as if he didn't receive a message from Vivian last night? Her heart beating madly in her chest, she let her anger lose and lashed out at him.

"If you're going to lie to me about your conversations with Vivian, then why are you here? Huh? What are we doing in this relationship? Did she finally get back with you after I left? Did you guys rekindle your love affair? I feel like such a fool. To think I actually believed that you were serious about us..."

Iben listened in disbelief as Fey spat out one accusatory question or comment after another. The anger that he had been trying to get under control, boiled to the surface.

"That's enough!" he finally said, raising his voice, causing Fey to stop talking. Then he met her fiery gaze and said in a voice as calm as he could muster, "Just so we are clear, I am *not* in a relationship with Vivian. *You* are the only woman I love."

"Oh please, that's a load of crap!" Fey scoffed dismissively.

At her words, Iben's voice got icy and an octave deeper than usual, "Don't *ever* say that again! There isn't another woman in this entire world that I would fly across continents to be with right now."

He thought about all the work he had painstakingly completed in advance so that he could take the next few weeks off. He knew that he had to head back to Nigeria to begin working officially as the CEO of Ariri Corporation very soon. Jetlag wasn't the only reason he was exhausted yesterday. He hadn't slept properly in over a week. And it was all so that he could spend time with her. But here she was, spouting nonsense.

"It hurts when you cheapen my feelings for you like that," Iben said and walked off, angrily to the bathroom. *So much for getting to the bottom of things,* he thought bitterly to himself as he got in the shower.

While he was gone, Fey began to feel guilty about everything she had said to Iben. Why on earth was she acting this way? Did she truly believe that Iben was cheating on her with Vivian? She had practically accused him of cheating simply because of a text message that she didn't even know the contents. Mortified by her bad behavior, she covered her face with her palms. She took a deep breath and tried to think rationally. She had to fix this.

When Iben came out of the shower, he was already half-dressed, wearing a pair of shorts. Fey tried to meet his gaze, but he wouldn't even look at her. He rummaged through his luggage and found a t-shirt to put on. Afterward, he started to leave the bedroom.

"Iben, please let's talk," she said, stopping him in his tracks.

Without looking at her, he shot back, "For real this time? Or do you plan to continue to accuse me of something I didn't do?"

"I'm sorry about what I said earlier," Fey said sheepishly. "Can you forgive me and hear me out, please?"

Iben slowly turned around. "Fine, I'm listening," he said before taking a seat on the opposite side of the bed from where she was.

"Last night, when we were at the bar, I saw that Vivian had sent you a message. I didn't know what was in it, but when I asked about it, you just brushed me off. It made me feel like you were hiding the fact that Vivian had messaged you. When you brought me here afterward, I thought maybe I was just overthinking it, so I summoned enough courage and tried to… you know… come on to you. But you rejected me. I felt like you rejected me because of Vivian, and I guess my mind just went crazy after that. I know it was wrong of me to accuse you in the way that I did. I'm really sorry."

She sighed before she continued, "I have a confession, Iben. Ever since Vivian showed up at your apartment in Munich, I've felt this unease at the back of my mind. I hate the fact that she has access to you in the way that she does—texting you, calling you. It really upsets me. I admit that I'm jealous. But it's sometimes tough for me to deal with. Plus… Vivian is very beautiful, and..." Fey let herself trail off.

Iben, who had been listening quietly to everything Fey said, got up and picked up his phone from the nightstand. He unlocked it and gave it to Fey to read last night's message from Vivian. Fey took the phone and scrolled through almost a hundred unanswered messages from Vivian in the previous two years.

"I didn't tell you about the message last night because I didn't want to ruin the mood by bringing up Vivian. I'm sorry it came off as a brush-off. As you can see, there isn't a single time where I bothered to respond to her. She's been doing this for so long that I'm just used to ignoring her. I didn't realize that it bothered you that she has my phone number. But I don't feel like I should have to change it just because of her."

"Why don't you just block her number instead?" Fey asked.

"I never thought of that," Iben admitted. "Can you do that for me, please?" he asked.

Fey nodded and immediately blocked Vivian's number on his phone before handing it back to him.

"Thanks," he said. "Is there anything else you want to say?"

"Did Vivian ever show up at your new apartment?" Fey asked. That was another unknown that was eating away at her.

"No," Iben responded, meeting her questioning gaze head-on. He wanted her to see that he was honest and open with her. "Anything else?"

"Yes," Fey responded. "What's *really* going on with informing your grandfather about Vivian's abortion? Obviously, you haven't told him yet. Otherwise, she wouldn't continue pursuing you."

Iben sighed. "I have everything I need to settle that account with Vivian, but it isn't exactly a matter that I can handle with just a phone call to my grandfather. It needs to be done in person, and that's my first order of business as soon as I return to Nigeria. I promise I will let you know as soon as it is taken care of. Okay?"

Fey nodded. "Okay… I guess that's it," she said.

"Good, now it's my turn," Iben said. He reached out to hold her hands in his before he continued. "You said that you're jealous of Vivian. I wish you wouldn't be. As far as I am concerned, you are the most beautiful woman in the world. You're the only woman who turns me on and the only woman that I want. You can't even begin to imagine how hard it was for me to stop you last night. We haven't been together in so long that I was tempted to take you right then. But I knew that you were drunk, and I didn't want our first time together after so long to be alcohol-driven."

He leaned in and kissed the back of her hand before he said, "I love you, Fey—so very much. For me, it's only you. So, please—don't ever doubt my feelings for you again…"

Fey's eyes began to tear up at Iben's words. He had always been so sincere and honest with her. Yet she had acted so childishly.

Iben moved closer before wiping her tears and hugging her. Fey hugged him back and held onto him tightly. They stayed like this for a while until Fey felt better and eventually pulled away from Iben's embrace.

"Why don't you go and take a shower?" Iben suggested. "I'll try to scrounge up something for us to eat when you're done."

Fey nodded and went to the bathroom while Iben went to the kitchen. Unlike a regular hotel, the Airbnb condo had a full kitchen with everything he needed for cooking. Pots, pans, plates, and so on. The refrigerator was also stocked with a few essential items like milk, eggs, and sausages. At least for now, he didn't have to run to a nearby store to buy food. He made a mental note to remember to leave a good review for the host.

When Fey came out of the bedroom, he had just finished dishing out the eggs and sausages that he cooked. When he looked up, he had to do a double-take as she was not wearing her clothes, but one of his shirts.

"Sorry, I had to put my clothes in the washer. It reeked of alcohol," Fey said as she made a face. "I don't have anything to wear until it's dry, so I hope you don't mind that I'm wearing this," she added apologetically.

Iben smiled. It wasn't the first time that she'd worn one of his shirts. It had just been a long time since he'd seen her like that. "You know I don't mind," he said. "Come, sit down and let's eat."

Later, as they ate, Iben asked, "So, what are your plans for today?"

Fey looked thoughtful for a moment, then she said, "Today is Thursday, right? I need to finish packing up my things. My flight leaves tomorrow evening, so between now and then, I need to empty my dorm room and hand in the keys."

Iben nodded and took out his phone. He asked Fey for her home address and saved it on his phone before he searched for flights to Delaware. He found one that would arrive on Saturday morning. Next, he looked for accommodations. With Fey's input, he found another Airbnb condo for rent in a neighborhood that was close to her family's. He planned to stay there until he left for Nigeria.

"How long will you be in the States for?" Fey asked.

"Three weeks."

Fey smiled, "That's great. I'll get to show you around and stuff."

"I look forward to it," Iben responded with a smile.

They finished their meal, and Fey helped with cleanup.

While Iben was putting away the last of the dishes, Fey walked up behind him and wrapped her arms around his waist. "I'm so glad you're here, Iben," she said as she rested her head against his back.

While taking a shower, Fey had some time to think some more about her relationship with Iben. Now that she had gotten her insecurities out in the open, she felt closer to him. She was glad that despite her harsh words and behavior the night before and that morning, he didn't ridicule or judge her. Instead, he calmly explained himself and helped her understand how he felt about their relationship as well as what he was willing to do for their relationship. If there was one takeaway from their argument, it was that she had to be straightforward when it came to Iben. Making assumptions would only cause her unnecessary grief. Since she wanted to be in this relationship, she had to trust him. He hadn't done anything to earn her distrust anyway. As she stood there with her arms around him, she had an epiphany.

She had fallen for this man.

"I love you," Iben suddenly heard her say.

His heart skipped a beat. He stopped what he was doing and turned around to look at her. "Say that again," he said softly.

Fey smiled, looked him in the eye, and repeated, "I love you, Iben."

Now certain that he heard her correctly the first time, Iben pulled her closer into his embrace. A big grin appeared on his face. It felt nice hearing those words from the woman he was in love with. *She's finally on the train*, he thought happily to himself and sighed contentedly.

"I thought I would have to wait until eternity before I heard those words from you," he teased, causing Fey to chuckle. "I love you, and you love me back. So, why don't we seal this moment with a kiss? Hmmm?" Iben continued, a smirk playing on his lips.

Suddenly in a playful mood, Fey smiled mischievously, shook her head, and backed away. But before she could get far, Iben reached for her hand, twirled her around, and next thing she knew, she was right back in his embrace. Her eyes met his smoldering ones.

His hand trailed down her back until it reached the plump, succulent flesh under the shirt she was wearing. Iben sucked in a breath and leaned in to kiss her neck. She moaned in response.

With Fey now flush against his body, coupled with the knowledge that she wasn't wearing anything underneath the shirt she had on, Iben's thirst went into overdrive.

"I need you, babe," he said, want and desire evident in his husky voice.

Unable to hold back the lust he had been keeping at bay any longer, Iben kissed Fey deeply, his tongue wreaking havoc on her senses. Then, he picked her up and walked to the bedroom.

A short while later, in the quiet condo, the only sounds that could be heard were the heavy breathing and moans from the couple as they expressed their mutual love and desire for each other.

16 | Making Memories

Saturday rolled around, and Fey excitedly waited for Iben's arrival. On her way back from a grocery store errand, she received a text message from him that he had arrived at the airport and would let her know when he had checked into the condo. When she got back home, she gave Tutu an update on Iben.

Adaobi overheard their conversation and asked, "Your boyfriend—what's his family name?"

"His name is Iben Ariri," Fey responded.

"Ariri... Is he related to the owner of Ariri Corporation?" Adaobi asked, recalling the household name that she hadn't heard in a long time.

Fey nodded and smiled. "Yes, Iben is his grandson."

Adaobi seemed to be impressed, but then she quickly said, "Are you sure he is serious and not just playing around with you? These handsome, rich boys can't always be trusted."

"Yes, Mom. He's a good man. Besides, we love each other..." Fey responded bashfully.

Her mom scoffed and said, "Love... What can that do when you are both living on different continents? Hmmm? Or is your plan to sit here and wait for him to come for holidays?"

At her words, Fey and Tutu gave each other a knowing look.

Fey took a deep breath and exhaled before she said, "Mom, I'm going to relocate to Nigeria."

"What?!" Adaobi spat in disbelief. "You're just going to follow that boy to Nigeria? Didn't I raise you better than that? Ehn? You must be joking!"

"I am not joking, Mom. And I am not just *following* him to Nigeria."

Adaobi stared incredulously at her daughter. What nonsense had this Iben been filling her daughter's head with? Now she regretted having allowed her to study abroad last year.

"Really?! So, you think that country is so easy to just move to and live? It is not the same as living in the United States. How are you going to support yourself when you get there? Where are you going to live when you get there? Or is it your plan to shack-up with him?" Adaobi shouted angrily.

Fey had expected her mom's ire, so she was unperturbed.

"I already have a job lined up over there with the Ministry of Science and Technology. Demi is also moving back home, and her parents have agreed to allow me to stay with them," Fey responded calmly. Then, she hesitantly added, "I am also going to find Dad."

Adaobi glared at her daughter, and for a few seconds, she was at a loss for words. Granted, she seemed to have considered where she would stay and how she would make a living for herself. But Fey's last sentence was what drove her up a wall.

"You are going to find who?" she asked rhetorically. "You will do no such thing! Why are you so insistent on getting in touch with that man? Didn't I give you the letters that he recently wrote to you? What else do you want? It's bad enough that you are deciding to go back to Nigeria. But don't go looking for trouble. Leave your father and his crazy family alone. Those people are dangerous. Do you hear me?!" By the time she was done with her tirade, Adaobi was shrill from yelling at the top of her lungs.

Fey said nothing. There was no point in giving her mother a response. They were going to forever be on opposing sides when it came to her father. If her mother was, in fact, right, and her father's family was dangerous, then Fey would just have to find out on her own.

A few minutes later, Adaobi had calmed down. She knew that her daughter was stubborn, so she decided on a different course of action. She would have a frank conversation with Iben when he came over for dinner later. Maybe she could get him to convince Fey to change her mind about her move.

With that comforting thought, she said, "Let's table this discussion for later and focus on getting things ready for the dinner party tonight." She then rattled off some tasks for Fey and Tutu to get done.

***

Later that evening, when Iben arrived at 6:00 PM, the other guests were already there. It was a small dinner party. The guests included two of Adaobi's good friends, one of Tutu's friends and Iben. Tutu had decided at the last minute to invite her friend because she didn't want to be a third wheel since Iben was coming, and her mother would be entertaining her friends.

Fey introduced him to everyone, and he politely shook their hands with a smile.

"What a pleasant young man," one of Adaobi's friends commented.

When it was her mother's turn, he bowed in greeting and handed her a gift bag. "Good evening," he said with a warm smile.

Adaobi accepted the bag and saw that there were two bottles of expensive wines in it.

"Hello, Iben," she said with a welcoming smile. "Glad you're able to make it."

"Thank you for inviting me."

"Go ahead and make yourself at home."

He bowed respectfully once more before he left with Fey.

"That went well," Fey said after they were out of earshot. Last night on the phone, she told Iben about the argument she had with her mother regarding her relocation to Nigeria.

"Why wouldn't it? Nobody can resist my charms," Iben said and gave a playful wink.

Fey deadpanned at his egotistical comment and said in a flat tone, "Seriously, dude?"

Iben gave a short laugh, as they walked to the table of hors d'oeuvres.

"Which one of these did you make?" Iben asked as he picked up a small plate.

"Nada," Fey responded. She almost sounded proud of the fact. "This is all Tutu. Just like you, she loves cooking. Maybe you guys should exchange notes."

"Really? I'm impressed, Tutu," Iben said as he saw Tutu coming up to them with her friend.

Tutu smiled. "Thanks, Iben."

Fey, who was now standing between both Iben and Tutu, smiled and put her arms around them at the same time. "I'm so lucky to have two people in my life who love to feed me."

Tutu scoffed jokingly. "Don't get too full of yourself. You're just my guinea pig half the time." Then she turned to Iben and said, "I feel sorry for you, man. Be careful not to spoil her so much."

Fey and Iben laughed.

For a while, the young people chatted and joked with each other. Tutu found that behind his polite exterior, Iben could be very playful, but only with Fey. From the banter between them, it was clear to see that the couple were very comfortable and very much in love with each other. More importantly, for Tutu, she now felt a little better about her sister being in Iben's care when in Nigeria.

While chatting, they all decided to go to the beach the following weekend since Iben was going to be around for a few weeks. Delaware had many beaches, so they had quite a few choices. After much deliberation, they all decided on Rehoboth Beach.

"You should invite your brother," Fey said to Tutu's friend, Sandra. "He can bring his girlfriend. The more, the merrier."

Sandra rolled her eyes and said, "Uh... I don't think so... Those two are obnoxious."

Everyone laughed.

Just then, they heard Adaobi suddenly call for Iben. "Iben, can you please help me with something over here?" she asked.

Iben and Fey shared a look before he walked over to where Adaobi was.

"Sure, how can I help?" Iben asked.

"You're the only male here, so I have to lean on you," Adaobi said. She gave him a large serving bowl and gestured for him to follow her as she walked down the hallway to a storage room. She opened the door and asked him to put it on the topmost shelf. Iben did as requested, and once he was done and had stepped out, Adaobi shut the storage room door and asked him questions. This was the main reason why she had asked for his help. She wanted a chance to talk to Iben alone, without Fey around.

"Yesterday, Feyisayo told me that she was moving to Nigeria. What are your thoughts on that?" she asked. "She just graduated from college, and now she wants to move halfway around the world to a country that she has little knowledge of." Adaobi knew that Fey must've mentioned their conversation to him. So, she was curious to see how he would respond.

Iben gave a small smile and said, "To be honest, I admire Fey's courage in this respect. And yours as well, if I might add. When you allowed her to study abroad in Germany last year, it was a huge leap of faith on your part. Faith that she would thrive and focus on what her goals were while she was in Munich, even though it was a new environment where people speak a different language. And I think you will agree with me that she was very successful in that regard. I view her move to Nigeria similarly."

His response wasn't what she had expected. *Did Feyisayo not mention their conversation to him yet?* Adaobi thought doubtfully to herself.

"But Nigeria is not as developed as European countries such as Germany and the UK. How many students have you heard of who are going to Nigeria for a study-abroad semester?" Adaobi responded provocatively.

"That's true. Hopefully, in the future, we will get there. I believe Nigeria has a lot to offer the rest of the world in that regard. In light of that, the government program that Fey applied to is trying to improve things in the country so that it becomes attractive to foreigners and expats alike. I am well acquainted with the program, and it is very competitive. That she was selected is a testament to her abilities and what she has to offer."

Adaobi didn't respond, so Iben continued, "We need more folks like Fey, who have been educated overseas, back in Nigeria to help us out in the government. They can bring their knowledge and experiences from overseas to bear in improving things back home. Nigeria has such a bright future with so many capabilities. She'd be doing a great service to the country, and as a young person, I can see why she would want to be involved in that."

Adaobi sighed, "I suppose so..." Then she added, "And let's not forget the fact that her moving to Nigeria also works in *your* favor, doesn't it?" She gave Iben a questioning look.

Iben smiled but said nothing.

"So, what about you and her? I can't help but worry."

Iben responded in a serious tone, "I am aware of what a mother's concern would be. I'll keep that in mind always and make sure that Fey is safe."

"Do you plan to marry her?" Adaobi asked pointedly.

"Mom, please stop!" they suddenly heard Fey say.

She had come over to check on them, as she had an inkling that her mother might be giving Iben the third degree. Both Iben and Adaobi turned around to see Fey standing there looking extremely mortified at her mother's last question.

Iben smiled, and his eyes softened as they met Fey's. Then, he reached for her hand and said, "I love Fey very much. And if in the future, we both feel that's where we want to go with our relationship, there will be no hesitation from me." Then he turned to Adaobi and added, "And as her mother, you will be the first to know."

Fey stared at him in shock. *Wait, did he just indirectly admit that he wouldn't mind being married to me in the future?*

"But right now," he continued, "We're just going to focus on getting her settled in Nigeria and situated with her career."

Adaobi sighed defeatedly at the couple. The conversation with Iben hadn't gone exactly as she had hoped. However, for some inexplicable reason, speaking to him had reduced most of her apprehensions about Fey's relocation to Nigeria. *At least, this Iben boy seems to have a good head on his shoulder,* she thought to herself. She had no choice but to take a wait-and-see attitude.

"Fine... fine," Adaobi finally said. "Let's just go and eat."

The rest of the dinner was quite enjoyable. Excellent company, good food, and drinks were always the recipe for a pleasant gathering, and this was no exception.

***

Over the next few weeks, Iben visited Fey's home a few times and had dinner with her family. Other times, Fey would hang out at his condo or take him sightseeing. Although Iben had visited the United States a few times, he had never been to Delaware. He was fascinated with the small-town vibe that most of Delaware gave. Compared to other places he had been, like New York and California, Delaware seemed very laid back. It reminded him of some of the quaint little towns he had visited while in Germany. Together they visited the famous Dupont Mansions that are historical landmarks in the state, as well as a couple of museums.

Fey also took Iben to a few shopping malls and outlets in Delaware since he wanted to buy souvenirs to give to people back home. She pointed out to him that one of the remarkable things about shopping in Delaware was not paying sales tax on purchases. This meant that if something had a price tag of ten dollars, that was precisely how much you would pay. No more and no less. She mentioned that many other states in the US did not have that, and based on his recent memory, Iben agreed.

Occasionally, while shopping, Fey would show interest in a piece of clothing, jewelry, or shoes. However, whenever Iben wanted to buy them for her, she would refuse.

"Why do you make it so difficult for your man to spoil you?" he complained after being rejected a few times.

Fey chuckled and looped her arm in his. "Don't be like that. You're spoiling me already by being here and hanging out with me almost every day."

"Fine," Iben conceded begrudgingly with a sigh. "I'll just have to settle for feeding you, then. You *will* allow me to do that, right?"

"Yes... But I was going to treat you to lunch today," Fey objected softly.

"Really? A jobless and broke college graduate wants to buy me lunch. How amusing..." he said, his voice dripping with sarcasm. He was still feeling salty about not being able to buy her those items.

"Ouch!" Fey responded, feigning being hurt by Iben's comment. "Which reminds me. I need to apply for some summer jobs so that I can save up some spending money for when I leave in August."

"What are your options?" Iben asked as they walked to the food court.

"I got in touch with a construction management company that I interned with last summer to see if they had any openings. I should hear back from them soon. But even if I do get a position there, I still need another part-time job. So, I'm thinking maybe a bank teller, retail store cashier or waiting tables," Fey responded.

"No waiting tables at bars," Iben commented, as he suddenly had a flashback to her drunkenness when they were in Atlanta.

Fey tossed him a side glance and asked, "Is that an order?"

Whoa?! Iben's spider senses tingled as he realized that his comment might have caused some misunderstanding on Fey's part, based on her tone. He had to answer very carefully. "No, babe—just a suggestion," he responded in his best nonchalant tone.

Fey seemed to be okay with his answer, so she continued, "I don't like working at bars anyway. I was more thinking about waiting tables at a restaurant. They're a dime a dozen here in this city, so it shouldn't be too hard to find something."

As Fey continued talking, Iben quietly sighed in relief. One of the things he had learned about Fey was how quickly she could go from chill to fiery hot if she felt like someone was trying to control her decision-making process. One had to gently ask guiding questions if you wanted her to consider a particular decision path or option. He couldn't help but worry about how she would handle situations like this in the workplace.

As they continued to chat, Fey asked Iben what the cost of living was like in Nigeria. She was trying to figure out how far her money could go, relative to the exchange rate. But she quickly realized that he was probably not the best person to answer this question. She was asking a wealthy man what the cost of groceries, rent, and transportation would be for the regular working class. Although Iben wasn't a very ostentatious person, one couldn't deny the fact that there were just some things he never really had to worry about.

***

Time flies by when you're having fun. And before long, it was time for Iben to return to Nigeria. Although he was regretful that he had to leave Fey, Iben was glad that he decided to take some time off to spend with her. From his perspective, this trip was well worth it, as it deepened their relationship, and he also got a chance to meet her family.

He was taking a red-eye flight back to Nigeria, so Fey had spent the whole day with him until it was time to go to the airport in the evening. Although she wanted to go with him to the airport, he refused because he didn't want her to have to journey back from the airport during rush hour traffic. But if he was honest with himself, it was because he couldn't bear to walk away from her at the airport. It was okay if he was the one watching her leave. So, they said their goodbyes after the Uber driver that was taking him to the airport dropped her off at home.

Later, as he sat on the plane, waiting for takeoff, Iben thought about Fey. An amused smile tugged at the corner of his mouth as he recalled how she had shyly given him a quick peck on the cheek when he had dropped her off earlier. Considering that the Uber driver was in the front seat, it must've taken a lot of courage on her part. He chuckled to himself.

He also thought about what her reaction would be once she received the packages he had scheduled to be delivered tomorrow. For a moment, he relished in the fact that she wouldn't be able to refuse or return the items as he was no longer there, and he did not include store gift receipts. She would have no choice but to keep them. In his dating experience, Fey was the first woman who seemed to have a problem with him buying her things as gifts unless it was a special occasion like a birthday, anniversary, or holiday. He wasn't sure if it was an American thing, or just a Fey thing.

He continued his musings and remembered the first time he met Fey at the cafe in Germany. The first time he kissed her and their first fight. The first time they made love. He smiled at the memory. As his first love, he was undoubtedly going to miss her. But unlike when she had to go back to the States last year, Iben knew that he would see her much sooner. It was now the last week of June, so he had a little less than two months to settle the issue with Vivian before her arrival in August. He hated the fact that Fey felt a bit insecure in their relationship because of Vivian. So, he vowed to himself that by the time she arrived in the next two months, all traces of his prior relationship with Vivian would be non-existent.

Just before his plane took off, he sent a message to Fola.

'I'm heading back. Do we have everything in place for next week?'

A moment later, he received a response. *'Affirmative. I'm almost done with handing off things over here. I should arrive in two days.'*

'Got it. Thanks.'

17 | The Setup

When Iben arrived at the Lagos airport, he was met by a small entourage in two luxury vehicles. After his luggage had been cleared through customs, and one of his assistants secured them in an Autobiography SUV, Iben gave instructions to have them delivered to his home in Lekki. He then boarded the black Maybach SUV and instructed the driver to take him to his grandfather's house on Banana Island. On his way there, he received a message from Fey. He had sent her a message as soon as his plane landed, letting her know that he had arrived.

'Hey, babe. Glad you arrived safely. So, I received the packages you sent to me. You're so sneaky...'

She was referring to the clothes, jewelry, and shoes that Iben had purchased and were delivered to her. They were the same ones she had shown interest in while they were out shopping. The same ones she had refused his offer to purchase on her behalf. She was impressed that he even got her sizes correct.

'You left me no choice,' he responded unapologetically.

'Well, thank you for giving them to me even though you didn't have to.'

'It's my pleasure. Don't forget to send me pictures. I'd like to see you in those dresses (wink emoji).'

'Hmmm... I'll think about it,' came her teasing reply.

Iben sighed, a bit irritated. This woman always did that to him whenever he asked her to send pictures of herself.

'I'll be waiting with bated breath,' he responded hopefully.

'Haha - Anyway, I have to go. I start work soon.'

Although it was already afternoon in Lagos, it was morning in the United States, as Nigeria was six hours ahead.

'Okay, have a good day. I love you.'

'I love you too.'

A few hours later, Iben arrived at his grandfather's residence on Banana Island. It was the same home he grew up in after his parents and sister died many years ago. However, after he graduated college, as a gift, Edafe bought Iben a residence of his own, at nearby Lekki. Although he was tired from his twelve-hour flight, Iben had to go and say hello to his grandfather first. It was the respectful thing to do.

As soon as Iben arrived, he was met by the long-time housekeeper.

"Good evening, Master Iben. Welcome home," she greeted Iben with deference and a warm smile.

"Good evening, Aunty," Iben responded with a smile. "How have you been?" he asked.

"I'm doing well, sir. Chief is about to eat dinner. Should I set a place for you?" she asked.

Iben nodded, "Yes, please." Then he walked off to the dining room.

As soon as Iben saw his grandfather, he said, "Good evening Papa. I'm back."

Edafe's face lit up in a smile as soon as he laid eyes on Iben. "Ah... Iben, my son. Come..." he said as he gestured for Iben to come closer. When he did, he hugged him. "Welcome back. How was your trip?"

"Thank you, Papa. It wasn't too bad," Iben responded after pulling away from the hug.

"Good... good. You came just in time. Sit down and let's eat."

After dinner, Iben and Edafe chatted a bit.

"When is Fola coming back?" Edafe asked.

"He's still handing off things after his resignation. He said he'd be back in the next couple of days," Iben responded.

As planned, Fola was resigning from his position on the Interpol financial crimes investigation team that he had been a part of for the last few years. However, he would continue to work at the EFCC in a different capacity upon his return. This way, he could stay close to the goings-on at Ariri Corporation without worrying about being sent on an international mission at only a moment's notice.

Edafe nodded. "Let's schedule Starlight Shipping's proxy voting for the first week in July. Next Monday, to be precise."

Iben looked thoughtful. It was currently Wednesday, and Fola would likely arrive by Saturday, which would give them just two days to finalize things. The proxy voting would allow Ariri Corporation to take over Starlight Shipping in a merger. Iben smirked, a smug look on his face. He'd been preparing for this for a while now. The earlier they got this over with, the better, he thought to himself.

Edafe continued. "Since you are now back, I'll invite the Iberes over for dinner on Sunday evening. I hear Vivian has been looking forward to your return."

Iben clenched his jaw at the mention of Vivian and her father before he forced a smile and said, "Sounds good."

After another thirty minutes of chatting, Iben excused himself. "I need to get going, Papa. I came here straight from the airport, so I'm exhausted."

"No problem. See you on Sunday."

"Good night," Iben said before heading toward the exit.

His driver was ready and waiting when he got outside. He climbed inside his Maybach, and in thirty minutes, he was home. He thanked the driver before dismissing him and giving him the next day off. Then he went inside the house. Compared to his grandfather's mansion on Banana Island, his four-bedroom house in Lekki seemed very modest. Although he hadn't lived in it for the past two years while he was studying in Germany, it was well maintained and cleaned in preparation for his arrival.

His housekeeper greeted him as soon as he walked into the house. "Welcome back, Master Iben."

"Thanks, Mobi," Iben responded with a smile as he patted the younger man on the back. "Long time, no see."

Mobi smiled and asked, "Would you like to have dinner?"

"No, I'm good. I already had dinner with Papa. I'm exhausted, so I'm going to head to bed."

"Okay, sir. Your luggage is already in your bedroom."

"Thanks, good night," he said as he started walking up the stairs. He turned around after a few steps and added, "By the way, I am not receiving any visitors. Turn everyone away until I tell you otherwise."

"Okay, sir," Mobi responded.

Later, Iben took a shower and went to bed.

The next day, he slept in and did not leave his bedroom until around noon. When he came downstairs, Mobi said to him, "Good afternoon, sir. Miss Vivian came by earlier, and per your instructions, I told her that you were not receiving visitors."

Iben nodded and said to Mobi, "Good job." He had an inkling that Vivian might try to show up at his house, which was why he gave the order last night. He had blocked her number, so she didn't have a direct way to reach him anymore. Coming to his place was all she could do.

Mobi inwardly sighed in relief. As far as he knew, Vivian was Iben's girlfriend, so he was conflicted about turning her away when she stopped by. Afterall, in the past, although she rarely visited, she had been free to come and go as she pleased. Unfortunately for him, he had to remain apologetic while listening to her acerbic tongue as she yelled at him for his refusal to let her in. Were they having a lover's quarrel or something? Anyway, that wasn't his problem. As long as his boss was happy, everything was good.

Iben spent the next few days relaxing and completing final preparations for the Starlight Shipping merger. On Saturday, Fola came over to Iben's in the early afternoon. He didn't have a problem gaining access, as Iben remembered to inform Mobi that he would be stopping by.

Fola had arrived late at night on Friday, the day before he came to Iben's. He owned a flat at Lekki as well, so he was close to Iben's house. His penthouse was in one of the most expensive luxury apartment buildings in the area. It was built and managed by MorningStar Realty, an Ariri Corps subsidiary.

After Mobi brought them refreshments, Iben and Fola began chatting.

"Vivian seems to think that you may have blocked her number," Fola started with an amused smile.

"Yes, I did."

"Wow, took you long enough," Fola responded.

Iben shot him a look before he said, "It was Fey's idea."

Fola raised a brow and teased, "I see... Someone is *definitely* whipped!"

Uncharacteristically, Iben broke into a sheepish smile and said, "Yeah... I guess."

Fola made a face as if he just smelled something nasty and said, "Ugh... You're no fun, bro!" Where did his brooding Iben disappear to? Fola complained inwardly. That's what made teasing him enjoyable.

"I'm in love with that woman," Iben suddenly said. "I want to marry her someday."

Fola shook his head defeatedly before he took a sip of his beer and said, "How about we deal with your love triangle drama, first. Okay, Romeo?!"

Iben chuckled at his words.

"Anyway, enough with the mushy stuff, let's talk business."

**

On Sunday, Iben and Fola arrived at the Ariri mansion early for dinner with Edafe, Vivian, and her father.

When the father-daughter pair arrived, Iben greeted Charles Ibere with a handshake. "Good evening, sir."

"Iben! It's good to see you again. Welcome back!" he chirped.

"Thank you, sir," Iben responded politely.

Vivian, who had been quiet since her arrival, finally said something to Iben after her father walked off to say hello to Iben's grandfather. "Hi Iben," she started cautiously.

Iben's face was unreadable, his tone almost flat. "Hello, Vivian."

"How have you been?" she asked, trying to make small talk.

"You should go and greet Papa first. It's rude for you to just stand here," he said, ignoring her question.

Vivian sighed helplessly. She could do nothing but watch him as he walked away.

During dinner, Iben avoided eye contact with Vivian. Whenever Edafe or Charles brought up his relationship with Vivian in a teasing context, he would force a small smile and try to steer the conversation toward another topic. All of this wasn't lost on Vivian, so she just ate her dinner quietly. She couldn't wait for the dinner to be over so that she could have an opportunity to have a private chat with Iben. For one, she wanted to know why he blocked her number. She also wanted to know why he had refused her entry to his house the other day.

After dinner, everyone moved to the living room that Edafe used for receiving and entertaining most of his guests. Edafe sat in his favorite armchair, and Iben also selected an armchair to sit down instead of one of the sofas. He didn't want Vivian to get any ideas about sitting next to him. After some small talk, Edafe asked Charles if everything was ready for tomorrow's proxy voting.

"Absolutely! I have given appropriate monied payments to all parties involved," Charles responded with a nod.

Iben chimed in and said to Edafe, "That is correct, Papa. I took the liberty of monitoring the financial transactions."

Charles was shocked and a bit upset at Iben's words. However, he tried to calm himself before he asked, "Why would you do that?"

"Just precautionary measures, sir. But you have nothing to worry about, right?" Iben smiled, but it didn't reach his eyes.

The cold look in Iben's eyes caused Charles to feel uncomfortable. He had wanted to show his displeasure and complain about the invasion of his privacy. But instead, he decided that first thing Monday morning, he would speak with his accountant about closing and switching some of his bank accounts.

Charles also didn't want to continue this line of conversation as it might cause too much friction between him and Edafe. Tomorrow was the proxy voting for his company, Starlight Shipping, and he didn't want anything to destroy all their plans. He had worked hard over the years to build his shipping company to where it is today. And now, he was looking forward to the prestige of being under Ariri Corporation, as it will also give Starlight Shipping more business opportunities across the board.

He forced a laugh instead to smooth things over and said, "Iben, you're ever so diligent. You didn't have to go through such lengths. Your grandfather and I have been doing business for a very long time, and we trust each other."

Iben nodded. "Of course," he said, the smirk not leaving his lips at all.

For the last couple of years, Charles and Edafe had been discussing how the merger between Ariri Corps and Starlight Shipping would happen. They had been business partners for so many years, so Charles didn't have a problem with the merger. His daughter and Edafe's grandson would be getting married as well, so it just made sense. At the time, Edafe had proposed a proxy takeover of Starlight instead of having to buy a majority stake in the company. He offered Charles four billion naira in monetary compensation to convince the majority of board members and shareholders to vote for Ariri's management team when the time came to vote.

Charles continued, "Besides, you and Vivian will be getting married soon. So, we are practically family. We should formally announce your engagement and start the wedding preparations as soon as the merger is underway."

"That won't be necessary," came Iben's response. "I will *not* be marrying Vivian."

Everyone turned to look at him in surprise, except Fola, of course.

Vivian was the first to speak. She hadn't expected that Iben would drop this bombshell at this time, so she had to do damage control. "Iben, how can you say that?" she began, sounding very hurt. "We've been together for so long. If you are upset with me about something, why don't you just tell me, and we can talk about it in private. We don't need to drag the elders into this."

Iben chuckled in amusement at Vivian's acting. "You already know what you did, so I'll give you the opportunity to confess here in front of everyone. As your father has just said, we are all practically family, so there's nothing to hide. Right?"

Vivian stared at him, slack jawed. She knew he was talking about the fact that she had broken off their engagement, was pregnant by another man, and had an abortion. How could she confess to that here in front of Edafe Ariri? She looked to her dad for help, a signal, anything.

Iben followed her gaze and then added, "Or perhaps, Chairman Ibere will do us the honor. He is also aware of what I am referring to."

The room was silent.

Finally, Edafe spoke up. "Iben, what is going on? Tell me everything!" he commanded. His voice was sharp and authoritative. From Edafe's perspective, Iben had never gone against his wishes before, so whatever happened must've been something rather egregious for him to foot stomp like this.

"Vivian broke off our engagement two years ago," Iben began.

"She has no say in reversing a decision that was made by elders," Edafe responded dismissively.

Vivian took the opportunity and quickly added. "Papa, I didn't mean it when I told him that I wanted to break up with him. I only said that because Iben had been very distant from me. I thought saying that might move him to deepen our relationship. But instead, he took it literally."

"Is that why you went ahead and got pregnant with another man's child?" Iben shot back.

"I was just being dramatic when I told you that, Iben. There hasn't been anyone but you."

"Just so we're all clear, first you pretended to break up with me. Then you pretended to be pregnant and have an abortion," Iben said, his tone mocking and laced with contempt. He then shared a look with Fola, who stood up from where he was seated and handed Edafe some papers.

"Papa, that's medical proof of her pregnancy and abortion," Iben continued. "After she broke things off with me, she ran off with Damola Oyeniyi of Hygro Pharmaceuticals. But his family didn't want him to marry her, so she came running back after having an abortion."

The sneer on Iben's lips couldn't be missed.

"That's all fabrication!" Vivian said, raising her voice in an attempt to defend herself. "It's not true! Iben, why are you tarnishing my reputation?"

At her denial, Fola produced another envelope which had pictures of Vivian and Damola. In many of the photos, they were kissing, cuddling together at the beach, or entering a hotel with their arms around each other. There were also pictures from the security cameras at the hospital where she had the abortion. In the envelope was also proof that the payment for the procedure came from Damola Oyeniyi's account.

Vivian sat there in shock. How had Iben been able to get all this evidence? Her father had assured her that everything would be kept secret. Iben hadn't mentioned anything to her, so she thought he had nothing. She felt that if it came down to it, it would just be her word against his. And once they were married, they could iron out their differences over time.

Realizing that she was backed into a corner, she broke down in tears and got down on her knees. "Iben, I'm sorry. I know I was wrong. Please forgive me. I promise that it will never happen again. If you take me back, I'll be loyal to you forever. Please…"

It was the first time that Vivian had apologized to Iben for cheating on him. She had done nothing but tried to play it off and act like it never happened. However, Iben wouldn't even spare her a look, which made her cry even more.

Edafe, who had been sitting quietly in his chair, watching the show in front of him, finally opened his mouth to speak. "Vivian, I am very disappointed in you. It is obvious that you were unfaithful to Iben, and it is no wonder that he is upset with you."

He then turned to Iben and said, "Vivian is like… an unruly mare. You were too soft and have failed to tame her, Iben."

Iben frowned at his grandfather's words. He didn't want a woman that he had to tame. If letting her move freely meant that she would leave and become another man's, then such a woman wasn't meant for him, and he was okay with that.

Edafe then turned to Vivian's father and said in a measured tone, "Charles, what are your thoughts on this issue? Your daughter's indiscretion has greatly upset my grandson."

At this point, Charles Ibere was sweating profusely. It suddenly felt sweltering in the room even though the air-conditioning was running.

"Chief... As you can see, Vivian feels terrible about what she has done," he began, dabbing his sweaty forehead with his handkerchief. "I know that she has been trying to resolve this issue with Iben for a while now. But please do not blame her. Unfortunately, her mother, who would have taught her the ways of propriety, died when she was very young. And I have been so focused on my business that I neglected to teach her these things. She is my only child, and I have spoiled her too much." He looked down apologetically, away from Edafe's piercing gaze.

Everyone in the room was silent for a moment.

Edafe finally spoke. "I wonder how this affects our merger..."

Charles quickly replied and said, "Chief, don't worry. Everything is in place as we had originally planned. Our business deal is of utmost importance. If the children don't want to get married, and you are okay with it, that's fine with me as well. It would've been nice if we could become family, but many prosperous business ventures have been made in the past without family ties involved." Charles tried his best to plead his case.

"Hmmm..." Edafe said, nodding.

"Papa, I have some news regarding the merger," Iben suddenly declared.

Edafe raised an eyebrow and said, "Speak."

"Thank you. First, I'd like to ask Chairman Ibere some questions," Iben said, sounding very much like an attorney. He then turned towards Charles and asked, "You mentioned earlier that you disbursed the funds to the appropriate majority shareholders at your company. How will they be voting tomorrow?"

"Exactly as we had agreed. They will vote in favor of management by Ariri Corporation," Charles responded with confidence.

"And what about you? How will you be voting tomorrow?"

Charles did not like this line of questioning, so he said, "Iben, what is the meaning of this? I can't help but feel disrespected by your question."

Iben gave a small smile, "I don't mean to offend you, sir. I just want to hear it from you, for the record."

Charles sighed and said exasperatedly, "I will be voting the same—for Ariri Corporation management."

"Great!" Iben exclaimed, excitedly. Then he walked to the media system in the living room and plugged in a USB drive that Fola just handed to him. Soon, the entire room was filled with the voices of

Charles and someone having a conversation.

Charles: 'The proxy voting will be happening next week. Don't forget what we discussed.'

Person: 'I have not forgotten. We will vote for the merger, but we shall be voting against Ariri's management.'

Charles: 'Good, I'll be sure to transfer the additional funds to your account once everything is done.'

One after another, similar phone conversations were heard where Charles was convincing different shareholders and members of the board to vote against Ariri and to vote for him instead.

By the time the recordings finished playing, Charles looked like he had just seen a ghost. Dread hit his core, and he was sweating profusely. He finally looked up at Iben and met the sneer on the young man's face.

"So, Chairman Ibere, based on the conversations we all just listened to, it is obvious that you did *not* plan to keep your end of the bargain with Ariri Corporation."

"You bugged my phone?" Charles asked a moment later.

"Yes, and your office," Iben responded, smugly.

Charles suddenly started laughing. He couldn't believe that this young man had seen through his plans and exposed them so flawlessly. Iben even dared to infiltrate his own company and get damning evidence. He supposed Edafe's training and his law degree wasn't a waste after all. Edafe must be proud.

Speaking of Edafe, Charles looked towards him where he was seated. He hadn't said a word the entire time. Edafe's current expression was one of mild amusement.

"When did you find out about my plans?" Charles asked Iben.

"After Vivian ran off with her lover."

Vivian suddenly laughed derisively, a sneer on her lips. Then she said mockingly to Iben, "Were you so upset that I refused to sleep with you that you had to go and spy on my family? That's pathetic, Iben!"

Iben glanced over at her and said, "Aren't you getting too full of yourself, Vivian? I may not have sampled your wares—" he paused for effect as he looked her up and down in disgust. "—but I'm certain it's nothing spectacular. Otherwise, your lover would have kept you by his side, right?"

Vivian glared at him. She never knew that Iben had such a venomous tongue. "You…" her lips were trembling in anger, but she couldn't form any words.

"Sit down and be quiet before you make things worse for your father. This shit is way out of your league!"

Under the pressure of Iben's piercing gaze, Vivian shrank back in her seat and said nothing else.

Iben then turned to his grandfather and said, "Papa, I felt it was important that you were made aware of this development." Then he calmly went back and sat down in his seat.

18 | Motive

After Iben was seated, Fola glanced over at him and smiled to himself. Truthfully, Iben could've been more straightforward in his reveal of Vivian and Charles' betrayal by simply giving all this information to Edafe beforehand. But instead, he chose to put on a show and toy with them first, because he wanted to see Charles and Vivian squirm and backtrack on their words. Iben was very loyal, and sometimes to a fault. But once he branded you a traitor, he was a very vindictive person, and there was no getting away from his ire. He would lay in wait patiently to eventually serve his brand of retribution. He was very much Edafe Ariri's grandson in that respect.

Fola then glanced over at Charles Ibere. The man was too preoccupied with his issues to even defend his daughter's honor as Iben dressed her down verbally. Well, at least what was left of her honor.

"Explain yourself!" Edafe demanded of Charles after a moment.

The cat was now out of the bag, so Charles decided to speak plainly. "Chief, this is all your fault," he began.

"My fault?" came Edafe's incredulous response, as he leaned forward in his seat.

"Yes, if you hadn't tried to double-cross me first, this would not have happened."

"Double-cross you?"

"Yes! You were going to make Iben the Chairman of the Board of my company! My sweat and blood!"

Charles felt that he was justified in his actions because it would be a slap to his face if a 'small boy' like Iben took over the company that he built over the years. It would make him Iben's employee, and his pride would not allow it!

Edafe leaned back in his seat and chuckled before he said, "That was always my plan. When did this suddenly become news to you? What did you think voting for Ariri Corporation Management meant?"

"You promised me that nothing about our business relationship would change after the merger. How could I have foreseen that it meant losing my position as Chairman and CEO of my own company?!" Charles shot back angrily.

"We made a deal, Charles. You knew what the playbook was. You just didn't know *who* I was going to install as the new chairman after the merger. Obviously, you assumed it would be you. It would seem that the almighty Chairman and CEO didn't properly read and understand the contract that we agreed upon," Edafe responded with a smirk.

Charles frowned at his comment. He understood precisely what Edafe was saying. In his haste to solidify this merger agreement with Edafe, Charles had made the biggest blunder in his entire career. He did not properly read and understand the details of the contract before agreeing to it. He had erroneously put his trust in Edafe above his common business sense. He only found out about his oversight much later after his lawyers had taken a fine-tooth comb through the entire contract.

"I don't know what you mean," he lied.

Edafe ignored him. "I have set my eyes on acquiring your company for a while now. So, this was originally meant to be a hostile takeover of Starlight Shipping. But I decided that in light of our past business relationship, I would allow you to save some face by proposing a proxy voting situation. Surely, you didn't think that I was unable to acquire all of the shares needed to have a majority say in Starlight Shipping and kick you off the board. Did you?" Edafe said mockingly.

Ariri Corps had a long-standing contract with Starlight Shipping to import and export various goods for the Ariri conglomerate. The items were not limited to clothing, footwear, supermarket products, hair care products, etc. After the merger with Ariri Corps, one of the benefits for Starlight Shipping was that some of the shipment contracts that were currently given to other companies would pass on to Starlight Shipping.

Edafe continued, "And I paid you handsomely. So, now we need to talk about the four billion naira that I had transferred to your account."

"That money can be considered as dowry for Vivian since she is going to be marrying into your family."

Edafe let out a loud guttural guffaw at Charles' comment. After his laughter died down, he cocked his head to the side and said in a tone that made Charles' hairs stand on end. "Your daughter sought to make a fool out of my grandson, and now you want to make one out of me?"

He looked over at Vivian with distaste written all over his face before he continued, "Your daughter is not worth a dowry of four billion naira! She doesn't even understand what the word *loyalty* means. Her engagement to my grandson is now annulled!"

Hearing those words, Vivian's tears began anew. Despite everything, she still held a sliver of hope that Edafe would uphold her engagement to Iben.

Charles was a smart man, and he could see that using Vivian as a bargaining chip was no longer an option. He had hoped that Edafe's fondness for Vivian would cause him to overlook her indiscretion. As for Iben, he had hoped that Vivian's apology would do the trick. Afterall, many couples had made a comeback from a cheating issue and subsequently been married for many years. In his mind, everything was simple.

"Chief, the way I see it, we have two options. First, we can still go ahead with the merger, but I will remain chairman of the board, and Iben can be the CEO. That way, we both manage the company, and we all reap the benefits to be gained from this merger. Or we can forget about the merger and go our separate ways. I will return your money over time, and we can call it even."

While Charles was speaking, Edafe reached for one of his pipes. It was in an ornate wooden case sitting on top of the side table next to him. Iben saw this and immediately got up to light the pipe for him before going back to his seat. Even after Charles was done with his proposal, Edafe sat there quietly, smoking his pipe. He appeared to be contemplating Charles' words. After a while, he finally spoke in a voice befitting an emperor talking down to his subjects.

"Charles, you dare to disrespect me with your so-called options!" Edafe began. "I am preparing my grandson to run the entirety of Ariri Corporation, and this is to be his proper training. What better place to start than Starlight Shipping, a jewel in the crown of my empire? And yet you *think* that you can decide for me, *how* to sharpen this young man, who is to be my *sword*?!" He ended his sentence gesturing at Iben.

In general, larger businesses acquired smaller ones for various reasons ranging from expanding their market share to increasing their buying power. Starlight Shipping was a well-established and very profitable business, and Edafe was determined to bring it under his control sooner, rather than later. Doing so now was essential for Iben's final training.

Edafe took another puff of his pipe before continuing. "I was contemplating ignoring your daughter's indiscretion, but then I find out that *you* are fucking with my plans. You thought you could play me? Or did you think that because I have been taking a back seat in the daily affairs of the businesses, that I have become soft?"

Edafe suddenly raised his voice and yelled, "I. Am. Edafe. Ariri!"

Charles Ibere's eyes were lowered as Edafe spoke. He couldn't bear to see the scary look that was no doubt in Edafe's eyes. His voice didn't leave much to the imagination. Listening to him, there was no mistaking the fact that he was outraged.

Edafe continued, this time in a normal voice. "Here's what will happen. You will go through with this merger according to my terms. And then you're going to pay the price for your insolence!"

Edafe was a man that would not tolerate setbacks to his plans, especially when it was a result of a betrayal.

"I will not have the son of the *morning star* lording over me in *my* corporation!" Charles responded at the top of his lungs. "Over. My. Dead. Body!" he added vehemently.

Edafe's eyes lit up when he heard Charles refer to him as the devil, the morning star. A sinister smile appeared on his face as he clasped his hands together and said, "Ah... at least you know how to address *my son and me* properly. As for your last statement, you *shall* have your wish."

Charles is no doubt agitated, and he could see that negotiations have broken down, so he got up to leave. "Vivian let's go. We are done here!"

As the father-daughter pair attempted to leave, two guards blocked the exit leading out of the enclosed living room. After failing to get the guards to move, Charles turned around and faced Edafe.

"What's the meaning of this, Chief? Please call off your guards!" he demanded.

Edafe sat in his chair, calmly smoking his pipe. "You cannot leave until I say so. You are both going to be my—*guests*—until after the proxy voting is over tomorrow."

"Is that so?! Well, let's see what will happen when the police get here!" Charles said before he took out his phone and tried to make a call. However, there was no cellphone signal. He did not know that a hidden cell phone jammer in the room had been turned on since they first walked into the enclosed space, essentially blocking all incoming and outgoing cell phone calls. It was a safety measure that Edafe always took when speaking with business associates. After several tries on his phone and Vivian's phone, Charles finally gave up.

"The only calls that you are going to be making tonight are to those shareholders. And you're going to instruct them to vote for Ariri's management team tomorrow. If you are unable to reach any one of them, then your daughter here will pay the price," Edafe said, definitively.

"Chief, this is crazy! It is so late at night. You cannot expect me to call these people and wake them from their slumber," Charles deflected.

Edafe raised his voice and said, as he pointed his index finger at Charles, "I do not care if they are in bed with their wives right now! You will call every single one of them and reverse your instructions to them regarding the proxy voting tomorrow!"

He snapped his fingers, and one of the guards came up to Vivian and tied her hands behind her back before shoving her onto the cold marbled floor. Vivian yelped in pain as she hit the floor. At this point, intense fear etched on her face. She looked up at her father and begged him to make the call.

Panic struck Charles Ibere. Was Edafe really going to keep them hostage and hurt them? Charles was almost out of his mind at this point. However, after a few minutes of assessing the situation, he decided that their lives were more important than any business deal. Charles shook his head bitterly as he realized that he had erroneously made a deal with the devil, tried to renege on it, and now he was paying the price.

When Edafe saw that Charles had calmed down and accepted that he could do nothing about the situation, he gestured towards one of the guards and said, "Bring me the telephone."

A moment later, a landline telephone was placed in front of Charles, where he sat. He sighed deeply as he picked up the phone and started calling each of the shareholders. He explained to them that the reason for his decision was that he had come to an agreement with Edafe Ariri that would work in everyone's favor. Although some of them were hesitant, while others were irritated with the back-and-forth, they all eventually gave their promise to vote as he had asked. Their rationale was that if the Chairman/CEO of the company felt that voting for Ariri was the best choice, they were willing to go along with it. It could only mean more profits for all involved.

After Charles made the final call, Edafe said to him, "Now, call your driver and tell him that you will be spending the night here as my guests. Tell him to come and pick you up tomorrow at 8:00 AM." Charles picked up the landline and did as he was told.

Charles said to Edafe, "I have done as you asked. Please untie my daughter."

"Not yet. I need both your cell phones. You can have them back tomorrow when you leave," Edafe said in response. When he saw Charles' hesitation, he added with a sneer, "Surely you don't think that it was just a coincidence that you did not have any signal when you wanted to make a call earlier."

Charles immediately understood what he meant. Their cellphones were useless as long as they were in the Ariri mansion. He then handed them to the guard who was waiting.

"Take them away!" Edafe ordered.

The guards came over and led Vivian and her father out of the living room. Then, they locked them in separate guest rooms where they would be spending the night.

The room was silent for a while after the Iberes were taken away. Edafe was now quietly enjoying the glass of whiskey that Fola had just poured for him.

Iben had watched the goings-on quietly. He knew that his grandfather was ruthless when it came to betrayals, and while he might not have used the same tactics, Iben felt that Charles Ibere and his daughter got what they deserved. Vivian was a thorn in his side, and he was glad to be officially free from the shackles of his betrothal to her. He had also bested Charles Ibere at business combat, and he was very proud of himself.

"Iben, you did well for your first major assignment," Edafe finally said.

"Thank you, Papa."

"I like how you and Fola worked together on this. I am proud of both of you."

"Thank you, Papa." It was Fola this time.

Although Edafe gave Iben and Fola kudos, he had mixed emotions about the entire situation. He was happy that Iben proved that he was capable, as it validated the rigorous training that he had put Iben through over the years. He was also pleased that his decision to pair Fola with Iben worked out flawlessly. He had raised them together, and to regard each other as brothers, especially for days such as these. They each had a role to play, and they acted accordingly.

However, he was a bit displeased that he was left in the dark until the eleventh hour. Also, in terms of Iben's betrothal to Vivian, he did not like the fact that Iben had dared to take a stand without consulting with him first. While in the middle of gauging his feelings, Iben spoke.

"Papa, I have someone that I want to marry!" he declared.

Fola's eyes widened in surprise. He hadn't expected that Iben would play his card so soon. They had barely moved Vivian off the board, and now he was bringing in Fey. He leaned back in his chair, wondering how Edafe would take the news.

Edafe also leaned back in his chair as he met Iben's determined gaze. Instead of being upset, he was actually quite amused that Iben had the guts to bring this up when they had just gotten rid of Vivian. He thought to himself: *This boy dares to ask for what he desires despite what is going on around him.* This very characteristic that Iben possessed was the spark that Edafe saw in him since he was a young boy. It was the spark that solidified Edafe's belief that Iben was his perfect heir.

Edafe slowly rubbed his chin. "Is that so?" he asked.

"Yes, I met her in Germany. Her name is Fey."

"Which family is she from? Who is her father?"

"She is of modest background. I have only met her mother, but her father's name is David Ademola."

"David Ademola..." Edafe repeated. It didn't ring a bell.

Edafe turned to Fola and asked, "Are you aware of this... Fey?"

"Yes, I've met her a few times. She's a great girl. I've even asked Iben to hook me up with someone like her, but he refuses," Fola teased.

"Why the hell would I do that? You're such a player, man!" Iben shot back.

"Bro, I am who I am. But I guarantee that she will have a good time in my care."

Iben tossed him a nasty look and said, "Seriously?! If you carry on like this, you're never going to find someone to settle down with."

"That's fine with me. Your kids will just have to be my surrogate kids, and as their Uncle Fola, I can teach them the ways of the world."

"Like hell, I'm going to let you near any of my children!" Iben tossed back.

Fola laughed at Iben's outburst.

Edafe smiled as he watched the two men banter. "All right... settle down you two," he gently chided. "Tell me some more about her," Edafe said. He was curious to know more about this woman who seemed to have captured Iben's heart and Fola's admiration.

"She just graduated with a bachelor's degree in civil engineering from Georgia Tech in Atlanta."

"I see... she was the reason for your recent holiday to the United States?" Edafe asked.

Iben smiled and said, "Yes. And while I was there, I met her mother, who is a university professor and her younger sister, who is still in university."

"Where does her mother teach?"

"Wilmington University in Delaware," Iben answered. Then he continued, "Although she was born here, Fey has lived in the States all her life. But she will be moving back to Nigeria in a couple of months. She was selected for the expatriate program with the Ministry of Science and Technology."

A realization dawned on Edafe. "She is the friend you mentioned last year who was thinking about relocating back here?" When Iben nodded, he said, "Well then, I look forward to meeting and assessing this young woman that you have both spoken so highly of."

Iben and Fola shared a look. They knew that even with Vivian out of the way, Edafe wasn't going to cosign Iben's marriage to anyone easily. But at least, he was not dead set against Fey.

Fola wondered what Edafe's assessment of Fey would entail. He somehow felt sorry for her because, knowing Edafe, he wasn't going to make it easy. He hoped Fey would be able to handle it.

Iben also had similar thoughts. But he had confidence that no matter what his grandfather threw at Fey, she'd be fine. She was no pushover.

After a moment, Edafe said to both Iben and Fola. "I have raised you both as my sons... as brothers. Today, you have demonstrated to me with the way you handled the Starlight Shipping merger, that you are a competent team. As I get older and take more of a backseat in the organization, I feel confident that my legacy is in good hands."

19 | Retribution

The next morning, Charles and Vivian were served breakfast in their rooms. The guards also delivered the change of clothes that Charles' driver had brought to them. They were asked to get ready by 9:00 AM. Later, an entourage of three luxury vehicles left the Ariri estate for Starlight Shipping headquarters. Charles and Vivian rode with Edafe in the first vehicle, while Iben and Fola were in the next one. Lastly, Charles Ibere's BMW sedan, which was empty, followed.

Sometime later, they arrived at their destination. Charles and Vivian were very quiet during the entire drive. Just before they alighted, Edafe said, "Charles, you will be held responsible for the outcome of today's voting. For your sake, I hope that everything works out in my favor. Otherwise, Vivian will pay the price on your behalf. Understood?"

Upon hearing this, Vivian became misty-eyed. Never in a million years would she have thought that she would be treated in this way by Edafe. He had always treated her like a daughter, but now she was nothing more than a bargaining chip to him. Vivian reminded herself of her resolve last night as she lay in the room that she was locked in, that she had to survive this whole ordeal no matter what. Unlike before, she was now quite fearful of Edafe, and she knew her father's ego could potentially get in the way of them coming out of this in one piece. Based on her understanding of what transpired last night, they might not be the same financially by the time the day was over, but at least they would be alive and could pick up the pieces. With this thought, she quickly composed herself and fought back the tears that were threatening to fall. She looked to her father, who was sitting next to her and squeezed his hand reassuringly.

Charles responded solemnly, "I understand, Chief." It seemed that all the fight in him from the previous night had deflated by morning.

The Iberes were still not allowed to have their cellphones. So, while Vivian sat in a private waiting room, she could only watch TV and enjoy the light refreshments that were provided by her father's secretary while being accompanied by one of Edafe's guards. The men then made their way to the conference room to meet with the shareholders.

Sometime later, after all the introductions, greetings and pleasantries were out of the way, Charles Ibere kicked off the meeting by giving a short speech. Iben and Fola then took turns presenting different aspects of the merger between Ariri Corps and Starlight Shipping. At the end of the presentation, everyone present had a good understanding of the critical details of the merger, as well as the advantages it would bring to both parties.

After a short break, the proxy voting began. The purpose was to decide which party would determine the composition of the board of directors. The composition of the board would determine who would be making the strategic decisions that would affect the future success of Starlight Shipping.

Hours later, when all was said and done, Ariri Corporation emerged as the winner. Edafe nodded and smiled happily as the congratulations came his way. While Fola and Iben were busy setting up press releases for the merger, Edafe went with Charles to where Vivian was waiting. They gave her the news, and she slumped in her seat, relief evident on her face. At Edafe's signal, the bodyguard who had stayed with Vivian returned their cellphones.

"It was a pleasure doing business with you," Edafe said to Charles, with a sneer. Then he added, "As for your punishment with regards to your treachery, that will be given later. Behave yourself in the meantime." With those words, Edafe left with his bodyguard in tow.

Charles sat defeatedly in his seat. While he was relieved that everything went as planned and his daughter was safe, he was also depressed about the future. Now that he had begrudgingly given complete control of Starlight Shipping to Ariri Corporation, he was doubtful that he would be given a place on the board of directors. He was essentially reduced to just a shareholder in his own company. He was already in his late fifties, so perhaps it was time for him to retire. Since his shares were reasonably significant, being the founder of the company, he would survive financially. He called his secretary and gave instructions to cancel all his appointments for the rest of the day.

Then he said to his daughter, "I am tired. Let's go home."

As they were about to exit the building, a young man who appeared to be flustered and, in a hurry, bumped into them, knocking Charles to the ground. The man landed on Charles while the papers in his hands were strewn everywhere. It was quite a scene. The chairman of Starlight Shipping was knocked on his bottom in the most undignified way. Vivian and several employees rushed to push the man off her father and checked to make sure that he was okay. Charles felt a slight pain in his side, but other than that, he was alright.

The man was very apologetic. He bowed and prostrated profusely to Charles as he explained that the reason for his carelessness was that he was in a hurry for an interview, that he was running late for.

Indeed, today was just a bad day for Charles Ibere, but he was too mentally exhausted to make a big deal about it. He just wanted to get home and rest. He waved the poor guy away, and a moment later, he left in his car with Vivian.

***

Later that night, after a celebration dinner with his grandfather, Iben dropped Fola off at his flat before he went home. As soon as he settled down for the night and was in bed, he sent a message to Fey.

'Hey, babe. I got a chance to talk to my grandfather about Vivian.'

He was in the middle of typing a follow-up message with details when his phone rang. He smiled when he saw that it was Fey.

"Hey, beautiful," he said when he picked up the call.

"Hey babe," she responded. "Sorry to call you so late, but I got your text, and I just had to talk to you."

Iben smiled. "It's okay. You know that you can call me anytime. How are you doing?"

"I'm good… so… um… is… um…" Fey began, unsure of how to say what she was thinking.

Iben smiled at her sudden lack of words. Then he answered the question he thought she was trying to ask. "Yes, my grandfather has officially annulled my engagement to Vivian. So, she is out of our lives for good. We don't have to worry about her from now on."

After a pause, Fey finally said, "That's the best news I've heard in a long time…Thank you for letting me know…" After he left for Nigeria, she did not know how long it would take before Iben had the opportunity to tell his grandfather everything about Vivian. And until that conversation happened, although she trusted Iben, she believed that Vivian might try anything. Vivian was desperate and a desperate person couldn't be underestimated. Also, she didn't know if Iben's grandfather would try to set him up in another betrothal. So, instead of worrying, she simply focused on being busy and working.

Hearing the relief in her voice, Iben suddenly felt very emotional and said, "Babe, I know I've said this before, but I want to say it again. It doesn't matter how many Vivians there are out there. You don't ever have to worry about my feelings for you. You are the only woman who has my heart." He remembered the night that Fey had expressed her insecurities about Vivian, and he swore that he would do whatever he had to do to make sure that it was no longer something that she had to worry about. It was also very important to him that she understood that she was the only woman that he wanted to be with.

"Iben..." Fey said, feeling emotional as well when she heard his heartfelt words.

"Hmmm?"

"I love you very much," she said softly.

Iben smiled, "I love you too..."

***

That same night, when Edafe, Iben, and Fola were celebrating their successful acquisition of Starlight Shipping, Charles Ibere and his daughter were having a quiet and solemn one.

When dinner was almost over, Vivian asked, "Dad, what are we going to do now that the Ariris have control of the company?"

Charles sighed and said in a low tone, "Vivian, let's talk about this tomorrow. A lot has happened, and I need some time to think. Okay?"

Vivian nodded. She looked at her dad and noticed that he seemed very lethargic. "Daddy, are you okay?" she asked, a worried look on her face.

He waved his hand dismissively. "I'm alright. Just very tired." He got up soon after and retired to his bedroom for the night.

The next morning, when her father was late for breakfast, Vivian went up to his room to check in on him. When she got there, he was still in his bed, but he was not breathing.

***

Two weeks after the acquisition of Starlight Shipping was Charles Ibere's funeral. He had died in his sleep, and the doctors determined that it was due to cardiac arrest. The funeral rites took a few days according to the customs of Charles Ibere's ancestral home. Iben, Fola, and Edafe attended the funeral after assisting a very distraught Vivian with the funeral arrangements. Despite how things turned out between her and the Ariris, they supported her throughout the whole process.

On the last day of the funeral, Edafe was invited to say some kind words about the deceased. Immediately after he did, he went back to Lagos before the ceremony ended, while Iben and Fola stayed until later.

When they were saying their goodbyes before they left, Vivian said, "Thank you both for everything."

Despite everything, Iben felt sorry for Vivian. He knew firsthand what it was like to lose a parent. He remembered how he felt so lost for a long time after his parents died in that accident so many years ago. If not for his grandfather's support, he might not have recovered from it as well as he did at the time. "Papa has offered to help, so if you need anything, just reach out to my personal assistant. He will deliver your message."

Vivian nodded in response before she hesitantly added, "I've been thinking… The autopsy report mentioned that my dad had a small mosquito-like mark on his side. That is such an unusual place to have a mosquito bite, don't you think?" As far as she knew, mosquitoes tend to bite around exposed skin like the neck, arms, and ankles. She looked at Fola and Iben as if gauging their reactions.

Fola was the first to respond. "Yeah, but the report also mentioned that your father was giving himself insulin shots for his diabetes. Sometimes injection sites can swell like bug bites. Didn't you know that he had diabetes?

"No, I did not. My dad was healthy as far as I knew."

"The elders tend to hide illnesses like that from the younger generation because they do not want us to worry," Fola responded.

"I know… but why would he give himself an insulin injection on his side?" She had looked into the locations to administer insulin shots on your body, and the side wasn't a particularly popular one.

Iben was the one to respond this time. "What are you trying to say, Vivian?"

She opened her mouth to say something but changed her mind. She sighed instead and shook her head before saying, "I just feel like something is off, you know."

Fola spoke next. He knew what she was getting at. "Vivian," he said as he placed his hand gently on her shoulder. "I know that your father's sudden passing away must be difficult for you to accept. Iben and I have both experienced a loss like this in the past, so we know how you feel. But you cannot go around kicking up dust and ruffling the wrong feathers over a *feeling* that you have. Your father was almost sixty, and he lived a good life. He left you a good legacy that you can build upon if you want. My advice for you is to focus your energy on moving forward. Take your time, but make sure that you are moving forward with each step that you take. Dwelling in the past is not a good thing."

Vivian sighed and nodded. After both men left, she thought about what Fola had said. Maybe he was right, and she was just reading too much into the circumstances surrounding her father's death. Like Fola said, she would be okay financially, even after paying off her father's debts. Iben was installed as the new Chairman of Starlight Shipping, and her father's shares in the company would be transferred over to her so that she would receive dividends periodically.

Looking at things from a different perspective, perhaps the shock of losing his company to the Ariris caused her father to have a heart attack. Even if her father's death did involve foul play, what could she do about it? She had brought it up to Iben and Fola because she hoped they might want to help her investigate her doubts. But they obviously didn't want to touch it with a ten-foot pole.

Would Edafe even allow them to help her investigate? She doubted it. Although she was glad for his assistance with her father's funeral, she had developed a fear of the man. She couldn't stomach being around him any more than he probably wanted to be around her.

Vivian appreciated all the help they gave her in the last few weeks, but she also felt like it was the least that they could do. No matter how she looked at it, Edafe Ariri was the cause of her father's stress and subsequent death. Going forward, she vowed to stay away from the Ariris while she healed from this whole ordeal.

***

On their way to the airport, Iben was lost in thought. Based on Vivian's suspicion, he couldn't think of anyone with a motive to hurt Charles Ibere. He thought about how ruthless his grandfather could be when it came to dealing with those who tried to double-cross him in business deals. He had even witnessed a scene many years ago where a man was flogged and beaten until he acquiesced and did as their original agreement had stipulated. Even then, he never killed the man. His grandfather already got what he wanted, control of Starlight Shipping, so why would he need to kill Charles Ibere? It just didn't make sense to him.

He asked Fola for his opinion, and his response was: "Don't tell me Vivian's ramblings got to you?" When Iben didn't respond, he added, "If you really care to know the truth, you know who to ask."

Iben turned to look out of the car window as he pondered Fola's words. He asked himself, *Do I really care to know the truth?* The only reason he was even thinking about this was because of what Vivian said. He had nothing to gain or lose from finding out the truth one way or another. He suddenly felt silly, realizing that Vivian had tried to manipulate them into looking into this on her behalf. That woman couldn't be trusted, and he didn't want to get tangled in her matters. If there was foul play in terms of her father's death, regardless of who it was, Charles Ibere had obviously offended someone enough that they wanted to kill him. And that had nothing to do with him.

20 | New Beginnings

August came around and the night before her flight to Nigeria, Fey sat at the dining table having dinner with her family. Her mother was repeating her list of do's and don'ts for when she was in Nigeria.

"Remember, don't stay out late at night. Don't go to the market by yourself. Only drink bottled water…"

Fey and Tutu exchanged a look as she continued. This was like the umpteenth time that she had gone through this list. They could both start mouthing the words along with her by now.

Fey sighed, "Mom, I know."

"Good! Anyway, I already asked Demi's father to help you exchange your dollars for naira when you get there," her mother continued. "Don't do that on your own. You can easily get swindled by unsavory characters once they see you are not a local and that you speak with an American accent," she warned. A few days ago, her mother had called and spoken with Demi's parents to thank them for agreeing to allow Fey to live with them during her move to Nigeria. "And if you run out of money, just let me know," she added.

"Thanks, Mom. But, I have enough money to last me for a long time," Fey responded. In addition to the money she made from working for the last two months, her mother also gave her two thousand dollars from the funds she kept aside from the money that their father had been sending over the years.

Just before she went to bed that night, Adaobi went to Fey's room to chat with her. She sat on the bed as Fey looked at her expectantly. The scene reminded her of when she would tuck Fey in at night when she was little. Adaobi suddenly had mixed emotions. Her baby girl was now a grown woman and making decisions about her life and her future. She was both proud of her and sad.

"I still wish that you would not leave," she began, "But I know I cannot stop you from going. While you are there, if you ever feel like it's not working out, just come back home. Okay? Don't try to prove anything to anyone."

Fey smiled at her mother's words but said nothing.

Adaobi continued, "And please while you are there, promise me you will *not* look for your father."

Fey stiffened at her last sentence. *Ugh! Not this again*, she thought to herself. "Mom, I can't promise you that," she said firmly. Finding her father was the major catalyst in her decision to move to Nigeria after all.

"Feyisayo, please, I beg you. Those people are dangerous," Adaobi pleaded.

"Who is dangerous? What makes them dangerous?"

"It's best if you don't know. Sometimes ignorance is bliss."

Fey was exasperated. "All you do is speak in riddles and half-truths. It's fine if you don't want to tell me. But you cannot continue to make demands of me with no explanation," she responded. "You need to let go of the past and allow me to make my own decisions!" she added as she crossed her arms defensively across her chest.

Adaobi sighed and looked like she was contemplating something. Then she finally said, "A couple of weeks after your father went to Nigeria, he called to let me know that his parents wanted him to take a second wife. He told me he refused them, and that he would be back soon. A few weeks after that, he called again and said that he was now in trouble and needed to stay back in Nigeria because he did not want us to be in danger. He said his parents had gotten themselves involved in some kind of business deal with some powerful and dangerous people. He also said that if he refused to stay back and work with them, we would be in danger."

Fey's eyes widened as she listened to her mother.

"Honestly, it all just seemed too crazy to believe," Adaobi continued. "I found it more plausible that he had given in to the pressure of taking a second wife and that he didn't want to come back to us because of that."

"So, what changed your mind?" Fey asked curiously.

"About a month later, I got a visit from someone when we still lived in Washington DC. It was the woman who was to be your father's new wife. She told me that as long as I stayed here in the States and out of her way, I would have no problems. I was so shocked that she found us. Then, I remembered what your father said, and I thought to myself, if this woman can easily find us, what about these dangerous people that supposedly want to hurt us? If what your father said was true, we could truly be in danger and I did not want to take any chances. So, I quickly planned to relocate. Luckily, I soon got a job at the university and moved us here to Delaware. I also changed my name so that nobody could easily find us again."

"That must've been so scary for you," Fey said as she listened to her mother's tale.

"Yes, it was."

"Mom," Fey said, holding her mother's hand in hers. "Thank you for telling me this. And thank you for doing everything to keep us safe over the years."

Adaobi smiled wryly. After a moment, she said, "Promise me, Feyisayo..."

Fey sighed defeatedly. "Okay, Mom. I understand."

Adaobi sighed with relief. "Thank you," she said before she stood up and left.

Fey sat up in bed thinking. She had told her mom that she understood what she expected of her and implicitly promised to toss the idea of finding her father. While having that conversation, she could see in her mother's eyes that her fear was real. So to lessen her mother's worry, she had agreed.

But being honest with herself, she really couldn't let go of her desire to find her father. Although she was happy to get more information, it only left her with more questions. Just what kind of trouble did her father find himself in? Was he okay now? Did he need help? Did he eventually marry the second wife? Was he happy? Would he be happy to see her? Regardless, if her father was in danger, she wondered if she might be able to help him somehow. With these thoughts in mind, she dozed off.

The next morning, Adaobi drove Fey to the airport. Her sister Tutu rode along as well to see her off. After saying goodbye, Fey checked in her luggage and went through airport security.

Later, as she sat on the plane, waiting for her flight to take off, she sent Iben a message: *'Hey, babe. My flight is about to leave. Looking forward to seeing you soon.'*

Iben was in a Starlight Shipping meeting when he received the message on his phone. Based on the notification sound, he knew it was from Fey. He couldn't help himself and read it right away. As soon as he did, his eyes softened and a smile spread across his face. When some meeting attendants noticed that Iben's countenance had changed from serious and inexpressive to a smiling one, they exchanged looks of confusion and curiosity, wondering what could have caused their normally aloof chairman to wear such a facial expression.

***

Fey's job interview was in Abuja, so it only made sense for her to head straight there upon arrival. For safety, Iben had pre-arranged for someone to pick her up from the airport and take her directly to the temporary accommodations provided by the government agency that was recruiting her.

Apparently, the job interview was just a formality, as they already accepted her for the position. Instead, she attended a three-day orientation soon after her arrival. Although she had dual citizenship, Fey had identified as a Nigerian national on her job application to improve her chances of getting selected. As a result, she had to attend the mandatory National Youth Service Corps (NYSC) boot camp training, which was required for any individual that would join the Nigerian workforce. According to the information that she received during orientation, the purpose of the NYSC scheme was primarily to teach Nigerian Youths the spirit of oneness and selfless service to the community, regardless of cultural or social background.

The three-week boot camp period was a very interesting experience for Fey. It reminded her of the time when she went camping and hiking with a group of friends while in the States. During this time, she met several people who had also been accepted into the expatriate program. After boot camp was over, all NYSC participants were released to continue their service in Abuja, except for those who had been accepted into the expatriate program. Instead, Fey and others like her were instructed to continue the rest of their one year NYSC service at the different government agencies where they had accepted job offers.

After boarding the plane, Fey called Demi and Iben to let them know she was leaving Abuja and was now on her way to Lagos. Iben would pick her up from the airport while Demi would join them at Iben's place for dinner.

Demi had returned to Nigeria a couple of months before Fey. Although she had spoken to Fey many times in the last few weeks, today would be the first time they would meet in person since she arrived from the States.

Upon arrival at the Lagos airport, once Fey retrieved her luggage and started walking towards the arrival lobby, she spotted Iben almost immediately. He was standing with his hands in his pockets, scanning the crowds, looking for her. It was a Friday, and it looked like he had come straight from work. He was wearing a black business suit with a light blue shirt and a navy blue tie. The first couple of buttons of his shirt were undone where the tie was loosened around the neck. He hadn't seen her yet and so Fey stood still, just watching him from afar, with a smile on her face. When he finally did and their eyes met, a bright smile spread across his handsome face and he immediately started walking towards her. She then continued walking, luggage in tow, until they met midway.

As soon as he got close, he immediately pulled her into a hug and said in his usual fashion, "Hey, beautiful..."

Fey hugged him back tightly and after a moment, they parted. She then realized her luggage was missing, and she panicked.

"Don't worry, my guys have taken them to the car," Iben said immediately.

"Oh..." Fey said surprised, as she hadn't even noticed.

"So, Miss NYSC *corper*... Welcome to Lagos," Iben teased, as he noticed she was wearing her NYSC uniform. He stood with his hands in his pockets as he checked her out from head to toe. Maybe it was because he hadn't seen her in a while, but he thought she looked really cute in the full uniform of khaki trousers, crested vest, jungle boots, and fez cap.

Fey broke into a grin. She knew he wouldn't be expecting her to be dressed how she was. Then, she said with her hands on her hips, "Hey, I am very proud to have served my time! Plus, I wanted you to see me wearing my uniform."

"You could've just sent me pictures like I had asked," Iben replied, unamused.

"I know... I just wanted us to take some together while I was wearing this," Fey responded. Then she took out her phone, and they took some selfie pictures together.

Afterward, Iben led her out of the airport to the waiting vehicle. When Fey saw Iben's Maybach SUV, she raised her brows. *Just how wealthy are the Ariris?* she wondered to herself. Iben got in the driver's seat and started the car. Soon, they were on their way to his house.

"Thanks for picking me up, babe," Fey said as they drove away from the airport.

With his left hand on the steering wheel, Iben reached out to hold her hand with his right hand. "It's my pleasure," he said. "You know, I'm still pinching myself to make sure you're actually here in the flesh." He had imagined this day since when Fey had told him she was accepted into the expat program. And now he almost couldn't believe it was happening. His Fey was actually here in Nigeria, next to him.

Fey chuckled, "Don't worry, you're not hallucinating." Then she leaned in and gave him a peck on his cheek.

Iben turned to her and complained, "That's not fair. You only did that because you know that I'm driving and can't kiss you back."

Fey smiled mischievously and was going to give a snarky response when her phone rang. It was Demi. "Hello," Fey said when she picked up the call.

"Hey, girl. Have you arrived?" she asked excitedly.

"Yes, Iben and I are on our way to his place," Fey responded.

"Great! I'll meet you guys there by 6:30 PM. Don't start dinner without me." Demi's family home was in Ikoyi, which was a 30-minute drive to Lekki where Iben lived, so it wouldn't take long for her to get there.

Fey chuckled. "Don't worry, we won't. See you then. Bye."

The call ended.

"My grandfather wants to meet you," Iben said a few minutes after her call with Demi.

Fey turned to look at him. She knew this would happen inevitably, she just didn't think that it'd be so soon. "Will I be meeting him tonight?" she asked.

"We're going to my house tonight. But he has invited us both to dinner tomorrow. He's looking forward to meeting you," Iben responded.

Fey nodded and quietly let out the breath that she was holding in relief. She wasn't mentally ready to meet his grandfather today. Tonight, she just wanted to relax and enjoy the company of friends.

As Iben drove, he pointed out a few landmarks and places to Fey as they passed by. When they arrived at his house, it was almost 6:00 PM. As soon as Fey and Iben stepped into the house, they were greeted by Iben's housekeeper.

"Welcome, sir," Mobi said.

"Thanks, Mobi," Iben replied. Then he put his arm around Fey's waist and introduced her. "This is my girlfriend, Fey. Treat her well."

Mobi nodded and turned to Fey before saying with a smile and a slight bow, "Good evening, Miss Fey."

Fey smiled and said in response, "Hi Mobi. It's nice to meet you. Please, just call me Fey." She felt uncomfortable with the formality, especially since Mobi looked like he might be about her age.

At her words, Mobi stole a glance at Iben, but the look on his face told him not to even think about it. Mobi wasn't surprised, as his boss had told the household staff yesterday that the future madam of the house would visit the next day. So, how could he call his future lady boss by name? He wasn't trying to lose his job.

"When should I serve dinner?" Mobi asked, changing the subject.

"In about an hour," Iben responded. Then he turned to Fey and said, "Let me show you around the house."

Fey nodded and followed him.

When Mobi returned to the kitchen, the rest of the staff were eagerly awaiting his assessment of their boss's new girlfriend. They had all disliked Vivian Ibere and were quite terrified of her, as she was very haughty and rude to them the few times they had interacted with her. When they heard that their Master Iben was no longer dating her, they were relieved, but weren't sure what kind of personality the new lady would have. They were even more anxious when their boss told them she was going to be the future madam of the house.

"Well...?" asked the gardener impatiently.

Mobi lowered his voice and said, "She is nothing like Miss Vivian. Miss Fey seems very pleasant and nice. She even asked me to call her by name."

Everyone gasped in disbelief.

Alice, the cook, then said, "Hmmm, maybe it's because she is American. I hear they're very informal with each other over there."

Heads nodded in agreement.

Then she added, "We'll just have to wait and see if she changes. Worst-case scenario, she will turn out like that witch, Vivian. And we already know how to deal with that."

"I don't think that will happen," Mobi said. "Anyway, enough gossiping. We need to serve dinner in an hour." He then gave out instructions. As the housekeeper, he was in charge of the rest of the household staff, and although he was the youngest of them, they all liked and respected him.

***

Since her arrival in Nigeria, one of the things that stuck out to Fey was that unlike in the States, the houses here were built with cement bricks from top to bottom. Unless you were dragging furniture and throwing things around, it was relatively quiet when walking around no matter which floor of the house you were on.

As Iben walked Fey through his house, she admired the architectural design and decor. On the first floor of the house were two living rooms, a guest room, a home gym, a study, the kitchen and the laundry room. On the second floor were the remaining four bedrooms, each with its own ensuite bathroom.

At the end of the hallway was the master bedroom. Compared to the other bedrooms, it was very spacious, with a walk-in closet, lots of windows and a balcony which overlooked the backyard. It wasn't a large yard, but you could have a small gathering of about thirty people with plenty of room to spare. There were also some moringa trees and palm trees around the perimeter that provided enough privacy so that you could sit at the balcony without worrying about your neighbors seeing your every move.

Fey sat down on one of the cushioned wicker chairs on the balcony. The sun was setting soon and there was a cool breeze blowing. It was very picturesque. She then leaned back in the chair and closed her eyes.

A few minutes later, Iben joined her. He had changed out of his office clothes into something casual. He stood behind her chair and bent down to wrap his arms around her shoulders before tilting his head and planting a kiss on her cheek.

Fey smiled at his touch. "Hey…" she said with her eyes still closed. "You have a lovely home."

Iben smiled and said, "It's even lovelier now that you're here." Then he walked around to stand in front of her.

Fey opened her eyes and looked up at him. When their eyes met, he reached for her hand and pulled her up to stand before leading her back inside. As soon as they were in the privacy of the bedroom, Iben pulled her closer to him before leaning in for a gentle, yet sensual kiss. Fey eagerly wrapped her arms around his waist while he caressed her face with one hand, and placed the other hand on her lower back, pressing her closer to him. They held onto each other tightly, as their tongues slowly ignited the flames of desire within them.

When the kiss ended, Iben said huskily, "I've missed you… Can I pick you up tomorrow morning?" He knew that after dinner, Fey would leave with Demi, as Demi's parents were expecting her tonight.

"I'm not sure, babe," Fey began apologetically as she caressed his face. "I think Demi said her parents want us to attend a wedding with them tomorrow. I don't think I can get out of it. We should be back in time for dinner with your grandfather, though. How about Sunday?"

Iben sighed disappointedly before he said, "I'm actually leaving for a business trip on Sunday." He was scheduled to tour the different Starlight Shipping depots, offices and warehouses across the country. He had been putting off this trip since he began his role as chairman, but he could no longer do so. This trip was essential for strategizing the changes and improvements that will be needed for the company's growth. Because of that, tomorrow was the only opportunity they had to spend time together until when he would return.

"How long is your trip?" Fey asked.

"Three weeks."

"Oh..." It was Fey's turn to be disappointed.

Just then, the cordless phone in the bedroom rang. Iben moved to answer it. Mobi was on the other line. He told Iben that their dinner guest had arrived. Iben thanked him and hung up. Then he turned to Fey and said, "Let's talk about this later. Demi is here."

They both went downstairs to meet Demi. As soon as she saw Fey in her NYSC uniform, she burst into laughter. She wasn't expecting her to be dressed like that. "What's with the getup?" she teased.

Fey rolled her eyes at her and said, "I wanted to take pictures with Iben wearing this. Besides, I'm very proud of myself for not quitting midway during those three weeks at boot camp."

Demi let out a chortle. "Really? So you think you're a selfless soldier coming home from the battlefield?"

Fey turned to Iben and said, "Can we just make her *watch* us eat dinner and *starve* her instead? She's not being very nice!"

Iben laughed at her words.

Then Demi moved to hug her friend. "I'm sorry... I'm sorry..." she repeated insincerely, while failing at her attempts to stop her laughter.

Iben chuckled as he watched Fey and Demi joke around. "Let's eat before the food gets cold," he said.

Later, while eating dinner, Fey remembered something and asked Demi a question. "How was your lunch date with your boyfriend?"

Iben's ears perked up, and he looked up from his plate. He didn't know Demi now had a boyfriend.

Demi smiled happily and said, "It was great. I can't wait for you to meet him."

Iben asked curiously, "How did you guys meet?"

Demi put down her fork, clasped her hands together and said dramatically, "He's my knight in shining armor."

Fey rolled her eyes, and Iben almost laughed, but he quickly caught himself.

Demi continued, "So, a few weeks ago, I went to a party with one of my cousins. I met this really cute guy, and we hit it off right away. We exchanged Instagram IDs and chatted over DMs for a few days. Then, he asks me out to dinner. So we plan to meet at this restaurant on Victoria Island at 8:00 PM. I get there and wait, but the jerk *never* shows up!"

She stops to drink from her cup before continuing. "As I'm leaving to get back home, some guys with guns and knives tried to carjack me. Apparently, they had been watching me for a while as I was waiting for my asshole date who stood me up. Luckily for me, there was a police detective who happened to be nearby, and he saved me. He was so cool and handsome as he disarmed those bad guys. We kept in touch as I had to give my report of the incident. And a week later, we started dating."

Iben was speechless as he listened to her tale. And he almost chuckled when suddenly Fey made a comment that expressed his very thoughts.

"Sounds like a scene straight out of an action movie," Fey said dryly. She swore that every time Demi recounted this story, it had just a bit more embellishments.

"Whatever…" Demi responded before continuing her meal.

Iben pressed for more information. "So, in what arm of the police force is he a detective?"

"He's with the Special Anti-Robbery Squad," Demi responded.

SARS, hmmm… Iben thought to himself. He then nodded slowly and said before continuing his meal, "Well, I look forward to meeting him someday."

The trio continued dinner with light banter. Afterward, they moved to the living room to relax. When it was almost 8:30 PM, Iben called for Mobi and instructed him to move Fey's luggage to Demi's car. Soon after, Fey and Demi left.

Around 9:15 PM, they arrived at Demi's family home in Ikoyi. Demi's parents, Victor and Remi Oke, welcomed her warmly. While Remi, her mother, saw Fey during graduation, her father did not attend and so he hadn't seen Fey in many years.

Later, Demi showed Fey to her bedroom. It was next to Demi's with a connected, shared bathroom separating both rooms. The friends chatted till late into the night before they finally went to sleep.

21 | The Meeting

The next morning was Saturday, and after breakfast, Fey accompanied Demi and her parents to a wedding. For Fey, it was a very interesting experience. While she had attended a few weddings in the States, this wedding was on a whole other level. For one, she felt that everything took too long. By the time the church ceremony was over, she was more than ready to move on to the next event, which was the reception. Luckily it was on the premises of the church, so they only had to walk for a few minutes.

When they entered the reception hall, Fey was amazed. The beautiful decor almost took her breath away. Vibrant shades of pink and blue could be seen all round the room. It felt like a grand festival was about to take place. It was exciting. After they were seated, the MC welcomed the guests as music played in the background. After a while, the bride and groom arrived. Everyone watched as the couple happily danced all the way from the entrance to the stage where they would be seated.

Finally, the waiters began serving food to all guests. Although Fey wanted some pounded yam and vegetable stew, she opted for a plate of jollof rice with chicken and *moi moi* instead. The key factor in this decision was the terrifying size of the meats in the pounded yam plate. Fey wasn't confident that she could do justice to the meal without looking like a starved wench from the medieval times. If she were at home, of course, that would not be a problem.

Another part of the wedding that Fey enjoyed was the music and dancing. Coupled with the exquisite traditional outfits that people wore, it was a very colorful and enlightening experience for her. At some point, she couldn't help but imagine herself in the bride's shoes. After thinking about it, she was certain that she wouldn't want anything this grand when it was her time to get married. She suddenly blurted out her thoughts to Demi. "I wouldn't want something this elaborate for my wedding."

Demi smiled at her friend's comment and said, "I'm calling dibs on designing your wedding dress and traditional outfits when it's time for you and Iben to get married."

Fey shot her a glance. "Don't be ridiculous. Neither one of us is thinking about that."

Demi scoffed. "My dear. I think *you* are the only one who is not thinking about that. I am certain that Iben has thought that far ahead."

Fey rolled her eyes. "And you know this how?" she asked incredulously.

"I just know these things," Demi replied smugly. "Wasn't my intuition spot-on back then in Germany when I told you he was in love with you?"

"It's not the same thing," Fey countered dismissively. "Besides, we've only been dating for barely a year now. And half of it was long distance. I don't believe he's thinking about me in that way."

Demi looked at her friend as if she had suddenly sprouted two heads. "Why are you hell-bent on being in denial when it comes to that man? Didn't you say that he had hinted just as much to your mom when he visited Delaware?" Fey said nothing, so she continued. "Anyway, even if Iben is not thinking about it, you should be."

Fey just shrugged dismissively. Seeing her nonchalant response, Demi decided to turn things up a bit. Her friend needed a wake-up call.

"Okay. Let me paint a picture for you," Demi began. "Imagine that it's some time in the future and Iben is standing in front of the altar, about to get married. But the person he is getting married to is *not* you. The woman he is pledging his eternal and undying love to is *not* you. The woman that he has his arms around and is kissing passionately is *not* you. The woman—"

"Okay...Okay...you've made your point," Fey interrupted. *How annoying!* she thought irritably. She looked away from her friend's piercing gaze. The thought of Iben being with another woman was truly a sickening and heart wrenching thought. She loved him so much and wanted him all to herself. Even if Iben didn't feel the same way, she didn't see her feelings for him changing anytime soon.

Demi smiled as she watched her friend's reaction. *This girl can be so dense and in denial sometimes.* She felt it was her duty to enlighten her.

"So tonight," Demi continued. "You had better leave a good impression on your future grandfather-in-law."

Fey sighed, rubbed the space between her eyes and said, "Thanks! Until now, I was only mildly anxious about meeting Iben's grandfather. But no thanks to your *wise words*, I'm now completely terrified!"

Demi chuckled. "Don't worry, I have faith in you," she said reassuringly. "Besides, I'm sure that lover boy Iben won't let you go down in flames tonight. The *Fey-Ben* ship must sail!" She raised a fist in solidarity.

Fey was amused by her friend's words. "Was that supposed to make me feel better?" she asked with a soft chuckle.

Demi smiled. "Did it?" she asked with her brows raised.

Fey chuckled in response.

Mission accomplished, Demi thought to herself happily. She was wholeheartedly on the Fey and Iben ship, and would do anything to make sure that it sailed beautifully into the sunset.

After a while, Demi turned her attention to the other goal she wanted to accomplish today. Since her return to Nigeria a couple of months ago, she had been putting together her business plan. Although her parents had promised to help finance her fashion design business, they told her that she still had to put together a proper business plan for her brand and present it to them. They were going to be investors in her business, and she had to sell her dream to them. Demi had no problem with their request. In fact, she viewed it as a challenge. Afterall, if she had stayed back in the States and needed investors, she would have to do the same thing.

Normally, Demi would not attend events like this with her parents. However, she wanted to take this opportunity to see firsthand the different styles of clothing that people wore to weddings here in Nigeria. She was working on a new catalog of designs, so this was more of a research trip than anything else. In order to understand the prevailing fashion trends, she had also attended a few parties and events with some of her cousins so that she could get a sense of what the younger generation liked to wear.

***

Later that evening, Iben arrived at Demi's to pick up Fey for dinner with his grandfather. Once inside, he introduced himself as Fey's boyfriend to Demi's parents.

"Ah, nice to meet you, Iben," Victor said, as he shook Iben's hand. "Please, have a seat. Fey should be downstairs soon."

Iben smiled and said politely, "Thank you, sir."

After about five minutes, Fey came downstairs. When Iben saw her, he broke into a big smile. She was wearing one of the dresses he had gifted her back when he was leaving Delaware. It was a knee-length navy blue half sleeve dress with flower prints. She wore a pair of silver heels and held onto a matching silver clutch. She looked elegant as she walked down the stairs. Iben stood up to meet her and then pulled her into a hug. "Hey, beautiful…" he whispered.

After a few seconds, they heard Victor clear his throat, causing them to separate. Fey looked down, a bit embarrassed. Unperturbed, Iben then turned to Victor and said, "We'll be leaving now, sir. My grandfather is expecting us."

They said their goodbyes and left.

"That Ariri boy is too bold," Victor complained to his wife Remi after they had left.

"Stop being so old-fashioned," Remi chastised. "He seems like a nice boy. What are you going to do when your daughter brings her man around?"

Victor turned to look at his wife. "Ehn?! What man?!" he asked with a frown.

Remi rolled her eyes and stood up from where she was seated. She ignored his question and said, "I'm going to prepare dinner."

"Remi… Remi…" he called after his wife, wanting to continue the conversation. She didn't turn around, so he got up and followed her.

***

When they stepped outside, Iben said to Fey, "I'm sorry, I didn't mean to embarrass you back there. I was just so happy to see you in this dress. You look *amazing*!" he gushed.

Fey smiled and said, "Thanks, babe."

Iben then unlocked the car and opened the passenger door for Fey to get in. After she was seated, he got in the driver's seat and immediately leaned in to give her a kiss on the cheek.

"You look so sexy tonight and I really want to kiss you right now." Iben's gaze fell and lingered on her inviting lips. "But I can wait. We'll have time for that later," he added huskily, with a wink.

Fey stared at him, speechless. How could she have forgotten how much of a flirt this guy could be?

Iben smiled as he watched her reaction. *So cute*, he thought to himself.

Iben started driving and about thirty minutes later, they arrived at the Ariri mansion on Banana Island. Fey was floored by the opulence before her. The mansion was sitting on a sprawling estate with hotel style driveway curving around the front entrance. By her estimate, there had to be about ten bedrooms in the mansion.

"Welcome to my childhood home," Iben said as they walked into the house.

Almost immediately, they were met by the housekeeper. "Welcome, Master Iben."

"Good evening, Aunty. I want you to meet my girlfriend, Fey," Iben responded.

"Good evening, Aunty," Fey greeted the housekeeper, following Iben's lead.

The housekeeper smiled warmly at her and said, "Good evening, Miss Fey. It's a pleasure to meet you." Then she turned to Iben and said, "Chief is waiting in the study. Dinner will be served in about half an hour."

Iben nodded and led Fey to the study. Just before he knocked on the door, Fey took his hand and gripped it. She was suddenly very nervous. Iben turned to look at her and wrapped his arms around her in a hug. She buried her head in his embrace while he stroked her back. After about a minute, Fey's erratic heartbeat had calmed down. She pulled back and said, "I'm ready." Iben nodded, and then he knocked on the door. Hearing a response from within, he opened the door and led Fey inside.

When they walked in, Edafe was seated on a large, ornate leather armchair reading a book. When Fey saw him, he looked nothing like she had expected. He was not your average-looking, run-of-the-mill grandpa. He had an imposing air around him, and he was tall with broad shoulders, just like Iben. You could only tell his age from the wrinkles around his eyes and the salt-and-pepper hairs on his head and face. She could see where Iben got his good looks from. She imagined Edafe was probably very handsome when he was much younger.

Iben greeted him, "Good evening, Papa."

"Good evening, Iben." Edafe responded with a big smile. Then, he looked past Iben at Fey, who was standing off to the side.

Iben then turned around and gestured for Fey to come closer. When she was standing next to him, he put his arm around her waist and introduced her to Edafe. "Papa, this is Fey–my girlfriend."

Fey met Edafe's gaze and gave a small curtsey, "Good evening, sir. It's a pleasure to meet you," she said politely. She had received a few pointers from Demi. Apparently, the elderly liked the younger generation to show some respect and deference in the form of either bowing if you were male or bending your knees in a curtsey if you were female.

Edafe was unsmiling as he gave her a once-over before he said, "You're American, so I won't fault you for greeting me as you are accustomed to." The implication was that she had only curtseyed to try to impress him.

Fey was taken aback by his words, but she didn't show it. *This man is unpredictable*, she thought to herself. She smiled at him and said, "I appreciate the consideration, sir. But an American like me is not above learning new things."

Edafe raised a brow at her response. *She's a spunky one*, he thought amusedly to himself. He then gestured for the couple to sit down.

Iben smiled to himself as he reached for Fey's hand and led her to a two-seater sofa. He knew Fey could hold her own against his grandfather. However, he also knew that this was just the beginning.

No sooner had they sat down did Fola come strolling in. "Good Evening Papa," he greeted Edafe with a slight bow.

Edafe smiled warmly. "Fola, my son. Welcome. How was your trip?"

Fola had been away on business in the past week and had only just returned earlier today. "It went well. We have everything ready for next week."

Edafe nodded and said, "Good work." Then he gestured for him to sit.

With that out of the way, Fola then turned his attention to the couple sitting on the sofa. His signature grin lit up his handsome face as he walked up to them. "Bro!" he exclaimed excitedly as he and Iben fist bumped each other in greeting. Then he turned to Fey who was sitting next to Iben and said with a smile, "Hello, Fey. Long time no see!"

Fey smiled back. "Hi Fola. It's nice to see you again."

After Fola was seated, Edafe said to Fey, "I understand that you have just completed your NYSC boot camp." Fey nodded. "What are your thoughts on that farce of a program?" he asked provocatively. "I personally think that the government should scrap the NYSC and spend the money on other worthwhile endeavors."

Fey looked thoughtful for a moment before she answered him. "The boot camp was definitely a unique experience for me. Having lived overseas for most of my life, it was nice to meet people from different cultural and ethnic backgrounds. Americans can be very individualistic, so it was really nice to enjoy the feelings of inclusion in that temporary boot camp community, even though it was only for three weeks.

"I will not claim to understand the economic, social and cultural issues of the country, nor would I claim to understand the inner workings of the NYSC program. But I would definitely *not* call it a farce. I think certain aspects of the program could use some updating to meet the current needs of the country's youth. In my conversations with some people I met, they don't believe that the initial goals are being realized in every participant. So, from that perspective, it can seem like a waste of time. However, there are still many people who benefit from it. That alone, in my opinion, makes it a worthwhile program."

"I see..." was Edafe's response. *She appears to have a mind of her own*, he thought to himself. He knew that many expats and nationals who studied overseas would always try their best to get an exemption from serving in the NYSC, as they felt it was pointless. Aside from expats, many nationals who graduated from the country's university system feel demoralized and used by the government as cheap labor to staff primary and secondary schools in areas where there's little funding and resources.

Although he thought her analysis was a bit myopic, Edafe was impressed that she wasn't afraid to disagree with his opinion. He continued. "You seem like a freethinker. You should come and work for Ariri Corps when you have completed your indentured service to the federal government. We could use a civil engineer such as yourself."

Iben and Fola, who had been silent this whole time, shared a look. It was quite unusual that Edafe was complementing Fey so early in his assessment of her.

Fey, however, didn't miss the ridicule and somewhat dismissive tone in Edafe's words regarding her government job. She smiled politely and said, "Thank you for the offer, sir. I'll keep that in mind. I'm really excited about my new position with the Ministry of Science and Technology. For the next few years, I really want to do a good job while I'm there. I want to make a difference with the projects that I am assigned. My goal is to leave my mark in this world, regardless of whether I'm working for the federal government or not."

Fey didn't want any hand-me-down job offers. She'd rather make her own way if things didn't work out with the government job. So far, Edafe seemed like an unpredictable, royal pain in the ass, anyway. If she accepted a job offer from him, he might end up throwing it in her face at some point in the future and she didn't want that.

Edafe leaned back in his chair at her response. Many people would have jumped at the opportunity to get a job with Ariri Corporation. But here was this girl, acting like it was just another option to be considered. He was a tad irritated and wanted to take her down a peg. He smiled slyly and said, "Iben mentioned that you are living with Judge Victor Oke."

"Yes, his daughter and I are childhood friends."

Edafe nodded and said, "He is an excellent judge in our court system. But because he is a very nice man, it's a shame that people tend to take advantage of him. Over the years, he has taken in a few people with nothing to show for it, in my opinion. A few years ago, he took in a girl—about your age—and she almost betrayed him for some money. It was quite the scandal." He ended his commentary with a smirk.

Iben, who had been holding onto Fey's hand since they were seated, suddenly felt her stiffen at his grandfather's comment. "Papa, that's–" Iben began in an attempt to defend her.

"It's okay, babe," Fey interrupted him. She then met Edafe's gaze and thought to herself, *Is this sly old man saying this because I indirectly refused his job offer?* She then leaned back in her seat and crossed her legs before responding. "As an esteemed member of the Nigerian judicial system, wouldn't you agree that he is quite *capable* of identifying people who are just trying to take advantage of him?" She knew Edafe was lying about the girl who supposedly tried to betray Demi's dad. If such a thing happened, Demi would've told her.

"Uncle Victor has been like a father to me since I was young. When he heard that I was considering relocating here, he offered to get me a job, but I refused. Maybe it's the American in me, but I like to hold on to my independence and not rely on others to do everything for me. Iben knows this about me." When she was done speaking, she had a smug look on her face. She wanted Edafe to know that she knew that he was just being salty about her indirect refusal of his job offer.

Edafe suddenly chuckled. He was thoroughly enjoying his verbal sparring with this young woman. Obviously, he had been trying to feel her out. She was a beautiful girl, so he could see why Iben was attracted to her. But was she smart? Was she self reliant? Or was she looking to use Iben as a stepping stone? How did she handle adversity? Would she try to hide behind Iben or stand up for herself? So far, he could see that she was a very intelligent girl. She hadn't backed down from a fight, and she had held her own, with poise and elegance. "How old are you?" he asked curiously.

"I'm twenty three."

Edafe nodded and looked thoughtful for a moment. *She has more confidence and grace than some people older than her*, he thought to himself.

He remembered that Iben had mentioned that he wanted to marry her, and considering how he was feeling right now, Edafe felt that he would not be embarrassed if she married into his family. The only thing left now was to determine how she truly felt about Iben. From his perspective, many women in her shoes would do anything to marry into a wealthy family like the Ariris. He glanced over at Iben and thought to himself, *Let's see if this girl of yours is the real deal.*

Edafe suddenly asked, "Fey, do you want to marry Iben?"

For a few seconds, Fey was stunned by the sudden turn in the conversation topic. She hadn't expected that Edafe would ask her such a direct question. *Oh my gosh! This man is going to give me a heart attack*, she thought to herself.

Fey subconsciously glanced at Iben. Unlike when her mother, Adaobi, had asked him the same question, and she had protested, Iben did not stop his grandfather. In fact, he was very curious to hear Fey's answer to his grandfather's question. He turned to look at her, his heart pounding in his chest. *What if she says 'no'?* he thought to himself. *That would be so depressing...*

Fey looked at Iben as she responded. "I love Iben… and I hope that he continues to be in my life." Iben's eyes softened as he held her gaze. She then continued with a mischievous smile teasing the corner of her lips. "Right now, I want to focus on my career. However… if in the future, he summons enough courage to ask nicely for my hand in marriage, *maybe… just maybe…* I'll say yes."

Iben raised an amused brow as a smirk gently tugged at the corner of his mouth. Despite her bold statement, he watched as Fey bit her lower lip shyly under his gaze. His eyes hadn't left hers since she started answering Edafe's question about marriage. After a few seconds, she looked away self-consciously, but Iben gently caressed her cheek and slowly turned her face back towards him. He leaned in and then asked softly, "Is that a challenge?"

Now, more than ever, he wanted this shy, yet feisty woman to be his.

"Iben..." Fey protested quietly. She was quite embarrassed that he was acting as if they were the only two people in the room.

Edafe watched the interaction between the young couple in front of him. He had to admit that he had never seen Iben so taken with anyone before. He couldn't recall a single time when he had shown such an expression on his face when he was engaged to Vivian. *Any woman who has the confidence to speak like that to my grandson is a welcome addition to my family,* he thought to himself amusedly.

A smile blossomed on Edafe's face as he spoke, interrupting them. "Your family. I'd like to meet them!" he declared.

Hearing Edafe speak to her, Fey gladly turned away from Iben's gaze to look at him instead.

"Iben told me he has met your mother in the States," he continued once he saw that he had her attention. "How about your father?" he asked.

"Um...that's actually one of the reasons why I relocated, sir. I'm hoping to reconnect with my father."

"I see... Why are you not staying with him then? Is he domiciled outside of Lagos state?" Edafe asked curiously.

"I have no idea where he is living currently," Fey admitted. "My mother raised my sister and I on her own because my father has not been in our lives. I am actually trying to look for him."

"I'll be happy to help you with your search, Fey," Fola suddenly interjected. Iben had given him this task since the previous year when he was still in Germany, but he had reached a dead-end in terms of finding any clues to where her father could be. This was a very unusual situation for him, as there wasn't anything so far that he couldn't uncover. He knew that Iben hadn't wanted her to know about his investigation, but if Fey could give him more clues, he might be able to make some headway.

"I think that's a great idea, babe," Iben joined in. "Fola is pretty good at finding anything."

Fey looked back and forth between both Iben and Fola. It really warmed her heart that they were willing to help her with her search. But she didn't want them to feel obligated. "I don't want to impose–" she began.

"Nonsense!" Edafe interrupted her. "Fola will help you. Family is very important." He then smiled at her.

Fey looked at Edafe, surprised. For the first time since she had met the man, his smile right now seemed warm and genuine. She returned his smile and said, "Thank you very much, sir. I really appreciate it."

"Don't mention it." He moved to stand up. "Let's all go and have dinner."

22 | What Lies Beneath

After dinner, Edafe excused himself to attend to other matters while Iben, Fola, and Fey sat in one of the living rooms to chat and relax.

"Sister-in-law," Fola began, "I'm impressed that you made it through your NYSC camp in one piece. Romeo over here was stressing like crazy the entire time." He smiled impishly and shot a teasing look at Iben.

Fey, surprised at the way Fola addressed her, turned to him and said, "Um… until *Romeo* proposes, I am *not* your sister-in-law!"

Fola let out a loud guffaw at Fey's response. "Bro! That's the second time tonight that she has called you out on your lack of game!" he said, pointing at Iben in jest. He was laughing so hard that one could tell he was thoroughly enjoying himself.

Fey rolled her eyes at Fola's antics. Sometimes, she couldn't believe he was many years older. However, her curiosity got the better of her so she asked, "Was he really worried while I was there?"

After Fola stopped laughing he said, "Yes, he was like a mother hen, constantly fretting about your *delicate* nature, and whether you would be okay if the electricity goes out at night."

Iben's worries weren't unfounded. Depending on where you lived, power outages were a common occurrence in Nigeria.

Fey glanced over at Iben, who was sitting next to her. "Aww… how sweet, babe…" she said with a chuckle as she patted his hand in a very patronizing manner.

Iben sat quietly for the next couple of minutes, listening to Fola and Fey continue to rib and tease him. After a while, he leaned in and whispered something in Fey's ears, which caused her eyes to go wide in surprise, shutting her up. In the next moment, she quickly reached for her cup of unfinished coffee and concentrated on drinking it.

"What was that about?" Fola asked when he saw that his teasing partner was suddenly quiet.

"I just unleashed my secret weapon–her kryptonite!" was Iben's cryptic response. He had a smirk and a smug look on his face as he glanced over at Fey, who was now trying to avoid eye contact with him.

Fola quickly realized what happened and thought to himself, *Ugh, is this guy flirting right now?* He sighed defeatedly. Since things had turned out this way, he changed the subject. "Fey, can you tell me everything you know about your father? It'll be helpful in my investigation."

Fey's eyes lit up, happy for a change in conversation topic. "Sure. His name is David Ademola. He is from Ogun state and as far as I know, he is a civil engineer."

"Do you know of the last place where he lived?"

"I think my mom said his parents lived here in Lagos. Although, he may have moved away after he remarried."

"Do you know the name of his current wife?"

"No."

"Do you know the names of his parents?"

"No."

"Do you have a picture of him?"

"No, I don't. My mom pretty much erased all traces of him in our home." She sighed before adding, "If my sister wasn't already back in college, I could've called her to see if she can snoop around in the attic for me. My mom keeps a bunch of old stuff in there."

"That's okay," Fola responded. "I have enough information for now. Let me know if you can get a photo or if you think of anything else. No information is irrelevant when looking for someone."

Fey nodded in understanding. "Thank you for doing this for me. It means a lot."

"You're welcome," Fola replied. Then he stood up and said, "Well, I need to get going. I have a few things that I need to get done tonight before our trip tomorrow. See you lovebirds later." He left soon after.

The room was quiet for a moment after Fola left before Iben spoke. "Babe, as I was saying yesterday, I'll be away for three weeks. But, I'll let you know as soon as I get back so that we can hang out." Fey nodded but said nothing. Reading her facial expression, he asked, "What's the matter?"

"I'm going to miss you," she said, looking down at her hands. She had taken for granted that he would always be around. But he had a job to do. An entire company was depending on him to do his part, keep the business profitable, and pay salaries to their employees. And sometimes that required being away for long periods.

Iben placed his hand on her chin and gently lifted her face towards him before he said, "Babe, I'm going to miss you like crazy too." Then he kissed her. It was a very passionate kiss. Knowing that they would be apart for another three weeks aroused intense feelings in both of them. When they parted, Iben looked into Fey's eyes and was delighted that they mirrored the same desires as his. Then, he said in a voice that was low and husky, "When I get back, I want you all to myself. So, hold that thought until then… Okay?"

***

The next day, Iben and Fola left for their business trip early in the morning. For Fey, the rest of the weekend was quite uneventful and relaxing. However, starting on Monday, she was busy preparing for her first day of work.

First, at Demi's insistence, she opened an account at the same bank as Demi's. Next, she needed a car. Since she couldn't afford a new one, Demi's father, Victor had promised to refer her to a reputable used car dealership. He also graciously offered to have one of his drivers take her to wherever she needed if Demi was unavailable. Meanwhile, she had to obtain a driver's license. She presented her American driver's license, along with her passport, and took a skills test. Then, she returned at the end of the week to collect her temporary license.

A week later, Fey began working at her new job. During orientation in Abuja, she learned that she would do a series of twelve-week rotations at different agencies within the ministry. Sometimes, she might also work on joint projects with other government ministries and parastatals. These rotations would allow her to learn and gain first-hand experience in the functions of each agency. Her first rotation was at the Technology Acquisition office, which luckily was also in Ikoyi where she lived. This meant that her commute to work for the next three months would be a breeze.

By the end of her second week on the job, Lagos heat wave and crazy traffic aside, she had settled in and was getting the hang of things. While some of her coworkers seemed indifferent, others were eager to help her get acclimated to the work. Lastly, some people treated her with distrust because they regarded her as an outsider who would not be there beyond three months. Regardless, she enjoyed the work that she was given, and was eager to soak up all the learning that she could before moving on to her next rotation.

***

In the third and final week of the Starlight Shipping tour, according to their itinerary, Iben and Fola visited the Port Harcourt warehouses and depots. On the last day, after they had finished the tour and met with the relevant people, Edafe joined them and told Iben that he wanted to take him somewhere. Their entourage then traveled for about an hour and a half to a secluded area not in the original itinerary. They then drove through a tiny fishing village until they reached their destination. By the time they arrived, it was around sunset.

When Iben stepped out of the vehicle, he looked around curiously. "Where are we?" he asked.

"Come along," Edafe responded, and Iben followed him to a nearby warehouse. Once inside, Edafe signaled to some workers, and they opened a few shipping containers. When Iben saw the contents, he frowned.

Inside the containers were firearms of all kinds. Rifles, shotguns, machine guns, and many more were all in there. Iben looked to his grandfather and asked in disbelief, "Papa, what's all this?"

"Firearms," Edafe answered curtly.

"I *know* what they are," Iben replied through clenched teeth. "What I don't know is *why* they are here… and why *we* are here."

Edafe closed one of the opened containers and leaned against it for support. "It's time that you know what's going on. Since you have now officially taken the reins of Starlight Shipping, I need to keep you informed. These firearms belong to us and we sell them to the highest bidder."

Iben had a stunned look on his face. After a few seconds, he asked. "Are these legal?"

Edafe laughed and said, "We didn't steal them if that's what you are asking. Son, this is one of the reasons we acquired Starlight Shipping. Charles Ibere was my partner for a while in this business. For many years, he allowed me to conceal and move these items via his shipping network, and I paid him a hefty fee for his silence."

Iben looked to Fola and asked, "Were you aware of this?"

Before Fola could respond, Edafe answered, "Of course. He has always known!"

Iben sighed and looked down. Then, he placed his hand on his forehead before kneading the muscles around his temple to ease the tension that was forming. "Who are the buyers?" he asked after a while.

"Send them in," Fola suddenly instructed one of the bodyguards.

A moment later, two men walked into the warehouse. Iben couldn't believe his eyes. He had only asked about the buyers to understand what he was dealing with. But a transaction was actually about to take place right now.

Iben stood to the side and watched as the two men inspected a few of the containers in the warehouse. Once they were satisfied, they took out their smartphones and made wire transfers. Fola verified the payments and then instructed some men to move the containers to a truck waiting outside.

After the buyers left, Iben asked, "Is there another warehouse like this?"

But before he got an answer, they suddenly heard someone yell from outside, "We've got company!"

"Shit!" he heard Fola curse. "Suit Iben up right now!" he yelled.

Within seconds, someone came over and strapped a plate carrier on Iben. *What the hell is going on here?* he thought to himself in confusion. The next thing he heard was gunfire. Instinctively, he ducked and laid on the ground behind one of the steel containers close by. He looked over at his grandfather to see if he was okay, but he was stunned by the scene before him. Edafe, also strapped in a plate carrier, had a firearm in his possession and was expertly shooting back at the people who had attacked them. Iben's eyes widened in shock as he watched his grandfather go from calm and collected to savage in an instant. He looked over to where Fola was standing and he was also doing the same thing. *These guys are acting like this is a normal occurrence,* he thought to himself in disbelief.

During the ensuing gunfight, Iben took a peek around the warehouse and saw that everyone except him had a firearm and was returning fire against their attackers. Soon, many of their attackers were dropping like flies. After some time, the gunfire died down and Iben peeked from behind the steel container that had been acting as his shield. By now, there was a slight fog of gun smoke in the warehouse, so he couldn't see too well.

He suddenly heard someone yell, "They're getting away!"

Fola yelled back angrily, "Capture every one of those motherfuckers and bring them to me! Now!"

Iben heard footsteps as some guards ran out of the warehouse in pursuit of their retreating attackers. His tense muscles relaxed as he sat up to lean against the container he had been hiding behind. Suddenly, he heard Edafe yell, "Get down, Iben!" In an instant, he heard gunshots and two bodies fell.

One of the gunmen that attacked them, who was previously shot and was lying on the ground, had launched a surprise attack on an unarmed Iben. Edafe saw this and in the ensuing gunfire, he shot the guy in the head as he took a bullet in his shoulder while trying to protect Iben. When the gunshots ended, Iben ran over to where his grandfather had fallen. "Papa!" he yelled, panic-stricken. Trembling, he checked to see if Edafe was alright. "Oh my god! He's bleeding!" Iben said, alarmed.

"I'm alright," he suddenly heard Edafe say with great effort. By now, Fola and two guards had come over to them and were inspecting his gunshot wound. They stopped the bleeding with a surgical patch and sat him up against a nearby wall.

Now that Edafe was okay, the captain of their elite security guards joked and said to him, "Chief, you were incredible! You still have the fire in you!"

"Whatever, the bullet went straight through," Edafe said as he patted his bandaged shoulder as if it was nothing.

"Look at Chief. He's still acting like he's in his thirties," another guard said jokingly.

"Shut up, you little runts!" Edafe shot back and they all laughed.

Everyone except Iben. From his viewpoint, there was nothing funny about the entire situation.

Relieved that his grandfather was okay, all of Iben's energy was now completely drained. He slumped onto the ground, suddenly mentally and physically exhausted. He leaned against the wall and sat with his knees raised so that he could rest his elbows on them as he covered his face with his hands. As he sat there, he heard Fola give instructions to interrogate the hostages they had captured while they were trying to make a getaway.

Never in a million years would he have guessed that this day would end up like this. A few hours ago, he was happy to be done with the tour and was just looking forward to going back home and spending time with Fey. Thinking of her, he reached into his pocket for his phone. But it was missing. *It must've fallen out*, he thought to himself.

He stood up and searched for it, but when he found it, the screen had shattered.

Fola and Edafe gave instructions to their men to clean up the warehouse and notify the police. They had a few cops on their payroll, who were in the Anti-Robbery Squad. These cops would take care of the bodies and report whatever fabricated scenario was needed to keep their arms trafficking business hidden from the prying eyes of the authorities.

Sometime later, Edafe, Fola, and Iben were driven back to the guest house where Iben and Fola had been staying for the last couple of days. As soon as they arrived, they called in a private doctor to assess and treat Edafe's bullet wound. After he took the painkillers that the doctor prescribed, Edafe retired for the night.

Soon after, Iben and Fola sat down to talk.

Iben was the first to speak. "How long have you known about this side of the business?" he asked.

"Since forever," Fola replied.

"Why didn't you tell me?"

"Papa didn't think that you were ready. So, I was sworn into silence." Fola paused before he asked, "Now that you *do* know, do you wish you didn't?"

Iben looked thoughtful for a moment before replying, "Yes, ignorance *is* bliss. But I'm not sure that being in the dark forever would do me any good, unfortunately." He sighed and then asked, "Why were we attacked yesterday?"

"Some rebels in the area somehow got wind of the contents of the warehouse. Usually, we have airtight security and we only open things up for potential buyers and deliveries. They found out we were going to be there yesterday and tried to steal from us."

"Were you able to determine how they found out about the warehouse contents?"

Fola shook his head. "Not yet, we're still interrogating the assholes!"

Iben nodded in understanding before he asked, "What else are you and Papa hiding from me?"

Fola chuckled and said in ridicule, "Nobody has been hiding anything from you. You've just had your head in the sand for so long, pretending not to see the signs."

"That's bullshit! What signs have I ignored? Huh? Tell me!" Iben responded as he raised his voice.

"I'll give you a recent example. Charles Ibere!" Fola shot back. "You decided that you didn't want to know if there was foul play in his death. If you had asked Papa, he would never lie to you."

"Are you saying Papa had something to do with his death?" Iben asked incredulously.

Fola sighed and said, "All I'm saying is that you shouldn't be afraid to ask the hard questions, even if the answer might not be what you would like to hear. You're going to be the head of the company soon, so you need to man up, and stop ignoring that voice in the back of your head when something doesn't seem right! If you don't, the people around us, the people watching us, will realize this weakness of yours and destroy everything! Do you think Papa built Ariri Corporation and made it great because he was a nice guy who drank milk tea and ate biscuits with people?"

"I'm not that naïve!" Iben shot back angrily. "I studied Business and Law, remember? I know of a million different ways to screw someone over legally. But what I'm having a hard time with right now is understanding how firearms fit into the whole picture. It just makes no sense to me."

"Papa is the only one who can answer that question for you," Fola said in response. "All I can say is that he was the one who orchestrated the positions I've had in the past with the EFCC—and Interpol, to a lesser extent. My task was to learn how things worked so that I could be Papa's eyes and ears. That way, he knows who's sniffing around, what they're looking for, and how to avoid detection."

"And now that you're back in the country, what happens to all that intel?"

Fola smiled smugly. "I still have eyes and ears where it's required."

Fola's attitude irritated Iben. "Just so you know, when I take over the company, we're going to do things *my* way. So, prepare yourself!"

"That's the spirit!" Fola shot back with a smirk.

Iben glared at him and then walked off.

After Iben left, Fola sat in the same spot, thinking about his conversation with Iben. *Was I too hard on him?* he thought to himself. He truly cared about Iben like a younger brother and a friend. When they were younger, and Edafe took him in as an orphan, Fola was directed to protect Iben. At first, it started as a job that he had to do so that Edafe wouldn't throw him back in the streets, but he grew to truly care for Iben. He also had full confidence that Iben would be an outstanding leader. He just needed some tough love to wake him up from his slumber.

***

The next morning, Iben went to Edafe's room after breakfast. "Good morning. How's your shoulder faring?" he asked.

"I've been worse," Edafe replied, dismissively.

"Papa," Iben began solemnly. "Thank you for saving my life yesterday."

"It's nothing. I put you in that situation anyway, so we're even," Edafe said with a wry smile.

Iben didn't smile. The thought that either of them could have died yesterday kept him up half the night. Edafe was his only family, after all. "Papa, why are we trafficking firearms? It's so dangerous, not to mention, illegal."

Edafe sighed. He knew this conversation was bound to happen. He leaned back in his seat and said, "Whenever I mastered a new business industry and conquered the market or the competition, I would get bored and need another challenge. Then, I'd dabble in something else, and when I got good at that, I would move on to something else. That's how Ariri Corporation became the conglomerate it is today.

"Once in a while, I would get the rare opportunity to tangle with unprincipled businessmen, and I do get *so* excited! Why? Because I know they cannot help their nature but to try to double-cross me. And when they inevitably do, I take the opportunity to let loose. I teach them a grand lesson and I get to exorcise my thrill-seeking demons. So, it's a win-win for me.

"But over the years, I have found that business has become very boring and I occasionally need some excitement. Eventually, I got into firearms trafficking because over time, very few people would try to go head to head with me in business, and I needed other outlets for adventure and excitement."

As Iben listened to his grandfather speak, he almost sounded like a rebellious teenager. No—his grandfather sounded like a chaos demon trapped inside an aging, mortal body. "You're getting older, Papa. Shouldn't you be slowing down?" Iben chastised.

"I'll slow down when I take my last breath on this earth!" Edafe said with determination.

Nobody spoke for a few minutes.

Iben then asked Edafe, "Are there other warehouses?"

"Yes. We have three altogether. One each in the north, west, and east."

"Can you provide me with specific locations? I'd like to visit and see what we're dealing with."

Edafe's face blossomed into a grin. "You're interested in this line of business?" he asked expectantly. Although he had confidence in Iben's business acumen, he had always felt that the danger and illegality of firearms trafficking would repulse him.

"I just don't want to be in the dark anymore," Iben said as he met Edafe's gaze.

Edafe nodded at Iben's response. He felt that his grandson had matured. Unlike Fola, who was just as much a thrill-seeking, adrenaline junkie as he was, Iben was of a different personality. He wouldn't go looking for trouble. But if trouble came to find him, he wouldn't back down from a fight.

Iben chatted some more with Edafe to get more details on how the firearms dealings worked. By the time they were done talking, Iben decided in his mind that once he finished his training at Starlight Shipping and he took over the Ariri conglomerate officially, he would change things. In the meantime, he was an implicit accomplice, as he had no choice but to leave things as they were. He would not report his only family to the authorities afterall.

After Iben left his room, Edafe reminisced about the first time they met. Edafe had been estranged from Iben's mother for many years, and until a month before that day, he wasn't even aware of his existence. When he found out about him, he had been curious and had gone to his school to meet Iben for the first time. It was his tenth birthday that day and he had bought him a toy. When his mother introduced him as his grandfather, Iben had warmed up to him immediately and hugged him. And now that little boy had grown into a man that he was very proud of.

23 | Friends and Lovers

Due to the events at Port Harcourt, Iben could not return to Lagos until Edafe's injury had stabilized and the doctor declared that he could travel. As a result, they arrived in Lagos on Friday night of the fourth week after he left.

Since his phone was broken at the warehouse, Iben had to wait a couple of days before he could get a new one. During that time, he could not get in contact with Fey as he had never memorized her phone number since he saved it in his phone contacts. When he finally received her voice and text messages, he could tell that she was very worried. He called her right away to explain that his phone was broken.

The next day was Saturday and around 10:00 AM, Iben went to pick up Fey as they had agreed. When Fey saw him, she almost flew into his arms.

"I've missed you so much," she said as she hugged him.

"I've missed you too, babe," he said, returning the hug.

After they were seated, Demi teased, "I'm just glad you are back because it stressed this girl out that she couldn't reach you for a few days. You've spoiled her too much."

Iben smiled. His eyes met Fey's and held it for a moment as he thought about how distraught she would've been if he had been shot or died during the shootout at the warehouse. His heart ached at the thought.

Their moment was interrupted by Demi who said, "Ewww… I'm still here, you guys. Save your bedroom eyes for later." When she had the couple's attention, she said, "So are we still having dinner tonight? I'm so looking forward to the suya barbecue you promised us, Iben."

"Yes, dinner is at 7:00 PM," Iben responded with a chuckle.

Shortly after, Fey left with Iben to go shopping for the barbecue ingredients. When they arrived at Iben's home, she went up to sit on the master bedroom balcony, while Iben gave instructions to Mobi on preparing the ingredients for tonight's get-together. Later, he joined Fey on the balcony.

After sitting down next to her, he said, "It was around this time last year that I first met you in Germany. I never knew that I'd eventually fall in love with you that day when I saw a gorgeous, but penniless girl trying to buy breakfast at the cafe."

Fey smacked him playfully and said, "I was not penniless!"

Iben chuckled before he continued. "Do you know that I went to the cafe many times hoping to see you after that?" Fey raised a surprised brow before he continued, "And when you walked into the lobby of my office building a few weeks later, I felt like I had hit the jackpot." He moved closer to Fey and put his arms around her waist so that she was leaning against him. "Now that you're mine, I never want to let you go."

Fey turned to give him a peck on his cheek. "I'm not going anywhere, babe," she said.

Iben smiled at her chaste kiss. They sat in comfortable silence for a while until Fey heard Iben sigh uncharacteristically. She turned to look at him and said, "You seem kinda bummed. Did something happen during your trip?"

Iben sighed again before he said, "Sort of... I found out some things about the company that's not sitting well with me."

"I see... It must be something major to get you down like this."

"Yeah, it is. But I do plan to make some changes, although I honestly don't know where to start."

With his arms still around her waist, Fey intertwined her fingers with his and said, "My mom used to say that a journey of a thousand miles begins with one step. Even if this problem you encountered seems huge or insurmountable, just chip away at it a little at a time, and before you know it, the problem is no more. While I don't know the details of the issue, I do have faith that you can overcome it."

Iben smiled at her encouraging words. "Thanks for the vote of confidence, babe." Realizing that thinking about the firearms trafficking issue was affecting his mood, he changed the topic. "Anyway, enough about me. How has work been for you?"

"It's been good. Although, I never thought I'd get a bit of culture shock working here in the country."

"How do you mean?" Iben asked.

"People are so formal at work, and I have to retrain my mind to fit in. Mrs. This. Mr. That. Whenever someone calls me 'Miss Ademola', I cringe. It makes me feel like an old maid!"

She had a look of annoyance on her face, which made Iben chuckle. "Don't worry. You're definitely not an old maid."

After a moment, he hugged her closer to him and said, "Miss Ademola, may I kiss you?"

Fey turned around and smiled. "Mr. Ariri, I thought you'd never ask."

Iben smiled and then leaned in. As they kissed, Iben's hand caressed one of Fey's breasts, causing a moan to escape from her lips. She pulled away from the kiss and said with a coy smile, "Are you trying to seduce me?"

Iben's eyes flashed with amusement as she had thrown back his words from their first night together when they were in Germany. A sexy smirk played on his lips as he leaned in and said in her ear, "Mmm... is it working?" His voice was low and his warm breath sent tingles through her body. Next, he sucked on her sensitive earlobe and trailed kisses down her neck. Fey soon turned to putty in his hands.

"I've missed you so much, babe," Iben said in a low voice that was dripping with sexiness and desire.

"Mmm... How much?" Fey teased.

"This much," he said as he pressed his erection against her and moaned deeply. "Did you miss me too?" he asked, his eyes searching hers for confirmation.

Fey bit her lower lip and nodded.

At her answer, Iben didn't waste any time. He stood up and led her into the bedroom.

***

Hours later, Iben and Fey emerged from the bedroom to prepare dinner as Fola and Demi would come over to join them soon. Since Iben was grilling *suya*, they would have dinner in the backyard. Mobi had set up seating with tableware for four people, and a cooler with drinks. While Fey was hungrily watching Iben season and grill some *suya* sticks, her stomach growled.

Iben raised a teasing brow and joked. "Oh no! We may not have enough food for that monster in your tummy."

Fey poked his arm playfully. "It's your fault that I'm starving!"

Iben smiled sheepishly. He knew she was referring to the fact that he had kept them cooped up in the bedroom since her arrival that morning. He was unapologetic about it, though. Four months away from the woman he loved made a man *very needy*.

Ten minutes later, Demi arrived. Fola also got there soon after and Iben introduced him to Demi since this would be the first time they met.

When Demi turned around to meet Iben's best friend that she had heard so much about, she was shocked at the person standing in front of her. "You!" she growled at Fola.

Her reaction shocked Fey and Iben. "You two know each other?" Iben asked.

"Yes, what a small world we live in," Fola said sheepishly.

"*This* is the jerk that stood me up on that date I told you guys about," Demi said as she glared at him.

Fola, unfazed by her vitriol, met her gaze and said in a serious tone, "I'm truly sorry about that. I had an emergency that night, so I couldn't make it."

Demi scoffed, "And you couldn't call or send me a message?"

"I sent you a text message. Didn't you get it?"

"Yeah, *after* the fact! If you had sent it earlier, I wouldn't have gone to the restaurant and waited like a fool for two hours. And do you know what happened that night? Thanks to you, I almost got robbed!"

"You did?" he asked incredulously. As far as he knew, the neighborhood where the restaurant was located wasn't known for robbery or carjacking crimes.

Demi glared at him. To her, he didn't seem truly apologetic. Did he think she was making this up? She couldn't believe that she had once felt an attraction to this guy. She closed her eyes for a few seconds to calm down. Then she said, "Anyway, I made it out alive, thanks to a police detective nearby."

Fola nodded. "How can I make it up to you? Lunch some other time, maybe?" he asked.

"That won't be necessary. I don't think my boyfriend would like that at all!"

Iben, who was standing next to Fola all this time, watching the show before him, chimed in and said, "Yeah, she's now dating the *SARS* detective who saved her."

"All's well that ends well, then. Glad I could play cupid," Fola said with an impish grin.

Demi couldn't help but feel that he somehow seemed relieved that he didn't have to take her to lunch or dinner. And for some reason, that annoyed her.

Fola then added, "I'd like to meet him someday."

Demi gave him an incredulous look. "Why?"

"Why not? He saved my sister-in-law's best friend, didn't he?" he responded as a grin lit up his handsome face.

Fey, who had been quiet all this time, was going to complain to Fola about calling her 'sister-in-law' again. But she knew that the more she balked against it, the more Fola would get a kick out of doing it, so she just let it go.

"Have you guys met him already?" he asked Fey and Iben.

"No," Iben responded. "Why don't you invite him to our hangout next Saturday?" he suggested to Demi.

"Yeah, you've been dating him for over a month, and we still haven't met him yet," Fey chimed in.

"He's been pretty busy. But I'm sure we can work something out," Demi said.

"That's settled then," Fola added.

Demi then watched as he immediately turned his attention to the grill and the spread of food on the table. In addition to the suya that Iben was grilling, there were also sliced red onions and tomatoes, fruit salad, fried rice, and chicken.

"I'm starving! When do we eat?" Fola said, as he grabbed a beer from the cooler and sat down.

Why does he have to be Iben's friend? Demi thought in annoyance.

Soon, they all sat down for dinner.

While they were eating, Fey got Demi to talk about her fashion brand called 'Mila Threads', that she would launch soon. Demi decided to use the trio as a sounding board to practice her speech to potential investors. So after dinner, everyone moved indoors, and she retrieved her laptop from her car. Iben connected it to the flat-screen TV in the living room, and she gave her presentation.

She first talked about her goal and mission as a fashion designer. Then she showed pictures from her first catalog of designs, which seemed to have impressed her parents enough to give her the startup money that they had promised. With some of that money, she and Fey had gone shopping for fabric and sewing equipment so that she could begin sewing samples of the designs. Demi also pointed out that she was currently wearing one of her designs. It was a knee-length summer dress made from a floral Ankara fabric tastefully mixed with complementing chiffon fabric.

She mentioned that her next goal was to source funding for expansion purposes. Right now, she had an online shop, and she was getting a few orders. However, some of her designs were back-ordered as she couldn't keep up with the orders by herself without hiring help. Demi was thinking big. She wanted to hire and train three or four seamstresses and eventually open a store named after her brand, Mila Threads.

Contrary to her plans, her parents wanted her to continue working out of the house for now until she had a steady stream of online orders and a few boutiques willing to stock her designs. Essentially, her parents felt that it was too premature for expansion, so she was trying to do this on her own. To that end, Demi needed to source funds elsewhere.

When her presentation ended, Iben asked, "How are you planning to fund your expansion?"

"For now, just government grants," Demi responded. "I'm scheduled to present my proposal in a few weeks. I'm hoping that I catch the attention of some venture capitalists who will take an interest in my designs. I'm also planning to network like crazy while I'm there."

"Have you thought about entering for Lagos Fashion Week?" Fola asked. He remembered that the Ariris had received invitations to the fashion show for many years now. Neither he nor Iben was interested, so they never attended.

"Yes, that's my dream!" Demi responded excitedly. "That's another reason I need to put my brand out there now. When I first returned from the States a couple of months ago, I watched videos of the fashion show and it was amazing. I didn't realize that Nigeria—and Africa in general, had such a budding fashion industry. I totally want to be a part of it!"

Fola smiled at Demi's energy. Her eyes glowed as she talked about this dream of hers. He was intrigued by her drive and ambition. He raised his hand and said, "You're very talented, Demi. I don't mind being one of your investors."

Demi turned to him and looked him in the eye for a few seconds, checking to see if he was being serious. Although she determined that he was, Demi refused his investment offer directly. "No thanks! I wouldn't want you to have an emergency and then leave me high and dry when it's time to pay up!"

Iben almost laughed. Obviously Demi had not forgiven Fola about being a no-show on their date. Iben was secretly glad that there was someone who could give his friend a run for his money.

"Touché!" Fola said and gave a light chuckle. *What a feisty woman!* he thought in amusement.

Iben then gave Demi some suggestions on improving her presentation. He pointed out that she was too specific on her expenses and numbers, and that a detailed breakdown was unnecessary at this stage. Alternatively, she could use pie charts or graphs to show the percentages of the funds that would be spent on each expense. "Once you make the final changes, you can send me a copy of your proposal. I'd be happy to shop it around to a few acquaintances," he offered.

Fola raised a brow at Iben's comment. *Since when do we have acquaintances in the fashion design business*? he thought to himself.

A smile blossomed on Demi's face. "Thanks, Iben. I really appreciate it."

***

On their way home, Fey asked Demi, "How are you feeling about meeting Fola today?"

Demi sighed, and a frown slowly creased her forehead. "It was… weird." Thanks to Fey's question, she couldn't help but think about the night that she had met him for the first time.

She was at a party that she had attended with her cousin. At some point in the evening, she went to the bar to get a refill of her drink and he was sitting there looking completely aloof and bored, as he flipped through an app on his phone. Sitting next to him at the bar, she snuck a peek to see that he was reading a digital edition of Recoil magazine.

"Is that a Q Honey Badger?" she asked, after seeing that he was reading a review of a firearm.

Fola looked up surprised. "You know about firearms?" he asked.

Demi shrugged. "I had a friend who grew up around them. Whenever we'd hang out, he would talk me to death about all types of firearms and their pros and cons." This friend was technically an ex-boyfriend of hers, but she didn't need to divulge that information to a stranger.

"Do you shoot at the range?" Fola asked curiously.

Demi nodded and took a sip of her drink. "Not recently, but I have in the past. Although, I can still find my way around assembling and disassembling a firearm," she added proudly.

Fola then quizzed her on firearm safety and was impressed at her knowledge. "Most women aren't interested in stuff like this," he finally said.

"Yeah, if I had to choose, I'd rather be deciding between a yard of silk and chiffon fabric than between a Glock and an HK."

Fola chuckled at her analogy.

"So, why are *you* into firearms?" Demi asked curiously.

"I'm in the security department at my job, so it's my business to be up to date on the latest firearm models out here."

Demi nodded. She was curious to know what exactly he did and where he worked, but she didn't want to pry. She'd just met the guy, so if he didn't want to share, she could keep her curiosity in check.

After a moment, Fola said, "So… silk and chiffon. Are you a seamstress?"

Demi made a face. "Ewww, you sound like a dude from the 18th century. Nobody uses that word anymore." Fola chuckled at her comment. Then she added, "I'm a fashion designer."

Fola held out his hand for a handshake. "I'm Fola. It's nice to meet you, fashion designer…"

"Demi," she responded with a smile, returning his handshake. "Nice to meet you too."

They sat quietly for a while, sipping their drinks when Fola smiled impishly and said, "I'd like to talk some more about the difference between chiffon and silk over dinner sometime." This woman intrigued him. In his mind, she was quite the contradiction, and he wanted to get to know how her mind worked. He wanted to know what made her tick.

Demi turned to meet his gaze. For the first time since they had been talking, she took in his facial features. He was a handsome man with arched, expressive eyebrows. He had chocolate brown eyes and lashes that could rival most women's. They drew her in. She smiled and said, "Only if you promise to talk some more about the difference between a rifle and a shotgun."

Fola chuckled. "Deal."

"How are you and Akin doing?" Fey asked, jolting Demi out of her thoughts. "Do you guys even get enough quality time together? He seems so busy all the time."

"I don't mind. I'm busy too. I'm not a clingy type of girlfriend, anyway."

"Do you still like Fola?" Fey asked. She had caught her friend stealing glances at him all night.

"I don't. He's a jerk!"

"But he apologized."

"Whatever."

"Maybe you shouldn't have blocked his number back then. You guys might've been able to patch things up."

"Whose side are you on?"

"Yours," Fey responded. "I just want you to be happy. I remember you seemed excited about meeting him back then. You had called me to tell me all about it. I also know that you were furious and disappointed when he stood you up. But now that you've seen him again, I just wonder how you're feeling."

"I'm happy with the way things are. I'm building my career right now, and the kind of relationship that I have with Akin is just perfect!"

Fey thought that her friend sounded more like she was trying to convince herself. But she said nothing more.

***

"What emergency got *you* to stand-up a woman?" Iben asked curiously after Fey and Demi left.

"Papa needed something done urgently."

"And you couldn't wait until after you called to tell her in person?" Iben thought that would've been more polite than sending a text message.

"There was an issue at one of the warehouses and I had to take the next flight out of town."

Iben acknowledged his response with a nod. "She seemed attracted to you." Then he said in a teasing tone, "To think that she thought you were *really cute*." When Fola shot him a nasty look, Iben immediately raised his hands in surrender and added, "Her words, not mine."

"Whatever! I'm kinda glad she and I didn't get a chance to date. You know my relationships don't last more than a few months. Fey would probably hate me forever and it would just make things awkward between the four of us."

Iben nodded at his reasoning. "I suppose you *could* say she dodged a bullet there... Anyway, what do you think about her business proposal?"

"I think she's talented and has some good, creative designs," Fola replied honestly.

Iben nodded in agreement. "And now that I know you're the reason she's dating some SARS cop, I feel responsible by association, and want to help her." Since his experience at the Port Harcourt warehouse, Iben had developed a distrust of SARS cops. "Let's invest in her business," he declared. "I can see myself buying some of her dresses for Fey. They're pretty good."

"She wants nothing from me," Fola countered.

"That's why we're starting our own venture capital company."

"Seriously?"

"Yeah, you can contribute whatever you were going to give her had she been open to your offer. And you can do it anonymously."

"Sounds good to me," Fola said. Edafe paid him very well and coupled with his savings from his income at Interpol and the EFCC, he had a pretty sizable bank account. Perhaps it was time he dabbled in something other than stocks. "We should also invite more people like Tonna to invest as well. He thinks anything you touch turns to gold anyway, so I'm sure he will agree without hesitation. More money for the pot."

Iben nodded in agreement. Tonna was a friend in their circle who, aside from helping run his family's hotels, also owned a professional car wash and detailing company. He had several locations in the area, and most of his clientele were wealthy with expensive cars. Fey had met him at Vivian's party in Germany when she made her outlandish announcement about being Iben's fiancée.

The conversation between the two men soon turned into a business development session where they hashed out the framework of their new venture capital company. At the end of their discussion, they each had action items to take care of getting their new company registered and functional.

On his way home that night, Fola thought about Demi. Although he hadn't given it much thought since it happened, seeing her today and her reaction to being stood up by him made him feel bad. He supposed Iben was right and he should've called her instead. Back then, he only had the idea to do so a couple of days later. But when he tried reaching out to her, she never responded to his messages or returned his calls. So, he had just moved on.

Although he found Demi attractive, he wasn't interested in a long-term relationship. So, it was best if he kept things platonic between them. His career choices didn't afford such luxuries, anyway. He doubted there was a woman out there who could deal with his constant traveling and disappearance, as it related to his job. Aside from that, Fola thought about how boldly Fey had handled Edafe's assessment and admitted that Fey was even scarier than Vivian. He certainly didn't want to get on her bad side. He had also witnessed her ire towards Iben in the past, and he didn't want any parts of that.

Looking at the situation with rose-colored glasses, he thought it was a good thing that Demi was now dating someone else. Without worrying about any weirdness, he would get to know her as a friend. He looked forward to the opportunity to understand that mind of hers, which got him intrigued the first time they met. He had always wondered if he should have studied Psychology in college. He enjoyed reading people and trying to understand their motivations. One way he did this was by teasing people where appropriate to push their buttons. Demi's personality was one that he wanted to learn and include in his mental dossier.

24 | Feelings Change

The following Saturday, the group of four assembled to have their weekly dinner get-together. This time, it was at a restaurant. Fey and Iben arrived together and were the first to get there. Next was Fola and then Demi. When she got to the table, everyone looked at her quizzically.

She knew the question on their minds, so she said, "Akin is on his way. He should be here in about ten minutes."

Exactly ten minutes later, they all saw a young man who looked to be about twenty-five years old walking towards their table. Demi got up to hug him before he sat down at the only empty seat next to her.

"Everyone, this is my boyfriend, Akin," she said introducing him. Then, one by one, they took turns introducing themselves to him.

Akin smiled politely as he took turns shaking hands with them. "It's nice to meet you all," he said.

Iben signaled for a waiter. When he arrived at their table, they ordered drinks and their dinners.

"It's nice to finally put a face to the name," Fey said. "I know it's been a while, but thank you for saving my bestie."

Akin smiled and said, "It was nothing. I was just doing my job. Besides, thanks to the guy who stood her up, I gained an amazing woman as my girlfriend." He looked at Demi, who met his gaze and smiled.

"Flattery will get you nowhere," she joked.

Akin chuckled. Then he added, "Demi mentioned that you also just returned from the States. How has it been since? Are you settling in alright?"

"Pretty good. I have an amazing support system in these guys over here." She gestured to Iben, Fola, and Demi. "So it's made the transition pretty seamless."

Akin nodded. "So, Iben, what do you do for a living?" Akin asked, trying to keep the conversation going. He could tell from Iben's body language that he was probably Fey's boyfriend.

"I'm a businessman," was Iben's brief reply.

"That's vague. What kind of business?" Akin shot back.

"Akin…" Demi chided, nudging him.

"I'm sorry, Iben. I can't seem to turn off the detective in me sometimes."

"No worries," Iben responded with a small smile, not bothering to answer Akin's question. So far, he didn't like the guy at all.

"So, how exactly did you figure out that Demi was in trouble that night?" Fola asked. He had been quietly studying Akin since he arrived.

"You didn't tell them?" he asked Demi, surprised.

"I gave them the cliff notes."

"And I missed class that day. Would you indulge me, please?" Fola pressed with a smile.

Akin shrugged. "I was on a stakeout monitoring a gang of armed robbers that were on the department's watch list. It just so happened that Demi was their unfortunate target that night."

"That's interesting," Fola said, rubbing his chin. "Why would you be staking out that area? It's not known for such crimes."

Akin stared at him before he said, "We received an anonymous tip."

"I see…"

Demi chimed in and said, "Anyway, that's all in the past, Fola."

Although Fola had introduced himself earlier, now that he heard Demi mention his name again, Akin had a thought. "You're not the same Fola who put her in danger that night, are you?"

Fola chuckled. "Cupid, at your service!" he said smugly.

Fola and Akin had a staring contest for a good five seconds before Akin finally spoke. "I hope this isn't awkward for you, Fola," he said, as he put his arm around Demi possessively. Demi stiffened at his sudden touch, but quickly covered it up with a smile.

Fola didn't miss her reaction, though. He met Demi's gaze and said calmly, "Not at all. Demi and I talked things through. We're adults and know how to keep our emotions in check."

Whose emotions are in check? Akin thought to himself. He wasn't sure if Fola meant that he was still interested in dating Demi, or that she still had an interest in Fola. "You didn't mention that you had made contact with him again," Akin said, turning his attention to Demi.

"Didn't think it was important. Besides, I knew you'd meet him today."

Akin looked displeased but said nothing more to Demi. "So what do *you* do for a living, Fola?"

"Iben and I work together."

"Ah, *businessmen*," Akin responded dismissively. In his mind, he concluded that Iben and Fola were probably small-time hustlers who dress up and use their good looks to impress and trick women. He'd have to warn Demi about them later and press her for more details on what they did for a living.

Just then, their meals arrived, cutting the tension that was already building at the table. As everyone started eating, the restaurant's manager came to their table. He introduced himself and asked if everyone was satisfied with their meals. He had also brought along two expensive bottles of wine for their table. "Mr. Ariri, it's a pleasure to have you dine with us tonight. Please enjoy these complimentary bottles on the house."

"Thank you, Mr. Shotemi. It's nice to see you again," Iben said.

The manager smiled and said, "My regards to Chief Ariri."

Iben gave a small smile. "I'll be sure to deliver your message."

After the manager left, Akin had a look of surprise on his face. "You're Iben Ariri? Of Ariri Corporation?" he blurted out.

Iben nodded as he poured some wine in Fey's glass. "This pairs well with the seafood meal you ordered, babe," he said, turning his attention to her.

"Thanks, babe," Fey responded.

Akin sat there dumbfounded. These guys weren't small-time businessmen at all. These guys were some of the 'big boys' of the business world. He suddenly felt mortified by his attitude toward them. He looked from Iben to Fola, and he could tell that they weren't too impressed with him either. If he had known who they were, he would have acted differently. He suddenly went from feeling superior to feeling inferior in the presence of these wealthy and affluent men.

"Why didn't you tell me we were hanging out with the heir to the Ariri conglomerate?" he whispered to Demi.

"I didn't think it was important."

Fey, who was sitting next to her best friend, caught their whispers and wondered what the couple talked about when they hung out. Akin didn't seem to know much of anything about them.

After a few minutes into their quiet meal, Akin spoke again. "I watched the press conference when you took over Starlight Shipping. Congratulations on the acquisition."

Iben looked up from his meal. "Thank you." He could tell that Akin's attitude seemed to have changed towards him a bit, now that he knew who he was. This increased his dislike of Akin. But as usual, Iben had his poker face on.

"I watched the press conference about the latest scandal in the SARS unit of the police force. What are your thoughts on that, Akin?" Fola chimed in. He was happy to finally get a chance to push this guy's buttons.

His question caught Akin by surprise, and he almost choked on the food in his mouth. After composing himself, he responded. "It's rather unfortunate. There are always bad eggs in any agency."

"True... I hope the internal investigation weeds out the corrupt agents. Colluding with armed robbers to blackmail politicians and people of affluence is atrocious. The mastermind, Terence Ogochi, needs to go to jail at all costs."

Akin stopped eating. He met Fola's gaze and said, "Agreed. I'm sure the justice system will not fail in that regard."

Fola nodded and continued eating his food.

Akin couldn't help but be annoyed at Fola's question and comments about the SARS unit where he worked. Was he alluding that he was also corrupt? How much did these guys think they knew about him? Just because they were rich didn't mean their hands were clean. He dropped a few hints in that regard. "I've heard that Starlight Shipping has a good relationship with SARS agents in some parts of the country."

Without skipping a beat, Fola responded with one of his signature grins. "Yes, we need all the assistance that the police can offer. Would you be interested in some of our engagements?"

Akin glared at Fola. He had heard rumors. He also knew that many rich people would hire the police for security reasons. Why the hell did this guy think he would be interested in that? Was Fola looking down on him?

Akin signaled for his bill. He was done here. Meeting Demi's friends was a bad idea. When the waiter came, he yelled at the guy for taking so long.

A short while later, he got up to leave. "I need to get back to work. It was nice to meet you all," he said with a forced smile. Demi stood up to see him off.

When the couple was out of earshot, Iben said, "That was interesting…"

"I don't like him," Fey complained, voicing everyone's thoughts. She especially didn't like that Akin was unnecessarily rude to the Waitstaff. She'd been a waitress at restaurants before, and she despised customers who took their anger out on the people serving them.

Fola shared a look with Iben but said nothing.

Demi, who had walked Akin outside, said to him, "Thanks for coming to meet my friends."

Akin turned to her and said in annoyance, "I wish you had warned me that your ex was going to be here tonight."

"He's not my ex. We never dated." Demi said flatly.

"But he likes you still, yeah? I don't want you hanging out with him."

"Iben is my bestie's boyfriend. And Fola is *his* best friend. They're like brothers. What do you expect me to do? Tell Iben not to invite him to get-togethers?"

Akin sighed defeatedly. "Let's talk about this later. Come, I'll drop you off at home."

"Thanks, but I drove tonight. I can't leave my car here. Besides, Fey is riding with me. We live together, remember?"

"So you're going back in there to your ex? So you can continue your *double date*?" Akin spat angrily.

"Seriously?!" Demi said, getting frustrated. She turned to leave.

Akin quickly grabbed her arm to stop her. "I'm sorry, sweetie," he said. "I just can't help but be jealous in this situation… Any man would be."

Demi stopped her retreat and said. "I understand. But you need to trust me."

"Alright." He then pulled her into a hug and kissed her on her cheek. "I have to go. I'll talk to you later."

"Okay, good night."

***

On their way home, Demi asked Fey a question. "What do you think of Akin?" When Fey said nothing, she added, "I want the truth."

"I don't like him for you," Fey said without hesitation. "He's very outspoken—which is not a bad thing. But he can't seem to read the room, and he is quick to throw around his sense of superiority." She thought back to how Akin had belittled Iben's occupation as a businessman until he found out that his last name was Ariri. Even if Iben weren't an Ariri, everyone takes pride in what they do for a living, and Akin was wrong to regard him as inferior.

"He was angry about Fola being there tonight," Demi confessed.

"I don't blame him for feeling that way. Iben did the same thing when he invited me to Vivian's birthday party last year. It's not a good feeling to be in the dark about an ex."

Demi sighed. "I know it was wrong of me. But I kinda just wanted to see what his reaction would be. I don't feel the spark anymore, so I hoped it'd wake him up or something if he felt like there was competition."

"Are you feeling this way because of Fola?"

"No. I've been feeling this way for a while now. At first, everything was great. But I started noticing that whenever we would hang out, he'd flip out on people in a heartbeat. Waiters, cashiers, pretty much anyone in the service industry. He has a temper and I keep wondering, when will it be my turn to get a tongue lashing? It's not that I can't match him in verbal combat, but I don't like the feeling that I'm just one moment away from his anger. That's the real reason I haven't asked him to meet you guys.

"Relationships have difficulties, so I don't expect everything to be perfect. But I feel like there's a part of him that he's hiding from me. To be honest, we haven't gone out on a date in a few weeks. I know he's busy, so I don't mind. But I don't miss him. I am almost relieved that he doesn't seem to find time to hang out. Isn't that a problem itself?"

"I guess that's why you guys came off as platonic friends playing at being boyfriend and girlfriend," Fey said.

Demi chuckled at her friend's candidness. "Sadly, it looks like it's not going to work out between him and I. At this point, I'm just waiting for the wheels to fall off."

"This will be your shortest relationship ever."

Demi sighed. "Yeah…"

***

The following Saturday, Fey finally went to pick out a car at the used car dealership that Victor Oke recommended. She proudly drove out of the dealership in the first car she had ever owned, a two-year-old Toyota Camry. It felt nice to not have to rely on others to get her to wherever she needed to be. Although she still had a lot to learn in terms of navigating around Lagos, at least she was comfortable getting around where she lived and worked.

The next day was Iben's birthday, and Fey planned to surprise him by showing up at his house early in the morning. Iben had invited some friends over to celebrate later in the evening, so Fey wanted to spend some time with him first. Then, she would go back to pick up Demi in time for the party.

When she arrived at his house, Mobi met her at the door. "Good morning, Miss Fey. I have everything prepared for you in the kitchen."

"Thanks, Mobi," she said, as they walked to the kitchen together.

Alice, who was also waiting in the kitchen, said, "Miss Fey, I'll be here in case you need anything."

"Thanks, Alice."

Fey had brought most of the cooking ingredients with her, except for things like cooking oil, salt, etc. Soon, she busied herself with making Nigerian style pancakes, omelets, sausages, and a fruit bowl. Alice and Mobi, who were on standby in case she ended up ruining the meal, were instead impressed that everything turned out well. When Fey was done, she asked them to perform a taste-test. The food turned out to be good and their impression of her improved.

Felix, the gardener, came into the kitchen as soon as Fey left with the food tray. "So, how did it go?" he asked excitedly.

"She cooked a lovely meal for Master Iben. He's lucky to have her. What an upgrade from that witch, Vivian!" Alice responded happily.

"True talk?" Felix asked in disbelief. "I'm impressed!"

"She will be an excellent madam of the house in the future!" Alice declared.

"Now that you mention it, I haven't seen a ring on her finger yet. What is taking the boss so long to seal the deal?"

"I wonder, O!" Alice lamented. "He is not getting younger. Isn't he celebrating his 27th birthday today? If he's not careful, someone else will snatch her away."

"Stop your gossiping!" Mobi chided. These people talked too much, and he always had to get them focused. "We have much to get ready for the party tonight."

Meanwhile, Fey went upstairs and quietly opened the door to Iben's room. As expected, he was still asleep. She tiptoed to the bed, placed the tray on his bedside table, and kissed him on the lips.

His eyes immediately flew open. When he saw that it was Fey, he lifted his hands to touch the sides of her face. "Hey..." he said in a low voice.

"Happy birthday, Iben."

He smiled. "Thanks, babe."

"I made you breakfast," Fey announced excitedly. "I hope you're hungry."

Iben sat up and looked at the tray at his bedside. Then he slowly directed his unblinking gaze at her.

"What is it?" Fey asked, concerned. *Wait, why is he looking at me as if I'm breakfast?*

Answering her question, Iben said, "I was having a sexy dream about you before you woke me up. So… the only thing I'm hungry for now… is you."

Fey chuckled. "Iben Ariri. Get your mind out the gutters," she teased.

"If the gutters lead to heaven—" He paused as his gaze slowly traveled from her face to the rest of her body before he continued, "then I'd rather stay there."

Fey was speechless. *This guy's flirting and seduction skills are at an all-time high this morning,* she thought to herself. However, his words and the look in his eyes had stoked the flames of desire within her.

Iben moved closer, placed his hand on her thigh and whispered in her ear, "How about I show you what happened in my dream?" Then his hand slowly slid up under her dress as he gently kissed her neck. Fey closed her eyes and moaned as his warm hand continued its caress up her thigh. She surrendered to him as he kissed her deeply and slowly laid her on the bed.

Sometime later, after the couple was done with their lovemaking, Iben said cheekily, "Now that we have successfully worked up an appetite, let's eat breakfast!"

Fey rolled her eyes at him. "It's cold now. I'll go warm it up."

"What will you tell Mobi and Alice is the reason the food is cold, hmmm?"

At Fey's panicked expression, Iben burst into laughter. *She's so much fun to tease.*

Realizing that Iben was poking fun at her, Fey smacked his arm. "Fine, eat it cold then! All of it!" she said in a huff, before storming off to the bathroom.

How adorable, Iben thought to himself after she closed the bathroom door. He then turned his attention to his breakfast. His woman had put a lot of effort into it, so he showed his appreciation by eating it all.

Around noon, Fola came over. While he and Iben talked business, Fey busied herself with watching TV in the living room until she dozed off. A few hours later, she received a call from Demi, waking her up.

"Aren't you coming to pick me up?"

"Sorry, I fell asleep," she said groggily. "I'll be there in about 30 minutes."

After she hung up, she told Iben she had to leave to pick up Demi.

"I'll do it," Fola offered.

Fey and Iben both looked at him in surprise.

"Are you sure?" Fey asked.

"Yeah, give me your address."

"Okay."

After he left, Fey was going to text Demi that Fola would pick her up instead. But then she changed her mind. *Let's see what those two make of it*, she thought mischievously to herself.

Iben, who was watching her, said with a smile, "Are you thinking what I'm thinking?"

Fey nodded, returning his smile.

***

When Fola arrived at the Oke residence, he parked and honked the horn. A few minutes later, Demi came outside. To her surprise, the vehicle waiting wasn't Fey's silver Camry like she had expected. It was a black Rezvani Tank SUV. Leaning against the hood in a leisurely manner was Fola.

Demi stopped in her tracks. "Did Fey put you up to this?"

"No, I volunteered," he said with a smile. He walked over to open the passenger door for her.

"I'm going to kill that girl when I see her," she muttered through clenched teeth as she got in the SUV.

Fola got in and began driving. The drive was quiet for the first ten minutes. Fola spoke when he noticed something in his rearview mirror. "I need to stop at the supermarket real quick. I hope you don't mind."

Demi shrugged in response.

Five minutes later, he pulled up to the parking lot of a nearby supermarket. Then he turned to Demi and said, "Can I bother you to go inside and get something for me?"

Demi shot him a sidelong glance. "Do I look like your errand girl?"

Fola smiled sheepishly. "Actually, Fey asked me to stop and get her some pocky sticks on the way back. But, I have no idea what that is. It might be quicker if you went and got it. Here's my card."

"Fine," she said, snatching the card from him.

After Demi stepped inside the store, Fola also got out and walked towards a car parked on the other side of the street. The driver had a newspaper hiding his face, so Fola went to the driver's side and knocked on the window. The person looked up surprised before rolling down the window.

"This is a dick move, even for a douchebag like you, Detective Akin," Fola said with a frown. "How long have you been following her around?"

"It's none of your business!"

"It is when it's my vehicle you're tailing!"

Akin ignored his comment. "So you guys are going out on a date?" he asked with a snarl.

"That's none of *your* business!" Fola shot back. "You know, she and I were never together. But now, thanks to your behavior last week, I think I might have a shot," Fola said tauntingly.

"You bastard!"

Fola sneered at him. "If you keep following me, I'll have no choice but to tell her what you're up to. So fuck off and go do some *real* detective work that our taxes are paying for!"

If looks could kill, Fola would be dead many times over by now, as Akin glared at him. Fola noticed that Demi had come out of the store so he snapped, "Beat it!"

Akin started his car and drove off angrily.

When Demi came out of the store, she walked to Fola's SUV, but he wasn't in it. She looked around and saw him crossing the street back to where she was. She gave him a questioning look.

"Sorry, I went to say hi to someone I know." He gave one of his dazzling smiles.

Demi rolled her eyes and got in the vehicle.

Once he was seated, Fola looked inside the plastic bag. He saw that there were about twenty packs of pocky sticks in it and raised a questioning brow.

"You didn't specify what flavor, so I got all of them," Demi said with a smirk.

"Oh..."

A moment later, Fola was back on the road to Iben's.

"Demi," he said after a few minutes, breaking the silence between them. "I want to properly apologize for standing you up a few months ago. I really had an emergency that night, but I should've called you as soon as I knew I would not be able to make it. That would've saved you from being targeted by hoodlums. You could've had your car stolen or worse, lost your life that night. I feel terrible and I hope you can forgive me."

Demi turned to look at Fola as he spoke. This was the most serious he'd been since she met him. She nodded, accepting his genuine apology.

Relieved, Fola asked, "So, we're friends?"

"Maybe," she said, looking out the window.

"Fair enough." He hoped that she would at least stop giving him death glares and sassy remarks every time he spoke to her.

As soon as they arrived at Iben's house, Fola went to look for him. Some of Iben's friends had arrived, so he had to wait a few minutes before he could pull him away to talk to him. When they were in the privacy of the study, Fola recounted the afternoon's events regarding Detective Akin.

"We should monitor him," Iben suggested after hearing what Fola had to say. His instincts had been right about that guy.

"Already on it. I'll also have someone looking out for Demi as well."

Iben nodded in agreement. Then he smirked. "And you're doing all this *solely* for your sister-in-law, right?"

Fola just smiled.

Later, Fey cornered Fola with the bag of pocky sticks. "*Apparently*, I asked for these?" She didn't even like the coated biscuit sticks.

Fola smiled sheepishly. "I had to improvise."

Thinking that Fola had done that to improve his non-relationship with Demi, she chuckled and said, "I hope it was worth it."

"Yes!"

25 | Unveiled

After Akin got caught while stalking Demi, he went straight home. As soon as he entered his apartment, he hurled his keys against the wall and suddenly punched the center table in his living room. Subsequently, every piece of furniture either got a taste of his fist or a kick. A few minutes later, when his rage had calmed down somewhat, he sat down to think.

How did things become this way between him and Demi? Was it because he had been neglectful of her recently? It wasn't his wish to push her away. Life just conspired against them.

He thought back to when he first met her. As his team closed in on the situation that night, he could see that despite being frightened, she put up a brave front while she was held up by the carjackers. After the ordeal was over and he and his men had subdued the robbers, he was further impressed by her calmness. She was visibly shaken, but she kept it together. Captivated by her beauty, he was drawn to her. He had saved her phone number under the guise of the investigation so that he could ask her out on a date later on. Things were going well between them until Terence Ogochi got arrested and was charged for colluding with SARS agents to kidnap and blackmail the wealthy.

While people like Iben Ariri were born with silver spoons, Akin, on the other hand, had to struggle and hustle to get by. Back when he joined the police force, he had graduated from college for almost a year but could not find a job. His only other options were becoming a criminal or starvation.

Unfortunately, the police force paid him peanuts for a monthly salary and it wasn't adequate for reaching the goals he had set for himself. Yes, a detective made more than a regular street officer, but from his perspective, the difference was almost marginal. He couldn't even afford his flat in the decent neighborhood where he lived if he relied solely on his police force salary.

Goals required money, and he was always looking for an opportunity to gain the extra cash he needed. Soon after making detective rank, he found out about Terence Ogochi and his blackmail schemes.

After Terence selected a wealthy target, he'd meticulously monitor their daily movements. Once he had mastered their schedule, he'd have them kidnapped for ransom. The easiest targets were the wives and children of his mark. Sometimes, cops would assist in the kidnapping to ensure that the hostages were relatively safe and weren't at the mercy of Terence's trigger-happy goons. If people started getting killed, it would draw too much heat towards everyone involved.

Their goal was simple. Separating the rich from some of their money.

As Terence's operations became a growing concern in the community of wealthy people, naturally several investigations were initiated to figure out who was behind the kidnappings and blackmails. Whenever the SARS agents working with Terence caught wind of this, they would tip him off if they were getting close or if there was going to be a raid on his latest hideout. Other times, they would hide or destroy incriminating evidence.

Terence would, in turn, tip off the cops by letting them know which gangs or groups of criminals were planning some kind of heist in their jurisdiction. This gave the impression that they were doing their jobs, as they had more successful raids and arrests than many other SARS installments in their area. In fact, the *anonymous* tip that Akin and his team received on the night when Demi was carjacked came from Terence.

Terence's network of SARS agents was extensive, and Akin soon joined them. About a month after he started dating Demi, he found out that her father was a judge. That wasn't a problem until Terence's arrest and he found out that her father was going to preside over the case at the Lagos High Court.

It wasn't that he was afraid of being linked to Terence. He was smart enough to have kept his dealings anonymous between them. Only the other cops knew that he was involved. Even if they pointed fingers at him, there was no evidence. He always insisted on being paid in cash so there was no electronic paper trail in case things went bust and the

EFCC got involved. He also always wore a mask whenever they had to supervise a kidnapping, so he wasn't worried about being identified by the victims, Terence or his minions.

That was not the case for some of the other corrupt cops though, especially the ones who were in direct contact with Terence. From Akin's perspective, many of them were relatively good men who would go down unnecessarily. Some of these guys had families to take care of and were his comrades who had had his back for the last couple of years.

Akin's chief concern was that if Terence went to jail, his money stream would dry up. He was tempted to use Demi to blackmail her father into judging in Terence's favor. If he couldn't get him off, he at least had to get a reduced sentence. He struggled with this thought since he liked Demi and she seemed to like him back, despite the difference in their socio-economic statuses. The guilt was eating away at him, so he had unconsciously started distancing himself from her. But now, it looked like he was losing her to some rich guy. He laughed bitterly. *It always comes down to money at the end of the day.*

Seeing her out and about with Fola helped solidify his decision. He was certain she would not be his for very much longer, so he might as well go all out. She deserved it anyway, now that she was allowing herself to be seduced away by Fola's money.

With these thoughts, Akin started formulating his plans.

***

A few days later, Demi and Fey sat in the living room watching TV when Demi received a text message from Akin. It read: *'Hey sweetie, I've missed you. Let's go out to dinner this coming weekend.'*

She passed her phone to Fey so that she could read it. "What do you want to do?" Fey asked.

Demi sighed. "I think I'll just use this opportunity to end things with him."

"Are you sure?"

Demi nodded. *'Sure. I'm free on Saturday,'* she responded.

'Great. Let's meet at 7:00 PM. I'll send you the address to the restaurant before then.'

'Cool.'

***

Soon, it was the night of the dinner date between Demi and Akin.

She drove to the address he sent to her. It was a restaurant in a quiet cul-de-sac with three different compounds. Aside from the restaurant, were two story-buildings which looked to be office buildings that were no doubt unoccupied on a Saturday night. Demi imagined that the restaurant was probably very busy during the week, as the office workers in those buildings likely came to eat lunch there. As soon as she arrived, she was ushered to the garden-style outdoor seating area. Akin was seated at a table waiting for her. He stood up and hugged her when she reached the table.

"You look great, sweetie," he said admiringly. She was wearing a sleeveless, knee-length, ankara wrap dress, belted at the waist.

"Thanks," Demi responded with a smile. "It's one of my designs."

"Wow. You're really talented. How's your fashion business doing, by the way?"

"Pretty good. I have lots of orders, and I'm trying to expand. I'm working towards getting a storefront soon."

"You're such a go-getter! That's one of the things I admire about you." Akin reached out and held Demi's hand that was laying on the table as he spoke.

At his touch, Demi lifted her eyes to meet his. He smiled, and she returned his smile before looking away. This reminded her of their dates earlier on in their relationship. *This guy is being very charming tonight.*

Their food soon arrived and during their meal, they chatted lightheartedly. Akin was a bit of a jokester when he was relaxed, and tonight, he made Demi laugh so much with his stories and commentary about certain things that happened at work, and with his friends. Throughout the entire meal, he was very mild-mannered. Demi thought he must be in a great mood. He didn't even yell at the server when he forgot to bring the extra napkins he had requested. Perhaps his erratic behavior in the past was because of stress.

After they finished eating, Akin suggested a walk around the gardens. It was a very romantic evening, and Demi thought to herself that it was a shame. If only he'd been doing this before today, she might not be feeling differently about their relationship.

As they walked, Akin said, "Demi, I'm sorry I've been somewhat distant and unavailable these past few weeks. Lately, my job has been very stressful and demanding, so I haven't found the time to spend with you. But things are looking up at work, so I invited you out tonight to make up for everything."

Demi smiled and said, "That's okay, Akin. I understand. I've been busy myself, so…" she let herself trail off. *Maybe I'm being rash and I should just give him another chance*, Demi thought to herself.

"I was going to ask you to dinner last Saturday, but when I called, you didn't pick up the phone. Were you busy or something on that day?" It was the day he had an encounter with Fola, so he was curious to hear what Demi would say. Obviously, Fola didn't tell her he caught him following her. If he did, she wouldn't have come out to have dinner with him. Regardless, he wanted to see if she would be honest that she was on a date with another man.

Demi didn't see the sneer on his lips. She looked thoughtful for a moment before she said, "Last Saturday was Iben's birthday, so Fey and I attended his party in the late afternoon. I'm not sure how I missed your call, but if I'd known, we could've at least met for breakfast or something."

What a lying bitch! Akin thought. Why did he think she would be honest with him, anyway? Despite being on his best behavior tonight, she still didn't have the common decency to be forthright with a simple question. Well, it didn't matter. Tonight, she was going to get what she deserved. Just then, his phone beeped. He excused himself to check it and the message he had been stalling for since they finished dinner had come in.

'We're ready. You can bring her out now.'

When he went back to where Demi was standing, he held her hand and said, "Come, it's getting late. Let me walk you to your car."

Demi looked at him quizzically at the abrupt change. But because he was smiling at her, she said, "Okay," and followed his lead.

They walked back towards the entrance of the restaurant. When they got to her car, Demi leaned against the door before she said, "Thanks for inviting me to dinner, Akin. I had a great time." Before her arrival that evening, she was determined to break up with Akin. But she was now feeling undecided and considering giving their relationship another chance.

Akin smiled. "I had a good time as well. Thanks for coming out." He moved to hug her when suddenly, a black sedan drove up and stopped right behind her car, blocking it.

Demi and Akin stopped talking and watched as a masked guy suddenly emerged from the car with a gun pointed at them.

Demi's heart almost leaped out of her chest. *Not again!* she thought in despair. *Why does this keep happening to me?* Frozen on the spot from fear, Demi watched as the masked gunman pointed the gun at Akin's head.

"Get on the ground," he said. Akin did as he was told and lay down flat on the concrete with his head pressed down by the gunman. The masked man then turned to look at Demi. Just as he was about to point his gun at her, a gunshot went off and he fell to the ground, dead.

Demi screamed.

Akin, who was lying on the ground, was initially smiling internally as everything about the kidnapping was going as planned. He had orchestrated things this way to make it believable and to ensure that nobody would later question his involvement. If the gunman only attacked Demi and he was there but didn't help, suspicions would arise. The plan was that once her father did as they wanted, they would release her from their custody unharmed.

However, when he heard the gunshot, his heart almost stopped in his chest. His first thought was his masked accomplice had accidentally shot Demi. However, when he saw the guy fall instead, he knew something wasn't right. Wondering what went wrong, he stood up slowly and saw that the driver of the sedan and the other person in the car looked just as shocked as he was. Recognizing that an unknown party had breached their operation, the black sedan took off, leaving Akin standing there bewildered.

Realizing that their operation had gone belly-up, Akin immediately turned his attention to figuring out who made the shot. Suddenly a gray SUV pulled up behind Demi's car. Again, someone stepped out of it with a gun pointed at him. *What the hell?* Akin thought to himself when he saw who it was.

"Fola!" he blurted out. "Who's stalking who, now?" He then started moving towards Demi who had been sitting on the floor since the gunshot went off.

Fola immediately racked the slide of his gun. "Don't you dare move any closer to her!"

"How dare you point a gun at a police officer!" Akin shot back.

Fola then reached into his pocket and flashed his officer's badge.

Akin's eyes widened in shock. "You're with the EFCC?"

Fola nodded and said, "Hands behind your head, and get down on your knees. If you make any funny moves, you'll just be giving me a reason to put a bullet in your head!" His voice was cold and the look in his eyes made Akin's skin crawl.

Akin did as he was told. His mind was in turmoil. He thought this guy was just someone working for Ariri Corporation. But instead, he was with the EFCC? *What the fuck?* he cursed internally as Fola walked over and handcuffed him.

"Are you going to arrest me? I've done nothing wrong. Shouldn't you be chasing after the accomplices of the dead guy who ran off?"

Fola ignored Akin and holstered his gun before approaching Demi. She was still sitting on the ground in a fetal position with her eyes closed and her hands covering her ears. He squatted next to her and called her softly, "Demi...Demi..." When she didn't respond, Fola gently picked her up in his arms. Feeling his warmth, Demi opened her eyes and saw that it was a familiar face.

"Fola..." she whispered before she buried her face in his chest and let the tears flow. Fola stilled and hugged her close while she sobbed.

Akin on the other hand was glaring daggers at them in their intimate embrace. His jealousy was so intense that he didn't even think to consider the effects of the night's events on Demi's mind and body.

By the time she calmed down, several police cars had arrived at the scene and she finally noticed her surroundings. "Why is Akin handcuffed?" she asked.

"He's the one who set you up to be kidnapped."

"Is that true?" she asked in disbelief.

Akin chuckled. "I won't be admitting to anything. But you two look very comfortable in each other's arms. Please continue. Pay no mind to *your boyfriend* over here."

Suddenly self-conscious, Demi slowly moved from Fola's embrace. Fola frowned and signaled to one of the officers, who then brought the two accomplices who had run off in the black sedan. Akin's face turned sour immediately.

When Fola asked, "Who put you guys up to this?", both men pointed at Akin.

Demi's heart sank. "Akin, why?"

"You were going to leave me for him, weren't you?" Akin said with contempt.

"No. But you were going to kidnap me for that?!"

Fola cut in. "He was going to kidnap you as leverage to force your father to judge a case in his favor. He's one of the corrupt cops working with Terence Ogochi."

Akin frowned at the mention of him being a corrupt cop. He didn't see himself as one.

Sometime later, after giving her statement to the police, Demi called her father to let him know what happened. As expected, he was shocked and worried. She assured him she was fine and that she would come home as soon as she could leave. However, when she got behind the wheel, her nerves got the best of her as she was still shaken from the night's events. Fola offered to drive her back home in his SUV, but her father insisted on coming to pick her up instead.

While waiting for him, Demi sat in her car and recounted the events of the evening to Fey, who had called when Victor told her what happened. Fey thought it was ironic that last time, Akin saved Demi because of Fola's neglect. And today, Fola saved her from Akin.

In the meantime, Fola exchanged words with Akin, who was waiting to be transported to jail along with his accomplices.

"Everyone in your department was secretly being monitored by my team for a while now. The first time I met you, your reaction and attitude towards my mention of Terence Oguchi's case put you on my radar. And when I caught you stalking Demi, you moved to the *top* of my list. Unlike you, I'm good at my job and I easily figured out your plans tonight. I have phone conversations, text messages, cash exchanges, and video recordings putting you at the hot center of tonight's operation. You're going away for a long time."

Realizing that he couldn't deny his involvement in Demi's attempted kidnapping, Akin said, "Your accusation that I tried to kidnap Demi for Terence's sake holds no water. You have no proof that I was ever involved with him."

"Yes, you weren't the person at the forefront of your department's dealings with Oguchi. You were pretty smart and made it difficult for any electronic transactions to be linked back to you, unlike the rest of the simpletons at your station. But—the moment you brought Demi into your plans because of your *jealousy*, you exposed yourself. And all I had to do was connect the dots."

Akin snickered and gave a cynical smile as he said, "I suppose it takes a double agent like yourself to know or catch one like me."

Fola smirked. He knew he was referring to the fact that he was also working with the Ariris. "My surname may not be Ariri, but Edafe and Iben are like my father and brother. Their business is my business."

***

A week after Demi's attempted kidnapping, Victor and Remi invited Fola to their house for dinner. They wanted to thank him for rescuing their daughter from Detective Akin's scheming. At first, Remi was hesitant. She felt that Akin ended up being a dangerous person to be around their daughter. What if Fola turned out to be the same way? It wasn't until Fey and Demi explained that he was Iben's best friend did she relax a bit and agree to have him come to their house.

After dinner, Demi walked Fola to his vehicle.

"Thanks for indulging my parents and coming out tonight," she said.

Fola smiled. "No need to thank me. The delicious food was worth the trip."

Demi chuckled and then said in a serious tone, "Also, thanks for rescuing me the other day. I can't imagine how things might've turned out if you weren't there that night."

"Don't mention it, Demi. You're a very important person to my sister-in-law... And to me as well."

Hearing his last few words, Demi looked Fola in the eye and said, "I'd like to treat you to dinner as a thank you."

Fola raised a brow and asked, "Is the Oke family secretly trying to fatten me up by constantly inviting me to dinners?"

Demi chuckled. "Don't be silly... I promise I won't be a no-show."

Fola sucked in a breath. "Are you ever going to let that go?"

"Only if you say 'yes' to dinner."

He agreed without hesitation. "Yes."

"Does next Friday work for you?"

"Yes."

"Can I have your number?" Demi asked.

"I thought you already have my number."

"I blocked it and then deleted it from my contacts a while back."

"Damn! You were just like 'burn all bridges to hell' huh?" For some reason that he couldn't explain, Fola was hurt that she had completely written him off.

Demi chuckled. "I couldn't help it. I was so angry at you back then. It was the only thing I could do to get back at you and stay true to myself."

Fola nodded in understanding. She gave him her phone to enter his number. After returning it to her, he looked at the time and said, "It's late—you should get back inside."

Demi said, "Here's to the start of being friends."

Fola smiled and shook the hand she was holding out. When he didn't let go right away, Demi lifted her eyes to meet his. He smiled and said, "Good night, Demi."

A smile tugged at her lips, "Good night, Fola."

She turned to go back in the house as their handshake relaxed, but he didn't let go completely and his index finger linked with hers. Their eyes met again with Fola wearing a sheepish smile. *What the heck am I doing?* he thought to himself. For some reason, he didn't want to leave, and he didn't want to let go of her hand.

Demi looked at their linked fingers and smiled. "I'm looking forward to our dinner next Friday."

"Me too," Fola said before he finally let go.

When she got back into the house, her parents were waiting in the living room.

"That boy Fola seems to be a decent guy. But, your mother and I can introduce you to some nice boys who aren't policemen. Okay?" Victor said. He had noticed during dinner that his daughter seemed to like Fola. But he too didn't want a repeat of what happened with Detective Akin.

Demi glared at her dad before she turned to her mom and said, "Tell your husband to *stop* trying to set me up with someone. Stay *out* of my love life or I'm going to move out!" Then she turned to her father, smiled facetiously, and said, "Good night!" before walking off to her room.

Victor's mouth was ajar as he watched his daughter storm off. "What did I do wrong?" he asked his wife, who sat next to him.

Remi sighed and shook her head. It was obvious that her daughter liked Fola and while she didn't dislike the young man, Remi didn't want her dating another law enforcement man, even if he is Iben Ariri's best friend. But she knew her daughter well, and she knew it was very difficult to convince her otherwise once she set her sights on something.

"I have an idea," Remi said. "Our wedding anniversary party is coming up soon, so let's use that opportunity to introduce her to some young men we think she might like. It won't be like a one-on-one date, so she shouldn't feel pressured."

Victor nodded excitedly. He liked his wife's idea very much.

26 | Catalyst

Iben stood next to Edafe in front of his family's grave. Today was the anniversary of their death. After a moment of silence, Iben said, "I can't believe it's been sixteen years. I still miss them a lot."

Edafe turned to him and asked, "Do you not remember anything from that night?" He was referring to the events surrounding the death of Iben's mother, father, and younger sister.

Iben shook his head. "No… I don't know why, Papa. I can remember everything until that point. It's almost as if my mind is blocking it."

Edafe sighed. "Don't worry about it." Although Iben's answer was always the same, Edafe asked him this question every year because he was curious.

"I think I may be suffering from PTSD," Iben mused sadly.

Edafe nodded in agreement.

In his darkest moments, Iben sometimes wished his mind would forget everything about his family. Then, he wouldn't be tormented by his memories of them, now that they weren't around anymore.

Soon, they started walking back toward their vehicle.

"Papa, I'm going to ask Fey to marry me soon," Iben announced. At first, he was hoping to take a vacation with her so that he could propose to her then. But he knew she couldn't take time off until a year after she started her new job. He didn't want to wait that long, so he started making alternate plans.

Edafe smiled. "So you finally summoned enough courage?" he teased.

Iben chuckled. "I guess I have… Do I have your blessings?"

Edafe patted his grandson on his back. "She'll be an excellent addition to our family."

Iben grinned. "Thank you, Papa."

***

Fey had now been living in Lagos for about three months. Soon, she started a new rotation at the Ministry of Works. Her new office was about an hour and a half commute in the morning, due to rush hour traffic. When she arrived, she met the folks in her department, which comprised fifteen people. Her new position required managing contracts for fixing and maintaining roads and pedestrian bridges.

For her first assignment, she had to oversee a repair project from start to finish. First, she looked through all the proposals from the top contractors that had been selected before her arrival. Then she picked the best one. Although her choice was opposed by some people on her team, she defended her decision, and her new boss signed off on it.

After a few days of working there, she also realized that a lot of things were done on paper. So she busied herself with digitizing as many documents as possible whenever she wasn't on-site to check in on the repairs.

One afternoon, after getting back from a site inspection, Fey rushed to her weekly status meeting with her boss. "Sorry, I'm late. I ran into a bit of traffic on my way back."

Hawas Yaro smiled. "Don't worry about it. Have you had lunch?"

"Not yet. I'll get something once we're done here." She handed him an iPad to look at her report.

Hawas gestured toward some takeaway food in a bag. "Please, don't be shy," he said. "I ordered extra."

Fey peeked in the bag and saw a jollof rice fiesta platter from a restaurant nearby. She had ordered from their menu before and she thought the food was tasty. "Thank you, sir."

"No worries. It's thanks for all your hard work."

"How much do I owe you?"

Hawas looked up from reading Fey's report. "You want to pay me back for the meal?" he asked. When Fey nodded with a serious look on her face, he smiled and said, "Why don't you buy me lunch next time instead?"

"That's fair," she said in agreement.

The following week, Fey made good on her promise and came to their next status meeting with lunch. While they sat to eat, Hawas said, "I know you've only been at this office for a few weeks, but you've contributed a lot to improve our processes around here. You've also been doing a superb job with your current project. How do you feel about taking on another one?"

Fey's eyes lit up. "I would love to. What do you have in mind?"

"Our team needs to come up with a budget for the next set of projects to be completed in the next fiscal year. Being someone who is new and can see things with a fresh perspective, what projects do you think would be most impactful?"

Fey looked thoughtful for a moment. She then recommended a major road that was on an incline. She suggested this road for rehabilitation because she felt that when the rainy season came, the potholes would likely cause problems for passing cars. She also suggested some kind of drainage system to handle flooding.

Hawas seemed impressed. "You have some great ideas. Can you document them and let's have a meeting to discuss it tomorrow?"

"Sure."

The following day, Hawas missed their meeting because he had to attend another meeting at Headquarters in Ikeja. When he returned, it was almost time for Fey to leave for the day. He stopped by her desk and said, "Can we have a quick chat to go over your document before you leave?"

Ugh! Can't this wait until tomorrow? Fey thought in annoyance.

As if reading her mind, he added, "At the meeting that I attended today at Headquarters, the deadline for submitting our budget was moved to an earlier date. This means I have a shorter timeframe to get everything together."

Not wanting to look like she wasn't a team player, Fey reluctantly agreed. Later, when Hawas finally called her to his office, there was only one other person left on the entire floor aside from them. Fey sat at the small meeting table in her boss's office and set up her laptop while he wrapped up whatever he was working on at his desk. When he was done, he sat down next to her while she talked about the specifics of her proposal. Fey thought that he seemed a bit distracted, but she ignored it, as she just wanted to get through the meeting and head home.

At some point, Hawas stood up to pour himself a drink. When he came back to the table, instead of sitting down he stood behind her chair. Then he leaned over and put a hand on her shoulder. Fey stiffened at the contact and stopped talking. Almost immediately, he kissed her on the cheek. "I like you, Fey," he said. "Are you seeing anyone?"

Fey's heartbeat quickened. "Yes, I have a boyfriend," she said, her voice loud and clear, despite her mind racing a mile a minute. *What the hell?*

"Are you happy with him?" he asked.

"Yes, I love him very much."

Hawas then sat down and said, "If you change your mind, or he mistreats you, just know that I'm here."

Fey was speechless. Was this guy seriously asking her to confide in him if she was having issues with her boyfriend? As a boss, wasn't that out of line? The guy had crossed the boundaries of propriety all in one go, and Fey was worried that things might escalate. She stood up abruptly and excused herself to go to the restroom. When she returned, she told him she was not feeling well and left for home right away, ending their working session.

When she got home that evening, she confided in Demi, who was concerned that her boss might continue to come onto her. She suggested that Fey invite Iben to lunch at work so that her boss would back off. Without telling him why, Fey texted Iben, asking him to lunch the next day. He agreed immediately and said he'd pick her up around noon.

The following day, as Demi predicted, Hawas continued his wooing of Fey and had someone deliver flowers and lunch to her. Fey left the food untouched and later offered it to one of her coworkers who gladly accepted it. Iben arrived soon after, to take Fey to lunch. When she went down to meet him, she ran into one of the ladies she worked with. Fey made a show of introducing Iben to the lady as her boyfriend. She knew the lady was a gossip, and she hoped word would get to Hawas.

Not only did he hear about it, Hawas also saw Fey get inside Iben's luxury SUV. Watching them leave together, his blood boiled. Realizing that the boyfriend Fey had mentioned was Iben Ariri, Hawas suddenly felt embarrassed by his statement from the day before. Why the hell would she leave someone like Iben for him?

The next day, his attitude towards Fey changed, but it wasn't how she had expected. First, he took her ideas from their meeting and asked someone else to develop the plans when she was already done with it. He was essentially giving the person credit for her work. Then, he started nitpicking at her project and her reports.

The week ended with Fey feeling at a loss, as she'd never experienced something like this before. Despite Demi's advice to tell Iben what was happening at work, Fey refused as she didn't want him to worry. She then reached out to human resources instead, to report the sexual harassment. Unfortunately, that only made matters worse, as the office was soon filled with gossip that she was trying to seduce the boss.

Demi, realizing that things were going downhill, told Iben what was going on, since her friend's pride seemed to be getting in the way. Iben thanked Demi for the information and immediately gave Hawas Yaro a call. During the conversation, Iben introduced himself and threatened him that if he didn't stop his harassment of Fey, he would regret it.

The next day, Hawas called her into his office and said, "Looks like you're not as tough as you pretend to be. You had to send your rich boyfriend to threaten me? Just withdraw your sexual harassment complaint and continue to do your work quietly until it's time for you to leave for your next rotation. I want nothing to do with a spoiled woman like you, anyway."

Fey was speechless. Iben called him? How did Iben know what was going on? And why did he think it was okay for him to interfere with her job? Fey's fury boiled to the surface. She'd deal with Iben later, but right now, she needed to set Hawas straight.

"Who the hell do you think you are?" Fey asked with a sneer, as she eyed him disdainfully, chin raised.

Her sudden change in attitude took Hawas by surprise. He blinked speechlessly like a deer in headlights.

"Neither you nor the rumors you've been spreading will intimidate me." She leaned forward and slapped her hand on Hawas's desk, causing him to flinch. "I will *not* withdraw my sexual harassment complaint. If you think you've done nothing wrong, then let the HR investigation process work itself out. We'll see if you're still so smug by then." Fey eyed him from head to toe with disgust before she stormed out of his office.

When she returned to her desk, she sent Iben a text message: '*How dare you call my boss behind my back!*'

Shortly after, she received a response. '*I'm busy right now. I'll stop by your place after work so we can talk.*'

Around 8:00 PM, Iben arrived at Fey's and sent her a message that he was outside.

A few minutes later, when Fey was seated in the passenger seat, she said, "Why would you call my boss without checking with me? You have no right!"

"Is that so?" Iben asked, glaring at her.

"Yes, I have everything under control."

"I assume that means they took you seriously when you complained about the sexual harassment?"

"No, but I'm working on changing that."

"Great. And while you're doing that, I will not stand by and watch you become a sacrificial lamb in that office. You've worked too hard to get to where you are. Do you want that man to put a mark on your excellent record simply because you rejected his advances?"

"Of course not! What I don't like is that you felt it was okay for you to go behind my back to take care of the matter."

"I would never do that for anyone other than you. I protect those who are important to me, and I will not apologize for that!"

Fey glared at him, but she didn't have a response.

Iben continued, "And let's not forget that you kept this from me. Why? Do you like the guy?"

"Of course not!"

"Or did you feel sorry for him because you thought I might retaliate?"

"No!"

"Are you tired of being with me?"

"Stop it, Iben!" Fey said through clenched teeth.

Iben didn't back down. "Then, why didn't you tell me?! How do you think this looks from my perspective? When Vivian was scheming back then, did I hide anything from you?"

Fey's anger suddenly lost its steam. He had a point. "I'm sorry... I didn't tell you about what happened because I didn't want you to worry."

"Did he touch you?" Iben asked, without skipping a beat. While Demi had given him a summary of what happened, she didn't provide any details on the nature of the harassment.

Fey hesitated before she said, "He touched my shoulder and... kissed my cheek."

Iben's heart raced as rage boiled within him. He suddenly wanted to punch something. No, he wanted to punch a *particular* someone so badly! How dare that scumbag put his filthy lips on *his* woman!

Fey watched as Iben gripped the steering wheel tightly, his jaw also clenched tightly. She didn't know what to say, so she kept quiet.

After a while, without looking at her, he said, "Next time, don't keep something like this from me."

"Okay."

"I respect your independence, babe. But you *can* and *should* ask me for help when things get too difficult. As your man, let me take care of things like this for you. If Demi didn't tell me what was going on, I couldn't live with myself if something worse had happened to you." What if the bastard got bold and tried to rape her? The thought sickened him.

Fey nodded, her face downcast.

After a moment, he said, "You should get back inside. I'll see you later."

Fey knew he was still upset, as he didn't even meet her gaze when she was leaving.

After Iben left, he drove around for a while hoping that his anger would subside. But it didn't. Then he called Fola, who picked up on the second ring. "I need to pay a visit to Hawas Yaro. Find me his address."

"Are you sure this is a good idea?"

"He kissed Fey, damn it!"

After a pause, Fola asked, "Where are you now?"

"I'm in front of your building."

"I'll be down in ten minutes." Sometime later, Fola got in Iben's SUV, laptop in hand. As he performed his search, he listened to Iben's complaints.

"Why doesn't she ask me for anything? She doesn't let me buy her things. She doesn't let me help her when she's in trouble. It's so frustrating. Am I always going to force my way into matters that concern her?"

"Isn't that independence one of the things you've always loved about her?"

Iben sighed. "It's a double-edged sword," he said bitterly.

"I'm sure she won't be like that after you guys get married," Fola said, trying to reassure him.

Iben thought about his proposal plans and suddenly felt unsure. "What if she says no?"

Fola, now irritated, said, "Stop being chicken shit! You two are so in love with each other, it's disgusting. Just pop the question already!"

Iben nodded. He didn't want other men taking liberties with Fey. The sooner she was wearing his engagement ring, the better.

After a few minutes, Fola looked up from his computer. "I have the address. Do you still want to do this?"

Iben looked at him and said, "I won't be able to sleep tonight."

"Okay, let's go."

After driving for about thirty minutes, Iben arrived at a house on Lagos Island. Fola flashed his law enforcement badge to security, and they were allowed into the compound. When a man who looked to be in his early thirties came out to receive them, Fola asked, "Are you Hawas Yaro?"

"Yes, how can I help you, Officer?"

As soon as Hawas identified himself, Iben, who was standing with his back to him, turned around and in a split second, his fist connected with Hawas's jaw. Caught off guard, he stumbled to the ground and looked up, shocked. "Who the hell are you?" he yelled.

"Iben Ariri!"

Hawas's eyes widened in surprise. *How does he know where I live?* "What do you want now?" he spat angrily. "I already left that silly woman alone!"

Hawas's words did nothing but anger Iben more than he already was. He bent down, grabbed Hawas by his collar, and punched him in the face repeatedly as he said slowly. "Don't you *ever* put your filthy lips on *my* woman again!" By the time Iben was done with him, Hawas' face was bloody and swollen. Iben straightened himself and looked down at him. "Effective immediately, you *will* return Fey's projects to her and treat her fairly. If I hear that you're mistreating her before she moves on to her next rotation, I'll finish what I started tonight. Understood?"

Hawas, who now cut a sorry figure, nodded as he held his aching face.

When they got back in his vehicle, Iben closed his eyes, took a deep breath, and exhaled slowly.

Fola couldn't help but think about how Iben never bothered to confront the guy that Vivian cheated on him with back then. But now, he was about to lose his rational mind over this kissing issue with Fey. "Feeling better?" he asked.

Iben nodded. "Can you get me in contact with the HR director of that agency?" He wanted to ensure that Fey's sexual harassment complaint was investigated and Hawas Yaro was disciplined accordingly.

"I'll send it to you tomorrow." Iben was still wired, and Fola didn't want him calling up the person this late at night.

The following day, when Fey got to work, she was relieved when she found out that Hawas was out sick. She was glad to not have to deal with his hostility for the day. A few hours later, she received a visit from the Assistant HR Director regarding her complaint. Fey recounted what happened and was assured that Hawas would be disciplined accordingly. They also called a meeting to include the rest of the office staff, where they were told that they would get a new interim boss while Hawas Yaro was under suspension.

Afterward, as Fey sat at her desk, she thought about how everything seemed to fall in place after Iben got involved. She picked up her phone and sent him a text message: *'Babe, thanks for accelerating the processing of my HR complaint. Hawas Yaro has been suspended and we will be getting a new boss.'*

Iben sent a response right away: *'You're welcome. Glad to hear it.'*

Now that the issue with Hawas Yaro was resolved, Fey could relax. Initially, she was upset with Demi for tattling to Iben, but she later thanked her as she knew her friend was only looking out for her. Who knows how long the issue would have dragged on for before any resolution could be achieved?

She couldn't help but wonder how many women out there were in a similar or worse position, but didn't have someone like Iben who could use his influence to fight on their behalf. Having gone through this, she researched nonprofit organizations that specialized in helping victims of sexual harassment in the workplace. She wanted to do whatever she could to support these organizations.

***

That Saturday, Fey woke up to find Demi and her parents in the living room looking through albums. Victor and Remi's silver wedding anniversary was coming up, and they were planning a party to celebrate. Demi had come up with the idea to have a slideshow of pictures that represented each year of their twenty-five-year marriage. It was a trip down memory lane for the couple as they were looking through their old photographs.

Fey sat down and joined them. As she flipped through one of the albums, a loose photograph fell out. When Fey picked it up, she was shocked to see who was in it.

"This is a picture of me and Tutu when we were little!" she exclaimed in surprise.

Remi looked at the picture and smiled. "Ah, this is a picture that your mother gave to us when we were returning to Nigeria many years ago. She had given it to us to see if we could help find your dad.

But when we got back, his parents had moved away."

Fey looked confused. *How would a picture of me and Tutu help with finding my dad?*

Remi moved closer and took the album from Fey. "There should be another photo with your father in here," she said, flipping through the album.

Fey's heart skipped a beat. "You have a photo of my dad?" The excitement in her voice couldn't be missed.

"Yes," Remi said. However, after flipping through the album, the photo could not be found.

Disappointed, but not discouraged, Fey immediately started looking through the other albums. Half an hour later, it was the same result. Fey slumped in the chair and closed her eyes.

"I'm sorry you couldn't find the photo," Demi said. She knew how important it was for her friend to find her dad, and having a photo would move things along so much quicker.

Victor and Remi shared a look. Why was Fey acting this way about a simple photo? Then, Remi asked, "If I didn't know better, I'd think you don't have a photo of your father at all."

Fey opened her eyes and met Remi's gaze. "Yeah, I don't remember what he looks like. My mother put away all photos of him a long time ago."

"Why don't you just ask her for it?"

"She doesn't want me to look for him. So, I'm doing it without her." She looked at the photo of her and Tutu and asked, "Can I keep this?"

"Of course, it's yours anyway."

"Thanks," Fey said before she left for her room. Once inside, she plopped on the bed with the photo in her hand. *So, at some point, Mom tried to find Dad?* she thought to herself as she twirled the picture in her hand. *I wonder why she changed her mind.* She then noticed that the edges of the photo looked strange. She stuck her fingernail between the seam and it looked like two photographs were stuck together.

Fey sat up immediately. Her heartbeat quickened. What if the second photo was the one she had been looking for? She gently and slowly pried the two photos apart and once they were free, the second photo revealed a picture of Fey and Tutu standing next to a man who had his arms around both of them. He was her father. She ran a finger across his face and thought sadly that if she had crossed him on the street, she wouldn't have recognized him.

Just then, there was a knock on her bedroom door. "Come in," Fey answered. The door opened and Demi walked in. She had come to check in on her friend. She knew she was disappointed about not finding the photo of her father that they were looking for. However, she saw Fey sitting on the bed with a grin and holding up two photos for her to see.

Demi stared at her friend in disbelief. "Oh my gosh. You found it?"

Fey nodded with a grin. "They were stuck together!"

Demi hugged Fey tightly. She was filled with so much happiness for her friend. "You should tell Iben and Fola the good news."

Iben was away on business otherwise, Fey would've jumped in her car and driven to his house right away. She settled for the next best thing. She took a picture of the photograph with her phone and sent it to Iben with a message: *'Good news! I found a photo of my dad!'*

A few minutes later, she received a response: *'Awesome, babe. I will pass it along to Fola.'*

***

Hundreds of kilometers away in Abuja, Iben had just arrived at the hotel where he would stay for the next few days. He smiled to himself as he looked at the photo Fey sent to him. He thought she looked really cute as a little girl and wondered if they had a daughter in the future, would she look like her mother?

Fola caught his smile and asked, "Fey sent you a message?" There weren't too many people who could make Iben smile like that.

Iben nodded. "She found a photo of her father. I just forwarded it to you."

Fola opened up the message on his phone and said, "I think I know this man."

Iben turned to look at him. "Are you sure?"

The man in the picture looked like he could be a younger version of the person who came to Fola's mind. "I don't know his name, but he looks like one of the engineers working for the company."

Iben looked thoughtful. *What a coincidence...* "Don't Tell Fey until you've confirmed that he's the person we're looking for."

"Understood."

27 | Union

One Saturday evening, as Fey drove to Iben's house, she admired the Christmas decorations in the streets. Her first Christmas in Nigeria was right around the corner, and she relished in the festive air that permeated everywhere she went. She especially loved driving by the Lekki waterfront and seeing the lights at nighttime.

Later, as Demi and Fey were chatting in the living room, Fola and Iben were talking business in the study. Afterward, Iben asked, "How's Demi?"

"She's a great girl," Fola said with a smile. "I like her." After their dinner date a few weeks before, Fola and Demi got closer.

"You're welcome." When Fola looked at him with a questioning gaze, Iben smirked. "You asked me to introduce you to a *great girl* like Fey, and I have. So, you're welcome."

Fola chuckled. *Smartass!*

"Seriously, how are things going?" Iben asked. He liked Demi for Fola. Not only because she was Fey's friend, but also because he felt like her personality was an excellent match for Fola's.

"We're taking it slow."

"Why? I know she likes you a lot."

Fola sighed and ran his hand across his head. "It's me. I don't know how to do this serious relationship thing. I'm almost 30 years old, and I've never had a long-term relationship. I'm attracted to her, and we get along well, but what happens after the initial *honeymoon* period is over? We're probably going to get tired of each other, and then she'll hate me. And then Fey will hate me. I don't want both of them giving me death glares and shit!"

"So, you're just going to stay in the friend zone? Is the almighty Fola afraid of falling in love?" Iben teased.

Fola stood up. He didn't want to talk about this anymore. He'd always known what he wanted; relationships with no-strings-attached. It was easier that way.

"Well, I guess that means you're also okay with her dating other guys," Iben added.

"Why would I be okay with that?" Fola snapped. Somehow, the thought incensed him.

Iben shrugged. "I heard her mention to Fey that her parents had been trying to set her up with some of their friends' sons. And at their wedding anniversary party next weekend, some of those guys will be there."

Fola frowned. "Shit!" he cursed. Suddenly, he stormed out of the study and made a beeline for Demi, who was still chatting with Fey.

Iben smiled and followed.

"Excuse us," Fola said gruffly, to a surprised Fey, before grabbing Demi's hand and marching back to Iben's study. With the two of them alone, he asked, "Is it true that your parents are trying to set you up with other guys at their wedding anniversary party?"

"Has Fey been running her mouth again?"

"You were hiding it from me?"

"Yes."

"Why?"

"Because I don't want to pressure you. You said you needed time—"

"And you said you would wait."

"And I *am* waiting, Fola. But since I haven't introduced anyone to them as my boyfriend, my parents can't seem to help themselves." The entire situation was frustrating to Demi. She couldn't understand her parents' sudden interest in her love life. Even her mother, who was usually the more reasonable of the two, was on her dad's busybody campaign.

"I see..." Fola said, but his mind was in turmoil. *What if she meets someone she likes at the party? Shit, Fola. Why do you even care? You can't expect her to wait around forever while you make up your damn mind!*

Fola met her gaze and held it as he slowly closed the gap between them. By a sudden compulsion, he wanted to lay claim to her lips—lay claim to her. It wasn't the first time he'd felt the impulse to kiss her. They'd been hanging out and dating casually, getting to know each other, and during those times, he would sometimes want to kiss her. However, he told himself that it wasn't fair to her, and he would just be taking advantage of her feelings for him. But now, he almost couldn't hold himself back.

Sensing his motive and hesitation, Demi planted a kiss on his cheek instead. "Fola, I still like you…" she said softly. Ever since the incident with Detective Akin, Demi decided that life was too short to play games. She was determined to ask for what she wanted, instead of hoping that things would happen for her. Demi also admitted to herself that she never stopped liking Fola. Truthfully, part of her anger towards him back then was because she was projecting her anger at herself for not hating him despite standing her up that night. Once she came to terms with her feelings, she laid all her cards on the table.

***

On Christmas Eve, Iben picked up Fey for a dinner date. She was wearing a sleeveless wine dress with champagne lace appliques around the waist. Fey complimented the dress with a pair of champagne heels and a clutch. Iben was also wearing a black suit with a champagne pocket square and a wine bowtie.

Iben smiled when he saw her. "You look gorgeous, babe." He had sent her the ensemble she was wearing, asking her to please wear it and humor him for their date tonight.

Fey smiled. "You look handsome as well," she complimented. "What's the occasion? Why are we dressed up tonight?"

"You'll see…" he cryptically said as he opened the passenger door for her.

Soon, they were on their way to their dinner destination. When they arrived, Iben led Fey into the multi-storied five-star Eko Hotels, and they took the elevator up to the rooftop. The elevator doors opened to reveal a gorgeous view of Victoria Island and the surrounding area. The rooftop was decorated for the holiday season with garlands, a Christmas tree, and lights.

For a moment, Fey was mesmerized by the bright lights of the cityscape below. "Lagos is beautiful…" she said.

"Not as beautiful as you," Iben said, bringing her out of her trance.

Fey turned to look at him and smiled. "You're full of flattery tonight, Mr. Ariri. What are you up to?"

Iben chuckled. "I just want to give my lady a good time on this lovely Christmas Eve." Then he leaned in and kissed her on the cheek.

Fey smiled and shook her head helplessly. *This guy is laying the flirting on thick tonight.*

After sitting at the only table there, a server poured some red wine in their glasses. Iben raised his glass for a toast. "To the woman I love. Forever." Fey's eyes met his. She smiled. Their glasses clinked.

Sometime later, their meals arrived, and the couple chatted as they ate, enjoying each other's company. Afterward, they moved to sit on a lounge sofa that was closer to the glass railing, which spanned the perimeter of the rooftop. Fey leaned in and rested her head against Iben's shoulder, and he put his arm around her, hugging her close to him. They sat in silence for a while, just enjoying the light breeze and each other's closeness.

"This will be our *first* official Christmas together," Iben said, breaking the silence.

"Mmm… it is," Fey responded. The previous year, she had left Germany to go back home a couple of days before Christmas.

Iben continued. "I remember all our firsts. The first time we met. The first time we kissed after we had that cook-off…"

Fey smiled at the memory.

"… The first time we had a fight and that same night, I told you that I loved you… The first time we made love… The first time you told me you loved me…"

He kissed her softly on the forehead before he continued.

"Being in a relationship with you for the last fifteen months has been one of the best and most fulfilling experiences of my life. I'm the luckiest man alive to have you by my side and—I want this to be permanent."

Fey looked up at him. Her heartbeat quickened. *Wait, is he…?*

Iben smiled as he moved to answer the question in her eyes. His right hand that had been in his pocket since they were seated on the sofa finally moved to produce a beautiful platinum engagement ring. It had a red ruby in the center, surrounded by a shimmering bed of diamonds.

Fey watched speechlessly as Iben got down on one knee in front of her, ring in hand. "Fey, I promise to always respect you and to love you unconditionally. I want you by my side forever. Will you marry me?"

Iben's eyes never left Fey's in anticipation of her answer. He had just bared his heart to her, and despite his calm exterior, he was feeling very vulnerable internally.

Unexpectedly, Fey leaned forward and kissed him on his lips. After they parted, Iben asked expectantly, "Is that a 'yes'?" Fey nodded as a grin spread across her face, and she held out her hand. An elated Iben then slid the ring on her finger. It fit perfectly. He then hugged her tightly as he let out a relieved breath. Iben sent out a telepathic thank you to Demi. If it weren't for her help, he wouldn't have guessed Fey's correct ring size.

"I love it!" Fey gushed as she admired the ring on her finger.

"Let's take a picture," Iben suggested, still feeling elated. Immediately after, he sent it out to a group chat that included his close circle of friends. In the photo, Iben held up Fey's hand with the ring. 'She said yes!' the photo caption read.

A few minutes later, the chat blew up. 'Congratulations' and 'OMGs' came rolling in from everyone. Iben Ariri was now officially off the market.

Fey chuckled as Iben showed her the comments on his phone. "You told everyone?" she asked, amused.

"Yeah. That's to ensure you can't back out," he joked.

Fey chuckled. "You're so silly..." she said, snuggling close to him. Why would she ever want to back out? Her love for Iben was like a flame that had blossomed from a small flicker to a blazing torch. She loved him very much, and she couldn't see herself being with anyone else. As far as she was concerned, the only way they wouldn't be together is if fate played a cruel trick and tore them apart.

Fey did not realize that this seemingly offhanded thought was a foreshadowing of what was soon to happen. Her love for Iben was about to be tested in a significant way.

The next day, Iben and Fey went to the Ariri mansion to deliver the news of their engagement to Edafe.

"Welcome to the family," Edafe said to Fey with a warm smile.

"Thank you, sir."

"Call me Papa from now on."

"Okay... Papa," Fey said in response, which pleased Edafe greatly.

"Have you given your mother the good news?" he asked.

"Yes, we did this morning."

"Excellent. Excellent. Let's announce your engagement at tomorrow's party," Edafe declared.

***

The next day was Boxing Day, and the Ariris would host their annual end-of-year party, which was exclusive to guests, close friends, business partners, certain politicians, and select members of the press. This year, the party venue was one of the most exclusive banquet halls on Victoria Island.

Fey and Iben arrived at the party together. She was nervous as she had never attended something this grand before. Fey wondered how she would cope with events like this once she was married to Iben. Would there be an expectation that she would plan such events? She certainly hoped not.

"Penny for your thoughts?" she suddenly heard Iben ask.

"It's nothing," she said with a small smile. "Just a bit nervous."

Iben nodded in understanding. "Just be yourself, babe," he said with an encouraging smile. Then he added with a sly smile, "You know what'll help with the jitters?"

Fey could see the mischievous look on Iben's face. He was likely up to no good. "Uh...no thanks!" she responded, tossing him a side-eye.

Iben chuckled to himself as he watched her quicken her steps to their table.

As the Chairman and CEO of Ariri Corporation, Edafe Ariri gave his opening speech, welcoming all the guests. Then he announced that he was pleased to share the news of his grandson's recent engagement. Fey and Iben instantly became the center of attention, and the sudden barrage of camera flashes almost blinded Fey. Their engagement was undoubtedly news for the gossip columns. One of Lagos's most eligible bachelors was no longer available.

Shortly after, several guests came to congratulate the couple on their engagement. Fey swore that she had never smiled in her entire life as much as she did during this period. Her jaw was hurting.

At some point, Edafe pulled away Iben to meet some guests. Before Fey could enjoy some peace, she suddenly found herself surrounded by a few women.

"Your dress is gorgeous!" one of them complimented as she admired Fey, who was wearing a fitted black floor-length evening gown with an intricate black lace bodice.

"Thank you," Fey responded with a smile.

"Are you a model?" another lady chimed in.

Fey chuckled. "No, I'm not. I'm an engineer."

"It's such a lovely dress. Who's the designer?"

"Mila Threads."

"Oh, I've never heard of it."

"It's an up-and-coming designer that I patronize. The owner has a shop in Lekki. You ladies should look out for her designs at the next Lagos Fashion Week." The women listening took note, and Fey smiled to herself at the thought that Demi was about to get a rush of orders soon.

The conversation centered on fashion for a while until someone asked, "It's such a shock to hear that Iben Ariri is now engaged. How did someone like you bag such a catch?"

Fey turned her attention to the lady who asked the question. How was she supposed to answer a question like that? It had the connotation that Fey had somehow tricked Iben into their engagement.

Before she could respond, one of the other ladies said, "Watch out! The rumor monger is here."

"Is it because you are pregnant with Iben Ariri's baby?" came the next question from the lady who seemed unperturbed by the preceding comment.

Fey stared at the lady in shock. *Pregnant?*

Without waiting for an answer, she continued. "Aren't you responsible for the broken engagement between Iben Ariri and Vivian Ibere?"

What the hell?

"Wait, isn't she the lady that hangs around Vivian Ibere? Zara something…" someone suddenly said.

Hearing that, Fey now had a clearer picture of the lady's motive. She was likely one of Vivian's friends. Fey smiled to herself internally before she turned to Zara and asked in a flat tone, "Who the hell is Vivian Ibere?"

All the ladies listening burst into laughter when they heard Fey's question.

"She doesn't even know who this so-called *ex-fiancée* of Iben is. Hahaha. This is too funny."

"Vivian is probably one of those girls that were throwing themselves at him. This is hilarious."

"True O! It's just rubbish talk. If Iben was engaged to someone before, wouldn't we all know? Surely, Chief Ariri would've announced it."

As heads nodded in agreement, Zara glared at Fey, who had a satisfied smirk on her face. *How dare this bitch act like she doesn't know who Vivian is!* Although Vivian wasn't invited to the party, Zara was attending as the date of one of the invitees. Earlier, she was shocked when she heard Edafe's announcement that Iben was engaged. It had only been five or six months since the annulment of his engagement to Vivian. What was crazier was that he was now engaged to the same girl from Germany who Vivian had complained about. Neither she nor

Vivian truly understood how serious Iben was about her.

Zara's initial goal tonight was to embarrass Fey, but the evil girl had turned the tables on her. She now regretted coming over. Suddenly, she spied Iben heading towards them, so she quickly turned around and walked away.

When Iben arrived at the table, he smiled and said, "Ladies, I'm sorry, but I must steal my fiancée away for a moment."

"It was nice to meet and chat with you all," Fey said with a smile before she walked away hand-in-hand with Iben.

When they were out of earshot, Fey said, "Thanks for saving me."

Iben chuckled. "How are you holding up?" He was aware that this entire event could be overwhelming to Fey.

"I'm good... One of Vivian's friends is here."

Iben frowned. "I saw... Did she bother you?"

"It was nothing I couldn't handle," Fey said with a smile.

"Okay," he said as he placed a hand on the small of her back. He remembered how Fey handled Vivian in Germany, so he was confident that any of her friends would be no match. "I want you to meet my two favorite people here tonight," he said with a grin.

Fey turned to look at him. She was intrigued to find out who these people were. Iben led her to a table at one corner of the banquet hall. Seated there by themselves were two children, a boy and a girl. They looked to be about ten or eleven years old.

"Why do my two favorite people look so bored?" Iben said, announcing his presence.

"Uncle Iben!" the girl said with a smile when she saw Iben. She got up to hug him, but she was only tall enough to embrace his leg.

"Hey, you!" Iben said as he high-fived the boy who was still seated.

Fey smiled as she watched Iben's interaction with the children. After a moment, Iben reached for her hand and said, "I want you guys to meet my fiancée. She's the person I'm going to marry."

Fey smiled warmly at the children. "Hello, I'm Fey," she said. "What are your names?"

"I'm Olamide, and this is my little brother, Pariola," the girl said. She seemed like the talkative of the two.

The boy scowled. "I'm *actually* older than you."

"Whatever, that's not what everyone says."

"How so?" Fey asked, amused.

"We're twins, and he thinks that because he was born first, it makes him older."

"Doesn't it?" Fey asked with a chuckle.

"Our uncle says I'm older because we're Yoruba, and we believe that the second twin is older."

Fey slowly nodded as she tried to digest the girl's explanation. She just learned something new today.

"Are you American?" Olamide asked. She had picked up on Fey's accent.

"Kind of. I grew up in America, but I was born here in Nigeria."

"You're very pretty," Olamide said.

Fey smiled. "Thank you. You look pretty as well."

Pariola suddenly made a face and said, "Hmph! She looks like a toad!" He was still upset about his twin introducing him as her *little brother*.

Olamide turned to glare at her brother. "Say that again, and I'll turn *you* into a toad," she bit back.

Pariola had a self-satisfied smile on his face. He seemed happy to have successfully gotten under his sister's skin.

Fey chuckled. She thought these kids were cute.

Fey and Iben hung out with the kids for some time until an older gentleman who looked to be in his fifties came to the table. "Babe," Iben said to Fey. "This is Doctor Sijuwade, Papa's longtime friend."

"Hello, sir. It's nice to meet you."

Doctor Sijuwade smiled warmly. "Same here," he said. "Congrats on your engagement."

"Thank you."

He turned to Iben. "Thanks for keeping them company while I talked to your grandfather."

Iben smiled. "It's my pleasure, sir. You know I'm very fond of them."

After the couple said their goodbyes and were on their way back to their seats, Fey teased, "So, *Uncle Iben*, I didn't realize that you would be so great with kids."

Iben chuckled. "I'm not sure why, but I feel a close bond with those two. They've been orphans since they were babies, and their uncle had been taking care of them ever since. Having lost my parents when I was young, I can relate."

***

In another part of the banquet hall, Fola had just finished chatting with some guests and was heading to the restroom when he heard someone call out to him.

"Detective Afolabi Ogundele, may I speak with you for a moment?"

Fola turned around at the mention of his name. He frowned. Not only had the man in front of him called him by his full name, but he also knew that he was an EFCC detective. Not that he was hiding it, but few people here knew that he also worked for the EFCC. The man met Fola's gaze with a smile. Fola narrowed his eyes in suspicion. "Who the hell are you?" he asked coldly.

"I'm Detective Godwin Olaniyi, with the EFCC," he said as he flashed his badge so that Fola could see.

"How did you get in here?" Fola asked, irritably.

Godwin chuckled. "I'm surprised at your question. You, of all people, should know that a good detective has his ways."

"What do you want?" Fola snapped.

"You're very hostile, Detective," Godwin shot back. "The only thing I've done so far is introduce myself."

Uncharacteristically, Godwin was getting under Fola's skin, and he realized it was because the man caught him off guard. He calmed himself down and said, "Assuming the badge you showed just now isn't a fake, I'll entertain you for a few minutes." He put his hands in his pockets and asked, "How can I help you, *Detective* Godwin Olaniyi?"

Godwin met Fola's icy stare with a smirk. "First, I want to congratulate you on closing the Terence Ogochi case. Your team's swiftness at resolving a case that previously assigned teams had difficulty with, is a testament to your leadership." He paused for Fola to say something, but when he didn't, he continued. "My team was tasked with interrogating the suspects, and I got the opportunity to speak to Detective Akin Oladele." He paused again as if expecting a reaction from Fola, but he remained the same and continued to regard Godwin with an icy gaze.

"He seemed to think that some illegal dealings were going on at Starlight Shipping and suggested that I look into it. In case there *was* something to his suspicions, I did look into it, and do you know what I found out?" He paused again before he continued, "Absolutely nothing!" Godwin then put his hand on his chin as if he were pondering something. "Which got me thinking. Why would someone like Detective Akin focus on Starlight Shipping? He obviously had something against the company. So, I did some digging and found out that the Ariris own it and that you *also* work for Ariri Corporation."

Godwin paused again and said as he looked Fola in the eye, "Isn't that a conflict of interest?"

"First of all," Fola began, "I work at Ariri Corporation as a *consultant*. It's not against the rules. Second, let's suppose in some alternate universe, the EFCC was tasked with investigating Ariri Corporation. As long as I *recuse* myself from such an investigation, there cannot be a conflict of interest."

This guy's a tough nut to crack, Godwin thought to himself. *I'll have to go with a direct approach.* "Detective Akin seems to think that you are a double agent for Ariri Corporation," he suddenly said.

"Detective Godwin, if you're trying to accuse me of some sort of wrongdoing, you're doing a shitty job of it," Fola said with a smirk. *This guy is just fishing for information. What an amateur!*

Godwin frowned. "In my opinion, the company just seems too squeaky clean. I have a background in Forensic Accounting, and in my experience, large companies like Ariri Corporation generally have some questionable accounting discrepancies in their financial records. It's usually not enough for prosecution. But I found it odd that there was absolutely nothing of the sort. Instead, it was—*perfect*!"

"You seem like a skeptic. Do you think a company can't act ethically? I take it you've never met Edafe Ariri. If you had, you'd know that nobody gets away with fraud at any of his companies."

"But my gut tells me there's a story here—"

"Let me get this straight," Fola said, cutting him off. "You've come barging in here with a bunch of accusations, based on what? Your *gut* and the ramblings of a corrupt cop who's just trying to make a deal to get his sentence reduced? Did your boss sanction this?"

Godwin's frown turned into a deep scowl. "I've reached the limits of my clearance and rank in terms of what I can do to pursue my investigation. You're not Ariri; you're just consulting for them. So, as a civil servant, your loyalty, first and foremost, should be to the country and justice. Work with me to uncover whatever the Ariris are hiding regarding Starlight Shipping."

Fola cocked his head to the side and asked, "How long have you been a detective?"

"Two years."

"Mmmm... So your goal is to make a name for yourself by attempting to bring down one of the wealthiest and affluent families in the country?"

Godwin blinked a few times, surprised that Fola saw right through him. He quickly composed himself and countered with, "We can *both* make a name for ourselves if we work together."

"My answer is no," Fola said flatly. "We're done here." He turned around to leave.

Godwin quickly walked around him to block his retreat. "Here's my card," he said. When Fola wouldn't take it from him, he put it in the breast pocket of Fola's suit jacket. "Please, call me if you change your mind." Then he walked away.

Fola watched Godwin leave. He had to give him kudos for the element of surprise, but other than that, as a young man in his early to mid-twenties, he was still very green. He took the business card from his pocket, tore it to shreds and tossed the pieces in a nearby trash can. *I'll need to let Papa know about this.*

28 | Decision

The next morning, when Fola woke up, his first thought was Demi. Today is the wedding anniversary party of her parents. Today is the day she would meet the guys her parents wanted to set her up with—his competition. He hated that. *Why does it matter anyway? It's probably best if she turns her attention to some other guy instead of waiting around for me. Then I won't have to worry about the aftermath of a relationship that's reached its end of life*, he thought pessimistically, as he tried to convince himself. But when he imagined the scenario where she showed up to their hangouts with another man, he quickly changed his mind. *Shit, Fola. Make up your mind. What are you so afraid of?*

He smiled wryly to himself. He never imagined that he would ever be in a situation where he was contemplating turning down a woman who had a genuine interest in him. A woman who didn't care about his money or status. A woman who was beautiful, smart, witty, and independent. A woman he also had feelings for.

If Demi weren't Fey's friend or Fey weren't Iben's fiancée, he wouldn't have this dilemma. Some people might think Fola was allowing his relationship with those two to affect his decision. But was he wrong in considering that, though? He was a very pragmatic and realistic person. He couldn't just pretend that it wasn't a real possibility that if a relationship with Demi failed, the dynamics of his relationship with Iben and Fey could also change. Of course, Iben would always be his brother, but what about Fey? Would she keep a grudge?

Born in these thoughts was the fact that Fola had a deep-seated assumption that a romantic relationship with him *would* fail, no matter what. Perhaps it was just a convenient excuse, but given his past experiences, could one blame him?

Fola continued with his internal dialogue until finally, he sat up in bed and shook his head to clear his thoughts. He then leaned over and picked up the book on his nightstand. It was the same one he'd been reading for the last few days since he found out about his potential competition. It was titled 'Love and Sense: A Man's Guide to Lasting Relationships.' He had been browsing a magazine in the books section of the supermarket when it caught his eye. He bought the book on a whim.

He flipped over to the page he last read. It was a chapter about communication and how important it was to share your fears, your emotions, and feelings in a relationship. After a few minutes of reading, Fola tossed the book aside and mumbled, "This is bullshit!"

He then sent a text message to Demi. *'Hey, we need to talk. Can we meet up in an hour?'*

'Sure. Where do you want to meet?'

'I'll pick you up at home.'

'I'm at my shop right now.'

'Ok. I'll head over there.'

An hour later, Fola was standing in front of Demi's shop, Mila Threads. He smiled at the thought that she still didn't know that he had a hand in the venture capital company that funded it. As an investor, he was happy that the store was doing excellent in sales. Aside from the fact that Demi's designs were amazing, she was also a guru at marketing. For instance, designing a dress for Fey to wear to the Ariri Corporation party was an excellent marketing strategy. There was a closed sign at the glass door, so he texted her that he had arrived. A few minutes later, she let him in and he followed her to her office in the back.

She gestured to the sofa and said, "Please make yourself comfortable. There are drinks in the fridge over there. I'm just finishing up a few things."

Fola nodded, but he didn't move from where he was seated. For the next ten minutes, he just sat there quietly and watched Demi as she worked. She had such a focused look on her face that Fola thought was cute. *Dude, if she farts, I bet you'd think it was cute,* he thought derisively.

"Sorry about that," Demi said when she was done.

"No worries."

Demi sat down beside him. "What did you want to talk about?" she asked.

"Us," he said, meeting her gaze. "I have an answer for you."

Demi's heartbeat quickened. She had an inkling that was why he wanted to see her. Since the last time they hung out at Iben's, she felt like he'd been distant, avoiding her. That was the reason she didn't want to tell him about her parents' plan to introduce her to potential boyfriends. She didn't want to put any undue pressure on him.

"Tonight is your parents' wedding anniversary party, and I want you to have my answer beforehand."

"Fola, don't rush to give me your answer because of that."

"I think you've waited long enough, Demi. It isn't fair to continue like this."

Oh my god, here comes the rejection, Demi thought dejectedly. She suddenly felt like crying, but she swallowed the tears and schooled her facial expression to hide it. She looked down at her hands as she listened to him speak.

"I've enjoyed getting to know you these last couple of months. Your ambition and the passion you have for your career, your laughter, and your witty sense of humor, your feistiness, and straightforwardness…"

Demi sighed. *But it isn't enough for you…*

"…Throughout this time, you've been very open with me, but I've been holding back and hiding a bit of myself from you. But if we're to have a meaningful and worthwhile relationship, I need to let you know some things about me."

Demi looked up at him. *Wait, there's still a chance?*

"After I've told you everything, if you decide to change your mind, I won't hold it against you."

Demi nodded.

"As you know, I'm an orphan, and I've been one for as long as I can remember. When I was around nine or ten, I ran away from the orphanage in my hometown and took to the streets. I was a bit of a mini thug back then. One day, I tried to rob a wealthy man and got caught. I figured it was the end of me, but the man was so impressed by my boldness and cunning that he offered to hire me. That man is Edafe Ariri. My choices then were to either work for him or be delivered to the police. Of course, I chose the former.

"He brought me to his home, educated me, and told me that my job was to protect his grandson, Iben. As long as I kept up with my education and training, and watched out for Iben, I had three meals and a roof over my head. Over the years, I've come to see those two as my family. To this day, there isn't anything I wouldn't do for them.

"You also know that I work for the EFCC and Ariri Corporation. I am Iben's deputy and Papa's go-to guy for certain security-related issues. Sometimes, I have to deal with unsavory characters at both jobs. But my loyalty to the Ariris is far greater than my sense of duty to the government. Because of this, I've done some questionable, unethical things over the years. I've also avoided serious relationships because let's be honest, what woman wants to deal with a man who disappears for long periods and is secretive about his job?"

"As a judge, my dad doesn't talk to my mother about his cases," Demi interjected. "They have an understanding that there are some secrets that he has to keep."

"Your dad's an upright man. He's a judge, upholding the laws of the land. I'm the opposite—some of the time. In a way, I'm not that different from Detective Akin."

Demi frowned at the memory of her attempted kidnapping. "Have you ever hurt an innocent person?" she asked.

Fola gave a light chuckle as he said, "No, I don't go around hurting and killing people for sport." Then he continued in a serious tone, "When situations like that arise, I'm doing it to either fulfill my duties on the job or to protect the people I care about."

"Then, don't compare yourself to that scumbag, Akin!" Demi retorted. "Look, everyone has a past. We've done things we're not proud of, but what's important is how we choose to live going forward."

Fola nodded. "Iben is trying to work things out to move me out of that security role, but until that happens, I'm going to continue to do these *questionable* things. Things I can't talk to you about."

The most significant gray area in Fola's work is the firearms trafficking that Edafe engaged in. Given his law enforcement position, he should've reported Ariri's warehouses to the authorities, but that would never happen. Since the warehouse incident a couple of months back, Iben had been working to reduce his involvement in that aspect of Starlight Shipping. The plan was for Fola to train someone to take over his role. And if Edafe needed him, it would be because no one else could handle the situation.

"Do you feel trapped?" Demi asked.

"No, I do not. I'm a bit of an adrenaline junkie, so I kind of enjoy the thrill that the job provides. I do enjoy working with Iben on business-related matters, but I think I'd die of boredom if that were the only thing I did. And unless people suddenly stopped committing financial crimes, I think my EFCC position will be enough," he joked.

"Or we could just go bungee jumping or skydiving together."

Fola raised a surprised brow. "You like doing stuff like that?" he asked.

Demi turned to look at him. "Sometimes… It's both scary and thrilling, so I understand the adrenaline rush you talked about."

He nodded before he asked, "Do you have questions for me?"

"No. But thanks for explaining your relationship with the Ariris. They are your family, and it would be crazy for anyone to question your loyalty to them. Besides, I do care about Fey and Iben, so if I trust anyone around them, it would be you. But—*you* need someone to have your back, too. And I still want to be that person—your person." She met Fola's gaze for a moment before she continued. "Last time we hung out, and you got upset about my parents setting me up, it made me happy. I knew that you cared about me more than you let on. So, let me be the person who you can turn to if you can't go to Iben or his grandfather… And you can be mine in return…"

Fola smiled. Her words were sweet as honey in his ears as she spoke. He leaned in and kissed her on the cheek. "Thank you," he said softly. *She's only twenty-four years old, but she has a very mature outlook on life.*

Maybe it was his primal male instinct, but Fola suddenly felt the need to protect her at all costs. If things ever went awry with the warehouse, he wouldn't want her to be implicated. Thinking about it now, Fola finally realized that perhaps this was the *real* reason he had been hesitating.

"So… what's your answer?" Demi hesitantly asked after a moment.

Fola reached for her hands and said, "Yes, you can be my person."

Demi rolled her eyes and attempted to free her hands from his.

"What's the matter?" he asked.

"Show me you're serious by saying it properly," she said firmly.

Fola nodded. He understood what she meant. Still holding her hands in his, he said, "Demi, I like you very much. And I would love to be your boyfriend."

Demi looked him in the eye and smiled, "I accept."

At her answer, Fola smiled and put his arm around her shoulder. She leaned in closer to him and rested her head on his chest. Demi sighed contentedly. She couldn't help but grin from ear to ear. Finally, he was hers. As they sat there, they discussed the dynamics of their new relationship.

"I occasionally have to travel for work, sometimes with little notice,"

Fola said.

"Okay. Just send me a text message or something."

He shook his head before he said, "No, I'll call you." Like hell, he would simply send a text message. The memory of the consequences of him not calling her to cancel their first date was still vivid in his mind. "Also, let me know if you need anything from me. I don't read minds," Fola continued.

"Likewise. I hate it when people think they know what I'm thinking," Demi retorted.

"I like to have my space every once in a while. Please, don't take it to mean that I'm cheating on you, ignoring you, or that I want to break up with you." Many past relationships of his had ended due to this misconception.

"I understand." Demi smiled at the fact that they were alike in many ways. She couldn't be happier.

"Make sure tonight that you let those losers know that you're taken," Fola said, changing the subject.

Demi smiled and raised her head to look at him. She kissed him on the cheek before she said, "Why don't you just come to the party? Nothing sends the message across better than you being there *in person*."

Fola sighed. "I would love nothing better, but after I leave, I need to pursue a lead in Fey's dad's investigation."

Demi's face lit up. "You found her dad?"

"I think so, but please don't tell her anything. I don't want her to get her hopes up unnecessarily."

Demi nodded in understanding.

Fola looked at the time and said, "I need to get going soon."

They stood up to hug each other. Fola thought it felt nice having her in his embrace. After a moment, he suddenly heard her say, "I wish you could stay…"

He leaned back from the hug and said, "Do you know my wish right now? To kiss you…" Those pecks on the cheeks they'd been giving each other wasn't cutting it for him now that they were an item.

"Me too," Demi said, looking away shyly.

Fola chuckled internally. He couldn't believe this woman could be shy about anything, but it was cute and refreshing, seeing that expression on her face. He lifted her chin so that their eyes met, and then he leaned in for a proper kiss.

Sparks flew everywhere when their lips made contact. *Mmmm…*

delicious, Fola thought to himself.

Demi felt him press her close to him, and she responded by putting her arms around his waist as their kiss deepened, slowly stroking his back.

The sensations from her touch drove Fola wild, and his tongue ravaged and explored every inch of her mouth. Every secret fantasy that he'd had about kissing and touching her didn't compare to the intense euphoria that he was experiencing right now.

It was almost as if all the sexual tension that had been building up between them in the past couple of months wanted to explode at this very moment. By the time they slowly climbed down from the high of their first kiss, they were both breathless.

I want more, Fola thought to himself as he continued to hold Demi close. He then trailed kisses down her neck. She arched her back and moaned as she felt his warm tongue on her skin. "Let's continue this… *conversation* later," he said, in a low and husky voice, sending waves of delight through Demi's body.

Demi nodded as she looked into his eyes. Although she didn't want him to leave, this wasn't the right time or place to express their mutual feelings for each other. Besides, they both had responsibilities needing immediate attention. He had some investigating to do, and she needed to finish the dress she was working on for a customer before heading home to get ready for tonight's party.

After Fola left, Demi found it difficult to concentrate on her work. The kiss she and Fola shared kept replaying in her mind. She sighed as she thought to herself. *Now I understand what the phrase 'hot and bothered' means…*

29 | Temidayo

After leaving Demi's shop, Fola drove to the mainland. Based on the information he had gathered, the man who he suspected could be Fey's father worked for Ariri Corporation. However, according to the employee records, his name was Temidayo Ademola, not David Ademola. Initially, he wondered if they were related. Maybe brothers? Or did he change his name? Even if that were the case, most people changed their last name, not their given name.

Fola had been surveilling Temidayo for a few weeks now to answer some of the questions he had. Where did he live? What was his personal life like? Did he have a wife or children? Did he have any hobbies?

When Fola discreetly enquired about him at work, he found out that his colleagues and subordinates had great respect for Temidayo. They described him as a brilliant civil engineer who kept to himself mostly. He was easygoing, and nobody thought he was married, although he sometimes talked about his children.

So far, Fola had gathered that on weekdays, Temidayo's routine comprised going to the office, sometimes to the gym, and then home. On the weekends, he mostly stayed indoors except for going to the gym and eating lunch or dinner at one of his favorite restaurants. It was clear that the man took his fitness and health very seriously. He was in his early fifties, but he looked very fit, almost as fit as a man fifteen years younger than him. Temidayo would occasionally have drinks with a few colleagues from work, but other than that, he didn't seem to have much of an active social life.

Also, the man didn't seem to have any wife or kids. Based on Fola's surveillance so far, he lived alone. This differed from the information that Fey had given him. According to her, her father had remarried, most likely with at least one child. Maybe he was now divorced?

Fola approached Temidayo for the first time at the gym where he had a membership. He had purposely asked Temidayo to spot him a few times on the bench press equipment, as he wanted to get a feel of his personality. After that, Fola joined the gym and subsequently timed his visits to the gym to sync with Temidayo's. He would also offer to spot Fola and soon, they became gym acquaintances.

Today, Fola was meeting with one of his men who he had assigned to tail Temidayo in the last few days. When he arrived at the meeting place, his man told him that Temidayo had traveled to Sagamu, Ogun State to visit his parents. Fola instructed him to let him know as soon as he was back. His informant also mentioned that before Temidayo left, he had gone to the post office to mail something. Curious, he had gone in after Temidayo left to ask where the mail was going? After showing his badge, the postal clerk reluctantly told him that the letter was going to the United States.

Fola thought to himself, *What could he possibly have mailed to the States?* Temidayo Ademola, by most indications, seemed to likely be the same person as David Ademola, despite some discrepancies in the information that Fola had gathered and the information that Fey had provided. He thought it was fortuitous that Fey found a photo of him. Otherwise, he never would've guessed.

Fola decided to meet and speak to Temidayo Ademola as soon as he returned from his trip.

***

After the security guard let him in, Temidayo drove into the gated compound where his apartment building was located. He parked his car and took out his travel suitcase before heading to his two-bedroom flat. He had just returned from visiting his parents in Sagamu, Ogun State. He was exhausted from his drive, and just wanted to eat dinner and relax. But when he opened his fridge, he realized it was empty. The caterer he usually ordered cooked meals from wasn't due to be back from vacation for another week. Now he wished he hadn't refused the cooked food his mother had wanted him to take back with him. He went out to dinner instead.

Soon, he was at his favorite restaurant. After he placed his order, he sat quietly reading an article on his phone while taking sips of the beer that the server had brought to him.

"Good evening, sir," he suddenly heard someone say to him. He looked up from his phone to see a handsome gentleman smiling at him. Temidayo raised a surprised brow when he recognized the man. "Ah, you're my spotter at the gym!" he said with a smile as he held out his hand for a handshake. He took a quick look around the restaurant before he asked, "Are you here with someone?"

"No, I'm not."

"If you don't mind, you can sit with me so you don't have to wait for a table. It gets pretty crowded here around dinnertime." Temidayo didn't mind some company tonight, so he had offered to share his table.

"I think I'll take you up on your offer. Thank you, sir." He sat down and introduced himself. "I'm Fola, by the way."

"I'm Dayo."

Although they had met at the gym several times, they never introduced themselves.

"I didn't see you at the gym this past couple of days," Fola said, making conversation.

"Yes, I traveled to visit my parents. I just returned this evening."

"Oh, I see. I hope they are well."

"Yes, thank you," Dayo said with a smile. "What about your family? Do they live here in Lagos?"

"Yes, they do. They're doing well." Fola signaled to a server to come over. He ordered a drink and his meal and continued chatting with Dayo.

"Your wife and children are still visiting with your parents?" Fola asked. He wasn't here to eat after all. He needed to confirm once and for all if the man sitting across from him was Fey's father. He had also noticed that Dayo was now wearing a wedding band, but he had seen him without the wedding band at times, so he couldn't make a determination either way.

Dayo didn't seem surprised at the question, though. "My wife and children are out of the country at the moment," he replied.

"Oh, I see... I assume they're on vacation or something? You must miss them this holiday season. I bet you can't wait for them to return."

Dayo smiled wryly as he had a faraway look in his eyes. Fola didn't miss his facial expression and the fact that Dayo did not give him a response.

Dayo abruptly changed the subject before Fola could ask more probing questions. "So, Fola, what do you do for a living?" He'd met the guy at the gym, but they never had time to talk.

"I'm a detective with the EFCC."

Dayo raised an impressed brow. "How's that going for you?"

"I enjoy the work. I get to travel once in a while, but I also get to do my own thing. Sometimes I consult with others. For example, I am currently investigating a case for a friend who hasn't seen her father in a very long time. She'll be getting married soon and would love to have her father walk her down the aisle."

Fola's words struck a chord in Dayo. He hadn't seen his daughters in a very long time either. His eldest, Feyisayo, was almost of marriageable age now. He imagined that she had probably graduated from college as well. What he wouldn't give to see her again. He wondered if he would ever get the chance to walk her down the aisle on her wedding day. *That's a pipe dream, Dayo,* he thought sadly to himself.

"My friend's name is Feyisayo Ademola," Fola suddenly said, without taking his eyes off of the man in front of him.

Dayo snapped out of his thoughts instantly, and his eyes met Fola's. "What did you just say?" Dayo asked in disbelief. He asked himself, *Am I hearing things?*

"What?" Fola asked, feigning ignorance.

"Your friend's name. What was it again?"

"Oh, her name is Feyisayo Ademola. Do you know her?"

Dayo looked wide-eyed. His heart was beating madly in his chest. "Did she tell you her father's name?" he asked after a few seconds.

Fola smiled. "Yes, her father's name is David Ademola."

Dayo suddenly felt all the energy leave his body. He sat frozen in his seat, staring at the young man in front of him.

"Are you alright, sir?" Fola asked, seeing Dayo's reaction.

After a few seconds, Dayo composed himself and asked, trying to hide the emotion in his voice, "Is—is your friend here in Lagos as well?"

"Yes, she just moved back from the United States a few months ago."

Another bombshell hit Dayo's heart. *Oh my god! My baby girl is here!*

Fola could see from Dayo's reaction that he recognized the names he had mentioned. He slid his phone across the table to him. "Here's a photo of my friend with her father and her younger sister, taken many years ago."

Dayo slowly looked down at the phone in front of him. He recognized the photo. His wife had taken the picture a few days before he left the States for Nigeria to see his supposedly ailing father. Dayo's eyes softened as he looked at the photo with both his daughters. Unknowingly tears welled in his eyes.

This was the final confirmation that Fola needed. Temidayo Ademola was certainly David Ademola.

"Your daughter wants to meet you, Mr. Temidayo David Ademola," Fola said after a moment.

Dayo raised his eyes to meet Fola's. He wiped away the tears that were now streaming down his face. He pushed Fola's phone back towards him on the table. Then he asked, "When did you realize that I'm the person she's looking for?"

Fola smiled. "Based on my initial investigation, I thought you *might* be her father's brother, but your parents only have one child. And when I found out you had recently mailed something to the United States, I felt it was too much of a coincidence. Besides, the only major difference between Fey's description of you and what I found out is that she expected that you would be married. You actually never remarried, did you?"

Although Dayo did not like that someone had investigated and surveilled him without his knowledge, he had to admit that Detective Fola was good at his job. "No, my parents wanted me to, but I refused," he responded.

Fola nodded. He wanted to know why he never went back to his family, but he didn't want to pry. That was something Fey would have to ask him herself.

"So, my baby is getting married, huh? Who's the lucky guy?"

Fola chuckled. "It's not my place to say. You'll have to hear that from your daughter."

Dayo smiled. "When can I meet her?" he asked.

"How about her birthday?" Fola suggested.

Dayo nodded. "Her birthday is on Saturday." That was three days from now.

***

Saturday rolled around and Fey excitedly waited at Iben's house for the birthday surprise that he and Fola had promised her. They were lounging on Iben's bedroom balcony, and Fey had tried to rack her brain to try and figure it out, but she couldn't come up with anything.

"Babe, I'm dying from anticipation here. Can't you just tell me what it is?" she begged. "I promise to still act surprised when I see it." She batted her eyelids for effect.

"No, your acting skills are yet to be verified," he said, appearing unfazed by her sudden coquettishness.

"Ugh, you're no fun! Party pooper!" she said as she stomped into the bedroom and flopped on the bed, pouting.

Iben chuckled. He walked to the bed, sat next to her, and whispered suggestively in a low voice, "I think I know what can take your mind off the surprise until Fola gets here."

Fey scooted away from him and said, "Get your mind out the gutters, Mr. Ariri."

Iben chuckled again. "Future Mrs. Ariri, I think *you* are the one with the dirty mind." Then he reached into his pocket and produced a small lilac envelope. "Happy birthday, babe," he said with a teasing smile.

Realizing she had gotten his intentions wrong, Fey poked Iben in the arm and said, "You tricked me! I thought…"

Iben raised a brow, still smiling. "You thought…?" He slowly waved the lilac envelope still in his hand.

Embarrassed, Fey looked away after she took the envelope from him. Iben smiled as he watched Fey take out the contents of the envelope. It was a black no-limit VIP card for unlimited services at one of the most exclusive spas in Lagos. Fey's mouth was ajar for a few seconds. She had mentioned in passing that she had gone to the spa with Demi some weeks back and that she enjoyed it. It was more of a splurging moment for her, as it was too expensive for her to afford regularly with her civil servant salary.

Fey tried to refuse it. "I love it Iben, but this is too much."

Iben sighed. "We're getting married, babe. You cannot refuse a husband who wants to spoil his wife," Iben complained.

"We're not married yet," Fey countered with a mischievous smile, although deep down she loved hearing Iben refer to himself as her husband.

Iben wrapped his arm around her waist and pulled her closer to him. "Okay, let's go to the courthouse and get married tomorrow then," he declared seriously.

Fey stared at him wide-eyed. "Of course not, don't be silly."

"So, will you accept the gift and go to the spa and pamper yourself as I expect?" Iben asked.

Fey smiled and nodded.

"Good," Iben said before kissing her on the cheek. Then he added, "Oh, and you have to go at least once every month."

Fey chuckled amusedly. "Why?"

Iben raised a brow and stared at her, indicating that she should know the answer to her question.

"Fine, fine, I will," she said. Then she added jokingly, "In fact, I'll bring all my girlfriends and run up an enormous bill at your expense."

To Fey's surprise, Iben said, "I would love nothing more. Because that means you have accepted that you and I are one and that all I have is yours."

Fey looked him in the eye. His words touched her heart. Then she leaned in and kissed him.

After the kiss ended, Iben held her close and asked, "Babe, when are you going to move in with me? We're getting married, so it's okay, right?" They had only been engaged for a little less than two weeks, but now whenever she came over, he didn't want her to leave. He imagined coming home to her every day.

"Let's pick a wedding date first," Fey said. "Do you have a preference?"

"No, I don't. Papa doesn't either," he responded.

Fey nodded. "Okay, I'll let you know after I talk to my mom."

A moment later, Mobi called Iben to let him know that Fola had arrived. "Let's go," Iben said to Fey. "Your surprise is here."

***

Fey eagerly followed Iben downstairs. When they reached the living room, she saw an older gentleman seated next to Fola. He was dressed casually, in a black pair of slacks and a tailored shirt made from Ankara fabric. His head was shaved, but he had neatly groomed facial hair. It was Dayo Ademola.

As soon as Dayo saw Fey, he stood up. Their eyes met, and he smiled ruefully as tears welled up in his eyes. "Feyisayo..." he said softly.

When Fey heard her name from his lips, her heart skipped a beat. She immediately knew who he was. "Dad...?" she said in disbelief.

Dayo nodded as the tears streamed down his face. Fey was on autopilot as her legs immediately carried her to his outstretched arms. While in his embrace, she let the tears flow. Iben and Fola quietly watched the emotional reunion between father and daughter. After a while, the pair let go of each other.

"You look so much like your mother," Dayo said admiringly.

Fey chuckled. "You think so? We hardly get along."

Dayo smiled. "I bet. You were always very strong-willed when you were little. Just like her."

"Figures," Fey said with an eye roll as they sat down.

"How's Tutu?"

"She's doing great." Fey took her phone out of her pocket and pulled up a picture of Tutu for her father to see. "She's studying Material Science at CMU."

Dayo's eyes softened when he laid eyes on the photo. "My baby's all grown up…" he said.

Fey thought his voice sounded sad.

"How's your mother," he asked after handing Fey's phone back to her.

"She's good. She's a tenured professor at Wilmington University."

"No way," Dayo said with a light chuckle. "She hated teaching when we were doing our NYSC." He had a faraway look in his eyes as he said, "That's where we met, you know." He sighed. "I bet she hates me now."

"I think she misses you a lot. She just always expresses it as anger," Fey said.

Dayo said nothing, so Fey asked, "Dad, what happened? Why didn't you return to us? Mom said you remarried? Is that true?"

Dayo sighed and said, "It's a long story, my dear. I promise I'll tell you some other time."

Fey nodded. She didn't want to press him, so she let it go.

"So, I hear you're getting married," Dayo said, changing the subject.

"Yes." Fey smiled and looked towards Iben, who was seated across from them. Iben stood up and walked towards Dayo and Fey. Fey looped her arm with Iben's and introduced him to her father.

"Dad, this is my fiancé, Iben Ariri," she said.

Iben bowed respectfully and said with a smile, "It's nice to meet you, sir."

Dayo stood up slowly. He glanced from Fey to Iben with a look of disbelief. *What?! I must be hearing things*, he thought to himself in alarm.

"You're Edafe Ariri's son?" he asked, looking wide-eyed.

"His grandson," Fey corrected. She noticed Dayo's distressed look. "Dad, is everything okay," Fey asked.

"Have you met Chief Ariri? Is he okay with your engagement?"

"Yes, he gave us his blessings," Iben responded.

This is bad! This is really, really bad! He must not know that she's my daughter, Dayo thought to himself. *Maybe he does and is doing this on purpose!*

"Do you know Papa?" Fey asked.

Dayo met his daughter's questioning gaze and quickly composed himself. "Yes, I work for Ariri Corporation in the R&D division. So, I've met him many times."

"Really? What a coincidence. To think that I've been looking for you for the past few months and you were so close."

"Your dad goes by Temidayo Ademola at work, so nobody could've made the connection that he was David Ademola," Fola chimed in. "If not for the photo you found, we'd probably still be searching for him."

"David is my middle name," Dayo explained. "I used David when we moved to the States since it was easier for Americans to pronounce." Dayo looked away from the gaze of the couple standing hand in hand in front of him. *This marriage cannot happen. What a twisted fate this is,* he thought sadly. *I finally get to see my daughter, but she's engaged to the devil's son. Ha! What gods did I offend in this lifetime? Have I not suffered enough? Why bring my innocent daughter into this quagmire?*

Iben, Fey, and Fola watched in confusion as Dayo's expressions changed between disbelief, sadness, anger, and determination.

Iben hadn't expected that Fey's dad would be thrilled at the thought of his long-lost daughter getting married to some guy he didn't know. But he hadn't expected this. From his perspective, his future father-in-law's reaction was just odd. He shared a look with Fola, who raised his brows and shrugged, indicating that he had no clue what was going on either.

After a moment, Dayo finally looked up and spoke in a very solemn voice. "Feyisayo, this man's father is the reason I couldn't go back to the States many years ago!"

30 | Secrets

Iben's heart skipped a beat. His father died many years ago. Besides, Dayo was the first person he'd met who claimed to know his father. "You knew my Dad?"

Dayo furrowed his brows. *Why is he talking about his father in the past tense?* "I'm talking about Edafe Ariri."

It was Iben's turn to look confused. "My grandfather? What did he do?" he asked.

Dayo sighed. He hadn't expected that he'd be talking about this to anyone, least of all, today. After they were all seated, Dayo began.

"Fifteen years ago, I returned to Nigeria temporarily to take care of my ailing father. When I arrived, I found out that he wasn't sick and that it was all a ploy to force me into taking a second wife and have a son. I refused and my parents claimed I was going to destroy everything they'd worked for all their lives if I didn't marry this woman. Her name was Kemi Olaniran, and we were childhood friends.

"At the time, my parents and Kemi's parents were working on submitting a bid for the construction of a five-star hotel that Ariri Corporation advertised. My parents owned a construction company, and Kemi's parents were looking to expand their business. Our parents wanted to form a merger between both companies to increase their chances of winning this contract. My refusal to marry Kemi put their alliance in jeopardy. Anyway, I told my parents that I would do my best to help them with the contract proposal, after which I was going back to my family in Washington, DC.

"Torrential rainfall was characteristic of the location chosen for the construction project, and the land designated had a five percent slope. The first phase of construction had to be halted because floods were compromising the integrity of the foundation. I came up with several ideas to fix these challenges, created a CAD 3D model, and presented it to the Ariri Corporation stakeholders.

"They were impressed and awarded the contract to my parents' company. Edafe also offered me a job with Ariri Corporation. I was flattered, but I declined, of course. I planned that when I returned from the States with my family, later on, I'd take over my parents' construction business instead."

"What hotel is this you're referring to?" Iben asked.

"Harmony House."

Iben raised a surprised brow. "Papa told me about the history of that building. It was the first structure that ushered in MorningStar Realty as a branch of Ariri Corporation. So, you're the brilliant engineer he mentioned…"

Dayo shrugged dismissively. "Anyway, during this time, Chief Ariri and I would meet periodically to discuss the construction and how things were going. And every time, he'd try to sweeten his offer to have me work for his company. Once, he joked about bethroting his *grandson* so he could marry one of my daughters in the future."

Fey and Iben looked at each other at Dayo's words. What irony…

"During one of our discussions, I complained to him that I missed my wife and kids, but my parents were still trying to force me to marry Kemi Olaniran. He said he knew her parents and that he would take care of the issue for me. I was so thankful—but what happened next destroyed everything. Kemi was murdered, and Chief Ariri framed me for her death."

"That's quite an accusation you're making," Fola chimed in.

"It's the truth! To this day, I do not understand the rationale behind his actions. Maybe he already had a grudge against her family or something. Although that woman was a pain in my rear, she didn't deserve to die."

Dayo sighed as he remembered that night. He had received a call from Kemi asking him to come and see her. They met up for dinner and she begged him to give her a chance. Dayo told her for the umpteenth time that he was happily married and not interested in her. After dinner, he walked her to her car and drove away in his shortly after. The next day, his parents told him that Kemi had died. She was found in her car and not breathing. They found her car in the same spot that he left her the night before. They said she died of cardiac arrest, but he thought Kemi was too young to die in such a manner.

The next day, he received a package at his office. It contained a video recording of him walking Kemi to her car, and after he left, Kemi had her head resting against the steering wheel. Perhaps she was crying. A few minutes later, someone who had the same build as Dayo went to the car and stabbed her arm with something that looked like a syringe. Dayo guessed that whatever was in that syringe killed her. In addition to the video was a note accusing him of murdering her.

Scared and distressed, Dayo went straight to Edafe Ariri. Someone was trying to set him up, and since Edafe had connections, he was going to ask him to help. He had to figure out who was trying to frame him so that he could get out of this mess. When he met with Edafe, Dayo found out he had asked the wrong person for help.

"You wanted me to get rid of her," Edafe said with a sneer.

Wide-eyed and angry, Dayo yelled, "I never asked you to kill her!"

"*Perhaps*—I was a bit heavy-handed," Edafe said, waving his hand dismissively. "But you weren't specific, so I did what I thought was best."

Dayo glared at him. *This man is the devil incarnate!* After calming himself down a bit, he asked, "Why are you trying to frame me for this?"

"Because I want you to work for me," Edafe said. "You see, I like to surround myself with intelligent people. You're a brilliant engineer and I want you on my team. If you agree, I'll make this go away. If you disagree, I'll send this recording to the police."

Dayo felt the energy drain out of him. "I have a family in America waiting for me," he said. "I cannot stay here."

"Then, have them return to Nigeria," Edafe countered.

Dayo looked alarmed. Why would he bring his family into this mess? He didn't trust that Edafe wouldn't try to hurt his wife and kids on a whim.

As if reading his thoughts, Edafe added, "If you try to escape to the States, your parents will pay the price!"

Seeing no way out, Dayo then made the hardest decision in his life. In order to protect his loved ones in Nigeria and America, he did as Edafe wanted. He stayed in Nigeria and started the MorningStar Realty arm of Ariri Corporation. Years later, he moved to the R&D division. Edafe forced Dayo's parents into retirement by buying out their company and folding it into Ariri Corporation.

"At least Edafe has been paying me well," Dayo continued. "It's been good enough to send money to my family in America so that I could support them financially since I couldn't be there physically."

"Mom told me about the money that you've been sending all these years," Fey said. "It's helped pay for mine and Tutu's college education and stuff."

"I'm glad to hear that," Dayo said with a wry smile.

"This doesn't make any sense," Iben suddenly said.

"Are you suggesting that my father is lying?" Fey asked, getting upset.

"No, that's not what I mean. I know my grandfather is not a saint, but why would he do something so despicable just to make you work for him?"

"It's a pointless endeavor to try to understand *evil*," Dayo responded.

Iben had no response.

After a moment, Dayo said, "Iben, despite what your—*grandfather* has done, I have nothing against you. My daughter fell in love with you, so you must be a really great guy."

Then he continued, "Feyisayo, you're a grown woman and I cannot force you to do anything. Beyond sending money to your mother, I haven't been in your life at all, so I have no right to make any demands of you. I am glad that you looked for me, and I am very happy that I got to see you again. It's your decision to make if you still want to marry this man, but knowing who he is, I cannot support this relationship. It might've been better if you found me *after* you both were married. But now that I know, I just can't." He glanced over at Iben and said, "His father destroyed my family, our family, and I cannot forgive that."

Complete silence enveloped the room.

After a while, Dayo stood up and handed a card to Fey. "Here's my phone number and address. Let's meet up soon so we can catch up properly."

Fey stood up and hugged him. "I will, Dad," she said.

Dayo nodded towards Fola and said, "Thank you for everything." Then he left.

Fey slumped back in her seat next to Iben. She was still trying to process all the information that her father had dumped on them. Her mind was in turmoil. What kind of fate was this? She finally found her father, but it turns out that her fiance's grandfather was responsible for tearing her family apart. She suddenly felt Iben hold her hand, so she turned to look at him.

"Babe…" he started, but he couldn't form any words. Everything he'd heard from Fey's dad about his grandfather repulsed him. If what Dayo said was true, then his grandfather was a different person than who he knew. He also knew his grandfather never did anything without a reason. Perhaps there was something that Dayo left out of the story, he thought. It wasn't until Fey stood up and was climbing the stairs did Iben snap out of his thoughts. He stood up to follow her.

Fola remained in the living room, deep in thought. *Who would've known that a joyous moment would turn out to be a depressing one?* In Fola's opinion, what Dayo said sounded like something Edafe would do, but only if someone double-crossed him. He, like Iben, wondered if there was any information about the situation that Dayo didn't tell them.

***

When Iben entered his bedroom, he saw Fey putting on her shoes. "You're leaving?" he asked, surprised.

Fey didn't look at him. "Yes."

"Can we talk first?"

"Not right now. I need some time to think." She reached for her handbag and started toward the bedroom door.

Iben panicked and shut the door, blocking the doorway. "Babe, let's talk about this before you go."

Fey sighed. She just wanted to be alone right now. Trying her best to speak in a measured tone, she said, "Iben, I really can't do this now."

"Please…" he begged as he reached for her hands.

Exasperated, Fey yanked her hands out of his. "Let go!" She stepped back and glared at him. "What part of *I need time to think*, don't you understand?!"

Iben looked hurt by her reaction. "I just want to talk…" he said softly.

Iben didn't budge from the doorway, so Fey snapped, "Fine! Talk!" She stomped to the bed and sat down in a huff.

Iben moved from the door to sit next to her. However, as soon as he sat down, Fey bolted for the door. Although he was surprised, Iben quickly caught up to her and wrapped his arms around her waist from behind in a tight hug, stopping her. "Babe, don't be like this…"

Angry and determined to leave, Fey thrashed her body and flailed her arms and legs to get away from his embrace, but Iben wouldn't let her go. Desperate, she suddenly wrapped her right leg around Iben's right leg and deliberately tripped both of them. Iben lost his balance and fell backward, taking Fey down with him. He landed on his bottom and winced at the impact. But unlike Fey had expected, Iben still didn't let go of her.

"Let me go!" Fey screamed.

Iben had never seen her this angry before, and it shocked him. However, he was worried that if he let go, as angry as she was and with the news they'd heard from Temidayo, he might not see her for a very long time. "Fey, please…"

"Let me go!" Fey yelled angrily and continuously, still trying to get away. Soon she started crying, out of anger and frustration. "I can't do this, Iben…" she cried repeatedly in between sobs.

Iben's heart ached at her words. "Please babe, let's talk about this."

"I can't…" she cried. "Your grandfather was directly responsible for breaking up my family. Because of him, my sister and I grew up without our father in our lives. Because of him, my mother was sad for many years…"

"I'm sorry… I'm sorry…" was all Iben could say. He truly understood how she felt. The woman he loved was hurting so badly and because of that, so was he.

Iben held Fey in his embrace for a long time until her crying subsided and she stopped trying to leave. When she had calmed down, she was sitting on the floor between Iben's legs, her back against his chest.

"I need some time to think, Iben," Fey said, her voice hoarse from crying.

"I love you, babe. Don't push me away. We can work through this together," Iben pleaded.

"It's not fair for you to ask me not to take time to think about this. Or would you rather I lie to you now and later change my mind?"

Iben sighed at her words. He realized that perhaps he was being selfish. "Two weeks," he said. "And then I'm going to find you if I don't hear from you."

Fey nodded in agreement. Two weeks was reasonable. "You can't contact me during the two weeks!" she added firmly.

Iben met her determined gaze. He could tell that she would not budge. "Okay…"

After Fey left, Iben stayed seated on the bedroom floor until Fola showed up. When Fola saw Iben's dejected body language, he knew that things hadn't gone too well with Fey. He wasn't surprised though.

She had sprinted down the stairs a few minutes before and would only look him in the eye for a couple of seconds to thank him for finding her father before she left.

"She doesn't want to see me for a while," Iben said sadly.

"Let her sort out her feelings, Iben," Fola said. "In the meantime, you need to focus on your own problems."

"Her problem is my problem," Iben countered.

"You know what I mean," Fola responded. He was talking about how they were going to deal with the situation, especially after Edafe found out who Fey's father is. "Remember our conversation in Port Harcourt about burying your head in the sand? This is one of those times where you do *not* want to do that!"

Iben looked up and met Fola's piercing gaze. "I know…" he said.

***

A few days later, Iben contacted Dayo, asking to meet with him for drinks after work. Dayo agreed, and when he arrived at the meeting place, he was ushered to a private room where Iben and Fola were already waiting.

Iben stood up and bowed respectfully. "Good evening, sir," he said in greeting.

Dayo was surprised at Iben's attitude toward him. He half expected him to be hostile since he had recently exposed Edafe's role in separating his fiancée's family. Dayo looked him in the eye and said, "Hello, Iben." He turned to Fola. "Hello, Fola." They shook hands.

After they were seated and had ordered drinks, Iben said, "Thank you for coming to meet with me."

Dayo nodded. "What do you want to talk about? If it's about my daughter, my position hasn't changed."

"I understand, and I'm not here to change your mind." He paused before he said, "I'm actually giving Fey some space so that she can decide what she wants to do about us." As Iben said those words, he felt a tightness in his chest. It had been a difficult few days since that fateful Saturday. He missed Fey so much and had been struggling to keep his promise to not contact her. But whenever he remembered her intense fury that day, he would get himself together. Throwing himself into his work had been a good distraction so far.

Dayo noticed the brief look of sadness that floated across Iben's features. He was surprised at Iben's statement. Although he had seen Fey and spoken to her a few times since last Saturday, she hadn't mentioned this development. Somehow, he felt sorry for the poor guy, as he seemed to truly care about his daughter.

Iben composed himself and said, "In the meantime, I want to know more about the Olanirans. The other day, you mentioned that the lady who died is Kemi Olaniran. What were her parents' names?"

"Oladokun and Tinuke Olaniran," Dayo responded.

"Do you know where they live?"

Dayo shot him a wary look.

Iben quickly added, "I'm not looking for trouble or anything. It's just that—I just want to see if I can make things right in some way. I know it's been a long time, but I don't want to just—"

Dayo cut him off and said, "They live in Festac." Dayo's guilt over what happened to Kemi made him keep in touch with them.

"Do you have a photo of Kemi or her parents, by any chance?"

"No, I don't."

Iben then asked Dayo for all the details surrounding his blackmail by Edafe. Dayo obliged.

"What do you hope to achieve by digging all this up, Iben?" Dayo asked at the end of their conversation. "The damage is done. Your money isn't going to bring back a dead person. Nor will it reverse time."

Iben didn't have any answers. "I don't know yet," he said in response.

***

Over the next few days, Fola verified Dayo's information regarding the whereabouts of Kemi Olaniran's parents. On Saturday, a week after Fey's birthday, Iben and Fola drove to the Olaniran residence in Festac. When they arrived, Iben parked his Maybach SUV in front of the entrance. He stepped out and looked around the neighborhood. As he suspected, it seemed familiar.

Iben stopped in his tracks as he suddenly had a memory flash across his mind. He was at the front of a house, riding his bike with his younger sister, and a woman who was not his mother was chaperoning them.

"Are you okay?" a concerned Fola asked.

Iben looked at him and said, "I think—I used to live next door…"

"Are you sure?" Fola probed. Iben had mentioned that the Olaniran last name sounded familiar when he first heard Dayo mention it. That was the primary reason they met with Dayo to see if they could get more details.

Iben nodded and then described the memory he just had to Fola.

Fola knew it had been a very long time since Iben had any vivid memories of his sister, mother, or father. He placed a hand on Iben's shoulder. "Are you sure you want to do this?" he asked.

Iben chuckled. "What happened to not burying my head in the sand anymore?" he asked in a teasing tone when he saw Fola's worried expression.

Fola tossed him a nasty look and said, as he brushed past him, "Asshole!"

Iben laughed. "For a second there, I actually thought you might be worried about me, bro!"

Fola scoffed. "We're getting older here while you joke around," he said irritably and then rang the bell.

After waiting a few minutes, the pedestrian entrance to the gated compound slowly creaked open. A young girl who looked to be in her late teens poked her head out and said, "Who is it?" She had an annoyed expression on her face until her gaze fell on Iben and Fola. Seeing the two well-dressed, handsome men standing in front of her, the girl's attitude quickly changed from annoyed and irritated to shy and demure. "Oh, hello," she said sweetly. "How can I help you?"

Iben raised an amused brow at the young girl's quick attitude change.

Fola, on the other hand, flashed one of his signature smiles at the girl and said, "Hi there, young lady. We're here to see Mr. Olaniran."

The girl smiled shyly at Fola and then let them into the house. After they were seated in the living room, she left for a few minutes and returned with a tray of refreshments. She made a show of serving Fola first, before Iben.

"He will be here in a few minutes," she said as she twirled the ends of her braids and smiled at Fola.

Fola smiled back and winked at her. "Thank you very much," he said.

"Were you just flirting with the baby chick?" Iben teased after the girl left.

Fola gave him the stink eye. "That's gross. She's just a little girl. Even if she wasn't, I'm now a one-woman man!"

Iben said nothing, he just smiled to himself. *Good job whipping this guy into shape, Demi!*

While they waited, Iben looked around the room. As was common in most Nigerian homes, there were family pictures on the walls. Many of the pictures were of a couple on their wedding day. Iben assumed they were Mr. and Mrs. Olaniran. There were also some pictures of a young woman. Iben stood up to see them properly. His heart skipped a beat. This was the woman in his memory.

Just then, he heard a man's voice. "That's my daughter, Kemi."

Iben turned around to see the owner of the voice. It was an older gentleman who looked to be in his early seventies. It was Oladokun Olaniran. Although he had a head full of gray hair, his voice was anything but frail. It was deep and commanded attention.

Iben bowed respectfully in greeting. "Good afternoon, sir. Sorry for showing up unannounced. My name is Iben Ariri and I think my family used to live next door when I was little."

Dokun's eyes blinked rapidly and his jaw dropped as he stared at Iben. "Iben? Oh my god! You are so grown now. Come, come," he said as he adjusted his glasses and gestured for Iben to come closer. Iben did as asked and Dokun hugged him. Iben was surprised at the warm reception and awkwardly returned the hug. Afterward, Dokun said, "Sit, sit."

"I'm sorry I don't remember you, sir, but I do remember your daughter. She used to watch my sister and me when we were playing outside." Iben furrowed his brow as another memory suddenly came to him. "Did she have a child?" he asked.

Dokun smiled and said, "Yes." Then he called for someone. "Deola! Deola!"

In a few seconds, the young girl who let them in earlier came. "Yes, Grandpa," she said.

Iben and Fola looked at each other at the same time, surprise evident on their faces.

"This is Kemi's daughter, Deola. I think she was around one or two years old at the time." He turned to Deola and said, "This is Iben Ariri. His family used to live next door when your mother was alive."

Deola nodded and said, "It's nice to meet you."

"Likewise, Deola. How old are you now?" Iben asked.

"Nineteen."

"Wow. So you're attending university?"

"Not yet. I am waiting for my JAMB exam results."

"What do you want to study?"

"Finance," she said.

"That's great... I'm glad I got to see you again," Iben said with a smile.

Deola nodded, and Dokun waved her away. After she left, he said, "You look so much like your father now that you're older. How is he these days?"

"My father died many years ago, along with my sister and mother," Iben said. "Did you not know?"

"Yes, that was very unfortunate." He paused at the memory before he continued. "But I'm not talking about your stepfather. I'm referring to Edafe Ariri, your biological father."

This old man must be getting senile, Iben thought to himself. "You're mistaken. He's my grandfather."

"Edafe Ariri is your *biological* father!" Dokun said firmly as he looked Iben in the eye. "Did that man not tell you the truth after all these years?"

Iben and Fola looked at each other. This conversation was getting more bizarre by the moment.

"Do you have proof of your claim?" Fola asked.

"Edafe does. He had a DNA test done to prove paternity at the time. I was the one who got your blood sample from the hospital for him. You were around nine."

At this point, Iben's heart was beating madly in his chest. "Can you please tell me everything you know?" he asked, his voice shaking slightly.

Dokun sighed. "There's not much more to say. I used to be the manager at the hospital where your stepfather Andrew worked as a doctor. Edafe found out about your existence and wanted to verify that you were his son. So, he requested a blood sample for a DNA test. After he confirmed that you were his child, he asked your mother to give you to him but she refused. In order to prevent a custody battle your mother knew she could neither afford nor win, she and your stepfather decided to move your family out of Lagos, as far away from Edafe's reach as possible. On the night before you all were scheduled to move, the accident happened, claiming everyone's lives except for yours."

Iben slumped back in his seat. He suddenly felt sick to his stomach. "So... Papa is my *father*?" he said in shock.

The room was silent for about a minute.

Dokun suddenly said, "Edafe still owes me a favor for helping him out that night. Maybe you can help with my granddaughter. She's very bright and I would like her to attend a private university. However, it's expensive and I am a retired old man living on a fixed income."

Iben, still in a daze, did not respond, so Fola answered for him. He handed Dokun a card and said, "Please call this number to speak with Iben's assistant whenever you need anything."

Dokun accepted the card and smiled. "Thank you."

After Iben and Fola left, Dokun shook his head as he thought to himself. *Rich people and their secrets!* Then he smiled slyly as he looked at the business card in his hand. *At least I got something out of this, even after all these years.*

Unknown to Iben and Fola, Dokun had purposely left out some details surrounding the events leading up to the accident, but he didn't care. He would leave Iben and Edafe to sort that out amongst themselves.

Since Kemi passed away, Dokun and his wife were saddled with the responsibility of raising Deola. While they loved their granddaughter, it hadn't been easy on them financially. When the merger between his and Temidayo's parents' company went bust, and Ariri Corporation awarded the hotel contract to the Ademolas instead, Dokun's finances declined. After all this time, he still had heartburn about the situation, even though Dayo would come to visit them periodically bringing gifts and money.

Dokun was always an opportunist, and although Edafe had ignored him for many years, he felt that at least, Iben seemed easier to manipulate. He smiled to himself again.

***

Iben walked out of the house, still in a daze. When they got to the vehicle, Fola said, "I'll drive." He took the keys from Iben, who didn't resist.

The drive was silent for a while until Iben finally spoke. "It now makes sense why Fey's dad kept referring to Papa as my father. But— why would my mother introduce him as my grandfather?"

Iben remembered the first time he met Edafe. It was a school day, and it was his tenth birthday. While he was waiting for his mother to pick him up, a man walked up to him wishing him a happy birthday. When his mother saw them together, she seemed surprised. She then introduced him as her grandfather.

Fola responded, "Maybe because she didn't want you to know that your stepfather was not your biological father."

"He loved me like I was his son. I never knew the difference." After a pause, he added, "Why didn't Papa just tell me who he really was after the accident?"

"Papa is the only one who can answer that, Iben."

The rest of the drive back to Lekki was silent. Iben was internally grappling with how his reality had been upended. Fola was thinking about the aftermath of Edafe finding out that they had come across these recent findings. He was also worried about Iben. All this news had to be affecting him psychologically and emotionally.

31 | Dilemma

A few days after Dayo revealed Edafe's sinister role in keeping him in Nigeria, Fey visited her father at his home. She had driven there straight from work and, as usual, she was exhausted from driving in traffic. She wasn't sure if she would ever get used to driving around Lagos. It wasn't an issue with directions; it was the stress of dealing with impatient drivers and those who flaunted the rules of the road. It was stressful always having to drive on the defensive. She used to think it was a bit ostentatious when some people hired drivers, but now she felt that if she could afford one, she wouldn't mind taking the back seat on most days.

When she arrived, Dayo welcomed her with a warm hug. "Hi baby girl," he said with a smile.

"I'm not a little girl anymore," Fey said with a chuckle as she hugged him back.

"You're always going to be my baby girl," he said with a smile as he pulled away from their hug.

Fey rolled her eyes, even though his words warmed her heart.

"I'm sure you're hungry," Dayo said and gestured to the food he had on the dining table.

Fey looked at the spread of dishes on the table. There was jollof rice, chicken and beef stew, vegetable stew, moimoi, and fried rice. "You can cook?" she asked, brows raised.

Dayo shook his head. "Nope!" he responded. "I usually order dishes from a caterer I know."

They sat down to eat and chatted, catching up and getting to know each other.

Fey gave Dayo a rundown of how she came to Nigeria. From finding the letters that her mother hid from them to her trip to

Germany, where she met Iben and her application to the Government expatriate program.

Dayo was impressed that Fey was also a civil engineer, and it warmed his heart when she said it was because she knew that was his profession. Fey also talked about her job and some challenges she faced, while Dayo gave advice and suggestions.

When it was a few minutes past midnight, Fey said, "It's almost time. Are you ready?"

Dayo looked at his daughter and gave a wry smile. His hands suddenly felt clammy, so he wiped them several times on his trousers.

Fey gave a light chuckle. "Are you nervous?" she asked, slightly amused.

Dayo sighed. "Of course I am. I haven't spoken to or seen your mother in a very long time. So, I…"

Fey reached out and touched his hand comfortingly. But she didn't know what to say. It wasn't like she knew how her mother would react. For one, it would probably upset her that she went and found her dad, despite promising her that she wouldn't. To add on to that, now she would call her out of the blue for her to talk to and see the one man that had caused her many years of sadness.

A few minutes later, Fey made the video call to her mother. Since Delaware was six hours behind, Fey and Dayo had to wait until after 6:00 PM over there, when Adaobi would be home from work. Fey had sent her a text message earlier in the day that she would call her. She just omitted the part where her father would join in.

After a few rings, Adaobi answered.

"Hi Mom," Fey said once her mother's face came into view.

"Feyisayo, how are you doing?"

"I'm good."

"How's Iben?"

Fey smiled wryly. "He's fine. I'll tell him you asked after him," she lied.

Adaobi nodded. "So what did you want to talk about? Your wedding?"

Fey sighed as she thought about the fact that Iben and she weren't talking at the moment. Given what her father had told them about Edafe, was there even going to be a wedding at this point? She self consciously glanced at her father, who was sitting next to her before turning back to her phone. "No, I called because someone wants to talk to you."

Adaobi looked puzzled as her daughter moved so that Dayo came into the video. When she saw his face, she froze. *What?!*

Dayo's heartbeat quickened as he and Adaobi stared at each other. After a moment, he spoke first. "Hello Ada," he said with a small smile.

Ada said nothing in response. She just stared at the screen in shock. Slowly, tears welled in her eyes and began streaming down her face.

"Mom…" Fey said softly as she saw her mother cry. In all her life, she'd never seen the woman shed a tear. She always seemed to have everything under control. But now, her genuine emotions were showing. Fey suddenly wished she could reach out and hug her mother.

Soon, Dayo started getting misty-eyed as well. After a few seconds, he pulled himself together and said, "Ada, I asked Fey to call you because I wanted to say I'm sorry… I… I'm sorry I couldn't be with you and the girls all these years… I also want to say thank you… for taking care of our children. Feyisayo has grown into a wonderful woman, and so has Tutu. I spoke with her yesterday… It couldn't have been easy on you, so thank you…"

Adaobi nodded and sniffed as she wiped the tears from her eyes. Hearing Dayo acknowledge her hard work as a single mother for the last sixteen years, made her feel validated in a way that she didn't expect, bringing more tears to her eyes. After a while, Adaobi finally stopped crying. She was about to say something when Fey spoke.

"Mom, I know you never believed him, but everything Dad said in his letters to you is true. Someone really kept him here in Nigeria by blackmail."

"Dayo, is that true?" Ada asked. When Dayo nodded, she asked curiously, "Who was it, and what really happened?"

Dayo glanced at Fey before he said, "It was Edafe Ariri." He then narrated everything that happened.

Ada stared in disbelief as she listened to him speak. At the end, she realized two important things. Dayo never remarried, and Fey was engaged to the grandson of her newfound enemy.

After Dayo stopped talking, Ada turned her attention to Fey and scolded, "Young lady, you lied to me. Didn't you promise me that you wouldn't go looking for trouble?"

Fey smiled sheepishly. "I'm sorry, Mom," Fey said. "But aren't you glad I found Dad? I'm glad I did because now we know the truth."

Adaobi shook her head helplessly and sighed internally. She paused as she thought, *That's true, but you also unknowingly jeopardized the future of your relationship with the man you want to marry.*

"Now that you know that Iben's grandfather is responsible for all this, do you still want to marry Iben?" Ada asked pointedly.

Fey lowered her eyes and said, "I don't know."

Adaobi sighed. "It's quite unfortunate that this has happened because I like Iben and I think you're both well matched. But I am not sure that I can be okay with attending any wedding between you both." As much as she wanted to be at her daughter's wedding, Ada wasn't sure she could be in the same room as Edafe without wanting to strangle the man.

It was now Fey's turn to become teary-eyed.

"I'm sorry, dear," Adaobi continued sadly. "I know that this is difficult for you. Life can be unfair, and we sometimes have to make tough decisions. But—whatever you decide, I promise I won't hold it against you. Because I know from my experience that when you're truly in love with someone, it's not so easy to let go."

The words that Fey just heard her mother speak shocked her. She was certain that her mother would blow her top about her engagement to Iben when she found out about Edafe's blackmail. She hadn't expected her to be so calm and sympathetic.

"I understand," Fey said through her tears.

Dayo's heart ached as he watched his daughter cry. He put his arm around her and she leaned in and cried on his shoulder. Adaobi stayed on the call until Fey calmed down and stopped crying.

After the video call ended, Dayo showed Fey to the guest room where she would spend the night. Before he left the room, he said to her, "I'm sorry you're stuck making such a hard choice, baby girl. But as your mother said, we won't hold it against you if you decide to follow your heart."

"Thanks, Dad," Fey said with a forced smile. After he left, she got in the bed and cried herself to sleep.

***

Fey sat on the armchair in her bedroom, coffee mug in hand. She looked out the window and watched the raindrops pouring down heavily outside. She'd gone through the past week on autopilot. Going straight home after work and then staying in her room, mostly. Remi was worried and was going to ask if she was sick or depressed about something, but Demi told her not to pry.

Fey sighed as she thought about Iben. She missed him so much. Although she had asked Iben not to contact her, a part of her now wished he would. She wanted to hear his voice and feel his warm embrace. It had now been a week and a half since her birthday; since the two-week countdown started. She only had three days left before time was up, and she'd have to face him again with her decision. She still didn't have one.

Despite her feelings for Iben, the news of what Edafe did to keep her father in Nigeria was a hard pill to swallow. She wondered if Iben already told him about her father. Of course, she still loved Iben, but it was difficult to ignore the fact that Edafe was an integral part of Iben's life. He's the only family Iben had left, and she didn't want him to have to choose between them.

She suddenly heard a knock on the door. "Come in," she said, and a few seconds later, Demi walked into the room.

"I'm surprised you're still awake," Demi said. "Don't you have to work tomorrow?"

Fey glanced at the clock on her bedside table. It was past midnight. "I didn't realize how late it was," she responded. "How was your date?"

Demi grinned. "Great!" she said. She had met up with Fola that evening and had just returned.

"So, did you guys try the restaurant I was telling you about?"

"I was working late, so we ended up just ordering in and having dinner together at my shop," Demi said. "And afterward, things got a bit… hot and heavy."

Demi said the last sentence suggestively, and Fey gave her a look. "Ewww…"

"Oh please, stop acting like a prude. I bet you and Iben get up to some kinky stuff whenever you guys are together," Demi teased. "Fola and I haven't even gone that far yet."

Fey chuckled. "Whatever, just keep the details to yourself."

Demi rolled her eyes. "You're my best friend. Who else would I tell if not you?"

Fey scoffed. "Lucky me. My ears are going to fall off with all the *unwanted information*," she said, stressing the last two words.

Demi laughed. "Speaking of Iben, have you made a decision?" she asked, suddenly changing the subject.

Fey sighed and shook her head.

Demi moved from the bed, where she had been sitting, squatted in front of the chair Fey was seated and held both her hands. "I know you haven't asked for my opinion, but I'm giving it, anyway. I think you should do what makes *you* happy. I know that probably sounds like an empty statement given the situation. I mean, you essentially have to choose between your family and Iben. But whatever you decide, make sure that you are doing it for *you*. Not for Iben, not for his grandfather, and not for your parents. Because you're the one who's going to have to live with that decision for the rest of your life."

32 | To Be or Not To Be

The next day, after Fey got home from work, she got a call from an unknown number. She ignored it but the number called again, so she picked it up.

"Hello," Fey answered.

"Good evening, Miss Fey. This is Mobi."

Mobi? Why would Mobi call me? Fey panicked. "Is everything okay? Is Iben okay?" she asked.

Hearing the anxiety in her voice, Mobi said, "I'm sorry to bother you so late at night, but Master Iben hasn't been feeling well for the last couple of days and he won't go to the hospital. He just stays in his room all day and won't eat anything. So I—"

"I'm heading over right now!" Fey said, cutting him off.

"Okay, see you soon," Mobi said, relief evident in his voice.

Fey grabbed her car keys and popped her head in Demi's room to let her know where she was going before she left. As she drove, her mind was filled with so much worry. *Iben is sick? He's hardly ever sick. Is it malaria fever?* Thirty minutes later, she was at Iben's house. As soon as she arrived, Mobi met her at the door.

"Hi Mobi, where is he?" she asked, worry written all over her face.

"In his bedroom."

"Okay, let's go."

Mobi nodded and walked up the stairs with Fey.

When Fey opened the door to Iben's bedroom, she saw him lying under the covers, slightly shivering. She walked over to the bed and placed a hand on his forehead. It felt hot to touch.

She turned to Mobi and said, "Can you please bring me some fever medicine and a bowl of water with ice? I need to get his fever down."

After Mobi left to execute her instructions, Fey unbuttoned Iben's shirt to prepare for the cold compress. "I'm sorry you're not feeling well, babe," she said.

Iben's eyes fluttered open. He furrowed his brows. "Fey?" he said groggily. He then lifted his hand to touch the side of her face.

Fey placed her hand over his feverish hand. "Hey," she said with a wry smile.

Iben suddenly groaned like he was in great pain. Fey watched helplessly as his eyes rolled to the back of his head and she could only see the whites. "No, please leave us alone... No..." he muttered deliriously.

Fey held his hand and patted it comfortingly, "It's okay, babe. It's just a dream."

Soon after, Mobi came into the room with the items she requested. She could get Iben to take the medicine, although he had his eyes half-closed the entire time. She then began administering cold compress to his forehead, neck and chest until he cooled down. But within the next half hour, his fever went up again.

Fey spent the next two hours cooling Iben down until his fever finally subsided. Exhausted, she slumped in the bed next to him and went to sleep. When she woke up the next morning, Iben had his arm around her waist, while her back was against his chest. She slowly turned around to face him and placed the back of her hand against his neck and forehead to check his temperature. She sighed with relief that it seemed to have gone back to normal. She then slowly disentangled herself from his embrace and quietly left the room.

Not long after Fey left, Iben woke up. He looked at where she had been sleeping and sighed. *She's not here*, he thought sadly. *I must miss her so much that I dreamt all of it*. He then remembered calling his assistant on Tuesday, telling him to cancel his appointments for the rest of the week. *How long was I sick for?* He reached for his phone, which had lost its charge, and plugged it in. After about a minute, he powered it on. It was Friday, 7:35 AM. *I was out for two days*, he thought in shock.

Realizing that his shirt was damp with sweat from the fever, he went to take a shower. Sometime later, as he walked toward the dressing room to get something to wear, the bedroom door opened and Fey walked in, carrying a breakfast tray.

The surprise on Iben's face was quickly replaced with a smile as his eyes softened. "Hey, beautiful," he said in his usual fashion.

Fey smiled. "Hey..." she said in response.

They stood still for a few seconds, neither of them saying anything. In that time, Fey couldn't help it as her eyes slowly traveled from Iben's face to his bare, toned chest and arms, down to the towel wrapped low around his waist. She cleared her throat self-consciously a few times as she spoke. "Um... I'll get breakfast set up while you um... go and put on a... um... some clothes."

An amused smile appeared on Iben's lips. "Sure," he said. "Just give me a few minutes."

As soon as Iben disappeared into the dressing room, Fey let out the breath she was holding. *Oh, my poor heart*, she thought to herself as a smile teased the corner of her lips. She certainly hadn't expected to see Iben standing there half-naked in all his manly goodness!

A few minutes later, Iben came out of the dressing room wearing joggers and a fitted tank top. When Fey saw him, her eyes lingered on his muscled chest and arms that were now accentuated by his top. Fey met his gaze, and his lips lifted into a smile. *Is he wearing that on purpose?* she asked herself. *Stay focused!* she chided herself. She turned around before asking him to sit down and eat. She finished setting up breakfast on the small table that Mobi had brought up for her last night.

Iben then asked, "When did you come?"

"Around 9:30 last night," she responded. "Mobi called to tell me you weren't feeling well." She placed the back of her hand against his neck to feel his temperature one last time. "Thank goodness your fever is over," she said.

As she moved her hand, Iben held it in place. Then he kissed the back of the hand he was holding. "Thank you for coming to take care of me," he said. "I thought I was having a lucid dream last night when I opened my eyes and saw you."

Fey avoided eye contact even though Iben was looking at her. She gestured toward the food on the table. "Mobi said you haven't eaten much of anything in days, so you need to eat something light. I have yogurt and fruit here."

"Thanks," Iben said and started eating. After a moment, he asked, "Will you be going to work today?"

"No, I called my boss and told her I have a family emergency."

Iben smiled and nodded. They ate quietly until Fey broke the silence.

"You were talking a lot in your sleep," Fey said, recalling Iben's deliriousness last night.

Iben furrowed his brows before he said solemnly, "I dreamt about my mother… and sister…"

Iben rarely talked to her about his family that passed away. Fey lifted her eyes to meet his, and she saw sadness in them. She had the sudden urge to hug him. But all she could say was, "Oh…"

Iben abruptly turned to Fey and said, "Babe, please don't ever ask me to stay away from you again. Do you know how difficult it was for me? So many things have happened since I last saw you, but I couldn't even text or call and talk to you about them."

Feeling guilty, Fey said, "You should've just called anyway if it was important."

"Really?" Iben asked incredulously. "So you could get mad at me anew and demand another two-week restriction? No thanks!" He then recollected her actions while trying to leave on that Saturday and added, "And—you're *so* scary when you're very angry!"

"I'm sorry about the other day," Fey said sheepishly. "I was a bit… aggressive. Hope I didn't hurt you?"

Iben raised a brow. "*Now* she apologizes," he said. Then he narrowed his eyes in suspicion before adding, "I thought you said you didn't have a black belt? Hmmm?"

Fey chuckled, "I honestly don't. Sorry, okay," she said.

"Lucky for me, I have buns of steel, so I was fine." Iben patted his butt to make his point.

Fey laughed. "Buns of steel?" she repeated and laughed again.

The corner of Iben's lips lifted in a smile as he watched Fey laugh. He'd missed hearing the sound of her laughter. When she finally stopped laughing, Iben said, "Babe, your two weeks are over. We need to talk."

"Technically, I still have until tomorrow," Fey responded. She knew they needed to talk about their future. But she wasn't ready to deal with the elephant in the room. Were they staying together or calling it quits?

Iben sighed. "Are you seriously going to split hairs about this? What difference will one more day make, Fey? Could your decision *really* change by tomorrow?"

Fey looked down at her hands. "Not really," she said in a low voice. "I'm just not ready to deal with this."

"Babe, this is so unlike you."

Iben thought about how Fey was usually the one who wanted to talk about issues and ask the tough questions. While he just wanted to bury his head in the sand, hoping and pretending that everything was okay. Now it seemed that their roles were reversed.

Fey said nothing for some time, so Iben raised her chin to look at her. When she lifted her eyes to meet his, he saw that she had tears in them. Iben's heart ached and his eyes filled with sadness, mirroring what he saw in her eyes. He immediately pulled her into a hug to comfort her.

Iben's heart ached because he hated to see her cry. His heart also ached because he now knew why Fey was hesitant to talk. Although she had come over to take care of him because she cared about him, she was going to decide to leave him. It was obvious, really. If that wasn't the case, Fey would happily have given him the good news. As Fey cried, Iben held her close. However, he decided that he would not allow her to do this to them.

Afterward, she pulled away from his embrace and said, without looking at him, "I think we should break up."

Even though Iben knew it was coming, it still hurt when he heard those words. "Look me in the eye and say that again," he responded calmly.

Fey looked at Iben, but she couldn't form the words. She looked down again and said, "Iben, you're making this difficult."

He gave a humorless laugh. "Are you seriously asking me to make it *easy* for you to break up with me?" he asked incredulously. He slowly lifted her chin, so that she was looking at him. Then he said, "Babe, I love you. I want to marry you. I want to have children with you. I want to grow old with you. Of course, I'm against anything that threatens these desires! So, instead of making such an *unappealing* statement asking us to break up, why don't you talk to me? Tell me what you're thinking and feeling."

Fey still said nothing, so a frustrated Iben said, "Fine, I'll talk if you won't." He sighed and leaned back in his seat before he continued. "What happened to your dad was despicable. It makes me sick to my stomach when I think about it. But, what happened between our parents does not reflect on *us*. And I refuse to sacrifice our relationship for the sins of others."

Fey scoffed. "Really? Your grandfather broke up my family, Iben. It's not a simple thing to overlook."

"So you'd rather *we* pay the price for *his* sins. Is that what you're saying?" Fey didn't respond, so Iben followed up with another question, "If your father and mother said they would forgive and forget what happened, would you still want to break up with me?"

"No, but—"

"So, you're doing this to make them happy?" Iben asked, interrupting her.

"My parents both told me to do what I want. But they also said that they cannot support our relationship. But I don't want to get married without their blessing. Am I not being selfish?"

"It's okay to be selfish sometimes."

"I'm not sure if this is one of those instances, Iben," Fey responded. "I also don't want you to have to choose between me and your grandfather. So, I'll bow out and we can each go our separate ways."

"Do you love me?" Iben asked.

"Huh?"

He repeated it. "Do you love me? Yes or no."

Fey sighed in frustration, "Iben—", she began.

He cut her off and asked again, "Do you love me, Fey? Does your heart still beat for me? Or, when you look at me, do I repulse you?"

Fey stared at him, brows furrowed slightly.

"Do you see that evil man who calls himself my grandfather in me? Is that it?"

"Stop it, Iben!"

"Answer me, Fey. I need to know!"

Fey was getting mentally exhausted. She hated it whenever Iben got like this. He'd push and prod until he got a response from you. She thought perhaps it was the lawyer in him.

"Yes, I love you, Iben," she finally said. "I love you so much that it hurts just thinking about being apart from you. But that changes nothing. Our situation remains the same!"

"I choose you," Iben declared. "I choose you and not him. What he did was wrong. And as his gr—" Iben paused before he continued, "I am ashamed of his behavior."

"Iben, this isn't practical. What are you going to do? Disown him? He's your only family. And when he finds out who I really am, he won't want us to be together anymore. Look, I'm glad you helped me find my dad. I know I wouldn't have gotten anywhere without you and Fola. Maybe… this is the reason we met. Fate wanted you to help me find my father. And now, we should just go our separate ways."

Iben was so frustrated that he wasn't getting through to Fey. Her words and her body language told him that she was making this decision because she felt it would please her family. Not because it was what she truly wanted. It reminded him of his relationship with Edafe. Everything Iben did was to please him. Down to his career choice and being engaged to Vivian, who he was never in love with. Being with Fey was the first time he did something significant for himself. And now, because of Edafe, he was about to lose the one person who was important to him—Fey.

Iben stood up and slowly pulled Fey up into a hug. As he hoped, she didn't resist. Instead, she closed her eyes and melted into his embrace.

Fey put her arms around him tightly as she thought back to the many times in the past two weeks that she'd wanted to do this. She sighed helplessly as her heart and body were betraying her head and mind. The former were screaming 'Iben' while the latter were urging her to be practical and realistic.

After a while, Iben leaned back from the hug and lifted Fey's chin. He looked into her eyes and said, "Don't leave me, babe. We love each other. Let's work together to come up with a plan." Before Fey could give a response, Iben suddenly captured her lips.

Now overcome with her feelings for Iben that she had been trying to repress, Fey kissed him back. Feverishly. Passionately. With abandon.

When the kiss ended, they were both raw with emotions.

Iben looked into her eyes and asked, "Do you still think we should break up?" When Fey didn't respond, he captured her lips again. Afterward, he said in a low voice, "Stay by my side, babe. Don't leave." Then he kissed her again.

"Is it your plan to kiss and seduce me into submission?" Fey finally asked with a chuckle.

Iben smiled mischievously and playfully wiggled his eyebrows. "Hmmm, that's not a bad idea." Then he began trailing kisses down her neck.

"Okay… okay," Fey giggled.

Iben stopped peppering her with kisses. "So, no more talks about breaking up, right?" he asked expectantly.

Fey nodded and said, "Let's see if we can find a better solution."

Iben immediately hugged her tightly. He sighed with relief and after a moment, he asked her to sit. Fey looked at him expectantly.

Iben gathered his thoughts and began. "Remember when I said I had so many things to tell you? Well, last week, I went to visit the parents of the woman who was killed, Kemi Olaniran."

"You did?"

Iben nodded and told her all he learned from his visit with Dokun Olaniran.

Fey stared at him wide-eyed as the news hit her. "So, Papa is actually your father?" Fey asked in disbelief.

"Yes, but that's not all," Iben responded. "Sixteen years ago, after the fatal accident that took my family from me, I couldn't remember anything about it. I've always believed that I was suffering from some sort of post-traumatic stress disorder surrounding the accident. I think my recent visit to Festac, where we used to live, and my conversation with Mr. Olaniran slowly brought back memories from that time."

He paused before he continued. "Earlier this week, I started having random flashbacks followed by intense headaches and stomachaches. So, on Tuesday, I took a few days off from work. I don't know much about PTSD, but I believe the flashbacks caused the fever, as my body tried to deal with the excruciating pain from the accompanying headaches and stomachaches.

"And last night, everything about the accident came back to me. Now I know why my ten-year-old mind could only deal with the intense trauma by blocking it. Fey, I now remember everything!"

33 | A Matter of Perspective

"It was my fault," Iben said dejectedly. "Because of me... they died."

"Iben, what are you saying?" Fey asked, puzzled.

Iben looked pained as he recalled the memory.

"That night, we were driving home from dinner at a restaurant when a black vehicle suddenly drove into our lane, blocking us. They wore masks, and we thought they were armed robbers. One of the men dragged my stepfather out of the car and the next thing I saw, he threw him to the ground. He hit his head and died.

"Another of the masked men then carried me away to another waiting vehicle off the side of the road. I remember hearing my mother screaming and running after me and my kidnapper. We got to the car and my grandfather—at least that's who I thought he was at the time—was waiting in the back seat. When my mother reached the car, he stepped out to talk to her. I don't remember what they said, but with everything I know now, I imagine it had to do with him trying to kidnap me. Whatever they talked about, my mother clearly lost the argument because Papa got in the car and drove off with me."

Iben sighed before he continued. "I remember crying and begging him to take me back to my mother... While I had met my *grandfather* once before, I didn't know him at all and was quite uncomfortable, given the situation. After a few minutes, I heard the driver telling Papa that my mother was chasing after us in her car. I looked out of the rear window and saw the car. I remember being so excited, but I tried not to show it.

"Anyway, my ten-year-old self kept hoping that my mother would catch up quickly so that I could go home. It was almost as if she heard me because she sped up and I was so happy. But, because of her speed, she lost control of the car and... she crashed into a tree. She died, along with my sister, who was also in the car.

"I must've blacked out from shock after that because when I woke up, I was in the hospital and had lost all memory of what happened that night. Papa told me everyone except for me died in a car accident and I believed him. He then said that since I was his grandson, he would adopt me. So my name changed from Iben Asinobi to Iben Ariri."

Iben raised his eyes to look at Fey and said self-deprecatingly, "I'm such a horrible son, aren't I? My mother died while trying to take me back and I promptly forgot her sacrifice because it was convenient."

"Babe, don't say that," Fey interjected softly. "You were just a kid, and your body was simply trying to protect itself from the trauma. You literally witnessed your entire family die in one night," she reasoned.

"All because of me…" Iben began, but he couldn't complete his sentence. Intense sadness and grief suddenly washed over him, and his eyes flooded with tears.

Fey saw this, moved closer to him and said, "Babe, it's not your fault…" She then put her arms around Iben and hugged him.

Iben cried for his mother, his sister, his stepfather, and for himself. It was the first time he truly mourned them after all these years. Fey hugged and comforted Iben for a while until he calmed down.

Later, while Iben was in the bathroom, washing his face, Fey was lost in thought. She knew it wasn't right, but she couldn't help but think that what Edafe did to her family almost seemed inconsequential compared to what he did to his own flesh and blood, Iben. She wondered if he ever regretted kidnapping Iben, given all the lives that were lost as a result.

When Iben returned from the bathroom, he hugged Fey and said, "Thanks for being here today, babe."

Fey hugged him back. "I'd rather be here with you than anywhere else."

After they broke away from the hug, Fey asked, "So, what do you want to do now? Will you let Papa know that you have your memories back?"

Iben nodded. "I have to. I can't pretend that things haven't changed. Anyway, I'll deal with that later." Fey nodded before he continued. "I think we should wait until everyone is okay with us getting married before we have a wedding."

Fey raised a questioning brow. "We're going to win them over with our stubbornness? What kind of plan is that? I don't know about my dad, but my mom is a force to be reckoned with. Apparently, I inherited my stubbornness from her, so she's the real deal!"

Iben chuckled at Fey's words before he said, "Babe, I can't go back in time to undo the damage that Papa did. But as a future son-in-law to your parents, I want to atone for what he has done. For starters, I want to get Papa to hand over or destroy the original incriminating video framing your father for Kemi Olaniran's murder. Then at least your dad won't feel trapped anymore. He's done so much for Ariri Corporation, and I'm sure he would love the freedom to move on to other things, if he so desires. As for the Olanirans, I have already set up an educational fund for Kemi's daughter to attend university—both bachelor's and master's degrees."

Fey nodded in agreement as she listened. There was no guarantee, but it was a start. Her parents weren't against the wedding per se. They just would not attend. Hopefully, Iben's attempts at trying to right Edafe's wrongs would soften their hearts a little and change their minds. "What about Papa?" she asked. "Since you haven't told him about finding my dad and meeting the Olanirans, we don't even know what his stance is on our engagement."

Iben looked thoughtful for a moment before he said, "Let me take care of Papa's side of things, okay?"

Fey frowned, so he asked, "Do you trust me?"

"I do, but I don't want any surprises. You have to keep me in the loop."

Iben nodded in agreement and then stood up. "I need to call the office and catch up on things since I've been out sick for a few days. I'll be in the study downstairs if you need me."

"Okay," Fey said, as a yawn suddenly escaped her lips.

Iben chuckled. "Sounds like *someone* stayed up half the night to take care of this other person."

Fey smiled as she stood up and stretched. "Yeah, and I think I'll be enjoying a nice long nap while that *other person* is working," she teased.

"Wow! Someone's rubbing it in," Iben responded as a smile teased his lips.

Fey chuckled as she walked to the bed and sat down. Iben came over and kissed her on the forehead before he left the room.

After Fey got comfortable in the bed, she sent a message to Tutu. It read, *'Iben and I talked and we're not calling off our engagement.'* She then forwarded the same message to Demi.

After a few minutes, a response came in from Tutu. *'Glad to hear that.*

Don't worry, I'll attend your wedding, even if Mom and Dad don't want to.'

'Thanks, munchkin,' Fey responded.

Demi's response came in soon after. *'Yay! You had me worried all this time. I'm so happy my FeyBen ship is still going strong!'*

Fey chuckled before putting down her phone and settling in for a nap. She thought about how supportive they were about her engagement to Iben. Even her parents weren't forbidding her to marry him, despite how they felt about Edafe. At this point, she could only hope for a miracle to change their minds about attending the wedding. These were her last thoughts as sleep took over.

***

Iben sat at the desk in his study. He was reading through some documents that his assistant had emailed to him. After calling to let the office know that he was feeling better, he asked his assistant to fax and email some documents for him to look over to prepare for some meetings the following week. He had been working for about an hour and a half when he heard the door to the study open.

Without looking up, he said, "Babe, I'll be done here in about half an hour. Do you want to go out to lunch afterwards?"

However, the voice that answered him wasn't Fey's. "I'd certainly like some lunch, but I prefer if you call me Papa."

Iben froze. He slowly looked up from his computer and met Edafe's gaze. The amused expression that Iben saw on his face was clearly because he had just unwittingly referred to him as *Babe*.

Iben's heartbeat quickened as he stared at his *father*. Seeing him standing before him, Iben was suddenly filled with a rush of emotions. Anger. Pain. Sadness. Love. Hate. Fear. Disgust. He clearly wasn't ready to face the man. He was still sorting out his feelings about what happened in the past and now, here he was. *Can't I just catch a break?* Iben thought, feeling sorry for himself.

Iben leaned back in his seat and said in a tone devoid of emotion, "I think calling you *Dad* would be most appropriate."

Edafe froze at Iben's words. Father and son held each other's gaze for a moment.

Edafe finally spoke as he took a seat. "How did you figure that out?" he calmly asked.

"Oladokun Olaniran."

Edafe frowned. "Did that old fool go looking for you?"

"No, I went to him after Temidayo Ademola told me that you

blackmailed him using Kemi Olaniran's death. Mr. Olaniran welcomed me with open arms and didn't seem to know that you had a hand in his daughter's death."

At Edafe's puzzled expression, Iben added, "Turns out, Temidayo Ademola is actually Fey's father who we've been looking for."

Edafe's face immediately blossomed into a bright smile. "That's excellent!" he said, to Iben's surprise.

"How so?" Iben asked with a bewildered look on his face.

"He's one of my favorite people. I'd be happy to have him as my in-law."

Iben stared at Edafe in disbelief. "Well, he doesn't want to be yours!" he snapped.

"Why not?"

"I think the part about you blackmailing him and keeping him away from his family in the States is kinda difficult to get over," Iben responded, sarcastically.

"Oh, that?" Edafe said dismissively. "Well, I *did* blackmail him, but I didn't force him to stay here in Nigeria. He made that choice."

"Are you saying that my father was lying?" they suddenly heard Fey say.

Edafe and Iben both turned their attention to the doorway and saw her standing there, lips pursed and frowning.

Edafe smiled at her and said, "Hello, my dear. Come and sit down so we can talk." He patted the seat next to him on the sofa.

Fey walked past him and went to stand next to Iben at his desk instead. She crossed her arms against her chest and said, "I'm listening."

Edafe chuckled. *Ah, this girl is perfect as my daughter-in-law*, he mused. *With her at Iben's side, nobody will be able to walk all over them after I hand the company over to Iben.*

"Your father chose his parents over his wife and children," Edafe said. "You can't blame me for that."

"Why would you give him such a choice to begin with?" Fey shot back.

"I think the real question is *why* did he choose his parents over you? Remember, these are the same parents who wanted him to abandon you, your mother and sister to marry another woman and stay here in Nigeria. Yet, he chose them."

Fey was speechless.

Edafe continued, "At the time, I really wanted to recruit your father for my company, but he refused. The blackmail was just a last ditch effort to meet this goal, and it worked."

"How could you kill an innocent woman just for that?" Fey responded.

Edafe smiled, "Who says I killed her? According to the police, she died of heart failure."

"What about the video? Isn't that what you used to blackmail my father?"

"Kemi had an illness that she kept from everyone and had gone to the States for diagnosis and potential treatment. I merely took advantage of the situation and seized the opportunity to make it look like it was I who killed her. In the right hands, you can doctor any video to add or remove people."

Fey and Iben looked at each other in shock.

"So, if my father had called your bluff…" Fey began.

Edafe nodded and completed her sentence, "He could've returned to the States."

Fey was speechless again.

After a moment, Edafe said, "I hear your father won't agree to you and Iben getting married. I don't see how what happened in the past has anything to do with you two."

Fey scoffed internally. She doubted Edafe would feel any different from her parents if the tables were turned. "He says I should follow my heart, but he just won't attend the wedding," she said instead.

"Hmmm, isn't that some sort of emotional blackmail in itself?" Edafe asked provocatively.

Fey frowned. *What kind of twisted logic is that?* she thought to herself. In her mind, her parents were simply being gracious and honest with her.

Without giving Fey an opportunity to answer, Edafe added, "So, what have you decided?"

Iben gently put his arm around Fey's waist and said, "We're not calling off our engagement."

"I'm happy to hear that," Edafe said with an approving nod.

"Why are you *so happy*?" Fey blurted out, suddenly. "Don't get me wrong. I love Iben and I still want to marry him. But—it's just *strange* not getting even a smidgen of resistance or reluctance from you. Don't you feel weird that your son is getting married to the daughter of the man you blackmailed?"

"Why should I?" Edafe asked. "You see, I'm a very practical person.

I do not indulge in burdensome social, ethical, and emotional ideals. I like your father and have great respect for him. He's one of Ariri Corporation's top engineers, and I have compensated him accordingly. Not because of the blackmail, but because I admire his work ethic. Despite what I did, he always put in his best effort at any and every challenge or task I threw at him."

Edafe leaned back in his chair before he continued. "I like you, Fey. You're no coward. You love my son and are willing to remain engaged to him despite how your family feels. You're spunky, and not afraid to speak your mind. I couldn't ask for a better daughter-in-law."

Fey was speechless after Edafe's explanation. She didn't know what to think of the man.

"Will you hand over the *fake* blackmail video so I can destroy it?" Iben suddenly asked.

Edafe's eyes snapped to meet Iben's. "Sure," he said. "You can stop by the house and pick it up anytime. You haven't called or visited in a while. Nor have you been answering my phone calls. When I heard you haven't been to the office because you were sick, I stopped by. Are you feeling better?"

"I had a fever for a couple of days. But I'm better now." Iben responded. After a few seconds he added, "Thank you for burying everyone who died in the accident on Ariri family graves even though you aren't related to them."

Edafe was silent for a moment after Iben stopped speaking. "Did you get back your memories?" he asked, finally. He wasn't sure if Iben's comment was based on Dokun Olaniran's expose of what happened that night.

"Yes," Iben responded. "Why didn't you tell me that you are my father?"

"Back then, the doctors said you were suffering from trauma. They advised that I should try to retain some sense of normalcy in your life after the accident. So, I just kept up with the lie that your mother told you about who I was. The years went by while I hoped that you would remember on your own."

"I suppose that's why you would question me about the accident every year at the anniversary of their deaths."

Edafe nodded.

"Mr. Olaniran said you kidnapped me that night because we were moving away. Why didn't you just work out some kind of custody arrangement with my mother?"

Edafe smiled as he recalled a memory, but it was a smile that unnerved you. "I gave your mother a chance to work things out with me. Her answer was to run off with my son. When I found out, it became clear to me that she didn't want me in your life at all. She had her reasons, I suppose.

"But was it really *her* choice to make? She was deciding for you and I what *our* relationship would be. Or if we would have *any* relationship at all. Nobody gets away with that kind of hubris when I'm involved! Now, I never meant to harm her physically. I just wanted my son. I also wanted to let her know that she didn't have the right to make such a decision on her own. Unfortunately, things just turned out the way they did."

Iben listened to Edafe quietly. He knew how the man operated. He just wished his mother hadn't gotten in the crosshairs. Having heard everything Edafe had to say, Iben had a better understanding of the situation. Unfortunately, his mother wasn't here to defend her perspective. She was gone and never coming back. How he wished there was someone who knew and could tell him. He doubted if such a person existed.

34 | Ijemma

Twenty-eight years ago.

Twenty-three-year-old Ijemma Oha arrived at the party venue with her friends. She wore an off-shoulder bodycon dress that hugged her petite frame. On her feet were high heels, which masked her height deficiency just a bit. She was quite nervous as she had never been to an event like this before.

"Don't worry," Sade, one of her friends said. "Just relax and you'll have a lot of fun tonight."

Ijemma looked anything but convinced, but she followed her friends aboard the yacht waiting on the docks. Soon after they boarded, another one of her friends ordered her a light alcoholic drink and warned her not to leave her drink unattended. Then she disappeared to find her male target for the night.

Ijemma took a sip of her drink and almost choked on it. She was shocked at how strong the alcohol tasted in her mouth. *If this is light, I wonder what a strong alcoholic drink tastes like?* she thought to herself in dismay.

Ijemma sat by herself in a corner as she watched men and women dancing, drinking, and flirting. She thought about why she was here tonight. She had always been the teetotaler of her friends, who didn't like to attend exotic parties such as these. However, she was going to graduate university in a few months and had wanted to try something different for a change. Now she was regretting it.

After a while, Ijemma was getting stifled with all the debauchery and cigarette smoke permeating the lower level of the yacht where she was. She moved to the top deck for some fresh air. Hopefully, she'd also stop getting propositioned by random guys up there. She soon found a quiet spot on the backside of the deck and leaned against the railing, drink in hand. As she enjoyed the cool breeze, she brought her drink to her mouth again and finally decided that she couldn't get used to it. So, she slowly poured it into the murky waters below.

"Not your cup of tea?" she suddenly heard a deep male voice behind her say.

Surprised, she spun around and her eyes locked with the owner of the voice. He was a handsome man, and he was much taller than her small frame. He could probably carry her in his arms like a little child without breaking a sweat. He was dressed smartly in a pair of black slacks, matching blazer, and a light blue dress shirt which was unbuttoned at the collar. He looked to be in his mid-thirties. His sharp eyes seemed to pierce through her as he held her gaze.

Ijemma broke eye contact and said, "No, I'm not much of a drinker." Then she added with a sigh, "This party isn't my cup of tea either."

"Would you like to leave?" he asked.

Not understanding the meaning behind his question, Jemma naively said with another sigh, "Yeah, but my friends are nowhere to be found." Then she realized that she had unwittingly exposed herself as helpless prey to this man. So she quickly added, "I mean, I'm waiting for them before we all leave together."

The man smiled at her obvious attempt at cleaning up her blunder. "Can I keep you company while you *wait* for your friends?" he asked. When she didn't respond, he held out his hand and introduced himself. "I'm Edafe. It's nice to meet you."

Ijemma reluctantly accepted his handshake as she didn't want to seem rude. *So much for some peace and quiet*, she thought to herself. "I'm Jemma," she said politely.

"That's a pretty name," he said with a smile, still holding her hand.

Jemma rolled her eyes and took back her hand. *He certainly didn't waste time before he started flirting*, she thought to herself. She turned around and faced the open waters again.

Edafe moved to stand next to her. He didn't say a word, but he would steal glances at her once in a while. She was much shorter than he was, with the top of her head barely reaching his shoulder. She had a small mole by her left eyebrow and wore her long hair in a side-swept hairstyle. Her tight-fitting dress showcased her modest curves.

It suddenly got cooler, thanks to the ocean breeze that just blew through, and Jemma began shivering a little. Edafe took off his blazer and put it around her shoulders. Jemma warmed up to him a bit after that gesture.

"Thank you," she said with a small smile.

After a few more minutes of staring at the cityscape from the shoreline, Jemma said, "Lagos is so beautiful from here. I'm going to miss it when I go back home."

"Where's home and why are you going back?" Edafe asked.

"I'm from Onitsha. I'll be graduating from UniLag in May."

Edafe and Jemma continued chatting for some time, learning a few things about each other. Jemma told him she was an only child and was studying Accounting at the University of Lagos. Edafe told her that he was also an only child, but his parents had died many years ago. He also told her that he was a businessman who was based in Lagos, but traveled a lot and had been to Onitsha in Anambra state a few times. Edafe asked her questions about her career goals after graduation, and Jemma said she wanted to work at a bank. Edafe thought she had set a modest goal for herself.

After a while, Edafe looked around, and as expected, the yacht was almost empty. This party was the type where people left soon after they found their partners for the night. He had approached her earlier because she was dressed provocatively, and he was curious to know why she was off to the side by herself. After having talked to her, he realized that Jemma was different from the girls that frequented these parties. Although he wouldn't classify her as pure and innocent, she certainly was out of her element here, and for some reason, he felt bad for her. He thought her friends were wrong to bring her.

Edafe looked at the time and said, "I don't think your friends are coming back for you."

Jemma sighed at Edafe's statement of the obvious. Now more than ever, she wished she had stayed behind at the flat she shared with her friends. *How on earth am I going to get back home this late at night? Do I even have enough money to afford a taxi?* She was so angry with herself for not thinking things through.

"Let me call you a taxi," Edafe said, and stepped away.

Jemma was surprised. She was almost certain that he was hanging around just for this moment when her lie would be exposed. Then he'd jump on the opportunity to offer to take her home. And then, he'd use that opportunity to proposition her. And then she'd have to do something she never planned...

"Jemma?" Edafe called, jolting her out of her thoughts.

"Yes?" she answered.

"Your taxi will be here soon. Let me walk you to the pickup spot."

Jemma followed Edafe off the yacht to what seemed like an unmarked taxi. He opened the door and after she got in, he told the driver to take her home.

"Thank you, Edafe," Jemma said sheepishly after she sat down. "It was nice to meet you."

"You're welcome, Jemma. It was a pleasure to meet you too," Edafe said with a smile and a wink.

When Jemma got home, the driver told her that she didn't have to pay for the trip as Edafe already took care of it. Although she was relieved, she also felt bad that she had burdened him with the cost. When she entered her flat, as expected, her friends weren't back. She knew they wouldn't be back until tomorrow.

The next day, when her friends returned home, although they apologized for ditching her at the party, Jemma refused to speak to them for a few days. She wasn't one to judge their social activities, but she was furious at them for not telling her what kind of party they were attending. She thought about Edafe and how, thanks to him, she could get out of a prickly situation relatively unscathed.

The following week went by uneventfully, but on Saturday, before her friends returned from their usual Friday night partying, Jemma received an unexpected visitor. It was Edafe. After the initial shock of seeing him at her doorstep wore off, she suddenly shut the door in his face.

Edafe stared at the door, stunned. He had never received a reception like that before from any woman. He was both angry and amused at her audacity. He took a deep breath to calm himself and knocked on the door again.

Jemma wouldn't open the door. "Go away, Edafe!" she said.

Edafe continued knocking, but after about two minutes, the knocking stopped and Jemma heard footsteps. She sighed with relief that Edafe had left, but now, thanks to him, she was having a headache. She decided to go to the supermarket to get some medicine and maybe something to eat. She was getting hungry anyway. To be sure that Edafe had left, Jemma waited about five more minutes before she stepped out the door and locked it. However, as soon as she turned around, a strong arm suddenly blocked her way. Shocked that Edafe was still hanging around, she instinctively tried to get around him, but he was an immovable mountain for her small frame.

Edafe then leaned in and said calmly, in his deep voice, "How dare you shut the door in my face?"

"How dare you just randomly show up at my doorstep?" Jemma shot back as she glared at him.

Edafe chuckled humorlessly. "I thought you'd be happy to see me. Afterall, I didn't take advantage of you the other night."

Jemma sneered at him. "I suppose you're here now to collect on your good deed, ehn? And by the looks of it, you're going to *take advantage* of me out here in the open?"

That's when Edafe realized that in his attempt at preventing her from getting away, he was pressed up against her, trapping her petite frame between the door and him. He collected himself and moved back. "I'm sorry," he said as he met her fiery gaze. "That was not my intention. Please forgive me."

Relieved that there was now some space between them, Jemma crossed her arms against her chest defensively. Then she asked, "How do you know where I live? Did you follow the taxi that brought me home the other night?" Before Edafe could respond, she added, "You know what? I'll just pay you back for the taxi so then we'll be even. How much do I owe you?"

Edafe shook his head and said, "No need. Your driver that night was actually my personal driver."

Jemma raised her brows in surprise. "So that was your car that he drove me home in?"

"Yes."

"Oh… I'm sorry to have burdened you with my troubles that night," Jemma said with an apologetic look on her face. "Thank you for helping me out."

Edafe chuckled internally. This young woman before him never ceased to surprise him. It was refreshing for him to see someone with such honest emotions. No matter what Jemma was feeling, it was clear as day, no guesswork. "It's no problem," he said.

"So why are you here, Edafe?" Jemma asked.

"To ask you to go out to lunch with me," he said. At the surprised and slightly suspicious look on Jemma's face, he added, "I really enjoyed chatting with you the other night, and I wanted to see you again. You didn't attend the yacht party yesterday, and I don't have your phone number, so coming here was all I could think of."

The clear look in his eyes, as he said those words seemed to pull a chord in Jemma. Truthfully, until Edate suddenly showed up at her doorstep like a stalker, scaring the crap out of her, she had been thinking about him on and off during the week. She just never imagined that she'd ever see him again.

"Okay," she said finally. "But I'm buying lunch so you'll have to eat what I can afford," she added firmly. She said this because she didn't want to feel indebted to him anymore. She also wanted to have some control over where they went so that she could easily get home if things went downhill. As much as she found him attractive, she didn't quite trust him entirely.

"I agree to the lady's terms," Edafe responded with a smile.

And that was the start of the relationship between Jemma Oha and Edafe Ariri.

Edafe was drawn to Jemma's beauty, honesty, and calm nature. Jemma was enamored by the way Edafe's mind worked. He was meticulous, fair, and logical. She soon found out that Edafe was very wealthy. At thirty-four years old, he was one of the country's richest, self-made bachelors. He constantly showered Jemma with gifts of clothing, shoes, handbags, and jewelry. But what Jemma enjoyed the most was the time they spent together. Since Edafe had a business to run, he traveled frequently. So whenever he was back in Lagos, she looked forward to hanging out with him.

Edafe was surprisingly quite romantic. Whenever Jemma visited him at his home on Victoria Island, they would sometimes go to nearby Bar Beach for picnics. Other times, they would have candlelight dinners in his backyard. Once, she mentioned that she would love to ride a motorcycle, and he went and bought one so that he could learn how to ride it and then teach her. After a couple of months, whenever Edafe had any banquets or events to attend, he would bring Jemma along, introducing her as his girlfriend.

Despite the eleven-year difference between them, they got along very well. And as their relationship got deeper, Jemma would sometimes spend the weekend with him. Then, he'd take her back home on Sunday night so that she could easily get to campus on Monday morning.

Before long, Jemma graduated from university. By Edafe's persuasion, she agreed to stay in Lagos instead of moving back home to Onitsha. She told her parents she had found a job in Lagos and wouldn't be going back home. Her parents seemed happy that she was settling down fine in Lagos. From their perspective, there were better job opportunities in Lagos, anyway. She promised to visit them periodically.

Jemma's job was at First Bank on Lagos Island. Although she could afford a one-bedroom flat with her salary, Edafe suggested she move in with him and send the money to her parents instead. They were just regular folk, who had a small trading business. But they could send their only child to university, making her the first university-educated individual in her family. It was her duty to give back to them, and she reasoned that living with Edafe would allow her to save a lot of her money and do just that.

Everything was going well with the couple until one evening when they were out having dinner at a restaurant. They sat at their regular table at a quiet corner of the restaurant, giving them some privacy. Suddenly a man came over and yelled at Edafe.

"You bastard!" he spat. "You think just because you are rich, you can swindle me and get away with it? I will destroy you! I will expose you for who you are, Edafe Ariri."

Edafe was unperturbed. He calmly looked up at the man from his seating position and said in his deep voice, "You are disturbing my dinner with my woman. Please leave."

The man became even more outraged at Edafe's attitude. "I toiled for you and did everything you asked. Why did you double-cross me? You bastard!" Suddenly, the man swung a fist at Edafe, but he could not land it because one of Edafe's bodyguards tackled the man, bringing him to the ground.

"Bring him outside," Edafe ordered as he stood up. "I'll be right back," he said to Jemma before he walked away.

Jemma, who was shocked at what just happened, could not contain her curiosity. So, after a couple of minutes, she went outside to see what was going on. By some bushes nearby, she saw Edafe's men beating the man ruthlessly to where he didn't seem to move anymore.

Edafe noticed her presence and said to his men, "Get rid of this garbage!" Then, he walked over to Jemma and said, "Why are you out here? Come, let's get back inside." He put his arm around her shoulder and led her back inside the restaurant.

After they sat down, Jemma watched Edafe as he continued eating. For him, it was as if nothing happened, but for her, she had lost her appetite given what she just witnessed outside. "Who was that man?" she asked after a while.

"Do not concern yourself with that, Jemma," Edafe responded. His tone was calm, but the look he gave Jemma indicated that he didn't want to talk about it.

Jemma said nothing more. They finished their dinner and went home. For the rest of the evening, Jemma kept to herself and when Edafe spoke to her, she would only give monosyllabic responses or short-phrases as answers. This continued for a few days until Edafe finally realized that something was wrong.

"What's the matter, Jemma?" he asked after she had rejected his advances in bed for the third day in a row.

Jemma shrugged and turned her back to him. "Just tired," she lied.

"You've been tired a lot lately," he complained. Then he suddenly had a thought. "Wait, are you pregnant?!"

"No!" Jemma responded, irritably. She snapped her head around, ready to give him the stink-eye. But when she met Edafe's disappointed facial expression, she regarded him suspiciously. "Have you been *trying* to get me pregnant?"

"Not really, but I wouldn't mind it if you were," Edafe responded easily as he rubbed his hand across the imaginary baby in her tummy.

Jemma was partly happy and partly annoyed at the fact that he wanted a child with her. "We're not married, so no babies right now. Who knows if you even want to marry me?"

Edafe was quiet for a moment. Then he said, "When I return from my trip in two weeks, let's go to Onitsha together to meet your parents." That was his way of letting her know he wanted to marry her.

Jemma was speechless. She met his gaze for a few seconds, checking to see if he was truly serious. She knew he was, as Edafe would never make such a commitment offhandedly. "Do you mean that?" she asked, anyway. When he nodded in the affirmative, she smiled happily, kissed him on the cheek, and said, "Okay."

Thinking that Jemma's issue with him was now resolved, Edafe proceeded with fulfilling his desire to be intimate with her. However, Jemma still had other issues on her mind. But since she was feeling overjoyed about Edafe's promise to meet her parents, she didn't want to ruin the moment, and would talk to him about it later.

The next morning was a Saturday and Edafe was scheduled to leave for a business trip to London. He would leave for the airport later in the evening and return in two weeks. Jemma woke up early to prepare his favorite breakfast. She wanted him in a good mood before she broached the conversation she wanted to have the night before. Now that Edafe indicated that he wanted to marry her, Jemma felt a surge of confidence.

After breakfast, they moved to the living room to relax. Jemma snuggled up to him as he put his arm around her. After a moment, she gathered her thoughts and began.

"Edafe, can you tell me more about your businesses? I know you own supermarkets and stores around the country, but what else do you do?"

Edafe raised a brow in mild surprise at her question. "Do you want to invest some money in my business?" he asked jokingly.

Jemma pouted at his teasing, "I'm serious."

Edafe chuckled lightly. It pleased him that Jemma seemed interested in the one thing that mattered to him most. "Okay, let's see... I also have a few steel production plants, some real estate investments, and I am in the process of setting up a construction business as well."

Jemma nodded as Edafe spoke. When he finished talking, she said cautiously, "So, you're not doing anything dangerous or illegal?"

Edafe turned to look at her. "Why would you ask that?"

"Well, the guy from the restaurant the other night. He seemed very violent."

"As a businessman, I have enemies, so it's normal," Edafe said easily.

Jemma furrowed her brows in confusion. Her parents owned a business as well, and they never had enemies. Did he mean his market competition? Even so, why would they be so upset that they'd want to harm him physically?

"Is that why you have bodyguards?"

"Yes."

"I'm worried about your safety," she said after a while.

Edafe smiled. He was touched by her words. "I'll be okay," he said and gently patted her on her head.

"I know he swung at you first, but is he okay?"

"Probably," Edafe responded with a dismissive shrug.

"So, which one of your business deals is the man from the other night upset about?"

Edafe's voice dropped an octave. "That's none of your concern, Jemma."

Jemma pressed. "Edafe, if we're to be married in the future, you shouldn't keep things like this from me."

Edafe's voice got frosty. "If we're to be married in the future, you'll do well to know *your* limits as it relates to *my* business!"

Edafe's tone and the look in his eyes unnerved Jemma, and she instinctively wanted to shrink back in fear. However, she forced herself to press on. "What limits? And *why* are there limits?" she asked. "Is it because you're doing something illegal?"

"Even if it's illegal, it doesn't concern you. Why are you suddenly so nosey?"

"It's because I care about you!" she responded. "And—what I saw the other night was scary, Edafe. It was almost as if you became a different person. I've never seen you like that before."

Edafe cocked his head to the side as he looked her in the eye. "If you don't like it, you can leave!" He got up and started walking away.

"Edafe!"

He turned around.

"Do you really mean that?"

He didn't respond. He just turned around and walked up the stairs. Sometime later, he came down with his travel bags. "I'm going to the office first and then I'll head to the airport from there. I'll see you when I get back."

Jemma didn't respond. She wouldn't even look at him, so he left.

For a while, Jemma sat rooted to her seat. Edafe was hiding something from her, and she was disappointed that she couldn't get it out of him. He talked about everything else but what she wanted to know, and it bothered her. Was she being nosey by asking about his business? Should there be limits placed on her? From her perspective, if his safety was involved, she had a right to know.

The other thing that bothered her was the way Edafe just switched from warm to icy-cold. It unnerved her. The look in his eyes as he regarded her like she was some stranger, and not his girlfriend. She knew he had a bit of a temper, but it was one thing to be angry and another to look like he could murder you without batting an eyelid. She was also hurt that he told her to leave if she couldn't deal with the limits he had set for her. Was she so disposable to him?

Jemma pondered these things on and off for the rest of the weekend and during the week. When the following weekend came, she had made up her mind. She had no intention of being there when Edafe returned. She requested some unpaid leave from work, packed her things, and went back to her parents in Onitsha.

***

A week later, Edafe returned from his London trip and went straight home. He hadn't spoken to Jemma the entire time he was gone because he wanted to give her time to calm down from the argument they had before he left. However, when he arrived, he was surprised that she wasn't there. When he asked the housekeeper, she handed him a note from Jemma.

It read, 'Edafe, I hope you had a safe trip. I thought about what you said and I have decided that I don't want to be in a relationship where I have to abide by limits as you have set them. Thank you for a wonderful time this past year. Take care. Jemma.'

Edafe's face was expressionless as he read the letter. When he was done, he crumpled it up and threw it in the trash. As he sat calmly in his seat, nobody could tell what he was thinking.

Edafe realized that he had underestimated Jemma's willpower. Although they had gotten along well and she generally did as he asked, he now understood that he never really tamed her as he had thought. In his hubris, he had been quite certain that Jemma would agree to his rules and was now surprised that she refused to. Despite that, he admired her for sticking to her principles. How many women out here would make the same decision, given the status and opulence that would be theirs as the woman by his side?

After a few minutes, Edafe summoned his housekeeper and told her to pack up any of Jemma's things that she didn't take with her and put them in one of the guest rooms. He would decide what to do with it later. He then called for his driver and told him to prepare the car for a trip to the location of the yacht party. He hadn't been there since he started dating Jemma, but now that she was gone, it was time to let loose.

35 | Entangled

Jemma looked out the window of the taxi she was riding as it weaved through traffic. It had now been a month since she moved back to Onitsha. In the first couple of weeks of her arrival back home, she was sad as she quietly mourned the end of her relationship with Edafe. She missed him but she knew that she could not be truly happy being with him any longer.

She sighed as she thought about the news she just received from her visit to the hospital. *I can't believe I'm eight weeks pregnant!* she thought as she rested her head in the palms of her hands. She badly wanted to cry. Why now? Why after she had broken up with Edafe? What was she going to do? Would she keep the baby or have an abortion? If she kept it, should she tell Edafe that he was going to be a father? If she did, would he ask her to move back in with him for the sake of the child? Did she want to be a parent with him? She had so many decisions to make.

As the taxi stopped in front of her parents' house, Jemma realized she would also have to let them know she was pregnant. They were already shocked that she had returned from Lagos so suddenly. She had lied to them that she came back because her job situation changed and she missed home. She would now have to tell them that they were about to have a grandchild. How would they feel when she also told them she was no longer in a relationship with the father of the child? How did her life become so messed up?

Jemma paid the taxi driver and went inside the house. After helping her mother prepare dinner, she tried and failed to summon the courage to tell her parents about the pregnancy during dinner. She was still undecided on what to do, and her thoughts kept her awake for most of the night. But, in the following days, she came to a decision.

She told her parents she was going to Lagos temporarily to get some things that she had left behind and would be back in a few days. When she arrived in Lagos, she went straight to see Edafe. She had called his house a couple of days earlier and left a message that she would come by today. She didn't have a phone, so he could not return her call. She hoped he wasn't out of town.

It was a weekday and, as expected, Edafe wasn't back from the office. However, the housekeeper said she could wait for him, as he was expecting her. He arrived an hour later, and as soon as he walked in, their eyes met.

Jemma stood up and said, "Hello, Edafe."

His face was expressionless as he responded with, "Hi, Jemma." He kept walking as he said, "I'll be right back." He returned some minutes later after he had changed out of his business suit into casual clothing.

"Let's talk over dinner," he said, and gestured for her to follow him to the dining table. The housekeeper had just set the dinner table for two.

Jemma was too nervous to be hungry, so she put just a little bit of food on her plate.

"I'm surprised you came to see me," Edafe said after he started eating.

"I'm sorry I left the way I did," Jemma responded. "It was very… cowardly of me."

"Perhaps…" he said.

They continued eating quietly. Meanwhile, Jemma was trying to figure out how to ease into what she wanted to say to Edafe.

"Why are you here, Jemma?" Edafe suddenly asked. When he received a message that Jemma would stop by, he was intrigued. Why did she want to see him? Was she here to apologize and beg him to take her back? Would her pride allow that? Perhaps being away from him opened her eyes to the error of her ways? He was ever so curious.

"I've been doing a lot of thinking in the last month or so, and I wanted to see you again to talk to you." She paused for a bit before she continued. "Now that we've been apart for a while, I wanted to know if you felt any different about our last conversation. I wanted to know if you would be willing to compromise. Assuming, you don't already have a girlfriend."

Edafe gave a small smile at the 'girlfriend' comment. "It depends on what you have in mind."

Jemma was quiet for a moment while she gathered her thoughts.

This was much harder than she had thought. Finally, she said, "I do not expect you to tell me all the details regarding your life and business on a daily basis. But I think nothing should be off limits, though. I would like to be able to ask about them if there are any issues or concerns."

"Do I have to answer you when you ask?"

Jemma stared at him wide-eyed. *Why would I ask a question if I don't want an answer?* "Yes," she responded.

"What do I get in return for this… compromise?"

"What would you like in return?"

"Your undying loyalty and commitment to me," Edafe responded. "And your obedience," he added after a pause.

"Would I have your obedience as well?"

Edafe raised an amused eyebrow. Was she now trying to tame him? Not in this lifetime. "No."

"Why not?"

Edafe's sharp eyes watched her like a hawk. She started fidgeting under his gaze and shrank back, subconsciously placing a hand on her tummy.

"You would have my undying loyalty and commitment," Edafe finally said in response. "There will be no other women. You will also have access to whatever funds you need. Aside from that, I can promise nothing else."

Jemma sighed. The reason she came to see Edafe was to get some closure on her earlier decision to leave him. She also wanted to see if his stance had changed so that she could decide whether to tell him about her pregnancy. He did not disappoint. She could clearly see that nothing had changed.

Not hearing a response from Jemma, Edafe said, "Listen, Jemma. You're the one who came back here. If it's not to abide by the terms I have laid out, you know where the door is."

His words jolted Jemma from her thoughts. She smiled wryly as she said, "Thanks for humoring me and agreeing to see me today, Edafe. But it seems we cannot agree." She sighed, "At least, I have some closure."

"Closure?" Edafe scoffed. "Well, just know that there will be no other opportunities to revisit this, Jemma. There are many other women who would take your place easily."

"I understand," Jemma said quietly.

Edafe gave a nod and continued eating his food.

Jemma also continued eating the rest of her food. However, as soon as she brought the spoon to her mouth, she suddenly felt nauseous. She put down her spoon and excused herself to go to the restroom. While in there, she emptied the contents of her stomach into the toilet bowl. When she was done, she flushed the toilet and rinsed her mouth. *Ugh! morning sickness,* she thought irritably. After checking that she looked presentable in the mirror, she stepped out of the bathroom and started walking back to the dining room.

Suddenly, she heard a deep voice behind her. "How far along are you?"

A surprised Jemma spun around to see Edafe leaning against the wall next to the bathroom with his hands in his pockets. It was clear that he had heard her vomiting.

"It doesn't matter," she said. "I'm not keeping it!" She turned back around and started walking away, but Edafe grabbed her hand, stopping her in her tracks.

"Why not? You think I don't want the child?" he asked.

"I don't want to have children with a man who does not view me as his equal."

"Why should the child suffer because of that?"

Jemma scoffed, "Don't you dare get moralistic with me!" She snatched her hand from his and walked off.

Edafe followed her to the dining room. When he saw her reach for her handbag, he said, "Jemma, I'll take responsibility for the child and I will marry you. Let's go back to Onitsha together to meet your parents."

"No need. The child isn't yours!" Jemma snapped as she headed for the door.

Edafe put his arm out to stop her. "You think I wouldn't have known if you were cheating on me?"

Jemma ran out of excuses, so she said nothing.

"Don't get rid of my child, Jemma," Edafe pressed.

Jemma sighed in frustration. What was this situation? Wasn't it usually the man who was skittish about having a child? Instead, it was the other way around.

"Move back here with me," he continued. "Marry me and I will take care of you and the child. You'll want for nothing!"

"Let me go, Edafe." She was so annoyed at his commanding tone of voice.

"Okay," Edafe said, a bit frustrated. "But it's already late at night, and you don't have a car," he reasoned. "Stay here tonight and think about what I've said. If you still feel the same way by tomorrow, I won't stop you from leaving."

Jemma hesitantly agreed.

Later, while she was settling in for the night in the guest room, she heard a knock on the door. "Come in," she said.

Edafe walked in and sat on the chair by her bedside. "Jemma, I don't like the idea of you destroying the life inside of you. But I understand that it's your body, so my limits are clear. However, it's my child too, and I want you to keep it."

"There are plenty of women who can give you another child."

"True, but I feel like this one is special," he said as his gaze fell on her abdomen. "… he's just meant to be."

Jemma scoffed internally. *Typical man*, she thought. *Already assuming it's a boy.*

"I will take your words under consideration," Jemma said.

After Edafe left, Jemma rolled her eyes. She had already made up her mind, and there wasn't anything that Edafe could say to change it. She felt that he was only appearing reasonable because he wanted to secure an heir. She didn't believe that Edafe Ariri could love anyone but himself, and she didn't want to be with him under his terms alone. She didn't want to be a wife who had to do as told, no questions asked. She also didn't like the fear Edafe elicited from her whenever he was upset.

If she decided to keep the baby, she would raise her child on her own.

***

Ten years and seven months later.

Jemma hurriedly left work to pick up her son from school. Today is his tenth birthday, and she had promised him that she would take him out for ice cream after school. The plan was to have a party the coming weekend, which was two days later. But for today, he could have a special treat.

At the end of each school day, students stayed within the fenced-in schoolyard. Parents and guardians picking up their children could easily see them through the fence and either go inside the schoolyard to get their child or have the child come out to them.

Jemma usually had her son wait very close to the fence so that she could easily see him when she arrived. Today, after parking her car, her eyes scanned the schoolyard looking for him. When she saw him, her heart nearly jumped out of her chest in fear. She quickened her steps and as soon as she was within earshot, she yelled, "Iben!"

Both Iben and the man talking to him turned around. When Iben saw his mother, a smile lit up his face and he ran to give her a hug. Jemma hugged him back tightly.

Iben then broke away from the hug to show his mother something. "Mommy, look. I got a birthday present!" he said excitedly.

"That's nice," Jemma said with a smile. "Is it from your teacher?"

"No, it's from him," he said as he turned around and pointed to the man he was talking to earlier.

The man walked closer to them and smiled. "Hello, Jemma."

"Hello, Edafe," Jemma responded flatly. *What is he doing here?* she thought as she held on to Iben tightly. *Did he somehow find out about Iben?*

"Didn't I tell you not to talk to or accept gifts from strangers?" she scolded Iben.

Iben pouted. "But Mommy, he said that he knows you. He didn't lie. You *do* know him."

Jemma sighed. That was besides the point, but she didn't want to upset Iben any further since it was his birthday. "We'll talk about this later," she simply said.

"Mommy, who is he?" Iben asked curiously.

"You're asking too many questions. Let's go!"

Iben looked unhappy at his mother's response. "Okay," he said reluctantly, before he suddenly walked to Edafe and gave him a hug. "Thank you for my present," he said.

Edafe smiled happily as he gently patted Iben's head. "You're welcome," he said.

Jemma glared at Edafe. For some reason, seeing Iben in his embrace turned her stomach. She wanted to get him away quickly, but she didn't want to cause a scene.

"Aren't you going to introduce us properly?" Edafe said to Jemma. He had been waiting patiently, while listening to Jemma and Iben talk all this time.

When Jemma didn't respond, Edafe said to Iben, "If you want to know who I am, I'll tell you. I'm your—"

"Grandfather!" Jemma said in a panic, cutting him off. "He's your grandfather!"

Edafe's expression turned frosty in an instant as he met Jemma's gaze. "His what?!" he asked coldly.

Jemma broke eye contact with Edafe and said to Iben. "Go and wait in the car."

"Okay," Iben said. "Bye, Papa," he waved to Edafe with a smile. "Come to my party on Saturday." Then he ran off, completely unaware of the tension between the two adults.

"You know full well that I am *not* his grandfather!" Edafe said, his deep voice laced with anger.

"That's right! You're nobody to him," Jemma responded. "So, please leave us alone."

"I know he's the child from back then," Edafe said, confirming Jemma's fears and suspicions. "I'm glad, you kept him."

"He is *not* your son!" Jemma lied desperately.

"I know he's *mine*!" Edafe countered. "I had a DNA test done, so I have proof. Give him to me, Jemma."

Jemma instantly felt goosebumps on her skin. How long had he known about Iben for him to have done a DNA test? How did he get Iben's blood, hair or skin? Had he met Iben before now? Jemma's heartbeat quickened. "How did you find out?" she asked.

"I have my ways."

"You can't have him," Jemma said, her voice shaking slightly. Iben is *her* son. She loved him dearly and had no intention of giving him away. "I'm sure you have other children by now. Please, just pretend that he doesn't exist."

"There are no other children."

Jemma's eyes widened in surprise. He had no other children? Why? How was that even possible? A man like Edafe could have women lining up to bear his children. Was it because he had always known about Iben and was just biding his time?

"I told you he's special, didn't I?" Edafe said with a smirk. "He is simply meant to be!"

Jemma met Edafe's gaze. Those were his exact words to her that night ten years ago when he found out that she was pregnant.

"You are his mother, so I am willing to work out a deal with you," Edafe continued. "But he shall live with me from now on."

Jemma's heart sank. She knew she couldn't fight him and win easily in court. Edafe was powerful and affluent. Furthermore, this was Nigeria, a patriarchal society where you would be hard pressed to find a judge who would oppose a man like Edafe. A wealthy man who wanted custody of his only son—his only heir.

"I need time," Jemma said, defeatedly.
"You have two weeks."

***

On his way back to the office, Edafe thought about Iben. He was thrilled to have met him earlier. *He looks just like I did when I was his age*, he thought with a smile. Then he suddenly remembered Jemma introducing him as Iben's grandfather. His countenance turned frosty again. *No matter, I'll fix that lie soon*, he thought to himself. Regardless, he felt fortunate to have found out about Iben. If it wasn't for Dokun Olaniran, he never would've known.

A few months before, Edafe was in his office when one of his men informed him that a man named Dokun offered information about a lady who claimed that he had fathered her son. Initially, he was going to dismiss the news because quite a few women had made similar claims over the years. Edafe did have a lot of women as the years went by, so he never outrightly denied any of the claims. However, he was no sucker and always insisted on a DNA test once the children in question were born. Unfortunately, none of them were his.

What got him to take this particular news seriously was the name of the woman. Jemma Asinobi. He had only ever been in a relationship with one woman named Jemma. So, he could only conclude that perhaps the Jemma he knew was now married but had kept the baby from many years ago.

In order to get more details, Edafe met with Dokun for the first time. He immediately had an aversion to the man, as he was an opportunist who was trying to sell information about another person. Apparently, Dokun had come across the information about Iben's paternity because Jemma had confided in his wife about who the biological father of her son was. And as married couples talk, Dokun became aware of the situation and decided to sell the information to Edafe. After all, the gossip columns were occasionally filled with claims of women who insisted that their child was Edafe Ariri's until proven wrong.

While Edafe was eager to confirm whether the said child was his, he made Dokun work for the reward money he requested. So, he pumped him for as much information about Jemma as possible.

According to Dokun, Jemma, her two children, and her husband, Andrew Asinobi had moved to Lagos a few years ago and were neighbors with the Olanirans. Additionally, Andrew was a medical doctor who worked at the same hospital where Dokun was a manager.

Since Jemma did not come forward to make her claim, Edafe had no choice but to figure out a different way to get DNA samples of Iben. Dokun offered to obtain that for him in return for payment. Edafe agreed.

It wasn't until almost two months later that Dokun could get the needed samples. It was during a sick visit when Jemma brought Iben to the hospital to be treated for malaria fever. The nurse, who was in cahoots with Dokun, had insisted on taking Iben's blood in order to confirm his illness.

***

After Jemma met Edafe, she told her husband what had happened. Although Andrew met Jemma after she had given birth to Iben, he never knew who exactly his biological father was. Jemma always said that the man was dead to her, so he didn't pursue it. After they got married, he had adopted Iben and had treated him as his own son ever since. Now that Andrew knew that Edafe was Iben's father, just like Jemma, he knew it would be a fruitless endeavor to refuse to give Iben to him.

Andrew loved Iben and although he knew Edafe had a right to his son, he also was hesitant to allow Iben to go and live with him. As a result, it didn't take much convincing for Jemma to persuade Andrew to sneak the family out of Lagos before the two weeks Edafe gave her were up. If only he had been more level-headed, he might've been able to avert the disaster that befell his family that night.

At Iben's birthday party a few days later, Jemma confided in Dokun's wife, Tinuke, that Edafe had found out about Iben. Although Dokun said nothing to her about his deal with Edafe, Tinuke immediately knew what her husband had done. They had been married for over thirty years, so she knew him well. *So that's why Ariri Corporation suddenly awarded our small side business a housekeeping contract at one of its hotels,* she thought to herself.

Tinuke felt bad because Jemma only told her about Iben's biological father to allay her fears about her daughter, Kemi. Kemi had divorced her husband and Tinuke was worried that she would have difficulty finding another man who would marry her with a child. While they were talking, Jemma told her about Iben's paternity, and that Andrew had adopted Iben even though he wasn't his. Jemma used herself as an example to show Tinuke that it was not the end of the world.

Tinuke's guilt, however, was not enough for her to tell Jemma that it was because of her husband that her family was about to be torn apart. But, when Jemma told her that their plan was to leave town, she was determined to keep that information to herself.

Unfortunately, Tinuke's silence this time would not make a difference because later in the week, Andrew's job transfer paperwork showed up for approval on Dokun's desk. There was no way he was going to allow his cash source to dry up. So, Dokun notified Edafe that the Asinobis were planning to move out of town before the two weeks he graciously gave Jemma to bring Iben to him was over.

Naturally, Edafe was furious. *This woman is always running away. She hasn't changed after all these years. Well, I'll show her just how I deal with people like her.*

***

On the night of the kidnapping, after Andrew's tussle with one of the masked men left him dead, Jemma ran after Iben's kidnapper to Edafe's car.

When he stepped out to talk to her, she yelled at him. "Edafe, this is wrong! Why are you so evil?"

"This is wrong? And I am evil?" Edafe said, his voice getting louder with each word. "How do you not see that what's wrong and evil is you trying to run away with my son?!"

Jemma scoffed. "He is *my* son, Edafe. I birthed and raised him! Not you! What if I got rid of the pregnancy back then, ehn? What would you do now?"

"Jemma, you're acting as though I had previously rejected this child of ours. I begged you to keep him then, remember? I was going to marry you as well. But your pride made you reject the safe haven I offered, both for your reputation and for our son. Yet, you're here acting as though you are some woman who was scorned in her time of need. You could've lived a life of luxury with me and *your* son every single day. Instead, you decided to raise him on your own. I'll applaud you. You've done a good job with him so far. But now I'm taking over."

Jemma never saw things from Edafe's perspective until now. "Okay," she replied. "Let's come up with a deal so that we'll both be in his life."

Edafe laughed, but it wasn't a humorous one. "No deal! If you hadn't tried to run off with my son, I was going to allow you to see him as you pleased. But not anymore. You'll be hearing from my lawyers if you so much as come near him without my permission."

"Edafe, please. Don't take him from me. He's my only s—"

"You have another child, don't you?" Edafe said, interrupting her. "Forget about Iben and pretend he doesn't exist!"

Jemma had no response when she heard Edafe throw back her previous words to him. She could only get down on her knees and beg him. "I'm sorry, Edafe. Please, don't do this."

"Goodbye, Jemma."

Jemma watched helplessly as Edafe got in his car and left with Iben.

Still on her knees, Jemma wondered if perhaps she had made all the wrong choices. Perhaps she shouldn't have been so upset about the way Edafe treated her back then. Perhaps she should've just married him for the sake of the baby—for Iben's sake. It may not have been the optimal marriage situation she dreamed of, but Edafe would've made good on his promise to not take another wife and to take care of her and their child. She could've saved herself and her parents the embarrassment of her being pregnant out of wedlock. Her husband Andrew would probably still be alive by now. But by convincing him to move the family away, she was in this mess and now he was dead as a result.

"Mommy," she suddenly heard her daughter Amara say.

"Yes, dear," Jemma said, wiping her tears.

"I'm scared," Amara said as tears rolled down her face.

Jemma's heart broke, and she pulled Amara into a tight hug. Her poor daughter no longer had a father, thanks to her foolishness. Thanks to Edafe's ruthlessness.

I can still fix this, Jemma suddenly thought to herself. She owed it to Andrew, Iben and Amara to make sure that everything that happened tonight would not be in vain. Jemma held her daughter by the hand and led her to their car. After they got in, she drove off, following Edafe's car. She would follow him home and try to convince him to change his mind. Maybe with Iben there, Edafe would be lenient.

She soon caught up to the car but Edafe's car sped up and when she tried to catch up again, she lost control of her car and crashed into a tree.

Jemma and Amara died on impact.

36 | Moments

Back to the present.

After giving his perspective on what happened the night of the accident to Iben and Fey, Edafe left Iben's house around 2:00 PM. Seeing that he still had some time, he told his driver to take him to the Ariri Corporation office at Victoria Island. People who saw him when he arrived wondered why the company chairman was there today. That office was the engineering arm of the company, and Edafe hadn't been there too many times in the recent past.

Edafe took the elevator to the office of the Director of Research and Development. The secretary greeted him and was about to notify her boss that Edafe was there when he said, "Don't worry. I'm not here on official business. Is he in a meeting?"

"No, sir," the secretary said.

Edafe then knocked on the door and entered the office before waiting for a response. Once inside, he shut the door behind him. A smirk appeared on his lips once his eyes met the wide-eyed look on the man sitting behind the desk.

"I was wondering how long before you came to see me," Dayo said once his initial surprise wore off.

Edafe took a seat in front of Dayo's desk and said, "Hello, to you too." Then he crossed his legs and continued, "Fate is a funny thing, isn't it, Dayo? Years ago, you refused the betrothal I offered between my son and your daughter. But they found each other, anyway. We are meant to be forever entangled, yeah?"

Dayo frowned. "And I suppose you're here to strong-arm me into agreeing to their marriage?" Before Edafe could answer, he added, "Don't bother. I'm not stopping them from getting married. Your son seems to be a better man than you, thank goodness. He must take after his mother in that respect."

Edafe chuckled. "I see you've become more vocal over the years."

Dayo ignored Edafe's comment and continued, "I'm not attending the wedding because I just can't stand to be in the same room as you outside of work. And I don't want to embarrass my daughter on her wedding day by being rude to her father-in-law."

"So you'd rather embarrass her by not showing up?"

Dayo sighed. "I don't expect you to understand my position."

"Oh, I think I understand very well. I just don't think your daughter should suffer for the decisions you made in the past. In fact, I think you *owe* it to her to put aside your *feelings* and take part in the wedding. Stop with the emotional theatrics."

"Don't act as if you care about my daughter. You're only here for Iben's sake."

"I actually like your daughter. For one, she's got more courage than you. She must get *that* from her mother!"

Dayo scowled when Edafe threw back his words.

Edafe smirked and continued, "To think she's bothered by how you feel about her wedding to Iben, despite the fact that you abandoned her, her sister and mother for many years."

"All thanks to you!" Dayo shot back.

"No, it's all you, Dayo. *You* made a series of decisions that had nothing to do with me or my blackmailing you."

Dayo scoffed, "Are you trying to rewrite history?"

Edafe leaned back in his seat and rubbed his chin. "Did you know that Kemi was sick with a heart problem? The police report was correct, but you believed my words instead."

Dayo frowned, "What the hell are you talking about? There's a videotape, remember?"

"What if I said that the videotape of her murder wasn't real?"

Dayo's face deadpanned. "Chief, I don't have time for your mind games today!"

Edafe continued as if he didn't hear what Dayo just said. "I knew about Kemi's illness, and when you asked me for help, I bargained with her. If she would stop pursuing you, I'd pay for her treatment in the United States. But do you know what she did when she returned? She broke our agreement and continued to chase after you. So I refused to pay for the rest of her treatment."

Like father, like daughter, Edafe thought to himself as he remembered Kemi and Dokun Olaniran.

Mouth ajar, Dayo stared at Edafe, and he was speechless for a while. Was he saying that he'd been trapped here in Nigeria, based on lies and a fake videotape? He could barely stomach it. "You are *amoral* and *irredeemable!*" he finally gritted out, disgust written all over his face.

Edafe nodded slowly, a serious expression on his face. "That *is* my nature, and I make no excuses. But you... you need to come to terms with yours." He leaned forward and continued, "I bet you can't stand me because my very presence reminds you of your cowardice and your inability to be with your family all these years."

Dayo's face hardened at Edafe's scathing words. He wanted to jump across his desk and punch Edafe in the mouth.

"Tell me, Dayo. What stopped you from verifying whether Kemi truly had a health issue? What stopped you from saying, *fuck Edafe*, I'm going back to my wife and kids? Frankly, if I had a family and my parents wanted me to abandon them for some business deal, those parents would be dead to me immediately. I wouldn't be sacrificing my wife and kids for their safety. The way I see it, you were a coward, and you took the easy way out. One that wouldn't require you to make any big sacrifices. But guess what? You still lost big time.

"Also, it's been how many years, now? Sixteen? Seventeen, maybe? Why haven't you tried to renegotiate with me? You could've gone on holiday to the States to see your family at any time. Did you think I was so invested in your life that I would monitor you *that* closely?"

By now, Dayo's facial expression had gone from furious to shocked to regretful. He slowly leaned back in his chair, feeling as if all the energy in his body was drained.

There was silence in the room for a while before Edafe said, "You're a good man, Dayo. And I'd be happy to have you as my in-law. Think of this marriage between our children as your chance to be a better father to your daughter. Put aside your *feelings* and do right by her."

Dayo didn't respond right away, but when he did, he asked, "What about the videotape?" That damned video was the bane of his existence right now. And although Edafe said it was fake, Dayo would only feel free once he destroyed it.

"I'll give it to Iben. He already asked for it on your behalf." Edafe stood up to leave. "As you've said, I'm here for Iben. He *is* my only son after all."

From Edafe's perspective, Iben was a dutiful son who did everything he asked. Being with Fey was the only thing Iben ever desired for himself, and he wanted to help fulfill that wish. Of course he liked Fey for Iben, so it wasn't a hard sell, anyway.

"Chief!" Dayo called just before Edafe opened the door. "If you or your son hurt my daughter in any way, I *swear*, I will not go easy on both of you!"

Edafe turned around, met the determined look in Dayo's eyes and smiled. Then he opened the door and left.

***

Dayo sat on the sofa in his living room as he stared intently at his cellphone. Yesterday, Edafe paid him a visit at his office and he had been doing a lot of thinking and soul-searching since then. The time on his phone clocked 3:00PM. Dayo took a deep breath, exhaled, and quickly made a video call before he chickened out. After a few rings, the person on the other line answered.

As soon as the person's face came into view, Dayo said, "Hello, Ada."

Ada smiled, "Hello, Dayo." Then she yawned.

"Did you just wake up?"

"Sort of, I had a late night. If you hadn't sent me a text that you would call, I'd still be asleep."

"Still not a morning person, huh?" Dayo said with a light chuckle. "You look great for someone just getting out of bed though."

Ada gave a small smile at the compliment. Then she asked in a serious tone, "So what did you want to talk about?"

Dayo cleared his throat self-consciously before he said, "Ada, I called to say I'm sorry about everything that happened in the last seventeen years."

"How many times are you going to apologize for that, Dayo?"

"As many times as needed."

"Look, it wasn't your fault. Edafe is to blame."

"Actually, I have to own up to some of that blame," Dayo said. "I stayed behind in Nigeria because I thought it was the right thing to do. But now, I'm not so sure."

Ada raised a questioning brow.

Dayo continued. "I shouldn't have been so scared of Edafe that I abandoned you and the girls. I've missed you all so much over the years, and I regret not doing more than just sending money. At the very least, I could've visited you all from time to time."

"We moved to Delaware, so even if you came, you wouldn't find us."

"Yes, but I should've given you my contact information in the letters I sent so that no matter how many times you moved, you could still reach me. Also, instead of being so secretive in my letters, I should've told you more about the situation I was in. But I was too ashamed. I was ashamed that I had to leave you and the kids to protect my parents, even though they didn't like you. So, I... I punished myself by making it difficult for you to forgive me."

He smiled wryly and continued, "What a twisted frame of mind I was in. I love my parents, despite what they had orchestrated. And I wanted to keep them alive, including you and the girls. But I shouldn't have wallowed in self pity. I should've been more courageous and perhaps looked elsewhere for help instead of letting Edafe Ariri bully me.

"Please forgive me, Adaobi. My failures put so much burden on you. I don't know how I can ever make it up to you. Tell me what I need to do to make it up to you."

After Dayo stopped talking, Adaobi didn't respond right away, as some of his words hit home. Although she was moderately relieved that Dayo didn't remarry like his parents wanted him to, she was still unhappy with him for not putting in more effort to reunite with them.

Ada sighed. "Although, I didn't agree with your decision to stay in Nigeria, I felt that you were just trying to protect us in your own way. But when Kemi Olaniran showed up at our house many years ago, it was difficult not to believe that you were going to marry her. And... I hated you for it."

Dayo looked shocked. "She did what? How did she find you?"

Ada shrugged. "Who knows? And that's what scared the hell out of me and made me move to Delaware."

"What did she want?"

"You," Ada said in response. "She must've really liked you because she came to warn me to leave you alone for her. So I did."

Dayo's face hardened. Here he was feeling guilty about Kemi's death all these years, but she was the reason his wife stopped communicating with him. No wonder Edafe looked down on him.

"You're not entirely to blame," Ada continued, snapping Dayo out of his thoughts. She looked away from the camera as she said, "I also could've called you. It's not like I didn't have your phone number in Nigeria. But I felt so betrayed and in my anger, I was determined to make it difficult for you to find us even if you wanted to. I changed my name and phone number, and I deleted yours. And even when I missed you and needed to talk to you, I couldn't. My pride wouldn't even allow me to reach out to you, even when you started writing letters to the post office box."

"You missed me?" Dayo asked, with a small smile.

Adaobi rolled her eyes, and she tried to stifle a smile. "Is that the *only* thing you got from everything I just said?"

Dayo chuckled. After a moment he looked straight at the camera and said, "I still miss you, Ada. Every day."

Ada looked away and said, "It's been too many years, Dayo. I—"

"I know," Dayo said softly, as he interrupted her. He didn't think he could handle the rest of what she was going to say. "I don't have any expectations. I just wanted to let you know how I feel."

Ada said nothing else, so he continued, "I acknowledge my failures and going forward, I want to rectify them as best I can. For starters, I want to support Fey. Much to my chagrin, she really loves that *devil's* son, so I am going to put aside my feelings and attend the wedding."

Ada's face went from surprised to suspicious. "Did Edafe try to force you?" she asked.

Dayo smiled wryly and shook his head. "No, I'm doing this because I know it would mean a lot to our daughter."

Ada sighed. "I have so much hatred for Edafe Ariri. I don't think I can stand to be around him."

"I understand," Dayo said in response. "I don't expect you to suddenly change your mind about the wedding. Although, I would love to see you again in person."

"I'll think about it," Adaobi said.

***

Three months later…

One Saturday evening, Fola heard a knock on his apartment door and went to answer it. It was Demi. After letting her in, he hugged her and asked, "Don't you have your key with you?"

"I do, but I didn't feel like digging it out of my purse." She tiptoed and gave him a gentle kiss on the lips. Then she walked to the kitchen, put down her bags and opened the fridge to get a drink of water.

Suddenly, her eye caught a book on the kitchen counter. "What's this?" she asked. She picked it up and read the title out loud, "Love and Sense: A Man's Guide to Lasting Relationships." She chuckled. "You're reading this?" she asked in amusement as she held up the book.

Fola scratched his head in mild embarrassment. "Sadly, yes," he said in response. *Damn, I forgot to hide it!*

Demi chuckled. "Is it any good?"

"Nah, it's mostly garbage!" he said dismissively.

Demi smiled and put the book down. Although Fola had played it off, the fact that he was reading the book showed her that he was committed to their relationship. It warmed her heart.

"What do you have in there?" Fola asked, turning his attention to the bags she had placed on the counter earlier.

"Chops and drinks."

"Oh, good thinking. I was going to order pizza or something for us later."

"This is better," Demi declared. "It's ofada rice and suya."

Fola's eyes lit up, and he started taking stuff out of the bags. Demi chuckled as she watched him.

"Whoa! Champagne too?!" Fola exclaimed. "What's the occasion? Did you win the lottery or something?" he joked.

Demi smiled as she walked up to him and put her arms around his waist. "It's our three-month anniversary since we started dating," she said.

"I didn't think you'd be sentimental about things like that," he teased.

Demi rolled her eyes. "I'm usually not. But considering how long I had to wait for you to agree to date me, I think it's worth celebrating," she said.

Fola chuckled and leaned in to give her a kiss. "It's been a great three months being together," he said softly.

To his pleasant surprise, Fola was enjoying his relationship with Demi. They had similar sensibilities and got along very well. Although earlier on in their relationship, they had both indicated that they didn't like people assuming what they were thinking, they were generally on point about reading each other. Motivations. Body language. Unspoken words. They were like tango dancers, with one responding instinctively to the other's movement.

Demi grinned and said, "Well, since you feel that way, I'll give you an extra serving of ofada rice and share my suya with you."

This earned a chuckle from Fola. "Come on, let's eat," he said.

After dinner, they moved to the living room to relax, each with a glass of champagne. Demi leaned in against Fola on the sofa and he wrapped his arm around her shoulder. They sat quietly for a few minutes until a notification came in on Demi's phone. It was a message from Fey. She wanted to confirm that Demi would accompany her to meet with her wedding planner the next day.

After Dayo decided to attend the wedding, it wasn't long before her mother, Ada, also changed her mind. With the wedding in three months, Fey was now in full wedding planning mode.

"Her wedding dress is going to be spectacular!" Demi suddenly declared, after sending a response to Fey.

"I see you're tooting your own horn again," Fola said with a chuckle.

"Hey, you know your girl is good at what she does. And my *investors* have been very happy."

"Indeed, they have," Fola said with a smile. He wondered if now was a good time to tell her he was one of the investors. He had avoided telling her, given how rocky their relationship started.

"Dee, I have a confession," he began solemnly. "I'm actually an investor in your company."

"I know," Demi responded with a smug look on her face.

"You do?" he asked in shock.

Demi smiled mischievously. "Yeah. I have a confession too. Every time you asked about Mila Threads, I'd always mention my investors because I enjoyed watching you squirm a bit. I wondered how long before you came clean."

"So I've been stressing out for nothing all this time?"

Demi chuckled. "Don't worry. It's been a source of entertainment for me."

"You don't say," Fola responded dryly, causing Demi to laugh.

Seeing that he looked annoyed, Demi leaned over and put her drink down on the side table next to him before putting her arm around his neck. "Thank you for believing in me," she said, and then she kissed him.

However, when she tried to let go, Fola held her in place and started tickling her. "This is for having fun at my expense," he said, as he continued tickling her.

As Demi laughed, she thrashed her arms and legs trying to get away when unexpectedly, her elbow poked him hard in his groin area.

"Uuuggghhh…" he groaned in pain.

"Oh my god! I'm so sorry, baby. Are you okay?"

"I think—it's broken," Fola gritted out, cupping himself with his hands. With his eyes closed, he peeked at Demi and smiled internally.

He continued to pretend that he was in pain while secretly enjoying Demi's utter mortification. *This is payback for being amused at my expense.*

Desperate to help, she suddenly pulled his hands away and started massaging his groin area to ease his pain. Fola closed his eyes and moaned with pleasure at her touch, but Demi in her panic, assumed it was because he was in pain.

She suddenly jumped up and said, "I'll go get some ice!"

Before she could leave, Fola grabbed her hand, stopping her. "Are you trying to freeze it to death?" he asked irritably. He was also annoyed that she stopped touching him.

"Oh, you have a point. What do we do then?" she asked, worry still written on her face.

"Let's just make sure it's not broken," he said. "I'll need your help with that."

"Hmmm?"

At the slightly confused look on Demi's face, Fola put his arm around her waist and pressed his hip against her. Thanks to her massage, he was now aroused. His voice was low and sexy as he said, "You're my girlfriend, so it's your responsibility to confirm that it's still working well."

It suddenly dawned on Demi that she just got played. She chuckled lightly at her gullibility and Fola's shamelessness. However, she didn't resist as he led her into the bedroom.

An hour later, as the couple cuddled under the sheets, Fola received a phone call. Demi snuggled closer to him in the bed while he answered.

"What?!" he suddenly exclaimed after a few seconds. Demi looked up at the shocked expression on his face. He sat up and said, "Okay, text me the details. I'll be there as soon as possible."

After he hung up, he turned to Demi and said, "Papa was arrested about an hour ago!"

He got up and started getting dressed. "Sorry, Dee. I have to go."

"No worries, baby," she said with understanding.

"I might not be back until very late or tomorrow."

"That's okay. I can let myself out. I have my key."

A few minutes later, he kissed her, and then he left.

37 | Drag Net

Earlier that evening.

Edafe sat with a glass of whiskey in his hand. He felt his muscles relax as an attractive, scantily clad woman massaged his shoulders. After a few minutes, she began caressing his arms and kissing him on his neck. Edafe's eyes snapped open, and he grabbed her hands, stopping her ministrations.

"*What's the matter?*" she asked in a foreign language. She didn't appear to speak any of the indigenous Nigerian languages.

"Leave," Edafe said in his deep voice, and waved her away. After she left, he leaned back in the armchair and took another swig of his drink.

Tonight, Edafe was feeling melancholic.

The recent happenings surrounding Fey and Iben's engagement, and the return of Iben's memories, put him in an unusually reflective mood as he thought about his life.

People say I am evil. But am I? I simply present options to them, he thought to himself. Ones that benefited him, of course. But what he found over the years is that people almost never did the right thing. Yet they blamed him for the consequences of their poor decisions. He merely viewed himself as a catalyst that exposed the weakness and real evil in men's hearts. And when they tried to blame him, he simply put up a mirror, showing them who they really were.

He stood up, put on his white suit jacket and left his cabin. He had come to the yacht party intending to meet up with an old friend tonight, but the man didn't show up. As Edafe made his way to the main deck of the luxury superyacht, he passed by men and women drinking, smoking, dancing, laughing and having a good time. The yacht parties had evolved over the years so that there were now private rooms for couples. Also, the yacht now sailed out to the open waters until the next morning instead of being docked.

When he turned a corner, he came across a couple who didn't make it to their cabin and were having sex right there in the hallway, against the wall. Edafe turned up his nose in disgust as he walked past them. *I shouldn't have come here tonight*, he thought to himself for the third time that night. Unfortunately, he would have to wait until their scheduled return in the morning.

Edafe walked to the stern of the yacht and stood by the railing overlooking the waters. He suddenly had a flashback to when he first met Jemma, Iben's mother.

He smiled wryly as he thought that Jemma was the only woman he ever really cared about. He wasn't sure if it was because he had seriously wanted to marry her at some point or if it was because she decided to give birth to Iben. *If only she wasn't so stubborn, she might still be alive today*, he thought to himself.

As he stood, drink in hand, he reminisced about the first time he met Jemma... and the last time he saw her. Edafe thought sadly that things could've been different. If only she had freely allowed him to share in Iben's life. He thought now that perhaps he shouldn't have been so hard on her back then when they were together. Perhaps he shouldn't have let his temper and his pride get the best of him, thus pushing her away.

What Edafe was feeling at this moment was loneliness, but he would never admit to that. He would go to his grave with these thoughts. Edafe wasn't a man to share these kinds of feelings with anyone.

He sipped his drink and whispered Jemma's name. Then he slowly poured the rest of his drink into the murky water below as a tribute to her.

A moment later, he heard helicopters in the distance. Shortly after, he heard the blare of another sea vessel's horn. As the helicopter drew closer, Edafe sighed. He knew what was about to happen. He took out his cellphone and made a call to his lawyer.

Although it was late at night, he answered. "Good evening, Chief," he said in greeting.

"Samuel, I need you to make preparations to bail me out from jail this evening."

"What?!" Samuel exclaimed. "You were arrested?"

"Well, not yet. I'm at a yacht party and the police are almost here."

Samuel sighed. *This is going to be a PR nightmare once this gets out*, he thought in frustration. "Chief, you're too old for these parties," he complained. "I thought you stopped attending them a long time ago."

"You're my lawyer, not my mother!" Edafe snapped. "Meet me at the harbor on Lagos Island within the hour and bring enough money for bail! I have no intention of spending the night at whatever hole-in-the-wall police station we'll be taken to!"

"Yes, sir! Should I notify Fola and Iben?"

"Yes, and tell Fola to find out anything he can about this operation."

After Edafe ended the call, he checked that his all-white ensemble was still immaculate and walked to the bar to get another glass of whiskey. Then he sat down and calmly waited for things to unfold.

***

The helicopter circled above the yacht until the police boat closed in on it. Several police officers boarded, and they instructed the captain to return the vessel back to shore. As the captain notified everyone over the public address system that law enforcement had commandeered the yacht, the police were busy breaking into and raiding the cabins. Several people were caught in embarrassing positions as the police abruptly disrupted their sexual activities. They also confiscated drugs and other paraphernalia. The only cabin where no one and nothing incriminating was found was Edafe's.

While still seated at the bar on the main deck, one police officer walked up and spoke to Edafe. "Sir, can I please see your ID?" When Edafe turned to face him, the officer recognized him. "Chief Ariri? You're here?" he asked in shock.

"Hello, Chidi," Edafe responded with a small smile. "How is your father doing?"

"He is doing better these days. Thanks to your recent help regarding his health." He bowed as a show of thanks.

"Don't mention it. He's a good friend of mine," Edafe responded. "So, what is this all about?" he asked.

Chidi glanced over his shoulder before he answered in a hushed tone, "It's a secret operation that we've been working on for months, sir. The only thing I can say is that it's unfortunate that you're here because there's human trafficking involved."

"Is that so…?" Edafe replied.

"Yes, our informant gave us a tip that tonight, there was going to be an event involving the parties of interest."

"I see," Edafe said. *That fool, Franklin, is slipping up in his old age. No wonder he's not here tonight.*

Just then, another officer came over and said, "Wow! A big fish got caught in our net. Am I lucky or what? Edafe Ariri, right?"

Edafe looked up and asked, "And you are?"

"Detective Godwin Olaniyi."

The name sounded familiar to Edafe, but he couldn't place it.

Godwin continued, "I'm with the EFCC on this joint operation with the Anti-Human Trafficking division."

Ah, he's the busybody Fola said had snuck into the Christmas party last year, Edafe thought to himself. He ignored Godwin and turned his attention to the drink in his hand.

Godwin was very excited at the opportunity to arrest Edafe. Although he couldn't get to him via the Starlight Shipping route, he was going to make the most of this opportunity.

He sat down next to Edafe. "It would seem that you're not so noble and distinguished, Chief Ariri," he said with a sneer. "How can someone like you attend an event like this? What would your son and soon-to-be daughter-in-law think? Hmmm? Your company is also going to take a hit once news of your proclivities makes the headlines. People aren't very forgiving of these kinds of indiscretion. They will either jump ship or eat you alive and spit out the carcasses. If you don't want everything you've worked for over the years to be destroyed, I would suggest that you tell us what you know so we can work out a deal."

Chidi, who was still standing around, stared in shock at Godwin's words. *Does this guy know who he's talking to so rudely?*

Edafe's face was expressionless as he listened to Godwin's taunts and insults. Finally, he said, "Surely, you don't think I'm going to speak with the likes of you without my lawyer present. Why don't you run along and find some other idiot to waste their time?"

"Detective Godwin, he's right," Chidi chimed in. "You cannot try to get a statement in this manner. We both know that's against protocol."

Godwin chuckled. "No need to be so serious. I'm simply chatting with the man." He stood up and said, "I suppose we'll get to chat again at the station." He sneered again before he left.

***

Fola went straight to Iben's house after he left home that evening. Barrister Samuel had given him the task of delivering the news of

Edafe's arrest to Iben. As expected, Iben was also shocked at the news. After getting more details from Edafe's lawyer, Fola also made a few calls to his contacts and found out about the EFCC's involvement in the arrest. When they arrived at the station, Iben went inside while Fola stayed in the vehicle so as not to arouse suspicion. While he waited, he made some more calls.

Detective Chidi showed Iben to the interrogation room, but he could only watch and listen to Edafe being questioned by two officers through a glass barrier. Edafe's lawyer, Samuel, was also in the room. Although Iben was nervous, he was confident in Samuel Adegbite's abilities, as he was one of the best lawyers in the country. Despite his somewhat tense relationship with Edafe these last few months, Iben still loved the man. He was his only family, after all.

"As I've said earlier, my client was unaware of any illegal activities happening on that yacht. He was there to relax with friends," Samuel said. "Furthermore, none of the pictures you took after boarding the yacht, nor the surveillance videos and pictures that your spies obtained had my client in a compromising position," Samuel continued. "So, on what basis are you charging him exactly?"

"He was relaxing with friends who do questionable things?" Godwin asked.

"Do you know *everything* your friends do in their private lives?" Samuel countered.

When Godwin was assigned to this case months ago, he was tasked with monitoring Franklin Ejike as he was a prime suspect and key player in the human trafficking ring. While doing this, he saw that Franklin made several trips to Edafe's house. Wondering what their relationship was, Godwin was excited to potentially link Edafe to his case. So, he planted a spy in Franklin's home and bugged his residence. He wanted to do the same at Edafe's residence, but the Ariri mansion had airtight security. He imagined it was probably on par with the Nigerian president's official residence at Aso Rock.

"We have surveillance videos which show that Edafe is familiar with Franklin Ejike," Godwin continued.

"Yes, and my client has not denied knowing him. Again, do any of these videos put my client in a compromising position?"

"We know that they're business partners."

Samuel shared a look with Edafe before he said, "Yes, but in a limited capacity. My client is simply a silent investor. He has his own multi-billion-naira company to run and is not involved in the daily business activities of Franklin Ejike's company."

"So, you're admitting to being partners with a human trafficker?"

"No. My client was not aware of such activities."

That was a lie.

Samuel was aware of the relationship between Franklin Ejike and Edafe Ariri. About thirty years ago, Edafe had invested in his good friend Franklin's business so he could start a luxury yacht rental and cruise business. When he realized that some of his renting customers were using the yachts for exotic parties, Franklin expanded his income by hosting similar parties for a fee. Edafe met Jemma at one of such parties.

Edafe and Franklin were cut from the same cloth—they were both adrenaline junkies. As time went on, Franklin used the cruises he planned as an opportunity to transport the women he bought and sold across several African countries. Many of them came from poverty-stricken areas where parents were willing to sell their children to Franklin for food or money. They sold the young ones as house helps while the older ones in their teens were forced into prostitution to service the exotic tastes of Franklin's customers.

When Edafe found out about Franklin's *side business*, he stopped attending Franklin's organized parties because it meant that those whores of his could be there, and Edafe didn't want to be caught in a sticky situation. Edafe wasn't averse to thrill-seeking and having a good time, but human trafficking was a line that he was unwilling to cross. That was his bottom line. However, that didn't stop him from assisting his friend by supplying him with firearms, as Franklin's human trafficking naturally attracted the attention of unsavory characters.

As decades went by, Franklin had become less wary and cautious. He had gotten away with what he'd been doing for so long that he rarely looked over his shoulder as often as he used to when he was younger. That was his undoing.

A few days before the yacht raid, Franklin had asked Edafe to meet up at the yacht to discuss something. Neither of them knew that Franklin was already under investigation by the police. On his way to the yacht to meet up with Edafe, Franklin was arrested.

Godwin turned his attention to Edafe. "You can deny your involvement all day long, and you might even prove that you were ignorant of the human trafficking. But news of your involvement with such a man will affect you negatively, Chief Ariri. The bottom line is that we actually have phone conversations that show that you were aware of the human trafficking part of the business. You knew about it and you didn't report it. You're looking at a minimum of five years imprisonment."

Edafe met Godwin's sneer with a frosty look. However, he understood exactly what he meant. Edafe wasn't worried about what people would think of him. He was concerned about a stain on his legacy. News of this would affect Ariri Corporation, and his business partners may disassociate themselves from the company. Edafe's company was his life's work, his legacy. He detested the thought of allowing any blemishes on it.

"I need to speak to my client in private," Samuel said after a moment.

"You have fifteen minutes," Godwin said and walked out with the other interrogator.

While Edafe and Samuel were discussing the situation, Samuel received a text message from Fola with information that could serve as a bargaining chip.

When Godwin and his partner returned, he said, "Are you ready to come clean and accept your fate?"

"My client would like to propose a deal," Samuel replied.

Godwin chuckled derisively. "You're in no position to bargain!"

"It appears that my client is not the only one who has a past relationship with Mr. Ejike. Aren't you also very acquainted with him, Detective Godwin?"

Godwin scoffed, "I'm no friend of his, if that's what you're implying."

"But you have met and spoken with him several times in the last couple of years since you joined the force, have you not?"

Godwin frowned? *What's he getting at?*

"He served as a witness on several cases you were involved with, correct?"

"So what?"

"His testimonies and evidence he provided even helped solve and win your cases, correct?"

Godwin's face now wore a full-blown scowl. "Get to the point!" he snapped.

"My client has proof that Franklin gave false testimony in many of those cases."

"That's impossible!" Godwin replied in disbelief.

"My client has multiple recorded conversations with Franklin Ejike to show this, and he is willing to provide them as proof. I wonder what would happen if the public found out that many of these high-profile cases that you recently solved had Franklin Ejike as a key witness. I know of many lawyers who would jump at the opportunity to expose this information and demand that all of those cases be reopened and retried, given your reliance on a witness such as Franklin Ejike, who is of *questionable* moral character. Your career as an investigator could end here, don't you agree?"

Godwin's nose flared and twitched as he stared Samuel Adegbite down. His eyes filled with malice and his hands balled into fists. He understood exactly what Samuel was getting at. *How the hell did he find out about my cases?*

Franklin was a key informant in convicting several corrupt Central Bank and private sector bank officers who were recently found guilty of financial fraud. Quite a number of these people were frequent customers on Franklin's cruises and yacht parties, and over the last couple of years, he had cooperated with the police to obtain evidence to indict them. Little did he know that he would later be under investigation himself.

"What do you want?" Godwin finally gritted out. Aside from all those cases potentially being reopened, his concern was that they could be putting convicted criminals back in the streets.

"My client will keep this information to himself, if you do not expose his business partnership with Franklin Ejike to the public."

"I cannot make that call."

"Then I suggest you get someone here who can."

Five minutes later, another officer walked into the interrogation room. He was a head taller than Godwin, and he sported a bald head and a bushy moustache. He sat down across the table from Edafe and Samuel. Then, he smiled and said, "Leave it to the distinguished Barrister Adegbite to *pour sand in our garri.*"

Samuel did not return his smile. Instead, he asked, "What's your answer, Detective Metuh?"

Detective Metuh sighed and said, "As long as you provide proof of Franklin Ejike's perjury in our prior cases, we will keep Chief Ariri's involvement with him from the media. There will be no trial. However, he cannot escape the million naira fine and imprisonment."

"How long?" Samuel asked.

"Five years in prison."

"Two years under house arrest," Samuel countered.

Detective Metuh scoffed, "You're asking for too much." He stood up to leave.

"Ten high-profile cases, eight of which are related to the well publicized Central Bank fraud, will be under scrutiny. Additionally, don't you have two more cases pending in that same investigation?" Samuel prodded.

Detective Metuh stopped in his tracks and met Samuel's sharp gaze.

Seeing that Metuh hesitated, Samuel continued, "My client will work with law enforcement to ensure proper adherence to the house arrest during the proposed two years. If at any time, he is in violation, you are free to cart him off to prison to complete his sentence."

Metuh looked thoughtful for a moment. Then he said, "Two years' house arrest and *four* million naira in fines. An extra million naira in exchange for each of the three years needed to make up the original five years."

"Deal," Samuel said without hesitation.

38 | Transitions

After he was released on bail from the police station, Edafe spent the night in a suite specially reserved for him at one of his hotels nearby. He did not return home until his entire mansion on Banana Island had been swept for electronic monitoring devices. Nothing was found, confirming that only Franklin Ejike's residence was bugged by the police. Edafe was relieved. He then asked Iben, Fola and Samuel Adegbite to meet him at the mansion later in the evening.

Samuel arrived first to discuss damage control with Edafe.

"I have the plea bargain documents ready for your signature," Samuel began.

Edafe took the file folder handed to him and put it aside without looking at it.

"Chief, it's imperative that you review the documents and sign them within the next few days," Samuel urged.

Edafe nodded in understanding.

Samuel was somewhat surprised by Edafe's calm demeanor given last night's events. Although Samuel knew that he did his best under the circumstances, he still half expected Edafe to rake him over the coals for not getting him a better deal or sentencing. *I suppose I shouldn't look a gift horse in the mouth*, he thought to himself.

"I want to talk about how the company will operate in the two years I'll be in confinement."

Samuel nodded. About two years ago, he and Edafe drafted a plan which outlined handing the company over to Iben in a gradual process. The first step was having him manage Starlight Shipping as training. Then, after a year, he'd systematically include other parts of the company over a few years until Iben was comfortable and Edafe could retire to the background.

"I assume we're going to fast track the original plan?" he asked.

Edafe nodded. "How long do I have before the official sentencing begins?"

"Two weeks. That's how long Detective Metuh and the judge will allow for converting your home at Ikorodu into a suitable... prison cell." He spoke his last two words with a measured tone. *That three-bedroom house was going to be one very comfortable prison cell*, he thought to himself.

Edafe didn't want the police in and out of his mansion during his house arrest, so he opted to serve his time at one of his other homes.

Samuel continued, "I'm still negotiating for you to be allowed to attend Iben's wedding in three months' time. While nothing is set in stone, they have assured me that if you're *well-behaved* by then, there shouldn't be a problem." Samuel paused before he added, "You *will* behave. Right, Chief?"

"I'll try my best," Edafe said with a smirk.

Samuel sighed. "Well, just remember that Iben is the one who will suffer for any misdeeds. And don't forget that the police are looking for any reason to ship you off to prison." Although Samuel made it sound like Edafe and Iben would be on the losing end if Edafe didn't follow the rules in the plea bargain agreement, Samuel also didn't want to be saddled with the responsibility of figuring out what lies to tell people if Edafe Ariri could not attend his son's wedding.

Edafe frowned as he thought about the situation. All his life, he'd been very meticulous and had avoided any run-ins with the law. Obviously, it wasn't because he was a law-abiding citizen all the time.

Edafe had always felt justified in his actions because he had a viewpoint that he brought a brand of order to the world by doing the things he did, regardless of whether it was good or bad.

What was most ironic was that he was now going to be doing time for a crime he didn't even commit. *I guess that old adage of 'watch the company you keep' rings true.* But Edafe figured it was a small price to pay for keeping his company unblemished by his friend's illegal activities. *I'll deal with that old fool, Franklin later, when he gets out of prison.*

"Questions will start flying when people cannot reach you after we announce that Iben will be the new CEO of Ariri Corporation," Samuel said, snapping Edafe out of his thoughts.

"We can just say that I'm overseas taking a sabbatical for personal reasons," Edafe suggested.

Samuel nodded in agreement.

"Look out for Iben," Edafe continued. "He has a tendency to avoid ruffling feathers. Some people will try to take advantage of that."

"Don't worry, Chief," Samuel responded with a reassuring smile. "Iben has been doing an excellent job with Starlight Shipping. Even your *side hobby* has been thriving with fewer incidents under his purview since he took over."

Edafe nodded slowly at the truth of Samuel's words.

"Perhaps you may want to consider a different hobby while you're under house arrest. I hear knitting can be very therapeutic," Samuel teased with a smile.

"I'd rather gouge my eyes out instead," Edafe responded, his deep voice sounding unamused.

Samuel chuckled. "Iben will be fine," he said, going back to their prior topic. "He has matured over the years."

Edafe and Samuel continued their discussion until Iben and Fola arrived. After greetings, they both took their seats. Samuel laid out the terms of Edafe's plea bargain and when his house arrest would begin. According to Samuel, during the nighttime newscast, Franklin Ejike's arrest and charges would be revealed. Thanks to the information Fola obtained, Edafe could make a plea bargain to avoid being on the news.

When Samuel finished speaking, Edafe said, "Fola, you did a good job getting us that important intel on Detective Godwin's cases."

Fola wore a solemn expression. "Papa, I'm sorry I couldn't do more. I should've known about the case earlier. Please forgive me." He bowed his head in apology.

Edafe gave a small smile before he said, "Don't be too hard on yourself, Fola. I can't expect you to know everything that's going on at the EFCC. Even if you were aware of the case, you didn't know about my relationship with Franklin Ejike, so you wouldn't have connected it to me."

He then turned to Iben and said, "It's time to hand over the reins to you, son."

Iben nodded in understanding. He had always known that was the plan, but it was supposed to be done gradually. And now, with Edafe's house arrest coming up, he was going to be thrown into the belly of the beast.

At first, Iben was angry at the way things turned out. He wondered why his father couldn't just stay out of trouble. If it wasn't blackmail or kidnapping, it was firearms trafficking or exotic yacht parties.

Eventually, he had no choice but to stop worrying about it. He reasoned that he now had his chance to run the company *his* way.

Unbeknownst to others in the room, Iben's heart was thumping loudly in his chest. He was both nervous and excited about taking on his new role as CEO of Ariri Corporation.

Edafe explained that he didn't want the police in his home on Banana Island. So, he instructed Iben and Fola to work with law enforcement to convert his Ikorodu house into his prison to serve his house arrest. While the updates were being made, Edafe and Samuel would work to transfer the company to Iben.

Hours later, after Fola and Samuel left, Iben stayed behind to chat with Edafe. When he saw Edafe reach for his pipe, Iben stood up and lit it for him. As he poured him a glass of his favorite cognac, Iben asked, "Papa, why didn't you ever marry?"

Edafe wore an amused smile. "Since when are you interested in my love life?"

"I think that perhaps you wouldn't feel the need to attend those yacht parties if you were in a committed relationship," Iben responded cautiously.

"What if I said that I met your mother at one of such yacht parties?" Edafe asked with a smirk.

Iben frowned. *Can't this man just answer the question without being nasty?* "Are you suggesting that my mother was a prostitute?" he asked.

"No, she was not. But it's true that I met her at a yacht party," Edafe replied. He then told Iben the events surrounding how he met Jemma, and how she refused to see him when he showed up unannounced at her apartment, to how they started dating. Iben listened attentively, hanging on to Edafe's every word as he spoke. He was eager to learn anything he could about his dead mother.

"Fey is a lot like her in some ways," Edafe said after he finished. "Strong-willed and fiery."

Iben smiled at the compliment. After a few seconds of silence, he suddenly asked, "Why didn't you and my mother get married?"

Even as Iben asked that question, he felt a pang of guilt. His stepfather, Andrew Asinobi, had treated Iben like his own while being happily married to his mother for about eight years before their deaths. And yet, here he was wishing his mother and Edafe had stayed together as a couple because it could've been the difference between her being alive or dead.

"Why do you think?" Edafe responded.

Iben looked thoughtful for a moment. Then he asked, "You didn't know she was pregnant with me?"

Edafe shook his head. "I did know, but when I asked her to marry me, she said no. Why do you think she refused?"

"She couldn't tolerate you," Iben said plainly. Thinking about it, he felt that perhaps few women could stand to be in a long-term relationship with Edafe. His mother was the closest that he was aware of, and even he could understand if his mother left Edafe because of his temperament.

Edafe smiled wryly. "I suppose that's what it was," he mumbled to himself.

"Hmmm?" Iben said, not quite hearing Edafe's response.

"Nothing," Edafe replied. Then he changed the subject. "Samuel will bring me periodic reports, so I look forward to hearing good things about the company while I'm away."

Despite the sudden change in conversation, Iben nodded and said, "Thanks for the vote of confidence, Papa." Then he added, "But, you should know that while I'm in charge, I *will* make some changes that you may not like."

Edafe met and held Iben's gaze. An understanding passed between them. He knew Iben was referring to his firearms trafficking. Since the shootout at Port Harcourt, Iben had reluctantly involved himself in the concealment of the shipment and warehousing of the firearms. With Edafe now going to be on house arrest and the police sneakily sniffing around the company, Iben couldn't wait to get rid of his father's dangerous pastime.

"Do what you want. I'm bored with it anyway," he said with a dismissive wave of his hand. "I need another hobby. Maybe I'll just take up knitting while I'm in confinement. I hear it's therapeutic."

Iben stared at Edafe, mouth ajar for a few seconds before he burst into laughter. This was the same man who sent him off to boot camp to learn how to become a man when he found out that Iben was spending his free time cooking in the kitchen. *Knitting my ass!* Iben thought to himself.

Edafe enjoyed hearing Iben laugh. Ever since he took custody of him when he was ten, he rarely saw Iben laugh so freely.

"Anyway, I'm sure you'll find something *riveting* to spend your time on in the next two years." Iben said after he stopped laughing.

Edafe smiled.

After a moment, Iben said, "I promise, I won't fail you, Papa."

"I know," Edafe said.

***

About two weeks after Edafe began his house arrest, Iben came home to find Fey pacing angrily up and down the bedroom. Just as she had promised Iben, she moved in with him once their wedding date was set. For about a minute, he watched her repeatedly pace from the bedroom to the balcony and back. Not once did she notice his presence. Finally, he stepped in front of her, blocking her path.

Surprised to suddenly see Iben, she said, "Oh... hi, babe." She gave him a hug. "How was your day?" she asked after pulling away.

"Very busy. How was yours?" he asked, eyeing her curiously.

The scowl that was on her face earlier returned immediately. "My boss pissed me off today!" she growled.

Iben led her to sit on the sofa and asked, "What happened?"

After her engagement to Iben was announced last Christmas, Fey became a bit of a VIP at work, as many people started treating her as if she were a celebrity. As a private person, she didn't care for the attention, but there wasn't much that she could do about it. Unknown to her, there were some on the other end of the spectrum who felt that her presence on the job was a waste of space.

Just before Fey left work that day, her boss, Mrs. Coker, asked to speak with her in her office. She wanted to know when Fey would hand in her resignation.

"Am I being fired?" she asked in shock at the question.

"No, but you're getting married soon."

"I don't see how that has anything to do with my job!"

"Look, Miss Ademola, or should I say, Mrs. Ariri to-be. We all know that once you're married to your billionaire fiance, you won't want to work here any longer. There is no point in taking up a position when someone else in need could benefit from it." Mrs. Coker also didn't believe that Fey would continue to put her heart and soul into her work for much longer.

Fey's jaw dropped. What was she hearing? "Am I to understand that I should resign simply because I am getting married? I am good at my job. And getting married isn't suddenly going to make my brain dull!"

Mrs. Coker, a woman in her fifties, looked exasperated. *What is this girl's problem? I'm just trying to make sure that I'm fully staffed by the time she leaves.*

Seeing that Fey was offended, Mrs. Coker forced a smile and said, "You're right, and you've been an exemplary member of our staff. I just thought you might think this job was beneath you, given your status as Edafe Ariri's daughter-in-law. Why would you need the small salary this government job pays?"

Fey was speechless. In one breath, this woman had offended all of her sensibilities as an independent woman. She wasn't marrying Iben for his wealth. And although she wouldn't lack money for the rest of her life, she would not be content with just being a housewife. Even if she didn't work for the government anymore, she'd be bored out of her mind from doing nothing.

After Fey narrated everything to Iben, he scooted closer to her on the sofa and put his arm around her. "I'm sorry to hear that, babe."

"Do you also think I should just stay home and take on the role of a rich housewife?" Fey asked.

Trick question! Iben thought to himself. Although he understood why Fey was upset, he secretly wanted Fey to stop working for the government. But it wasn't because he wanted her to stay home and be his trophy wife.

"No, babe," he said instead as he gently rubbed her shoulder. "So, what do you want to do?"

Fey sighed. "I've considered resigning and then finding another job, but after what my boss said, I'm not sure anyone would hire me once they figure out who I am to you. Who would've thought being wealthy had disadvantages?"

Iben chuckled. "I know one company that would hire you, *especially* because you are future Mrs. Ariri."

Fey's face lit up. "Really? Where?"

"Ariri Corporation," Iben responded with a small smile. This was the reason he wanted her to quit her government job. While her current job brought her to Nigeria, Iben felt it was time for her to move on.

"Oh..." Fey said simply as she met Iben's amused facial expression. Suddenly she started laughing at herself. Ariri Corporation hadn't even crossed her mind at all, even though her father worked there.

"I suppose you're right," she said after a moment. "Although, people will probably think that I got the job because of who I am to you."

"Who cares? Ariri Corporation is *ours*," Iben replied. "Why would anyone question you working there? Wouldn't it be odd if you were working for another company instead of your own?"

Fey nodded slowly as she pondered his words.

"Besides, you have so much to bring to the table," Iben continued. "Aside from your engineering skills, you also have your experience working for the government in the last ten months. Imagine the insights you can give Ariri Corporation regarding the government contracts and projects that we can propose and bid for. And if anyone thinks you got your position simply because you're my wife, I know you'll be able to prove them wrong in no time."

Fey met Iben's gaze. Every time Iben referred to her as his wife, she would get butterflies in her stomach. She still had to get her mind around her new social status as her wedding to Iben drew near.

"So, tomorrow morning, turn in your resignation and tell your boss to kiss your bumper because you're leaving to put your awesome engineering skills to good use where it will be appreciated—at your family's company."

Fey chuckled as she snuggled against him. His words made sense to her, and it was reassuring that she had Iben's support. "Thanks, babe," she said.

The next morning, Iben arranged for a driver to take Fey to work in his Maybach.

"Babe, this isn't necessary. I can get myself to the office just fine in my car."

"How are you going to floss on your boss if you just quit and then drive yourself away in your jalopy? You need to do it in style. If I wasn't swamped with work due to Papa's absence, I'd go with you and put on a show."

Fey chuckled. "Oh my gosh! You're so petty, Iben."

"Indeed, I am," Iben replied with a grin as he opened the door for her to get in.

"Okay," Fey said as she got in the back seat. She wasn't going to argue about something like this. Besides, it would be relaxing to not have to worry about driving in the mad morning traffic, anyway.

Iben leaned in to give her a goodbye kiss. Then he told the driver to bring her to his office when she was done.

***

Later, when Fey arrived at Ariri Corporation, Iben's personal assistant met her at the entrance. As he led her to the elevator, Fey said,

"Congrats on your promotion, Machie."

Machie was Iben's PA since last year while he was at Starlight Shipping. According to what Iben had told her, Machie had done such a good job that Iben transferred him over to Ariri Corporation headquarters as his assistant. He had Iben's trust, and as part of his new role, he was also in charge of the other two assistants assigned to the CEO.

Machie smiled and said, "Thank you, Madam."

Machie led Fey up to the top floor of the building. When they stepped out of the elevator, there was a waiting area to the right and three desks to the left. Two were occupied by the other two assistants. Fey smiled at them and said, "Good morning."

They stood up and politely returned her greeting.

When Fey was out of earshot, Tina, the younger of the ladies, said, "So she's the reason our *handsome* boss put Machie in charge of us. She must be a very jealous woman for her to want to control our access to him."

"And why does that bother you?" Tola, the other lady asked. "Were you hoping to work your way into the boss's bedroom?"

Tina smiled coquettishly. "So what? He's such a fine specimen of a man. And rich, too. And that British accent of his—" She paused dramatically to place a hand on her chest and fan herself with the other before she continued. "She can't keep him all to herself, even if she's his fiancée. Am I not a fine girl too? I can compete with her."

Tola wore an amused expression as she listened to Tina gush. "I admire your confidence, but obviously you don't know what happened when the CEO was at Starlight Shipping. His first secretary tried to seduce him and he fired her on the spot." Seeing the shocked look on Tina's face, she added, "If you want to keep your job, I suggest you focus on just that."

When Machie opened the door at the end of the hall, he said, "Mr. Ariri wants you to wait for him here in his office."

He then stepped out of the office to get her some refreshments, while Fey looked around the space. It was a large office suite. There was a conference room with glass doors and windows, an ensuite bathroom, a closet, two sofas and two armchairs arranged with a wall-mounted fifty-inch flat screen TV as the focal point. Two of the four office walls had floor-length windows, giving the space a bright and airy feel.

Fey sat down to wait for Iben.

A few hours later…

"Sorry, you had to wait for so long, babe," Iben said as soon as he walked into his office. "I've been in back-to-back meetings all morning."

"No worries," Fey said.

"How did it go with your boss?" Iben asked as he took a seat next to her. "Was your performance Oscar-worthy?"

Fey chuckled. "She was surprised for sure. She actually tried to convince me that she was only joking yesterday. And when I wasn't buying it, she got upset that I refused to stay on the job until she found a replacement or to hand off my projects. I calmly told her that wasn't a problem for soon-to-be Mrs. Ariri to solve and walked out."

"That's my girl!" Iben said excitedly and gave her a high-five.

Fey smiled sheepishly, "I feel like such a delinquent, though. I've never had to quit a job in that way before, but I'll admit that it felt good to get back at her. That woman really pissed me off on so many levels yesterday."

"By all means, revel in your delinquency until lunch is over, at least," Iben responded with a smirk. "Afterwards, I'll introduce you to your new team."

Fey pouted. "You're putting me to work already? Are you going to be a slave driver boss, Mr. Ariri?" she teased.

Iben smiled. "Stop complaining. I'm feeding you first, aren't I?"

Just then, there was a knock at the door. Iben answered and Machie walked in with their lunch. Afterwards, Fey attended a meeting with Iben where he introduced her to a handful of people. The plan was for her to work in the head office for six months while learning different aspects of the company before she transferred to the engineering department where her father also worked.

When the meeting was over, Fey asked, "Did you arrange all this today?" She was impressed at how quickly her orientation began.

Iben smiled. "Let's just say that I've been looking forward to this day for a while." Ever since Fey had the sexual harassment issue on her job, Iben had wanted to whisk her away to Ariri Corporation.

"Do you want the driver to take you home? Or do you want to wait until later so we can go home together?"

"I'd rather stay, if it's okay with you," Fey replied. If she went home now, she'd only be waiting for Iben to come home, anyway.

They returned to Iben's office and Fey busied herself with some reading materials that she received during her orientation. Iben worked at his desk until he left for another meeting. When he returned, he found Fey asleep on the sofa. For a moment, Iben watched her as she slept and a warm feeling slowly tugged at his heart. His eyes caressed her beautiful face as he thought with a smile, *I'm so lucky I found you.*

He leaned in to give her a gentle kiss on the cheek when his eyes wandered to her slender neck. His gaze travelled downward, and he took in her blush-pink silk blouse as it gently caressed the outline of her full breasts. His eyes spied at her cleavage as one of the buttons had become undone in her sleep. A mental image of him burying his face between the softness on her chest and kissing their peaks surfaced in his mind. Immediately, heat pooled within Iben and he longed to bury himself deep in the softness between her legs. He swallowed the lump that formed in his throat.

Iben realized just then that it had been a couple of weeks since he'd been intimate with Fey. He'd been so busy since Edafe's absence that when he got home in the evenings, he would catch up with Fey while they ate dinner and crash in the bed afterwards, too exhausted to think of anything but sleep. Even the weekends weren't spared, as he would be in the office all day. He looked forward to a time in the near future when he wouldn't be so busy.

Iben leaned in and kissed Fey. Her eyes fluttered open and when she saw Iben, she kissed him back, hungrily accepting his warm, sensuous tongue. Iben leaned in against her on the couch and deepened the kiss.

"I've missed you," he said in a deep, breathy tone as he pressed his hardness against her.

"Mmmm... I've missed you too, busy bee," Fey responded as she caressed his face.

"I'm sorry, babe. I realize I've been neglecting you lately," he said apologetically. But before Fey could respond, he added, "I'd like to remedy that now..." He then began unbuttoning her blouse.

Fey looked up to see the hunger in his eyes as he stared at her now bare chest. "We're in your office, Iben," she protested weakly.

"Mmmm, I know," he replied as his hands reached out to caress her soft mounds.

"Someone might walk in," she continued to object softly.

Iben chuckled, "First, it's already past closing time. Second, nobody just barges into the CEO's office." However, as soon as those words left his lips, Iben froze briefly as he suddenly had a mental image of his father walking into his office unannounced. He sighed with relief at the thought that he didn't really have to worry about that since Edafe was currently at Ikorodu.

Iben continued, "You see, I need you to keep that *prude* inside your head locked away for now. She's messing with my fantasy here." He wore a slightly irritated expression.

"What fantasy?" Fey asked in amusement.

"Making love to you in my office," Iben replied with a sexy smirk.

"Is this why you had me come here today? So you could seduce me and fulfil this fantasy of yours?" Fey teased with a chuckle. However, her laughter was quickly replaced with soft moans when Iben began kissing her neck and trailing warm kisses down her collarbone to her bare chest.

"Mmmm…" was Iben's response, as he now had his mouth over one of her breasts.

Fey arched her back as she felt Iben's warm tongue over her nipple. *Oh my god.* How she badly craved his touch. Because of Edafe's house arrest, Iben had been working overtime as he was inundated with extra responsibilities at the office and was exhausted by bedtime. Fey tried to be understanding and didn't make a fuss about their recent lack of sexual intimacy. After all, her love for him went beyond her physical needs and her attraction to him. But right now, intense heat was building up within her. "Iben…" she moaned.

"Mmmmm?" He was now trailing kisses down her tummy to her navel.

"Let's… go home…" she pleaded between moans. She wanted this. She wanted him. But not here. She wanted to be in the privacy of their home where she could express her desires for this man she was in love with. Where she could do so without worrying about being overheard by anyone.

Iben looked up at her and sighed. "Okay," he acquiesced. Then he whispered in her ear, "But you have to promise me that when we continue this in our bedroom, you'll let me do that *thing* I like."

Fey smiled shyly, "I promise."

39 | Doorway to Forever

Three months later.

Fey stood behind the closed double doors of the church. She was wearing an ivory lace wedding dress and holding a bouquet of luscious red roses. The backless mermaid style dress tapered into a V at her lower back with a modest, sweep train. Her hair was made up in an intricate updo style. The accessories that decorated her hair matched the dazzling diamond earrings and necklace she was wearing.

The bridal train had gone ahead of her and would soon end their walk down the aisle. And then the doors would open for her to enter. She nervously looked through her veil at her father standing next to her. He met her gaze and smiled as he gently patted her arm that was entwined with his.

"Getting cold feet?" he teased.

Fey chuckled, "Of course not." She turned to face the doors again.

She thought about the fact that Iben was behind those doors, waiting for her. They'd been through so much in the last year, with different things threatening to keep them apart. From Vivian's machinations to the secrets between her father and Iben's father, Edafe. But they'd somehow made it and were now here today, about to take their vows. About to pledge forever to each other in the presence of friends and family.

***

Iben stood at the altar of the chapel, patiently waiting for his bride to arrive. He was excited because he hadn't seen Fey in a few days.

As a surprise for Fey, Iben, with Demi's help, arranged for plane tickets to have her close college friends from the United States attend their wedding. All of them and her sister, Tutu, were currently boarded in their Lekki home. Two days before, he was told he couldn't see Fey until their wedding day. Although Iben could run a multi-billion naira company, he was no match for five ladies chirping at him about tradition and warding off bad luck. He tried to argue but failed miserably. At least Fey tried to console him a bit before he reluctantly moved in with Fola temporarily.

Today was the day he would officially be able to call Fey his *wife*. Iben suddenly felt emotional and his heart swelled with joy. His feelings for Fey got him believing in the idea of a soulmate and that she was undoubtedly *his* soulmate. Simply imagining her with another man tore at his heart. She was his alone, and he was committed to making sure that their union lasted forever. There was no other option.

Fola, his best man, noticed Iben's sudden somber expression and leaned in to say, "Bro, if you cry, you're going to lose *all* your cool points!"

Iben smiled at Fola's teasing and asked, his eyes not leaving the entrance, "When are you and Demi going to tie the knot?"

Fola scoffed, "Misery loves company, ehn? Just because you're getting married, everyone else should?"

"I suppose you are waiting for her to propose to you, then," Iben shot back, snarkily.

Fola's forehead knotted into a frown, "Not if I beat her to it!"

"Oh? So you *are* thinking about it. There's still hope for you, yet," Iben teased.

Fola chuckled lightly as he realized that Iben had sneakily goaded him into expressing his true feelings. He resisted the urge to smack Iben upside his head like he used to do when they were younger. "You ass!"

Iben's response was a smug expression. That look quickly transformed into one of awe as his jaw dropped when the doors opened and Fey finally came into view. His heartbeat quickened.

Damn! She's gorgeous!

***

As Dayo walked his daughter down the aisle, he grinned from ear to ear. At this moment, he was the happiest he'd been in almost two decades. He thanked the heavens for allowing him to reunite with his family. Walking either of his daughters down the aisle was a pipe dream this time last year. And now, here he was giving away his daughter to the man she had chosen. They reached the altar and Dayo placed Fey's hand in Iben's before going to sit down.

In his honest opinion, Iben was a good man. However, he couldn't say the same about his father. Dayo glanced over at the adjacent row and caught a glimpse of Edafe Ariri. For a moment, he was taken aback by the sheer joy emanating from the man. He was obviously ecstatic that his son was getting married today. Since he'd known Edafe, this was the first time that Dayo had seen him genuinely happy and it had nothing to do with anything he had orchestrated.

Dayo fought down the bitterness that was slowly rising within him as he thought about Edafe's role in separating him from his family decades ago. He owned plenty of blame as well, but seeing Edafe reminded him of that time in his life when he felt hapless. He secretly wished the man had remained under house arrest. Yes—even on his son's wedding day. In his opinion, that would've been justice. Karma. He sighed to himself, *No point in dwelling in the past. I need to focus on the future.*

With that thought, Dayo turned his gaze to the woman seated next to him. She was dressed in the traditional female Igbo attire, an embroidered blouse and two George wrappers. Her attention was on the couple at the altar about to say their vows. Dayo leaned over and said in a hushed tone, "You look gorgeous, Ada. Our daughter *definitely* gets her good looks from you."

Ada froze when she felt Dayo's breath near her ear. She turned to meet his gaze, and he winked at her. She rolled her eyes and said in a playful tone, "Stop flirting and focus on the ceremony."

Dayo did as he was told and smiled to himself. Now that Adaobi was vacationing in Nigeria for the next few weeks, he was on a mission to rekindle her love for him. They had had time to talk since her arrival a couple of weeks before, and he had been ecstatic to find out that Ada wasn't seeing anyone at the moment. Although he never stopped loving her all these years, Dayo knew he had a lot to make up for. He was acutely aware that he had to work hard to win her trust again.

***

As a bridesmaid, Tutu, Fey's younger sister, stood in a row close to the altar, along with the rest of the train. As the ceremony continued, Tutu noticed her father and mother talking once in a while. She was pleased that her father seemed to make a bit of progress in thawing her mother's heart towards him. She pitied him though, as she knew that woman could hold a grudge forever. Tutu shuddered as she remembered the cold and silent treatments she received from Ada after she found out that Tutu had gone through her things and found the hidden letters from Dayo.

She couldn't believe that it was already two years since then. Looking back, she was glad to have been nosy, glad to have found those letters, and glad she and Fey confronted their mother about them. She truly believed that the knowledge of Dayo trying to reach out to them was the main catalyst in Fey's decision to move to Nigeria and find him.

Although she had spoken to Dayo over video chat many times before her arrival in Nigeria for the wedding, Tutu couldn't help but burst into tears of joy when she finally met her father in person. And so far, she had enjoyed getting to know him. He was the opposite of her mother in many ways. He was calm, logical and very supportive. If there was anything he disagreed with, he would simply make his views known and leave it at that. Sometimes, she could tell that it drove her mother nuts. She swore the woman just loved the occasional verbal tussle just for the sake of it.

Tutu snapped out of her meandering thoughts and turned her attention back to the couple who were now exchanging their rings. She, just like everyone else there, was happy for the couple. She felt that they matched very well, and she hoped that fate would also bring her a man who would love and cherish her in the way Iben did Fey.

***

At the reception, Dayo proudly introduced Adaobi to his friends and colleagues from work. Adaobi didn't want to make a fuss and embarrass him, so she played along when Dayo introduced her as his wife. Legally, they *were* still married, as neither one of them had applied for divorce since their abrupt separation. But they both knew that their marriage had been anything but joyous in the last couple of decades.

Since Ada's arrival in Nigeria, Dayo had been trying really hard to please her. It wasn't lost on her, and while Ada appreciated the attention, she wasn't sure how she felt about getting back together with him. She had no intention of leading him on or giving him the false impression that they still had a future together. There was still so much hurt to work through, but she was trying to not dwell in the past. Gosh! It was really hard, though. Thankfully, Dayo seemed to be okay with taking things one step at a time.

Ada was especially glad that he did not invite his parents to the wedding. According to Dayo, he had informed his parents of their granddaughter's wedding, but refused to invite them. He told them he wanted to spend time with his wife and children, without their meddling. She was relieved at the news, and so were her daughters, although they tried not to show it so as not to hurt their father's feelings.

While Adaobi could deal with Edafe's presence, it would be difficult for her to do the same when it came to Dayo's parents. That duo tried to get Dayo to take a second wife and abandon her and the girls after all. If they hadn't summoned him back to Nigeria, Edafe never would've trapped Dayo in his web, and she would never forgive them for that.

***

At the wedding reception, after everyone had eaten their fill and the bride and groom had their first dance, Edafe mingled with the business partners, friends and family he had invited. When someone asked what he'd been doing the last few months, he said, "I'm just relaxing and taking it easy these days. It's time to leave all the hard work to the next generation." He laughed and others joined in.

"Chief, sorry to disturb, but I just received word that you have about an hour before we have to leave."

Edafe turned and gave a nod in understanding to the young man who had just spoken to him. It was Detective Chidi Azunna, who had been at the yacht raid months ago. Given that Edafe was currently serving his house arrest sentence, Chidi had volunteered to escort Edafe to his son's traditional and church wedding ceremonies.

Chidi knew that other officers would probably not be discreet and might make it obvious that Edafe was being chaperoned. This could undoubtedly lead to people asking questions and guessing at alternate reasons for Edafe's recent absence. The narrative that Edafe was taking a personal sabbatical had gone over well, and all parties would like to keep it that way.

With this in mind, Chidi had his eyes on Edafe, while still giving him enough room to breathe and mingle with wedding guests without making him feel stifled. Given Edafe's relationship with Chidi's father, and that if it wasn't for Edafe, his father wouldn't be alive today, this was the least Chidi could do to show his thanks.

After Chidi walked away, Edafe turned his attention to Fey and Iben. His heart swelled with pride. His son had found himself a woman that was worthy of being his daughter-in-law. He had also been very impressed with the reports that Samuel Adegbite had been giving him since his house arrest. Iben had stepped up to the plate, and he knew that the company would continue to do well under his leadership. And with a woman as grounded and level-headed like Fey as his wife, the sky was the limit.

He excused himself from his guests and went to say goodbye to the bride and groom. Soon after, he slipped away quietly.

***

As the reception progressed, Fola watched Demi as she chatted with her friends, family and other invited guests. Subconsciously, his eyes would pick her out from across the room, even while he was having conversations with other people. He thought she looked gorgeous in the fitted, burgundy gown she had designed for herself as the Maid of Honor. Fey had given her free rein to design the bridesmaids' dresses as well. Her only request was that they be in her wedding colors—burgundy and silver.

He recalled his earlier conversation with Iben at the church, and he felt a warm tug pulling his heart strings. *Yeah*, he finally admitted to himself. He was in love with Demi. Fola wondered that perhaps his emotional state of mind had to do with the amorous air that permeated weddings in general. Love was in the air.

Fola had always been a practical guy, and his ability to read people very well made him a bit cynical about newly formed human relationships. Experience had taught him that very few people didn't have an ulterior motive. Aside from Edafe and Iben, he was never close to anyone else, but now, he had included Demi and Fey in his close circle. It felt good. Knowing that there were people who loved him for *him*, and not for what they could get from him.

Before his relationship with Demi, Fola was prepared to be a bachelor for the rest of his life. But now, he was actually considering settling down and starting a family. He'd be a fool not to want that with the only woman with whom he had great chemistry.

He tore his gaze from Demi and directed it at Iben and Fey, who were seated at the stage. Iben whispered something to Fey and her eyes grew wide. When she turned to look at him, Iben picked up her ladies' fan and covered their faces while he kissed her. Fola scrunched up his nose in mild annoyance. *Why do I always catch those two when they're flirting? Get a room!*

Fola was happy for Iben, though. The poor guy had gone through an intense roller coaster ride over the last three years. First with Vivian's betrayal, then finding out that Edafe was his biological father, to his engagement to Fey hanging in the balance as they navigated the ramifications of Edafe and Dayo's history.

He recalled the first time he met Iben. Iben was very introverted back then, but as they became closer over the years, Iben opened up to him, and Fola naturally filled the best friend and big brother role. Today, he was a proud big brother. He was happy that Iben found the right woman for him. Unlike Vivian, Fey was loyal, logical, had a go-getter attitude, and didn't rely on Iben for everything.

Fola was also impressed with how Fey took charge of ensuring that Edafe got everything he needed since he'd been serving his house arrest. She organized cleaning and laundry services, as well as delivering groceries and household supplies to Edafe's *prison* in Ikorodu. She was doing a good job of fulfilling her role as Iben's partner—as Mrs. Ariri. This way, Iben could be free to focus on being his best self, for the company and for their relationship.

***

As the maid of honor, Demi had been shadowing Fey all day and working with the wedding planner to give guidance and answer questions, making sure that everything went smoothly. This way, Fey could enjoy her day, worry free.

The wedding turned out to be a tremendous success. It was bigger than Fey would've liked, but Iben had encouraged her to go all out. Demi would not let her best friend embarrass the Ariri family, so she had recommended a well-known wedding planner who took care of the major details like securing one of the most exclusive wedding reception venues, a wedding photographer and the musical entertainment at the wedding reception. Fey then focused on other details like the cake, wedding colors, food menu, wedding favors and so on.

Fey and Iben had just returned to the reception hall after changing out of their church ceremony attire. They were now wearing custom-made, matching silver and burgundy outfits and were getting ready to leave for their honeymoon night. They thanked everyone for coming and left soon after.

Demi finally had a chance to unwind and relax. She took a seat next to Fola at the table they occupied with the rest of the bridal party.

"Hey, baby," she said.

"Hey," Fola responded, kissing her on the cheek. "You should eat something," he said, pushing the plate of food he had saved for her in front of her. He noticed that she'd been too busy to sit down and eat much of anything.

"Thanks, baby," she replied and didn't need any extra nudging before digging into her meal.

A few minutes after she finished, Fola said, "Come with me. I need to talk to you."

Demi nodded, and they excused themselves from their table. They held hands as Fola led them out of the reception hall to one of the private rooms Iben and Fey had rented to use as changing rooms. Demi's feet hurt like crazy, and once inside, she sat down and quickly stepped out of her three-inch silver heels.

"What do you want to talk about?" she asked.

Fola pulled her up and said, "Dance with me."

"Here?" Demi asked in amusement.

"Yes."

There wasn't any music playing, but Fola held Demi in his embrace and they rocked side to side. Demi smiled to herself, wondering why Fola was acting this way. Since he said nothing right away, Demi had no choice but to be patient before she could hear what he wanted to talk about.

They danced for a moment before Fola leaned in and captured her lips. The kiss was gentle, unlike Fola's usual smoldering kisses. When the kiss ended, he said in a low voice, "Move in with me, Dee."

Demi met his gaze and smiled. "I would love to, but my father would probably kill you if I did so without a ring on this finger," she said, holding up her hand.

Fola held her hand and kissed it. "What size do you wear? You look like a... seven," he said, throwing out a random number.

Demi knew he was referring to her ring size. She chuckled and said, "I'm a five."

"Princess cut?"

Demi raised a surprised brow. "How did you know?"

Fola chuckled, "Lucky guess," he said. He twirled her around and she giggled. When she was back in his embrace, he asked, "Gold or platinum?"

"Platinum."

Fola nodded. "As you wish, Platinum Princess."

Demi chuckled.

They continued dancing quietly for a moment until Fola touched his forehead to hers and said in an almost-whisper, "I love you, Dee."

Demi wasn't surprised at his confession. They'd been dating for almost eight months now, and although Fola wasn't the type to gush, his actions toward her more than showed his feelings for her. She was happy to hear it, though. Guessing at someone's feelings and knowing are two different things.

Demi loved him back. She'd loved him since before they started dating, and her love for him had grown over time. She liked that Fola treated her with respect, and was very supportive of her passion, giving valuable insights into different aspects of running her business. She loved his confidence, loyalty and honesty.

Theirs wasn't a perfect relationship, but they were blissfully happy.

Demi grinned and said, "I love you too, baby."

***

Two months later, Fey and Iben arrived at the Lagos Airport. They had just returned from their honeymoon. Because of Iben's work, they could not leave for their honeymoon vacation until a few weeks after their wedding. Their honeymoon was in Germany, the place where they first met. After a week there, they toured Europe for the remaining three weeks before coming back to Nigeria.

Fola and Demi met them at their Lekki home the next evening.

"Oh my gosh, you guys are engaged?!" Fey exclaimed as soon as she saw Demi.

Demi nodded and grinned as she showed Fey her engagement ring.

"Why didn't you tell me?"

"I didn't want to disturb your honeymoon, girl. I figured it could wait until you guys returned," Demi replied.

"You move fast, bro!" Iben teased as he hugged Fola. "Congrats!"

"Thanks, bro!" Fola said with a wide grin.

"Tell me everything!" Fey demanded excitedly as she led Demi to a seat. They all listened as Demi recounted the proposal.

A few days after Iben and Fey left for their honeymoon was Demi's birthday. Fola called her early in the morning, asking her to come over and that he had a surprise for her. When she arrived at his apartment, he wasn't there, so she let herself in. Once inside, she saw a small wrapped box on the kitchen counter. She opened it to find a note and a jewelry box inside. *Marry me, please*, the note read.

Her heart skipped a beat.

When Demi opened the box, she saw a gorgeous platinum engagement ring with a princess cut setting. The inside was engraved with the words, *Platinum Princess*.

She put on the ring—it was the perfect size. She grinned as she admired the dazzling ring on her finger. She wondered if she should wait for Fola to return, but decided against it. She figured that he probably wasn't there because he was too nervous and wasn't sure of her response. She was going to enjoy messing with him a bit.

Then, she took out her lipstick and wrote the letters *'OK'* over his note, and stuck it on his fridge. She would not call him either and let him sweat a bit for an answer until he returned to his apartment to see her response. A few minutes later, she left for home with a bright smile on her face.

When she got home, she was shocked to find Fola already there. He smiled when he saw that she was wearing the engagement ring. Apparently, he had stopped by to inform her parents that he wanted to marry Demi, knowing that she was at his apartment. Her parents had no objections and congratulated them on their engagement.

Later, when they went out on a dinner date, Demi asked, "What if I had said no?"

Fola knew she was referring to the fact that he asked her parents for her hand in marriage without knowing her response. "Why would you?" he asked with a smirk.

"What confidence you have, Fola Ogundele," Demi said with a chuckle.

"Thanks, it's one of my greatest assets," he replied with a wink.

40 | Forever

Three months later.

One night, Fey showed up unannounced at Dayo's with an overnight bag. "Dad, can I please spend the night here?"

"What's going on?" he asked.

"Please, I don't want to talk about it."

Dayo sighed helplessly as he watched her walk to the spare bedroom in his two-bedroom flat. *Those two have only been married for a few months and they are already sleeping apart?* Since Fey didn't want to talk about it, Dayo didn't press the issue. He went to his room and settled in for the night when his phone rang. It was Iben. Dayo sighed again. He could already tell it was going to be a long night.

"Dad, is Fey with you?" Iben's voice was almost frantic. When he came home from work, Fey wasn't there, and she wasn't answering her phone. He had already called Demi who told him she wasn't with her.

"Yes," Dayo said.

Iben blew out a relieved breath and said, "Okay, I'm coming over right now."

A few minutes after the call ended, Dayo heard a knock on his bedroom door. It was Fey.

"Dad, if Iben calls, don't tell him I'm here," she said.

Dayo raised a brow. *Too late, baby girl,* he thought to himself. But he simply nodded and said nothing.

About an hour later, Iben arrived and after letting him in, Dayo gave him a once over. He looked like he hadn't slept properly in days.

After bowing in greeting, Iben asked, "Where is she?"

Dayo gestured toward the guest bedroom. "Good luck," he muttered under his breath. If Fey was anything like her mother when upset, Iben had a large wall to scale.

Iben knocked on the bedroom door and Fey answered it, thinking it was her father. When she saw Iben standing there instead, she immediately tried to shut the door. But he was fast and stuck his foot in the doorway. He winced and grimaced when Fey slammed and pushed the door against it repeatedly. Iben endured and didn't care that his expensive Armani shoes were getting scuffed to the point of almost being irreparable.

After a while, Fey gave up on her quest to keep him out. She huffed in frustration as she stomped away from the door, and Iben stepped inside the room. He shut the door behind him and leaned against it.

"Babe, what's the matter?" he asked, wondering what he had done to upset her. "Why didn't you pick up my calls?"

Fey just glared at him.

Iben could see that she'd been crying and his heart clenched. He moved closer to her and tried to hold her hand, but she avoided his touch and snapped, "Keep your hands to yourself!"

Iben sighed. "I know you're upset, but I can't fix it if you don't tell me what the problem is."

"I'm sick of repeating myself," she said.

Just then, his phone rang. He glanced at it and silenced the call. "Sorry about that."

"Who was that?"

"It's work. I'll deal with it later."

Fey scoffed. "Please don't do that on my account. Your work is *important*."

Iben didn't miss the sarcasm in her tone of voice. "It can wait," he said softly.

Fey rolled her eyes and sat on the bed. Iben took a seat on the armchair by the bedside. Fey said nothing, and Iben waited patiently.

"I feel like I'm married to myself, Iben," Fey finally said. "Your work takes precedence all the time."

This again? Iben thought to himself.

"Babe, I'm sorry, but I'm under a lot of pressure at work," he said. "Taking over the company has been very challenging. I really need you to be understanding and patient."

"I *have* been patient!" Fey replied.

Iben rubbed his hands across his head in a gesture of frustration.

"When was the last time you and I spent time together?" Fey asked.

Iben tried to recall but couldn't. Although they worked at the same company, it was as if they didn't. Fey had transferred from the head office to the engineering office. They barely saw each other, even at home. Most times, Fey was in bed before Iben came home from work. And he was usually gone by the time she woke up in the morning.

The only proof Fey had that he even came home was when she woke in the middle of the night and he was sleeping next to her. Or telltale signs in the bedroom that he had taken a shower and changed his clothes. If she was lucky, she'd catch him on his way out to the office.

"It's been two months, Iben."

No way, Iben thought in shock.

Answering the question in his eyes, Fey said, "Yes, it has, and I'm done being patient. Nothing has changed. Not even a little bit. If anything, it's gotten worse."

After a moment of quiet, he said, "I'm sorry, babe. I didn't realize that I have neglected you for that long."

"This isn't just about us. Your health is getting affected as well. Look at you. You've lost weight. You hardly get enough sleep."

"I'll do something about it."

Fey scoffed. "If I had a buck for every time you said that…"

Iben just sighed.

***

The next morning, Dayo woke up to find Iben asleep on the living room couch. When he returned from the gym a couple of hours later, Iben was cooking breakfast in the kitchen. "Do I get to eat some of that or is it just for Fey?" he teased.

Iben chuckled. "Of course, Dad," he said. He made him a plate and Dayo sat down to eat.

"So, you guys okay now?" Dayo asked. He had overheard some of their conversation the night before as they talked and argued.

Iben shrugged. "She's only just *half* angry with me now and she won't go back home until I fix the problem," he said dejectedly.

"How do you plan to fix the problem?" Dayo asked.

"I don't know. It's not like I can just quit my job. I know I've been busy, but I had hoped that she'll be a bit more patient with me until things settle down. There are so many people who rely on me to get things done."

"How much longer do you expect your wife to wait on the sidelines while you take care of others?"

Iben blinked speechlessly for a few seconds at Dayo's words. He hadn't thought of things from that perspective.

When Iben said nothing, Dayo continued. "There are two things I've learned to do in my career, over the years. Prioritize and delegate. There's always going to be something or someone needing your attention at work. Decide what are the most important things that nobody else but you can and should do. And delegate the rest. Hire competent people to delegate to, if you don't already have them. Otherwise, you'll one day find yourself a lonely old man with nothing except his work."

Iben sat quietly, digesting his father-in-law's advice. When he was Chairman and CEO of Starlight Shipping, he had a good handle on things fairly quickly. But Ariri Corporation was a different monster, and he truly was overwhelmed with all that needed his attention. Many times over the last few months, he'd been in awe of his father, Edafe. How had the man been able to effortlessly manage the conglomerate by himself for so many years? Perhaps that was why he never married—he simply couldn't have had the time.

Thinking of Edafe, Iben wondered what he'd think of him and the issues he was having with Fey. Would he say he wasn't man enough? And that's when it dawned on him. That's when he realized he'd been overworking himself because he'd been trying to prove something. He'd been trying to prove to his father that despite having to suddenly take over the company, he was capable of taking care of the business.

Also, Iben wanted to make the company even more profitable and greater than Edafe ever did. And he had ideas on how to do that. Lots of ideas. But maybe he was trying to do too much all at once. His marriage was already suffering and his health as well. He had developed ulcers and killer migraines.

Iben finally said, "Thanks, Dad. I know what I need to do."

Iben left soon after, and when he returned three hours later, a surprised Fey answered the door.

"I thought you went to the office," she said after letting him in.

"It's Saturday," Iben responded.

Fey scoffed, "That hasn't stopped you in the last couple of months." She sat on the living room sofa and continued watching TV, ignoring him.

Iben sat next to her and asked, "Did you get my text message?"

"What text message?" Fey asked without sparing him a glance.

"You were still sleeping when I left, so I sent you a message that I'd be back soon so that we can hang out together."

Fey turned to look at him.

Now that he had her attention, Iben said, "Fey, I'm really sorry about how things have been these last couple of months. I'm ashamed that you had to leave our home before I got the message and could see things clearly. Please forgive me."

Fey broke eye contact, refusing to get sucked into his pleading eyes. She asked, "So, you're really not working today?"

Iben nodded. "I'm not working the entire weekend."

"What of next weekend? And the one after that? And—"

"Babe, starting next week, I'm readjusting my workload," he said, interrupting her. "I will only take care of the really important matters. I'll still have to travel occasionally, but only if I need to. I have a great team of people at my disposal. It's time I let them do their jobs." Iben ended with a wry smile.

Fey looked at him again and nodded. She was satisfied that he had a plan beyond this weekend.

Now that Fey had accepted his apology, Iben slowly reached for her hand. He was glad she didn't reject his touch. "Let's go away for the weekend. Just you and me. No cell phones. No laptops. No distractions."

When he left earlier, he went home to shower, change his clothes and make arrangements for spending time with his wife. Since it was last minute, he couldn't plan anything elaborate. So, he called the manager at one of his hotels, reserving the penthouse suite for two nights.

Fey smiled when she heard his suggestion. She liked the idea. "Okay," she said. She stood up, sat in Iben's lap and hugged him, burying her face in his neck. "I'm sorry about slamming the door against your foot yesterday," she said.

Iben let out a relieved breath as they hugged. "No worries, babe," he said.

A moment later, Fey pulled back from the hug and kissed him. Although Iben had expected Fey to remain closed off for much longer, his surprise only lasted a couple of seconds. He instantly took control of the kiss, deepening it.

A moment later, Iben rested his forehead on hers and said huskily, "Let's head to the hotel where we won't have to worry about your dad walking in on us again."

Fey's eyes widened. "Oh my gosh, he saw just now?"

Iben smiled and nodded.

Dayo had quietly returned to his bedroom when he saw the couple in a passionate embrace.

Fey covered her face in embarrassment. Iben chuckled at his prudish wife. He still found that part of her amusing.

Fey stood up and went to pack her bag. Iben followed and once the bedroom door was shut behind him, he pulled his wife to him and kissed her again. This time, it was more needy, more urgent.

When Iben's hands reached under her t-shirt, Fey moaned as she melted into him. How she had missed his touch, his kisses. As she undid his belt buckle, he slowly backed her onto the bed.

Their departure for the hotel would have to wait a while.

***

Four years later.

Ariri mansion on Banana Island.

Edafe's face lit up in a smile as he watched eighteen-month-old Jemma try to wiggle out of her father's arms. Iben's phone rang, and he stepped out to take the call, leaving his daughter in the room with Edafe. Now free, she waddled over to the table where Edafe kept his magazines, picked one up with her chubby hands and handed it to Edafe.

"Papa, *wead!*" little Jemma commanded.

Edafe chuckled as he picked her up and sat her in his lap. This wasn't the first time he would read his magazines to her, but he offered to read one of the children's books his parents had brought instead.

"No!" Jemma said and swatted the book away. She reached for the magazine again. To her, that was more interesting, as she'd read her book several times today already.

"That's my girl," Edafe said, gently patting Jemma on the head. He opened to a page in the magazine and began reading.

After a few minutes, Fey walked into the room to this scene. "Papa!" she exclaimed when she saw the magazine cover. "How can you be reading that to her?" she chided.

Edafe scoffed. "It's only a firearms magazine," he said dismissively. "My granddaughter needs to learn how to protect herself."

"From what? You?" Fey shot back irritably.

Edafe chuckled and said, "If she inherits a mouth like yours, she'll need a few more skills to defend herself when she inevitably rouses someone's ire."

Fey could see the smirk on Edafe's lips and she realized he was enjoying this.

Edafe and Fey's relationship wasn't a typical father-in-law daughter-in-law one. Although he was very fond of her, he had developed the annoying habit of poking at her to rile her up and see her reaction. Sometimes, it was her stance on business matters, other times, politics. Today, it was Jemma.

But before Fey could respond with a sarcastic remark, she heard Iben say, "It's okay, babe. Jemma is just curious. She's too little to remember any of that stuff."

Fey turned around and shot Iben a glare. "You're defending him?"

He walked up to her and put his arm around her waist. "Babe, don't get upset, okay." Before Fey could protest, he kissed her, shutting her up.

"Eeewww!" drawled little Jemma when she saw her parents locking lips, causing everyone to laugh and easing the tension in the room.

"Why don't you sit and rest, babe?" Iben asked as he rubbed Fey's bulging belly. She was pregnant with their second child and was due in less than a month.

Fey sighed. *I'm pregnant, not an invalid.* But she said nothing and let Iben pamper her.

After sitting and propping her with pillows, Iben leaned in and said, "Let Papa define his relationship with Jemma." He reached for her hand before he continued, "He adores her, and we both know he won't do anything to hurt her. So let's not interfere too much, okay?"

Fey met Iben's pleading eyes. She understood where he was coming from. "Okay," she said finally.

Iben put his arm around Fey and continued in a low tone. "On another note, I'm looking forward to the little guy's arrival," he said, gesturing to Fey's tummy.

Fey smiled. "Me too. I can't wait to have my body back." Being a mother was a delight, but she could do without the pregnancy mood swings and the perpetual bloated feeling.

"And I can't wait to have my wife back," Iben replied. At some point, his hand had traveled down Fey's back, and at that moment, he discreetly grabbed her bottom, causing her to giggle like a schoolgirl.

As Iben sat there, he thought about the last four years. He stopped being a workaholic and his relationship with Fey had improved. He also realized that not being too involved in everything as he used to be, gave him the free time to dream up ways to grow the company.

For one, he was successful in converting the firearms trafficking operation into a legal entity called Executive Security. This new arm of the conglomerate provided security services to clientele. Services such as armed and unarmed bodyguards, private investigations, and state-of-the-art alarm and monitoring systems. They offered their services to both private and public clients, including law enforcement. Naturally, Fola was in his element as the Director after resigning from his position with the EFCC.

As Iben watched Jemma and Edafe interact, he couldn't help but think about his mother, sister and stepfather. Since Edafe's house arrest, Iben began a new tradition where he visited his family grave with Fey.

Despite his feelings about Edafe's actions in the past, Iben worked through his emotions and tried to improve their relationship. Edafe raised him, and Iben knew the man loved him in his own way.

And although Edafe was in retirement, Iben would occasionally involve him in some business matters. It was his way of making sure the man didn't get into any mischief due to boredom.

Fey leaned in against him, causing Iben to turn his attention to her.

She smiled, watching Jemma as she looked content with her grandfather. Then she looked up at Iben and said, "I love you."

Iben smiled and kissed her forehead. "I love you too, babe."

When she started out on her journey to find her father, Fey never imagined that she would end up here.

All the questions she had years ago were answered. And now, she was content settling into a life of blissful happiness, with Iben by her side.

THE END.

Author Notes

Thank you for reading our book. We hope you enjoyed it as much as we enjoyed writing it. If you could leave a review where you purchased the book, we would be eternally grateful. It's the best way to let us know what you think of it and to let others know about the book.

Before you leave, we would love to keep in touch. Be sure to visit www.eboniewayne.com for updates on future releases, book deals and to sign up for our mailing list.

And if you're curious about how things work out between Fey's parents (Ada and Dayo), we have a special gift for you—a free short story. Get your copy at https://eboniewayne.com/what-love-remains

Cheers!

~ Ebonie Wayne ~

Made in the USA
Monee, IL
03 December 2021

83764555R00217